Demon's Plague
By Will Keith

Preface

Hello, Readers. I would like to thank you all for choosing my story. This book takes place in a fictional alternate reality of medieval England, similar to the legends of Camelot and King Arthur. It is a low-fantasy world, with many characters and places that you will either love or love to hate. I hope you enjoy reading my book as much as I enjoyed writing it-

W. K.

Prologue
Winter of 1512 A.D
An oasis in Eastern Egypt
Late Afternoon

Sefu Najjar carefully worked the twigs, pinching each length of wood on either side of the small, leaf-green flower's stem, and he plucked it from the ground. His hands slipped and the flower fell from the twigs and gently began to slide towards him in the dry wind. With a desperate burst of speed, Sefu threw himself backwards, at the same time letting out a scream of mortal terror. He rolled down the grassy hill and crashed into a palm tree. The small, light flower lifted in the breeze, floating towards him, and he screamed again as he shoved himself away from the tree. The flower settled at the base of the palm, its long, attractive petals flowing gently. Breathing heavily and clutching a bruised rib, Sefu slowly, cautiously crawled back towards the flower. He managed to retain his twigs throughout his fall, and this time he tightly squeezed both twigs in his right hand. Sliding a finger of his left between them to separate the tips, he moved the twigs over the stem of the flower and removed his finger. The twigs snapped back into place, properly holding the flower this time, and Sefu sighed in relief.

He reached his left arm behind his back, removing his lumpy rucksack and depositing it on the ground. After some digging, he produced a small glass vial about the size of a child's fist, a large quantity of heavy cloth, and a long, thick rope. Squeezing the vial between his legs, he pried the cork out with his free hand and stuffed the vial into a patch of sand for stability. He shuffled backwards and slowly, gently deposited the green flower into the vial, and immediately hurled the pair of twigs further down the hill. Reaching again into the rucksack, he took out two more twigs of the same variety, and used them to place the cork back on top of the vial, then stood and used his boot to stuff the cork as far in as it would go. He then used his other foot to slide the boot off and kicked it hard down the hill, as well as tossing the second pair of twigs.

Next, Sefu took the thick cloth, wrapped it around his hands, and gingerly picked up the vial. He wrapped it in the cloth, folding it over, and over, and over until every inch of the heavy fabric was wrapped around it. Then he took the rope, wrapping it around the bundle from every direction, and ended by tying a series of complicated knots. He held the bundle at arm's length and began climbing back up the hill. He soon reached the edge of the oasis, vast desert spanning out in front of him. There, tied to one of the outer palm trees, was a large sand-colored camel, and a firepit with a large pot of boiling water sitting above it. Sefu walked to the other side of the camel, where a wooden box, about one cubic foot, was tied to the saddle. He reached to his side and unsheathed a curved dagger that he used to cut the box free from the saddle. The box was carved from a solid chuck of wood, except for one side that slid off to reveal the opening.

Sefu placed the bundle inside the box and proceeded to wrap the box in thick cloth and rope as well. Finally, he tied the entire construct to the camel's saddle and slowly walked to the firepit. Luckily, he had the light evening chill and shade of the palms to protect him from the sun as he stripped down to nothing, dumping all of his clothes into the pot. He then raised his hands in front of his face and saw them shaking involuntarily but understandably in fear of what was to come. However, the coming pain was nothing compared to what may happen if he did not suffer it. He squeezed his eyes shut and he roared in agony as he plunged his arms into the boiling water.

Chapter One
Summer of 1513 A.D
Central England
Kingdom of Valdus
The Village of Peydenal
Midnight

Bayard Travers slammed the hammer down again, sparks flying and red-hot metal shavings searing into his arm. A pain he was used to, barely feeling it as he brought the hammer down once more. Finally, he raised the blade and examined the length, width, and straightness, then plunged it into the quenching trough once he was satisfied. A couple more hours of detail work, and he was tying the hilt to the tang. He gave the light shortsword a few swings before taking it to the grindstone. Eventually he placed the completed sword on a wooden rack next to seven other identical blades, and he collapsed onto a wide, cushioned chair. Grinning at his work, he leaned back and closed his eyes. Figuring he'd go upstairs to his bed when his stiff legs woke him up as they did every night he passed out in this chair, he quickly fell asleep.

Knock, knock, knock. He thought he had dreamt it, but he jumped awake as the series of knocks repeated. Noting the abhorrent time for a friendly visit, he grabbed one of his newly forged shortswords and began to sneak up the stone stairs to the ground floor of his home and blacksmith's shop. He quickly ignited the lantern resting above the doorway and peered out the window. There stood a tall man, wrapped in a ridiculous amount of heavy clothing for a fine summer night. Only his head poked out of the mass of fabric, a face of dark skin and short, black hair. *An African,* Bayard thought. It had been a very long time since he had seen one. Bayard carefully held out the shortsword, steadying himself, and used the tip of the blade to flip open the bolt lock. "Come in," he said loudly.

The door creaked open and the large man stepped in. *Okay, not African,* Bayard thought quickly. His skin was dark, but it was the sort of dark you see in India, Egypt, or Turkey. He had seen many of these men when he used to live in the city of Valdus. Most of them were fine traders, mercenaries, and sailors. He seemed to be unarmed. Bayard relaxed slightly, lowering the blade. "I apologize for the hostility, but what in God's name brings you to me at this hour, can't wait till morning for a hunting knife? And why are you dressed like a Queen's bedspread?"

To his surprise, the man smiled a friendly, familiar grin. "Where I have been, this cold is completely unheard of." He spoke nearly perfect English, only the faintest hint of a foreign accent was audible in his deep voice. "This is the only way I can be comfortable here. But Bayard, do you really not recognize me, even in this darkness?"

The blacksmith squinted at the large man, quickly noticing the long, pointed nose and small scar crossing his right eyebrow. He broke out into the same stupid grin that the other man wore. "Bloody hell. I never thought I'd see you again, brother. It's been ten years now, hasn't it? I beg your forgiveness, my sight isn't what it used to be in the darkness. How did you manage to find me?"

Sefu lunged in and hugged Bayard, lifting him off the ground with ease. "Eleven years! Finding you only took some simple guesswork. I went to Valdus first, but nobody there had seen you since I left. You have always hated travel, so I knew you would be in a town close to the city. You always spoke of taking up smithing, and people in the city said that Peydenal had a skilled smith. So here I am."

"Travel doesn't get me coins and familiar ale, you bastard," Bayard grunted. He walked to the fireplace, quickly lighting the old wood with a flint and steel before collapsing onto another, even cushier chair. Sefu was removing his many layers of cloth and folding them neatly on the shop's counter, then he placed a lumpy package on top of it all. Bayard quickly noticed Sefu's arms, which were horribly scarred and disfigured up to the elbow. "What happened to you, there?"

"Boiling water," Sefu said simply. "I had to disinfect my arms, and it is the only thing good enough." He gestured towards the small parcel on the counter.

Bayard stood and walked towards the bundle of cloth and rope. "Disinfect them from what?" he asked cautiously. Sefu just shook his head and held an arm out to stop Bayard's advance.

"Where is your alchemy laboratory? I have need of your old knowledge."

Bayard pressed against Sefu's arm, trying to get a better look at the bundle. "It's all packed up in a chest upstairs. There's barely any useful or interesting ingredients in the forests around here. The last thing I used it for is trying to invent a new sort of quick-fermenting ale about three years ago. Damn near burned the building down. What's in here, Sef?"

"I thought you liked familiar ale?"

"Familiarity is a secondary concern when a traveling caravan drinks the tavern dry and they tell me to wait a month for the good shite. Now stop ducking my questions; what do you need, and what's in this thing?"

Sefu sighed. "A flower." Bayard settled back into his chair and blinked. "A flower that I believe to be responsible for a terrifying plague that afflicts anyone who contacts it. There is an oasis in eastern Egypt, near Velaconpolis, which is now an archeological dig site. The area has been mostly abandoned for more years than anyone can count, however recently many European scholars and students have begun to occupy the area for their studies. Ten months ago, a child born to one of the students there wandered off into the desert. They searched for days and were nearly ready to give up when a woman spotted an oasis in the distance.

"She and her search party ran into the oasis and found the child, but he was terribly ill. They reported grey skin, glazed eyes, a complete lack of reason or coherent thought. He acted violently towards anyone who approached, and they brought his mother in to try to calm him. She approached and attempted to embrace the child, but he bit into her arm without hesitation. She pushed him away and he tripped backwards down a large hill, breaking his neck on a tree. The mother, in her grief, jumped from the tallest ruin in Velaconpolis only two hours later, and that was the end of that particular incident."

Bayard stared at Sefu inquisitively, and despite his stubbornness against reverting to his old studies, many questions flooded his mind. "Where do you come in? Were you studying the ruins with them?"

"No, but please, I will explain as you assemble your alchemy table, time is of the essence. Every passing hour brings more potential danger to Egypt."

The serious, warning look in Sefu's eyes finally made Bayard stand. "Very well, follow me then." He saw the shortsword was still laying beside the fireplace, so he took it and placed it on one of the shop's racks, then started to pull himself up the stairs to the second floor of his home. Pushing open a door with the tip of his foot, he entered a large but simple bedroom with many tables and chests, a small bed, two large windows, and a rack containing a longsword, a hunting bow, a full quiver, many daggers and knives, and a woodcutting axe. Bayard lit two table lanterns and removed piles of metal ore and even more knives from two chairs, one of which Sefu settled into. He then moved to the largest chest in the room, pulling it open. Only wooden planks were visible at the top layer of the chest, and Bayard started removing them and assembling the base of the alchemy table. "Alright, I'm getting it ready, now talk."

"You are not making this easy on me, Bayard. It is hard enough to speak of such subjects as it is, not to mention the fact that I need to explain in a way that you will believe."

Bayard stood and looked to Sefu. "My friend, we are both men of science. We've each seen many then-unexplainable things and worked together to find the truth. Speak freely and without fear of being doubted, I trust your opinion as much as I trust my own. Also, if you please, tell me of your mother. Did you find her?"

Sefu grinned; it was true that Bayard had no reason to doubt him, no matter how absurd his claims. As a child of five, Sefu came to England with his trader father, to the Kingdom of Valdus to trade rare weapons, pelts, and spices. There he befriended the child Bayard, whose parents were great doctors and alchemists, known all over England and even some countries beyond. Quickly after arriving, however, Sefu's father was murdered by bandits trying to get at the unique Eastern weapons he brought to England. Poor and homeless, Sefu would have died in the street if not for Bayard and his family, who gladly took him in and trained him in the arts of medicine and alchemy. For fifteen years he lived with them, and he was just as devastated as Bayard when his mother and father died in a great fire that annihilated nearly all wooden homes and shops in the Lower Ring of the city. Sefu and Bayard survived the incident because they had been out collecting herbs and hunting, returning when they saw smoke rising thousands of feet above the castle.

Only weeks after, Sefu had dropped news of his intention to leave, to find his birth mother and finally let her know of his safety and his father's demise, as well as bring modern English medicinal techniques to Egypt. Bayard, alone and upset, fled the city and took up residence in Peydenal. Despite his aptitude for it, Bayard never appreciated Alchemy as a profession and instead took up apprenticeship as a blacksmith. Bayard was much more adept at the studious side of the alchemical art, able to deconstruct any potion or elixir or estimate the effects of any ingredients without ever having to consume them. And that was the talent that Sefu needed.

"Thank you, Bayard," Sefu said softly. "I will explain the chain of events just as they happened. I was in my village, having just arrived there weeks earlier. I found my mother quickly. She had remarried and given birth to three children, one of whom she had given my name. She said she regretted this when she saw I lived, but I told her it was the best thing she could have done, which I am sure you know is the truth." Bayard nodded silently as he continued building the laboratory table. "I stayed for many years, teaching the town's doctor my new methods, healing those who needed it and doing whatever else I could to help. Word of my medical talents eventually spread to other villages, and I was woken up by a late-night knock on my door, much like me coming to you tonight. To my surprise, it was a Frenchman. He came to me from the Velaconpolis archeological site, having heard of my advanced techniques and the fact that I spoke English and some French. He told me about how a plague unlike any he had ever heard of was killing off their community, victims turning into mindless animals and attempting to kill and consume anyone unaffected by the plague.

"I quickly agreed to visit their community, and left with him after saying goodbye to my mother. He would not tell me anything about the effects of the plague, saying that only seeing it with my own eyes would be enough to make me believe it. I have to say he was right. Two day's camel ride later we arrived, and the place was in chaos. Several headless bodies laid in the sand, the diseased wandered the ruins in a slow, drunken stumble, wooden barricades burned between the stone buildings. I have to admit I was terrified. As we approached, the camels began panicking and nearly threw us off. We managed to dismount and the animals sprinted off in the other direction. I could not blame them, really. The Frenchman, who named himself as Albert Hesen, strange name for a French, told me to stay back as he drew his scimitar, then star-"

"Drew his what?"

"A scimitar. It's a large, wide curved sword used by many Eastern countries. You have never seen one come through your shop?"

"I haven't seen your kind or any of their equipment since the city,

Sef. However I do remember seeing swords similar to what you describe, though I never knew their names. I want one."

Sefu smiled again. "I bet you do. Better than these twigs you make." Bayard just shook his head. "Anyway, he drew the sword and started walking towards the ruins. He shouted, and every one of the afflicted turned towards him and began..." He stopped and shuddered. "They began moaning. A terrible sound, a constant sound. Human lungs should not be able to sustain a vocalization like that. They began moving towards Albert, very slowly, as if their legs were filled with sand. Around eight of them, all together. The first of the group reached Albert and he quickly sidestepped the sick woman, then swung his blade into the back of her neck. She collapsed instantly, her head cleanly severed, but her face continued to move, jaws snapping and eyes wide in anger. He kept-"

"That's impossible. When the heart stops pump-"

"Please do not interrupt me. Everything I speak is the truth, save your questions for when I finish." Sefu was visibly shaking now, and Bayard nodded. "I stepped in, telling him that I should try to help them before we killed them. He pushed me back, shouting that they would rip the both of us apart and eat us, and that we would become like them. I was forced to stay back as he killed each of the diseased in almost the same manner. I made a mental note that they did not bleed, their flesh splitting cleanly, only dark, congealed blood could be seen within. They all lunged at him with teeth snapping, swinging their arms wildly in attempts to scratch him. He took the time to show me their nature, cutting off some of their arms, slashing some of their stomachs open, spilling their guts. Nothing slowed them down except damaging the spine or severing the head. Even after beheading, they were alive, and only cutting directly into the brain fully ceased their movement. It was as though their brains had become self-sustaining organs, without need of the heart, lungs, or anything else. He cut our way into the center of the ancient city, and there we saw another group of five, pounding on a stone slab covering the entrance to a large building. Albert dispatched them and had me help him slide the stone away from the door. The survivors of their community were inside, thirty of them, all severely malnourished, but alive and sane. Men and women of England, France, Venice, Spain, and some Eastern women as well.

"I was amazed by their community. The men and women were

considered equal, as were all the nationalities. There was no murder, no rape, no crime besides the petty theft of food and coins perpetuated by some of the younger students. A massive group of civilized academics. All study of the ruins had ceased, replaced by study of the plague, its victims, and its source. Albert had figured out that the child I told you about earlier had been afflicted by the same disease, but his head struck the tree he landed on with enough force to damage the brain, and his mother's brain was destroyed when she jumped from the high building and onto the stone ground. What he did not know yet, is that a woman in the search party had found a patch of unique flowers within the oasis. She picked them and passed them out among the other women and one man whom she fancied in the search party, who took to wearing them in their hair. Two hours later, they all began exhibiting signs of sickness. Not even a day after, they had become some of the monsters he had just killed.

"If they bit or scratched a healthy person, the person would fall ill and turn violent and insane within a day. It took nearly a week for them to figure out how the disease was transmitted, and how to effectively dispatch the plague carriers, before they had Albert block them into a shelter and come find me. In that time, almost all of the healthiest men had died fighting, attempting to capture or restrain the diseased. Over one hundred people traveled there, and thirty-one remained alive when I left Egypt months ago. Nearly all of them remembered seeing this flower in the hair of the first batch of victims, the flower taken from the same oasis where the first infected child was found.

"At first they thought it was the water there, but all the men and women had drank from the oasis pond, and only the women and the one man who touched the flowers became the monsters. Once I was filled in, I told them of you, of your talents in uncovering the properties of potions, poisons, and everything else mysterious. Right before I left, after I retrieved the sample of the flower in the bundle here, they used nearly their entire stock of lamp oil to burn the oasis to the ground, the infected bodies with it. We believe the threat to be over, but if possible, we need to discover an inoculation for this disease should this ever happen again." Sefu finally stopped talking and leaned back in his chair, staring blankly at the wall ahead of him. He pulled a short pipe and a vial of finely-cut dried tobacco from his vest pocket and ignited it in the flame of the table lantern, then took a long draw and offered it to Bayard.

Bayard took the pipe and puffed at it; he had finished constructing the alchemy table some minutes ago. He thought Sefu's words over and over and tiredly blinked his eyes. "The most logical culprit would be a parasite, probably," he mumbled. "It actively and intelligently seeks out more suitable carriers, to spread the sickness further. I've heard of parasites that can control the bodies of insects, but never something that could take over a mammal, and especially not a human being."

Sefu shook his head. "Of course, that was my first opinion as well. An undiscovered creature that invades and controls a host, but after some study, I no longer believe that to be so. Firstly, if its objective was to reproduce among hosts, it would simply implant the parasite with a bite and leave the victim to succumb. This is not the case; the afflicted attempt to entirely consume their victims, unless they escape. They do not willingly leave enough behind to create a walking carrier, it seems very counterproductive for their species. And that is not all.

"When asked by the community to dissect and study one of the creatures, at first I declined, in fear of being infected. However, they seemed entirely confident that I would not be, stating that whatever caused the transformations seemed to fade from corpses around two days after death. After I declined again, one of them went as far as rubbing the bloody stump of a dismembered arm against herself and willingly submitting to quarantine for two days. After seeing she remained healthy, I agreed to perform the autopsy. Moving one of the older cadavers onto an ancient burial slab, I first cut into the torso. It was strange how dark its blood was, but its organs seemed mostly unchanged. I expected strange nerves or veins originating from the brain, forcefully controlling the organs and muscles, but saw nothing of the sort.

"I then sawed into the skull. What I saw, and I am ashamed to say it, stumped me as a doctor, an alchemist, and as a scientist. The brain was almost entirely inhuman. The whole frontal lobe had been altered, swollen to nearly four times its natural size, covered in tumors and rips. The rest of the brain was compacted into the base of the skull. The only explanation is that the plague simply changes the complete biology of the human body. Just as an acorn bears no resemblance to the large tree it eventually becomes. The brain's new form allows the body to move without a beating heart, without breathing lungs, without tiring, without feeling."

He placed a hand over his forehead and closed his eyes hard in an obvious attempt to force away a headache. "The victims die, Bayard. And then they stand up. It is not possible to cure them, because they die less than a day after they become infected, and then they change, into another species entirely, with no similarities to our kind besides the shell of their skin. All we can hope to accomplish here is to find a way to protect the uninfected against it. Some of the Italians of the Velaconpolis site say that Hell has decided to claim our mortal plain. And despite my knowledge and reason, I am starting to believe them."

"This is no demonic uprising, Sefu," Bayard said solemnly. "Just like all new afflictions and plagues discovered, the common man always blames what he cannot comprehend, due to the fear of being forced to. Anyway, the laboratory is all ready, would you please bring the flower?" Sefu nodded and left the room. He returned quickly, carrying the bundle, as well as two pairs of blacksmith's gloves and tongs. Bayard took the bundle, cutting the rope off with one of his many knives.

"Be cautious, Bayard. Even the slightest physical contact with the flower or its spores will result in infection," Sefu said worriedly. "Wear the gloves, and only touch the vial and flower with the tongs." Bayard did as asked, pulling on the thick gloves. He slowly unraveled the cloth, revealing the wooden box. He slid the lid off, removing the second bundle contained within. After unwrapping this one, the vial sat alone in the center of the alchemy table. Bayard glared at it.

"When did you pluck this, Sef?"

"Nearly six months ago."

"Shouldn't it be...well, dead and dried?"

Sefu let out a soft chuckle. "It 'shouldn't' a lot of things, brother." The flower contained in the vial was flawless as the day it was plucked. The bright green pedals lightly curved down towards the stem, the white center puffing out above the leaves. "Cautious, brother...perform your tests on top of the cloth there, so at the end we can just bundle everything up and toss it in the fire downstairs."

"I know, Sef. Trust me." Bayard used the tongs to move the vial to the side of the table and removed a small, round beaker from the shelf of glass containers set above the work area of the table. He then removed two vials, one containing a brownish-red, sticky liquid and the other, a pretty shade of yellow similar to sunlight. He poured the entirety of the yellow liquid into the beaker, then added a carefully measured spoon of the red.

"What are these chemicals?" Sefu asked, peering over Bayard's shoulder. "They are unfamiliar to me."

"My piss and the blood of a pig." Sefu recoiled, and Bayard grinned. "I'm kidding. I'll explain the scientific process later, after I have some idea what this is. It's just a preliminary test to determine the toxicity of the flower, and I can figure out where to go from there. If it begins reacting, bubbling and such, I'll be able to tell just *how* poisonous this is by the intensity of it. I'm sure you know well enough, but I'd like to see it for myself." Sefu nodded.

Bayard slowly, carefully held the vial with his gloved left hand, then used the tongs to pop the cork from the small container. He upturned it over the cloth and the flower lightly settled, its evil nature entirely inconspicuous. Taking a knife, he cut off about one centimeter of stem, a bit of the leaves, and a shaving of the white, puffy center. He brushed the three parts of the flower onto the tip of his knife and dropped it into the beaker. Nothing happened. Bayard exhaled slowly. "I'm sorry, Sefu, but as of now it seems that the flower is just that, a pretty plant. Either you have the wrong culprit or whatever caused the infection died on the trip. I'll run more tests, but without the slightest sign of tox...what the hell?"

The mixture began to twist and swirl, the beaker nearly vibrating with the intensity of it. Then it began to change, turning first a dark red, then pitch black, and finally settled on a sickly brown. Sefu and Bayard, both of whom had retreated to the other side of the room and pressed against the back wall, stared at the concoction with eyes wide. "Well...that's new," Bayard gasped.

Sefu nodded. "I suppose the amount of time since it was plucked caused a delayed reaction." Once confident that the reaction was over, Bayard stepped away from the wall and back to the table. Sefu stayed put.

"You definitely have something dangerous here, Sef. I've never seen any reaction like this, and I've seen poisons where you could kill a Kingdom with a gram of it in a water supply," Bayard said softly. Sefu was still leaning on the wall, nursing his headache. "I don't even know where to begin. I suppose we need to determine-"

Crash

The sound of glass breaking, downstairs. Bayard and Sefu froze, staring at the closed door. Footsteps could be heard below, along with loud whispering. Sefu looked over to Bayard, his face livid.

"They followed me here. They want the key to the safe in my carriage. They likely intended to jump me when I left here, but got tired of waiting."

"What's in the safe?"

"Gold. A lot of gold. They probably saw me buying the carriage when I left the ship, followed me all the way from the coast." The footsteps entered the hall below, and the first footfall could be heard on the stairs. Bayard launched into action, sprinting along the wall and grabbing the longsword from the weapon rack. He ran for the room's door, slamming the lock shut and bracing against it just as the first kick made contact. Sefu joined him, jamming his boot against the bottom of the door. They pushed back against the repeated kicks, the wood around the lock splintering and buckling.

The kicks stopped for a few seconds, but were replaced by a loud crash, as the blade of an axe penetrated the center of the door, nearly cutting into Sefu's arm. He leaned, narrowly avoiding the second axe strike. "Bayard, hold the door!" Sefu yelled as he ran for the weapon rack. The axe struck again, opening a hole about half a foot wide. A dirty wad of light brown hair could be seen through the hole, and Bayard violently shoved the tip of the longsword through the opening. There was a yell, but the axe crashed into the tip of the blade, badly chipping it. Bayard withdrew the sword and cursed when he saw the lack of blood.

"GET DOWN!" Bayard turned and saw Sefu standing near his bed, the longbow in his hands and fully drawn. Bayard dropped, curling into a ball against the door as Sefu released the string. The heavy arrow sailed straight through the hole, and Bayard was glad to hear an agonized scream. The arrow seemed to strike the second assailant as the first continued swinging the axe into the door. Sefu fired several more arrows through the various holes in the door, but the attackers seemed to be standing out of the way, swinging into the door from the sides. The rusted hinges gave before the majority of the wood did, and the door toppled over Bayard's prone body. He grasped the hilt of the damaged sword, swinging upwards towards the burglars, but catching the side of the falling door instead. He felt a kick slam into his ribs and coughed, rolling over to see Sefu wrestling with a black-haired man with an arrow going through his arm.

The other, brown-haired attacker was standing over Bayard,

raising the axe over his head to finish him off. Bayard kicked forward, striking the man hard in his knee. He buckled, dropping the axe, which Bayard rolled away from just in time. Bayard grabbed a chair and quickly pushed himself to his feet, then swung the chair around, slamming it into the axeman with enough force to snap one of the chair legs. The thief collapsed and Bayard did not hesitate as he plunged the tip of the longsword into the man's chest. He turned to help Sefu, and saw that he had the second man by the neck with the bow string. It looked like Sefu was handling it, and afraid that he might hit Sefu if he swung at the remaining burglar, he decided to stay back. The black-haired man was turning blue, nearly choked out, but in an act of survival he managed to elbow Sefu in the solar plexus, and he released his grip. The man stumbled forward, tried to turn to attack Sefu again, but tripped over a fallen chair. He fell backwards, crashing into the alchemy table. The flower gently rolled off the cloth and landed innocently on the man's shoulder.

Bayard was sure that his heart stopped. He stared at the man, his eyes horrified, his mouth agape. Sefu had the same look. The flower rolled off the attacker's shoulder and silently came to rest on the wooden floor. The thief looked between them, wrinkled his eyebrows, then spoke. "What?"

"HE IS INFECTED, BAYARD! KILL HIM! KILL HIM RIGHT NOW!" Sefu roared. The man jumped to his feet with incredible speed at the anger and desperation in Sefu's voice, and he sprinted for the window. Bayard moved, diving through the air and slashing the longsword towards the running man. He managed to cut a deep gash into the man's lower back, but he didn't stop. The thief jumped, crashing through the window and collapsing onto the dark ground below. He was bleeding badly from the arrow wound, sword wound and broken glass, but he was slowly getting to his feet. Sefu was at the window now, drawing the bow. He fired an arrow and it struck the man in the thigh. In a fit of adrenaline, he managed to stay standing, and he began limping towards the trees surrounding the outside of the village.

Lanterns were being lit in nearby homes and shops, citizens alerted by the shouting. Sefu drew the bow once more, but screamed in pain as the string unhooked from the bow, striking him in the side of the face. *Damaged when he used it to choke the attacker,* Bayard thought. Sefu started hurling daggers at the limping man from the window, but none made contact, and he disappeared into the trees. "AFTER HIM!" Sefu grabbed Bayard's arm with great strength and pulled him from the room and down the stairs. They burst from the house and Sefu started towards the town stables, but stopped and turned to Bayard.

"Burn it, Bayard. I am sorry, but we do not have time to dispose of the equipment itself. If someone enters the house while we are gone and touches something, gets infected...I have more gold than you have ever seen, I will buy you a house twice this size once this is over and done with, but right now you have to throw your gloves in there and burn it." Bayard grimaced, looking up at the perfect old house. The home and forge he'd lived and worked at for the past eleven years, but he knew Sefu was right. Bayard shook the gloves off of his hands, letting them fall in the doorway, and he grabbed the lantern from inside the door, hurling it onto the straw-coated roof. It ignited instantly, flames spreading across the roof with great speed. Bayard turned away as he and Sefu sprinted towards the stables.

The town stable was a small, ratty building that was little more than ten poles and a roof, five horses resting peacefully inside of it. Three of the five were small and unhealthy-looking but Bayard's own brown steed and an unfamiliar exotic white horse, Sefu's, were large and strong. They mounted up and galloped into the trees, the early morning light pouring over the landscape. The blood trail was easy to follow, red spotting the ground and marking trees the thief leaned into. They were sure they would catch him at any second, when the trail stopped. Sefu cursed and dismounted, bending to look closely at the ground.

"They had a horse tied here. The hoofprints are obvious. He came this way, through the trees..." Sefu slowly walked through the forest, leading his horse behind him. They soon came to a dirt path, the hoofprints traveling off to the west. Bayard grasped Sefu's shoulder, looking terrified. "What is it, brother?"

"This path leads to a main trading and travel route...It leads to the city."

"GO!" Sefu yelled in a rage, throwing himself back on his horse, and they raced full-speed down the path. Soon they came to a wider, smoother road, and they followed the prints northwest. For hours and hours they pushed their horses onward through the day and finally, as the sun was getting low in the sky, the tall castle rose over a distant hill. Kicking the horses harder, they rushed towards the towering city. Twenty minutes later they arrived at the gates, nearly tumbling off their animals as they stopped. An armored guard ran forward, holding his sword to them suspiciously.

"What the hell are you two doing, rushing in here like this?" the guard spat. Sefu knocked the blade aside and gripped the much-smaller-than-him guard by the neck of his cuirass.

"An injured man. Arrow and sword wounds, and many small cuts. He arrived here very recently, I know you saw him," Sefu growled. The guard stuttered and recoiled.

"Y-Yes, sir. He arrived here not half an hour ago. Died right where we stand, after falling from his horse. Were those wounds your doing?"

"DAMN!" Sefu roared, and he pushed the guard away. "Where is he, where did the body go? And did you touch the body in any way?"

"No, I didn't touch him! I had my partner drag him inside, to get him ready for the corpse burning where we send off all the poor and homeless and unknown who die each day," the guard whimpered.

"When, when do they burn them?" Sefu asked pleadingly.

"Each day, at noon. Your, eh, 'friend' will be burned tomorrow."

Sefu shook the guard again. "No, you have to burn him now. Or just put an axe through his-"

"Sefu," Bayard interrupted. You said the afflicted change after about a day. What happens if they die through other means before then?"

Sefu shook his head. "I honestly do not know."

Bayard shut his eyes and groaned. Just then, the screaming started.

The guard turned towards the city gate, but Sefu held him back. "Do not go in there. There is nothing that can be done yet. We need to barricade the city from the outside, we cannot allow any to leave." The screams grew louder and the crash of collapsing wood could be heard.

"What are you talking about, Sefu? We have to go exterminate it now, before it spreads," Bayard hissed. Sefu violently shook his head, and a pained expression spread over his face.

"I am sure someone was bitten. Listen to the screams, Bayard. If it were just the thief we needed to put down, it would be one thing, but if we start trying to behead the town's citizens based on such an absurd claim, we will be burned at the stake."

"We can't just let the city die! We can quarantine the bitten. If they turn, we can convince the townspeople what needs to be done then."

"They WILL turn, brother. The panic has already started, people will be trying to flee the city. Even if they manage to kill the infected man, the bitten will return to their homes, or visit a doctor, and they'll turn tomorrow and infect even more people. We *cannot* let the plague escape the city. We know where the infected are, we need to contain them, wait it out, and we can handle the afflicted and any survivors once the initial panic, looting, and rioting fade out. Many of the men here are veterans or warriors, and there is a massive guard presence. We can do what we can to help from the outside, but we need to barricade the gates. I understand your need to help them, but you have not seen this plague in action. The afflicted seek out sights, sounds, smells. If even a few infected make their way out of the city and turn, they will wander to other towns, attack travelers. I am *not* overstating things when I say that nowhere on the continent would be safe."

"Damn this, Sefu," Bayard spat. "I know you are right, but this makes me sick."

"Er-" The guard was still standing there, his mouth open. "Would someone like to explain just what the hell is going on?"

Bayard spoke up. "Yes Sir, sorry. Me and my friend are alchemists and doctors. The man who died here, he, er...he was sick with a very rare plague. It quickly causes violent insanity in those it infects and makes them nearly impossible to kill or stop. It's loose in the city, and we need to stop anyone infected from leaving, or it could spread to other towns."

The guard stepped back. "Bugger that, I have family in there, I need to get them out!" He ducked under Sefu's arm and began sprinting towards the city gate, but Sefu easily ran him down and tied the guard's hands behind his back with his belt.

"I am so sorry, my friend. This is above you or the laws of your city. People will find shelter, and in a few days it will be safe enough for us to enter the city and help any survivors. Lay here for now, we will return soon." The guard violently and repeatedly cursed at Sefu, but he ignored it and jogged to the main gate, slamming the outer lock bar. "We are fortunate that these relics from the Black Death still stand outside city walls," he said, patting the massive steel plague bar. "It may have been a mostly conventional sickness, but the need for quarantine was still strong." They circled the city on horseback, blocking each of the gates as they passed. As they closed off the last, the screaming escalated, growing even more panicked. Suddenly, they heard something crash into the gate from the other side. Terrified voices could be made out.

"We're locked in! Where is the demon? Is it still following us?"

"I don't know, I don't hear it anymore. It must have gone after someone else. Who locked the gates, the guards?"

Another, stronger voice shouted out. "No. Our orders from the bishop for a demonic possession is to evacuate the city and try to force the possessed into the church for exorcism. I'm sure the other guards are preparing to do just that. Please do not panic, return to your homes, and wait for a town crier to deliver further instructions."

Bayard sighed. "I told you. It's always right to the demons with these people. Someone trips on the church steps: Demons. Someone flirts with a priest: Demons. Someone pisses themselves outside a pub: Yeah, it's probably demons," he whispered to Sefu, who shook his head. They returned to the front gate, the guard still wiggling against his bonds.

Sefu knelt over the man, and spoke softly. "What is your name, sir?"

The guard looked up at him, hate in his eyes. "I am Jacob Carter, member of the City Guard, and it is my duty to see the both of you executed as soon as I am able to," the tied man said, false confidence building in his voice. Sefu sighed again, then stood and took a massive breath.

"CITIZENS OF VALDUS!" he bellowed, his voice carrying loud and far in the open air. The scattered shouts ceased, and the men inside the nearby gate could be heard gasping and stumbling. Body and voice, Sefu was an extremely imposing man. "I assume some of you have witnessed the dead man seemingly returned to life. He is afflicted by a dangerous plague that must not escape the city. You have been quarantined, in order to preserve both the safety of nearby towns, and England as a whole. I ask that you do not shout back to me, as this will likely attract the infected straight to you.

If you see the infected man, do not approach him unless you are an experienced warrior. If you are such, you must either decapitate the man, or drive an arrow, axe, or hammer directly into his head. If you have been bitten by, scratched by, or otherwise contacted the afflicted man, I beg of you to enclose yourself in a sealed room for one entire day. You may encounter more citizens who are infected by this plague. Do not attempt to interact with them if you are not a combatant. Seek shelter, barricade yourself in, remain as quiet as possible, and do not enclose yourself with anyone who has been bitten or scratched. If any of you are family to a city guard by the name of Jacob Carter, please be aware that he is completely safe and in our care. He wishes to aid you, but I cannot allow the gates to open.

Once more: Seek shelter, do not contact the infected, and if you must do so, it is absolutely essential that you destroy or remove their head, as it is the only way to completely disable them. They cannot be reasoned with, they cannot be healed, and they most certainly cannot be exorcised by a priest or bishop of any caliber. My party will enter the city when we deem it stable in order to aid the survivors. Good luck, and may God have mercy on all of you."

Bayard was leaning on the city wall, his head in his hands. "I cannot believe what we are doing here, Sefu," he groaned in a strained, conflicted voice.

"An unbelievable method to prevent an unbelievable sickness," Sefu said, his voice solid and sure. "You will witness the infected soon enough, and then you will understand. I only hope my message helps them survive, but I doubt it will do much. Just like words cannot reach the infected, they also cannot reach those plagued by fear."

Bayard pushed himself off the wall and walked towards Jacob Carter, still wriggling about on the ground. "You've become a wise and cold bastard these past eleven years, Sef. For my own sanity, I'll believe you are right about this."

"I promise you, I am," Sefu said, placing a hand on Bayard's shoulder. "Come now, we have to get Jacob to shelter and take turns patrolling the walls, make sure no one tries to climb their way out with a ladder or rope down from a guard tower."

Bayard nodded. "What should I do if I find someone?"

Sefu handed Bayard the longbow, which he had repaired during their journey to Valdus. "You aim this at their heads and tell them to strip and turn in circles. If they refuse, put the arrow through their head. If you see any bite or scratch marks, put the arrow through their head. If not, tell them to come to that farm," he said, pointing to a large brown building a couple hundred meters away, "where we are going to leave Jacob. If they refuse to go to the shelter, *you put the arrow through their head*. We cannot have citizens alerting other towns, who may send guards or militia to aid the people here."

Bayard shook his head, shoving the bow back into Sefu's hands. "If we're killing live citizens, that's on you. I won't do any worse than hogtie someone who is not trying to kill me first." To his surprise, Sefu nodded.

"It is alright, Bayard. You will understand soon...you will see," he whispered, repeating the same line he used before. Bayard closed his eyes, secretly hoping that he would never have to understand.

*****

Gendrina Carter slammed the door shut behind her, collapsing against it and closing her eyes. The panicked screams drowned out the moans of the demon, and she was glad of it. As loud as it was, it was a sound she understood, it was a *human* sound.

"You alright, Gen?" She opened her eyes and they fell on Thomas Carter, her brother. "Is the bite okay?" She looked at her arm, a ragged strip missing from her sleeve.

"He didn't get me, just ruined my dress. I can't say the same for that guard. So much blood..." She quickly shook her head, as if physically trying to throw off the mental images.

"That was Sam. Me and Jacob trained with him. If it wasn't for my leg, it would have been me out there today." He rubbed his left leg, thick bandages wrapped around it. Just hours earlier, the sole of his boot had given out, and he crashed his leg with his entire considerable weight behind it into the corner of a stone step. It somehow wasn't broken, but it was swollen beyond belief and he certainly wasn't going anywhere fast. "God, where is Jacob?"

As if on queue, a distant, loud voice boomed out over the city, silencing the people in the streets. "CITIZENS OF VALDUS!" They listened quietly to the man's speech, growing more and more apprehensive with each sentence. Suddenly, the name Jacob Carter came up, along with news of his safety. Gendrina and Thomas both exhaled a laugh of relief, but quickly silenced themselves to listen to the yelling man. They looked at each other as he finished with an ominous "May God have mercy on all of you."

"Well, brother is alive, at least," Gendrina said happily. "And if we are to believe whoever the hell that was, it's no demon, but a new plague. That man was dead though, Thomas. He was sliced to ribbons and shot up like a target dummy. And then I saw him sit up and bite into that guard. Into Sam."

"It is unbelievable," Thomas whispered. "I do not know what sort of plague this is, but I think I know the identity of the shouter. I'd recognize that voice anywhere. There was a doctor here, long ago, an Eastern man. On his own time, at night, he would referee fights between off-duty guards. We had a betting game of it. Jacob was just a boy, it had to be around ten years ago. His name escapes me. See-foo, Seh-fah...something with an S and an F."

"Very astute, brother," Gendrina moaned sarcastically. "All we need to know is if he can be trusted." The shouts and shrieks had resumed after the man had ended his speech, his whole effort seemingly lost on the majority of the townspeople.

"I think so. He was a great healer, always treating the scrapes and bruises of the men after our fights, as well as supplying ointments and bandages to any guard who asked, many of which I ended up using on you. He was a friend of the city. If he says nobody can leave, this thing must be bigger than we can imagine."

Gendrina nodded. "If we're going to be trapped in here for days, we need supplies. Food, water. I'll go get what we need, before things get too bad out there. First I need to go upstairs and get out of this damn dress, I move slower than you do in this thing. While it may not be advantageous for a guard, Jacob is small enough where his spare uniform should fit me well." Thomas sighed as she bolted up the wooden stairs.

She returned soon after, wearing the decently-fitting cuirass and greaves, substituting the heavy and large iron boots with her own leather winter boots. The helmet fit her well, cushioned by her thick red hair that was rolled up into it. She wore a shortsword at her side, and a loaded crossbow across her back. "Ready," she said.

"Damn it, Gen, you cannot keep charging into danger like this. Despite your behavior, you're just a woman-" Thomas yelped as she kicked him in his injured leg with the tip of her boot. Not hard, but hard enough to get her point across.

"Don't call me that," she spat. "I've never considered myself anything less than a strangely-chested man. Now sit quietly while I bring you some potatoes to chew on," and she kicked her way out the front door, slamming it behind her again. She stood there until she heard the *click* of the lock, then proceeded down the crowded street.

Chapter Four
Summer of 1513 A.D
City of Valdus
Twilight

The district was in absolute pandemonium. Shop windows were shattered, homeless and poor citizens digging through the contents while the helpless shopkeepers tried to beat them away with canes and flagpoles. There were no guards in sight, probably all gathered around the demon-possessed man (if that was really what he was) trying to lure him to the church. Dead bodies scattered the sides of the street, some dry and some with pools of blood seeping from their motionless corpses.

One shirtless man with three visible bite marks on his left shoulder and arm twitched about on the ground, gurgling and moaning. Gendrina heard shrieking from down a side alley and saw two men attacking a small woman, ripping her clothes off and taking swigs from a massive bottle of absinth. She didn't want to waste time getting into a serious fight, but she managed to put a crossbow bolt into one of the men's arms, and they both turned and ran at the sight of her, obviously assuming she was a real guard. The woman squealed a quick thank you and retreated into a nearby door.

Gendrina reloaded the crossbow and slipped it onto her back, picking up her pace towards the market district, where she could find the water well and loot some produce. Turning a corner, she saw two women, obviously extremely drunk, shambling down the center of the road without a care in the world. She approached them, calling out- And they turned, their bloody, grey faces immediately opening in a deathly moan, their arms raised towards her, their eyes glazed, white, and dead.

Gendrina's breath caught in her throat, and she stumbled backwards, the word "demons" spilling from her mouth. She shook her head, raising the crossbow, remembering the words of the supposed 'See-foo' or whatever his name truly was. "Infected people. A sickness. Not demons," she whispered to herself. Praying that the man spoke the truth, she aimed the heavy wooden weapon and gently rubbed the trigger, felt the jolt as the string flew forward, propelling the broadhead bolt straight into the forehead of the woman on the right. She crumpled instantly and completely, like a sack of flour dropped from a house's roof. *Yes!*

She quickly reloaded the crossbow, and gave the second approaching woman the same treatment. *At least they're slow,* she thought. She jogged to the first body, grasping the end of the bolt that stuck from her head and pulling it free. She pulled her shortsword and cut off a wide strip from the dead woman's dress, using it to clean the blood off the tip of the bolt. Doing the same for the other, she put both bolts back into the quiver and kept moving towards the market, feeling much more confident if she had to face more of these people. And she did. On her journey to the market district, she encountered at least twenty of the infected. Each behaved the exact same way, turning directly towards her and unleashing their hellish moan. They all lunged towards her at their slow pace, their tactics unchanging as she put a bolt into each of their heads.

By the time she reached the market, the crossbow was nearly unusable. Two bolts had been lost, one in the arm of the uninfected man in that alley, and one in an infected that had toppled over a fence into the lower ring of the city. The other four were cracked, or their tips were bent and damaged from penetrating so many hard skulls. She disassembled the crossbow, salvaging the string and trigger assembly (it made a good lockpick), and then tossed the heavy frame along with the bolts. In front of her was the market, dozens of stalls lining the circular crossroads. There were nearly fifty people here, all seemingly healthy, wrestling over what little food was left.

Gendrina drew her shortsword and began striding towards the smallest group, two men and a woman who were punching the hell out of each other in an attempt to get at a sack of rice. They scattered at the sight of her and she was glad that she had a large frame, nobody seemed to recognize her gender at a glance. She lifted the sack of rice over her left shoulder, and made for the vegetable stand, which was occupied by four street urchins. She saw that the stand still had a good supply of food, so she stood at a distance until the children dispersed. Taking a burlap sack from the cabinet underneath the cart, she filled it to the brim with carrots, cabbages, onions, celery, and every potato that was left. Hauling the heavy sacks behind her, she made for the water well in the center of the circle.

Luckily there was nobody here, and she tossed the bucket down into the well where she was greeted with a disheartening *thunk*. The well was completely empty. Frowning, she started back for home. It was mostly clear on the way back, except for a pack of panicked dogs and a few scattering homeless. As she turned onto her street, she saw him.

The man with the three bite marks was standing directly in front of her house, pounding on the door. It held, the man was no match for the heavy and solid oak. This was a problem though, without the crossbow she would have to handle him with the shortsword. She remembered what the yelling man had said, decapitate them or destroy the brain. *I have to find a way to keep him still,* she thought. Looking around, she saw a wooden cart loaded with heavy stone bricks. She set down the sacks and grabbed the handles, wheeling it around and aiming it towards the man. She ran forward, the noise causing the infected man to turn towards her. She slammed the cart into him, pinning him against the thick door. He moaned even louder, swinging wildly at her with his hands bent in the shape of claws.

Gendrina stood back, waiting for the infected man to swing out again, and she lunged forward, slashing into his right arm. The arm came cleanly off, her strength combined with the man's own. She stepped to the disarmed side, and chopped the shortsword into the front of his neck. It didn't go all the way through. She withdrew the blade, and her mouth opened in amazement at the complete lack of blood pouring from the wound, not to mention that the man continued to snap and swing at her despite his missing throat. "*What are you?*" she asked the pathetic creature.

She only got a hissing moan in response. "Well, it does not matter. Demon or plague victim, I know how to kill you," and she swung the sword again, his head toppling over the cart and onto the ground. The body heaped forward, and she stepped back. The cart rolled away, and he collapsed at the base of the door. She reached out to knock, but jumped back as the head: The decapitated, lone head, opened its eyes and began chewing on her thick boot. She screamed and kicked out, sending the head flying down the road. Leaning on the door and clutching her chest, she felt tears welling in her eyes. She shook her head, picked the food sacks back up, and knocked on the door with the hilt of her sword. "It's me, Tom." It opened seconds later, and she ran inside just as the very top of the sun dropped below the horizon.

*****

"What do you think the royalty is doing right now?" Sefu asked, staring at the ceiling of the barn.

"Chances are they don't even know. I mean, they know something's going on what with the screaming, but I doubt they know *what* quite yet." It was Jacob who answered. They had dragged him to the farm, where Sefu explained the nature of the plague, repeating the whole story he told Bayard back in Peydenal. After this, the guard stopped fighting them. They cut him loose a while ago, and he had been entirely agreeable since.

Bayard had whispered to Sefu that he wasn't sure if Jacob truly comprehended the plague, or if he was just too afraid of Sefu to try anything funny. Bayard was now patrolling the wall, under agreement that he would restrain any escapees. "The dead man probably, er, 'woke up' near the entrance of the lower ring, judging by where the screams started from. Listening to it now though, I'm sure that it's reached the center ring. The castle will know of it soon."

"What do you think their response will be?" Sefu asked.

"I'm not sure. If they keep thinking that the infected are possessed by demons, they'll try to get them to the church. If they realize that isn't the truth, they'll respond with pure military force. Knights in full plate armor, carrying sword and shield and spear will be dispatched around the city. They'll employ the same methods they used during the Black Death. They'll lock infected people together to die, rather than killing them on sight. But if what you say is true, they won't really die. There will be buildings full of living dead, trying to tear down the walls. It will be complete chaos."

Sefu nodded, though unseen by Jacob in the dark. "You are right. We are going to have to enter the city earlier than I would have hoped. We must make it to the castle and inform the royalty and the knights of what the infected are, and how to deal with them, before they ruin everything. Jacob, I am unfamiliar with English military politics. How long do you think until they employ these methods?"

"Less than two days. Tomorrow they'll hold a warmeet, deciding what tactics they'll use and where everyone should be. The day after, they'll start their response, whatever it may be."

Sefu sighed. "By that time, the bitten will have turned, multiplying the spread of the plague by potentially dozens. Anyone who died early on has likely already gotten back up. Tomorrow we go in, then. Find a knight or any resident of the castle, and pray they will listen to us. Will you join us, Jacob?"

"Yes. I need to find my brother and sister. You help me get to our home, and I'll get you to the castle."

"Sounds fair," Sefu said. "Where is your home located within the city?"

"Center ring, same as all the other guards. Our home is right near the gate into the lower ring, so hopefully my siblings saw what was happening and barricaded themselves quickly. My brother's not the brightest candle on the alter, but he's strong and well-armed, and my sister is a complete spitfire. If anyone can survive, it'll be them."

"Very well. We will find your siblings and bring them back to this farm, then go for the castle. Another question has been tugging at me. Where are all the other outer guards? Should there not have been two at each gate?"

"You're right. You caught me seconds before I was to head back inside for the sunset shift change, and you shut the other gates before the replacements showed up."

"We just got lucky, then."

"If that is what you wish to call it."

Chapter Five
Summer of 1513 A.D
City of Valdus
Early Morning

"We need water, Tom. I have to find some before things get worse and I get weaker. The center ring's well is dry, the lower ring is overrun with infected and looters. I have to go up, further into the city, where I can get some from either their well or the underground stores beneath the castle."

"You can't go there, Gen. They'll kill you if they think you're a thief, and they'll kill you even faster if they think you stole equipment from a guard. I have to come with you. I'll get my armor on, and we'll go slowly."

Gendrina sighed, but nodded. "I'll get you your effects," she said, and ran up the stairs. Many loud clunks later, she dragged a large trunk into the room, containing Thomas's armor and weapons. He changed into his guard uniform, having to cut away the armored panels on his left leg in order to fit the great swelling. He began strapping the shortsword to his baldric, but Gendrina stopped him. "Don't bring the shortsword, it's hard to kill them with it. I'll carry it, just so we have a blade. Bring the axe, that thing can pike skulls easily. And let me at Jacob's crossbow," she finished, digging through the scattered objects in the bottom of the trunk. She handed him the hawk axe, one side a short, curved blade, the other a long, pointed spike. She took the other, smaller crossbow as well as every bolt there was, eighteen of them, and forcefully shoved them into a small quiver.

"Good thinking with this axe, it makes a nice cane," Thomas said, leaning on the weapon, his hand wrapped around the blunt inside edge of the head. "Also, my leg feels a whole lot better than it did last night. I won't be doing any acrobatics, but I can walk and I can fight." He lifted the axe and balanced on his legs alone, taking a few steps. He seemed stable enough.

"Think it's light enough to move around out there?" Gendrina asked. Thomas opened the door slightly and peered outside.

"I can see well enough. If we get there before the sun rises over the walls, chances are they'll have Pete guarding the gate. He's a friend of mine and it would be a lot easier than talking to some other unknown Castle Guard." He picked up the last bite of his breakfast of baked potato from a plate on the floor and downed it, then led the way out the door. Gendrina immediately noted that all the bodies she had seen before, with the exception of the headless one outside their door, were gone. Bloody footprints marked the entire housing row, doors were broken down, and improvised weapons scattered the ground. Gendrina lifted a pickaxe and slid it into her belt, the weight of the iron spikes reassuring her.

"We should head back through the market district. It was already mostly looted when I was there last night, so there shouldn't be anyone around. Nobody healthy, anyway." Thomas nodded, and they turned down the abandoned road. Soon they started passing bodies with holes in their heads, and Thomas crouched down over one of them.

"Crossbow wounds. Was this your doing, Gen?" She nodded innocently. "How the hell did you manage to pull the bow? I can barely load that thing."

"It's becaws I stronk," she said in a jokingly powerful Scottish accent, flexing her arms. Unable to disagree with her, Thomas just grinned and turned away from her, continuing to hobble down the road. After passing several more of Gendrina's kills, they heard knocking emanating from a dark alley to their right. Thomas stopped and squinted down the alley, unable to see anything in the shadows. Gendrina tapped his arm and tilted her head towards the market, mouthing "Forget it, let's go."

Thomas nodded and turned, but his leg throbbed and buckled. He caught himself with the axe handle, but the damage was done. From the alley, moans and footsteps started approaching them, and seven infected stumbled from the alley, shambling towards them. "In the name of Christ," Thomas whispered, seeing their white eyes and grey skin for the first time, their lifeless *moving* corpses lunging towards him in the street. A man in a butcher's apron, a woman in a nightgown, a tiny girl with a missing hand, a massive bearded man with five arrows protruding from his chest. Gendrina acted first, a bolt flying into the head of the bearded man. Thomas knew they should be running, but with his leg, that was not going to happen. He raised the axe and stood his ground, waiting for the first infected to reach him while Gendrina reloaded behind him.

The first to reach him, the child, was met with the spike of the hawk axe. She fell, the spike cleanly sliding from her corpse, and Thomas turned to the next and dispatched him the same way. Another bolt from Gendrina, downing the nightgown woman, and Thomas stepped forward and cut down the last three with an impressive combination. Retrieving her bolts, she clapped Thomas on the shoulder and helped him along the path. "This is horse shite," Thomas hissed, his face contorted into a display of anguish; physical or emotional, Gendrina couldn't tell. Probably both. "I just killed a little child."

Gendrina stopped, leaning him on the wall of a nearby home. A nearby cart loaded with pots, pans and cauldrons burned strongly, a broken lantern laying on the ground in front of it. "No. Whatever these things are afflicted with, they're not humans anymore. A *severed head* started gnawing on my boot last night. Ending their lives is the best thing we can do for them at this point, the same way you put an arrow in a rabid dog."

"These are *people*, Gen. I knew two of the men I just murdered. We have to try to help the infected, find the doct-" A window of the house Thomas was leaning on shattered, directly behind him. Six bitten, bloody arms reached out and wrapped themselves around his chest and neck. Gendrina was on them at the speed of sound, tearing the pickaxe from her belt and slamming it into the window, into the skull of one of the infected with a brutal crack. The heavy man fell, tearing the pickaxe from her hands. The remaining two creatures weren't strong enough to pull Thomas inside, and he wrenched his torso free from their grip, but they retained their hold on his left wrist. He kicked at the wall but they would not release him, and he roared in pain as one of them bit into his hand.

Gendrina was in a complete rage, grasping at the axe in Thomas's belt, but it was pressed against the window frame. She couldn't aim the crossbow around Thomas either. She drew the shortsword and slashed it into the darkness of the house. With Thomas in the window, she could not reach either of the infected, and she cried louder as they feasted on Thomas's hand and forearm. With no choice left, Gendrina stepped back, grasped the sword with both hands, and raised it over her head. Thomas looked up at her pleadingly, a stare of desperation and agony. Realization spread over his face, and he began to yell; "NO, GEN, PLEASE NO-" And Gendrina brought down the sword with all of her adrenaline-fueled power, cleanly severing his arm just above the elbow in one great slash. He collapsed instantly, blood spraying from the wound, whimpering and gasping in shock.

*****

His vision blurred, his voice missing, Thomas felt himself being dragged along the ground. Through the haze, he could see flickering light, flames. He closed his eyes and shook his head, and could see a little more clearly. Gendrina was standing over him, reaching into a flaming cart with the shortsword. He heard a clank, and saw a large, circular pan fall to the ground. Next, he was being jerked about as Gendrina tore his cuirass and undercoat off. She bundled the garment in her hands and lifted the pan. He had no strength left to resist as she pressed the red-hot iron against what was left of his arm, simultaneously cauterizing and disinfecting it. He made no sound as he blacked out completely.

*****

Bayard was asleep, laying on a pile of clean hay and dreaming of his past, dreaming of his time with Sefu. He sat in his old room with his mother beside him, teaching him the basics of alchemy.

"Damn it, Bayard, not that much!" Bayard grimaced as his mother slapped the vial from his hand. "How many times must I tell you to *measure,* someday you might be able to accurately judge it at a glance, but until you really learn, you have to check it! You will be saving lives someday, and if you give someone the wrong medicines, or too much of the right one even, you can kill them. Look at Sefu, see how he tracks exactly what he uses?"

Bayard turned to the large Egyptian boy, who was leaning over a notepad, quickly writing down quantities of herbs and oils. "She is right, Bayard," Sefu said, giving him a taunting grin. "You wouldn't want to be outdone by someone who is not even related by blood."

"How am I even supposed to tell how much I use? There aren't any marks on the vials or anything!" Bayard moaned.

"Use the chart and the ruler!" Marina Travers shouted, smacking Bayard's hand with said ruler. Just then, the door opened, and

Baeden Travers, Bayard's father, entered the room.

"Why always with the yelling, Marina?" he yawned. "The boy has Travers blood, so he has the capacity for this. If he does not respond to a particular sort of instruction, try something else."

"Why don't *you* try teaching him sometime, see how far you get?"

"I have patients, dear, or I would love to. Try leading by example, show him the proper methods and watch over him as he follows, rather than shouting orders like some sort of absurdly beautiful Guard Commander."

His mother sighed but smiled, and tried his method for the next few sessions. His father was not wrong, once he saw something performed it was easy for him to replicate it. Years passed in flashes, and then he was a teenager, sitting alone in the study surrounded by vials and pouches full of every extract, oil, and herb imaginable. He mixed this and that, examined the dark green shade and the soft, moss-like texture, and then stuck the very tip of his tongue into the concoction. Grinning, he corked the vial and ran from his room, and into Sefu's. He shook the large boy's bed, and Sefu sat up, blinking.

"What is want, you Bayard?" When woken up, Sefu tended to lose some of his ability to construct the English language. He spoke it neatly when he tried, but it was not his birth language, and still took some concentration.

"I've done it, I've put together a safe pain medicine and relaxer that does not cause addiction or lasting effects like milk of the poppy does. As you know, both pipeweed and root mushrooms can help relieve pain on their own, but each has its own problems. Mushrooms can cause people to go a little insane when taken in the quantities needed to block pain, and the weed lacks the potency to keep people relaxed when they have serious injuries. However, by mixing the oil of the pipeweed with water and blending in just the right amount of mushroom pulp so it will keep people stunned but not hallucinating, we can get the best of both effects. People who take the mixture should be rendered pretty much useless for a few hours, but the effects will wear off soon after."

Sefu was glaring. "You are telling me you just squished a couple of plants together and call them medicine?"

"Isn't that what ALL medicine is, Sef? It will work, I measured out every milligram to be proper for my own weight. I just need you to watch over me while I test it. By the time the sun rises four hours from now, I should be completely sober and the inventor of the biggest advancement in surgical aid since some heathen first figured out that whiskey was more useful on a wound than in his mouth."

"Have your parents watch you, I do not want to be a part of this."

"My parents would throw me to the pigs if they saw me messing with this stuff. Once I have the test results and a witness that it works, *then* we can bring them in on it," Bayard explained.

Sefu sighed. "Very well. But how are we to test it? Obviously I am not going to perform surgery on you, even though you might do well with a new brain."

"We only have to replicate the actions of a traumatized man under the effects of my medicine," Bayard said, ignoring him. "Once I take it and it sets in, slap me around a bit, shake me, pour water on me. If I don't react much to any of it, then we have our answer." Without waiting for a response, he downed the small vial and plopped onto his bed. Minutes passed as he stared at Sefu, but he slowly found himself sinking into his bed, further down than the bed physically went, and everything was up, and Sefu was in the ceiling, and the ceiling was above the sky...

When Bayard could next comprehend reality, he was still sprawled across his bed. Looking hazily to his left, he saw Sefu standing with his parents, his face worried. "It has been nearly six hours," Sefu was saying. "He said it would wear off in less than four. He must have measured wrong."

"It will wear off. Truth is, neither of the plants he took can cause lasting harm. Hopefully this will be a lesson to him though, to bring his ideas to me first. And it is not a bad idea, the theory is effective. Just look at him...but it needs fine-tuning, obviously," his father explained.

"It was *foolish*. He should know better than to handle those drugs, we need to lock them up," said his mother.

"Ooaar oh rrooaugh, hragga bor?" Bayard asked.

"Looks like he's getting himself back together. A little. Please do not get too angry, Marina. He needs to learn from his own experiences." His mother just nodded.

After a long struggle, Bayard sat on the edge of his bed, staring into the angry, disappointed face of his mother and the passive, slightly amused one of his father. "I'm sorry," he said. "I don't know what happened. I had it all measured perfectly. I had the vial chart, the ruler, the scale, everything. For my weight, what I took should not have lasted for longer than four hours."

"Let me guess," Baeden Travers said. "You measured the mushroom pulp the same way you would measure a whole mushroom, ignoring the fact that the pulp consists of only the strongest parts of the fungus. You likely took three times as much as you believe you measured."

Bayard squinted for a long time, then moaned and fell back into his bed. "Shite..."

His father sat next to him. "Do not feel bad, Bayard. Everybody makes these mistakes as they learn, and after this incident I can pretty well guarantee that you will not make the same oversight again, am I right? You came up with an idea that I should have figured out years ago, and I will investigate it further to see if it is indeed safe to use on patients. Thank you."

This made Bayard smile, and even more so when his mother stormed out in a huff. His father then turned to Sefu. "You on the other hand," he said to Sefu, who looked startled, "should have come to me first thing. From now on, remember that I support experimentation and innovation. If either of you come up with something new, *ask me*. Unless I know that the result is likely to kill you, chances are I won't say no to anything you can mix up." Bayard and Sefu nodded agreeably. Their father then left, there was a jolt, and Sefu was suddenly an adult, large, darker, muscular, and leaning over him.

"Bayard, we have a problem." Bayard blinked sleepily, looking up at Sefu's worried face. He pulled himself together and sat up, looking around. Jacob leaned against a wall, looking curiously at Sefu.

"What is it?" Bayard mumbled.

"The are some very strange noises coming from inside the city. It sounds like at least six horses, moving slowly, dragging something towards the western gate. A battering ram?"

Bayard shook his head. "Anyone with access to a battering ram would know it has no chance of breaking through the outer gates when the plague bars are down. The ram would collapse long before the gate does."

"Still, something is happening. We need to investigate it."

Bayard stood and yawned. "What we *need* to do, is find me some breakfast."

"Bayard!"

"Yes, yes, we'll check the gate," Bayard moaned. "But as soon as we're in the city, we're finding food." Minutes later, the three of them were collected outside the western gate, their ears pressed against it. Bayard closed his eyes, listening hard. Indeed, he could hear large, wooden wheels approaching slowly from a short distance along with the neighs and whinnies of very panicked horses. Every now and again there was the sound of a skirmish, muffled yelling and moaning, weapons striking bodies. "The sound is drawing the infected," Bayard whispered to Sefu.

Jacob was still listening to the sound, his face inquisitive. "That's not a battering ram. You don't need horses to move any ram that would fit inside a city. Our siege engines are kept in a special barracks miles away from here." Suddenly, a look of unwanted understanding spread over him, his eyes growing wide and worried. "God save us. They've brought out the Bombard." Bayard froze, but Sefu just blinked.

"The what?"

It was Bayard that answered him. "A cannon. And an absolutely ridiculous cannon at that. A four-thousand kilo iron tube that fires a ball as wide as a man's torso. If fired, it will demolish the gate, half the wall, and the next bloody town in that direction," he finished, gesturing away from the gate. "It was used in the Battle of Rhodes, long ago. A Turkish stronghold of four-thousand fought off seventy-thousand men and nearly two hundred ships with the help of their advanced artillery. How the hell did it end up *here?*"

Jacob nodded, and began his explanation. "After the Battle of Rhodes, word of the Turk's advancements in gunpowder spread quickly. Many European Kings and Lords purchased cannons from them at a great price. One ended up here, in anticipation of aggression from the North. The attacks never came, a truce was formed with the Northern Kingdoms and the weapon sat in the barracks as a landmark ever since. Been here longer than any of us can remember. We've kept it well-maintained, just as a precaution." Jacob looked over to Sefu. "What do we do?"

"There is no choice, we have to go in there and stop them from firing at any cost."

"We should yell over the wall first, try to talk them out of it," Bayard interjected.

Sefu shook his head. "That would draw every carrier in the district right here. It could cause them to panic and fire the weapon sooner. They are still far from the gate, we have time to talk them down, quietly. They should listen to Jacob, it is probably other city guards who are moving the cannon. We need to hurry though, the longer we wait, the closer they get." Bayard nodded and began wrestling with the heavy metal barricade. Shifting it upwards, Sefu took hold of it while Bayard and Jacob squeezed their way through the gate. Sefu followed and let go of the bar at the last second, hearing it fall into place. For good measure, he slammed the bar on the inside of the gate as well. They were now locked in along with everyone else.

Looking down the western road, Bayard saw the cannon. A ten foot tube of solid iron, mounted on an iron platform, being slowly dragged along by eight horses and pushed by fifteen men. They were about thirty meters away. Upon seeing the trio enter the city, they pulled the horses to a stop and waited apprehensively. Sefu, Bayard, and Jacob quickly walked forward, their hands held up as a sign of peace. The men behind the cannon walked around, forming a wall between them and the massive weapon. At this closer range, Bayard could see that they were a cobbled-together militia, armed with woodcutting axes, hunting knives, and crude clubs. There wasn't a decent sword among them. One stepped forward, his face full of rage.

"So you are the demons who keep us in as your kind feast on us," he said. It wasn't a question, the man was positive. The others hissed their agreement. Sefu shook his head. This wasn't going to end well.

"We are no demons, Sir," Jacob said, stepping out from behind Sefu. "I am a member of the city guard, a pious man. What haunts this city is a plague, just like the Black Death of years past. The Devil is not at work here, we do not want to fight healthy citizens. Help us get to the castle, help us explain to the knights what this is and how to fight-"

"LIES!" The scream came from one of the men in the line, pointing furiously at Jacob. "The dead are standing up and eating the living, their souls taken by Lucifer and turned against us! Listen not to these monsters, light the fuse!" One of the men ran backwards,

tearing a lit torch from the back of the carriage. Sefu charged.

The line of men scattered as Sefu crashed through them, tackling the torchbearer to the ground and knocking him out with a single thunderous punch. The other men recovered, drawing their simple weapons and converging on Sefu. Jacob and Bayard had drawn their own blades and had engaged the men who were still gathered in front of the cannon. Sefu rolled away from his attackers, retreating around the heavy iron stand. Sefu still carried the longbow, but had no close-combat weapon. He lunged behind one of the men who was striking at Jacob, grabbing his arm and twisting it backwards. The man dropped his long hunting knife, and Sefu quickly picked it up and plunged it into the man's chest. He dropped, and Sefu turned to engage the three who attacked from his rear. However, nobody was there, and he looked back to the other side of the cannon. One of the men stood holding the torch, somehow still alight after falling into the dirt.

Sefu roared, hurling himself behind the weapon and slashing the knife through the air. It connected, blood spurting from the man's arm, but it was too late. The fuse was lit. Sefu slashed at it with the knife, but it was too thick and loose, the blade just shifted it sideways. Dropping the knife, Sefu punched at the fuse with his hand, but got no result besides painful burns. The tip of the fuse retreated into the iron. He shook his head and turned to Bayard and Jacob.

"Run." When Sefu spoke, people tended to listen. Jacob and Bayard spun away from their attackers and rushed down the street. Bayard knew that cannons that size had very long internal fuses, they would easily make a safe distance, but the gun would fire. The plague would escape. Jacob looked over his shoulder, then stopped, yelling out. Bayard stopped and turned, his eyes growing wide with dread. Sefu hadn't followed them. Behind the cannon, his hands were wrapped around the sides of the breech, lifting with all his considerable strength as the remaining militia rained his back and shoulders with their crude weapons. Blood poured from the Egyptian man but he absolutely would not fall, and with a final, enraged scream, the breech fell loose. And then it fired, the entire force of the blast blowing back through Sefu and the militiamen. The massive cannon ball rolled slowly less than ten meters in front of the cannon, dust settling, parts of men scattered around the scene of the blast as the horses screamed and panicked. Sefu was simply gone, every part of him sent straight into Oblivion.

Bayard was finished. He just stood, unable to move, unable to think. Jacob had to physically drag him away as the moans of the dead converged on them from every direction.

Chapter Six
Summer of 1513 A.D
City of Valdus
Late Night

Thomas was laying unconscious on the floor of the wooden home, blissfully unaware of what had happened. He dreamt of his siblings, growing up in Valdus.

"You shouldn't do that, Gen," Thomas called, watching the small girl hang one-handed from the birch tree that grew next to the barn. "Soon you will be too big for me to catch." Almost every day, they would leave the city and travel the short road to the farms that supplied the citizens of Valdus. There, the farmer's wife would give them fresh milk and honey and let them ride her horses and climb her trees. She was the closest thing to a mother the three of them knew. It was a dry, sunny day.

"By then, I'll be good enough of a climber to not fall, I bet! As good as Jacob."

Thomas sighed and looked further up the tree, where his brother was resting atop the highest branch. "I wish you would at least climb a tree that bends over the lake, so if you fall out you won't break your neck."

"But then I would ruin my dress. You're the one who makes me wear this fucking thing," she hissed, pulling at the thick, loose skirts, which were tangled in the branches of the birch.

"Don't curse like that," Thomas scolded her. "And it isn't me who says you should wear that, every girl your age does."

"Oh *shut it,* Tom, or I'll tell father what you do with his sword every night."

Thomas sighed. "I am nearly thirteen. He should be training me, not keeping me from it. At least by practicing alone, I can get a handle on the motions and the weight of it. And you forget that I let you practice with it as well. He would be a lot more mad at you for using it than me."

"I'm just a stupid girl to him," she said. "He would flog you good for letting me anywhere near it. I wouldn't be blamed."

She had him. Defeated, he leaned his back against the cool tree. "You should start doing some of my mining work, gain some muscle. Wear a hat and a baggy shirt and you could pass as a boy to the foreman, at least for a couple of years. And eat some meat. You cannot swing a sword effectively if you're a bag of bones."

"She would eat meat," Jacob butted in from his place atop the tree, "if you would ever leave us any in the first place. You're always lurking outside the house ready to run in and steal all the good stuff."

"It isn't my fault that you two are so slow. Learn how to read the sun, and be there on time," Thomas laughed. Just then, a bell rang from the distance. "I guess I spoke too soon. Wait, no, the sun is still high, and the bell sounds different. Come down, both of you." Gendrina and Jacob made their way down the tree, Jacob landing like a cat and Gendrina like a sack of bricks. Circling around the patch of trees, they froze as they saw the smoke rising over Valdus, the alarm bell ringing continuously. Thomas snapped out of it first and began sprinting towards the city, Gendrina and Jacob close behind. Their running was interrupted by those machinations of the dream world that tended to avoid monotony, and then they were in the burning city, civilians and guards bolting about with buckets of well water. Thomas ran forwards and grabbed the arm of a passing city guard. "Sir, where is my father?"

The guard looked him over. "You are Liam's boy, yes? His party was dispatched to the Southern District, to try to save the grain. Stay on stone roads, don't go near any wood and keep far from tall buildings," he explained, then pulled his arm away from Thomas and continued on his way. Keeping his siblings close, Thomas weaved his way through the burning city. They quickly arrived at the gate to the Southern District, and the three of them pushed open the heavy wood. The fire here was lesser, with only a few pillars of smoke rising from the other end of the district. Thomas stopped another guard, who directed them to the granary. They began to run, and then they were in the granary with their father.

"You should not have come here, Tom," Liam Carter said, hugging his three children. "Luckily you're all alright, but the fires are not out yet. Get back outside of the city and stay near the lake until the smoke stops." The three protested, but Liam called over a large bearded civilian man, and he forcibly dragged the three of them from the city.

"I will join the city guard," Thomas said, two days later, after their father's funeral. "They accept boys my age for early training.

And Jacob too, in a couple of years. It will get us food, at least."

"I'll join too," Gendrina said through her tears.

"They don't take girls," Jacob explained.

"Why not?"

"Because girls are weak, and men are strong. If a lady guard tried to stop a thief, he could beat her up easily."

"I won't be weak. I'll become as strong as a man and when I'm grown, I'll fight in their recruitment drive hidden under armor and beat everyone there. Then they will have to take me."

"That isn't how it works, Gen," Thomas said, somehow wearing a grin. "The only place in combat a woman has is as a mercenary or bandit. The city has laws."

"Would you rather I become a whore?"

Thomas punched her arm. "Don't say that. You will marry a doctor, or a smith, or a guard captain."

"I don't *want* to marry a man. I don't like them like that," she moaned, collapsing back into her chair.

"You will soon enough," Thomas sighed. "I wonder how many bastards I'll have to punch in your honor."

"I'll do the punching myself," Gendrina spat, then she stood and stormed from the room. Thomas stood to go after her, but upon leaving the room, there was a jolt.

Thomas opened his eyes. He gasped as he felt the indescribable pain shoot through his left side. He tried moving his arm, then remembered. There was no arm. He fell back onto the hard ground, glancing about and taking in his surroundings. He was in a small wooden home, similar to his own. There was dim candlelight filling the room. Looking to his side, he groaned and tried to kick himself backwards as he saw a pile of three bodies, stacked in the center of the room. Two had crossbow bolts in their heads.

He tugged with his right arm, and saw that it was tied securely to the leg of a heavy oak table. Looking up, he saw a boarded-up window. Looking down, he saw his sister leaning on a wall, asleep. Placing everything together, he figured that she had dispatched the other two infected and dragged him into the house. He had been avoiding it, but finally he looked to his left arm. Wrapped in a clean white cloth, presumably scavenged from somewhere nearby, the stump wiggled uselessly as he imitated the 'thought' of moving his hand. At least his leg barely hurt anymore. He glanced down again. "Gen?"

She stirred and looked up, a weak smile growing on her face. "You're alright," she said quietly.

"Alright is *not* the word," he moaned. "Why am I tied up? Am I infected?" Gendrina stood and walked over, kneeling next to him. She gently unwrapped the end of the makeshift bandage, peering at his skin.

"I don't think so, Tom, but I had to take the precaution. There's no discoloration besides expected redness, none of the grey skin or darkened veins seen on the bitten." She lifted the shortsword and cut the rope tying him to the table. "Here, have some of this." She handed him a flask, and he took a swig. He squinted. He had expected whiskey or rum, but it was pure, clean water.

"Where did you get this?" he asked. Gendrina looked at it with a haunted expression.

"I saw someone carrying it. And I needed it. So I took it." Thomas just nodded and took another drink. He couldn't be bothered with giving her morality lectures at this point, and if the situation were reversed with Gendrina dehydrated and bleeding out, he might have done the same thing.

"How long was I out?"

"A little longer than twelve hours," she said. "Things are getting so much worse out there. There was some sort of sound this morning, soon after I got you in here. Sounded like thunder striking the west side of the city, but it was fine weather... After that, the infected moved away, towards the sound. However, many more started pouring out of houses and inns, taken by the plague itself. I've counted over one hundred just through the windows of this house. And the moans...they're quiet now, but every time they hear something, they start up again."

"Where are the knights? They should have evacuated the city long ago. What about the entire bloody Royal Army? Where is *anyone?*"

Gendrina shook her head. "I have no idea. I heard a lot of skirmishes throughout the day, but nothing on a large enough scale to think it was the knights. Some guards walked past a couple of hours ago but they were driven away by the infected, and I didn't want to risk drawing attention. I don't know what to do anymore, the castle seems an impossible task with this many infected out there."

Thomas pushed his remaining hand on the ground and stood steadily. "We will get to the castle. They have food, water, and doctors. We're already more than half way through the center ring, we can get there in fifteen minutes even at a slow run. Also, the barracks are less than a minute's run from here. We go there, get better armor and weapons, raid the food stock if there's anything left. Then we fight our way through the streets until we reach the castle."

Gendrina grinned at him. "Not feeling so bad about killing those things now, are you?"

Thomas nodded. "I'll cut down everyone in this godforsaken city before I let myself get bitten again. Human, Demon, I don't care anymore. If they come near me or my sister, they'll meet my axe."

Gendrina stood straight and grabbed Thomas's hand. "That's it, brother. This is the Thomas I know. You always talk peace but when it comes down to it, you'll fight to your last *limb*." Thomas laughed as he grasped the hawk axe.

"And that's the sister I know, telling terrible jokes 'till her last breath."

*****

Jacob quietly clicked the door shut, and turned to Bayard. "Shite," he spat, looking around the darkness of his home. "They've left here. Nearly cleaned out the equipment trunk and left a ton of food. With how many infected we went through to get here, I guess that's for the best. They would have probably broken down this door eventually, or gone through the windows."

Bayard stood in the center of the room, his bloody, broken longsword hanging limp at his side. His mind rushed with images of the dozens of infected he fought through as they slowly made their way around the Lower Ring, punctuated by flashes of the explosion that took his adopted brother. The eastern gate, where Bayard met Jacob, was almost directly across the gate into the center ring. But the Western gate, where they entered the city and where Sefu met his violent end, was very far away from any path to the center ring. It took a long while for Bayard to get himself together enough to fight, and was thankful to Jacob for protecting him while he was out.

When he did recover though, his wrath was great. As the day

wore on and night fell, the number of infected increased hugely. Pouring from doors, falling from windows, crawling out from under carts. They came from everywhere, but he killed every single one in his path. He knew how good his sword was. After all, he made it himself. But still, he killed and killed until the blade was little more than a rod and a handle. The last few infected he dispatched had their spines snapped rather than cut, as his sword was so blunted. He dropped the ruined weapon and took the last object from the trunk, an undamaged, decent-quality dagger.

"I'm sure they've gone for the barracks. There would be other guards there, and much more equipment. We'll hold here until morning, then go there. We can make it in less than an hour," Jacob explained. Bayard nodded wordlessly and slid down into a wooden chair. Jacob did the same and took a sip from a large bottle of ale he'd managed to procure from a tavern they took shelter in earlier, then tossed it to Bayard. "I'm sorry about Sefu, my friend. I doubt it helps, but he died in a display of honor and glory the likes of which are rarely seen. Only God knows how many lives he saved. He was a strong man, a good man."

Bayard took a great gulp of the ale, and placed the bottle on the ground beside him. "Thank you," he said simply. They both shut their eyes, and they rested.

*****

Thomas pushed the door open, advancing into the street, axe raised. Immediately, the moans started, first a single voice in the shadows of some building, then five, ten, dozens, each responding to the moans of the last. Converging on them, Thomas ran forward, slamming the axe spike into the skull of the nearest victim. Gendrina was ready with the crossbow, taking down another one, and reloaded just in time to dispatch one who was gaining on Thomas. There were too many now, and the crossbow took too long to reload. She swung it back over her shoulder, drawing the pickaxe that she had recovered from the house. At the proper angle, rather than sideways through a window, it was easy to spike the infected without losing her grip on the heavy tool. Thomas was like a typhoon, spinning, ducking, and swinging his way through countless infected. Gendrina was holding her own, taking out any that approached from behind.

"There," Thomas said, pointing to a dark iron gate around fifteen meters ahead. They rushed towards it, and Thomas reached into his pants pocket, withdrawing a ring with two large keys attached. Gendrina picked down three more infected as Thomas fiddled with the gate, and then retreated through it as Thomas shut and locked it behind them. The infected piled against the bars, and were easy victims for the hawk axe and pickaxe. Soon, there was silence.

*****

Prince Christopher Alento pointed down the street with his heavy steel gauntlet and motioned the crowd onward as the moans echoed through the dark alley. "Hurry! Abandon any heavy possessions and make for the church immediately! Torchbearers, keep to the front and rear, don't let the knights lose their vision!" There were numerous *thunks* as some citizens dropped chests and released wagons. His five most trusted knights, Zachery, William, Alexander, Richard, and Morgan were engaging the demon horde that assaulted the fleeing citizens from the rear. Behind armor, sword and shield they were untouchable, using shield bashes to knock over their attackers, causing the ones behind to fall. One stumbled forwards, grasping onto Morgan's shield. William spun, slashing his hand-and-a-half into the back of the demon's neck. Its head toppled, and the body followed.

"Try to behead them!" Morgan shouted over the crowd. "It seems to keep them down!" The other knights changed tactics, forming a shield wall and throwing powerful diagonal strikes with their heavy blades. As they moved, they quickly learned that cutting into the head, or even most of the neck, would drop any of the demons. As they turned onto the main road the crowd began to panic, demons approaching from every direction now, rather than just from behind.

Prince Christopher quickly glanced around, taking in the approaching hellspawn. Their numbers, their speed, and their apparent targets. "Diamond formation! Zachary, take point and keep pace to the church. Morgan on west, Alex on east, Richard on north, William on south. Keep the citizens in the center and try not to let the demons gain number!" The knights moved quickly, taking their positions around the crowd. Their shields rendered useless individually, they quickly slung them across their backs and gripped their blades with both hands. Stepping out and in as needed to strike down enemies before they reached the crowd, the whole group of people slowly made their way down the street. Soon, the tower of the church could be seen in the moonlight. His eyes adjusted to the dark, Christopher ran to the front of the group and looked along the road. "THE PATH IS CLEAR!" he shouted, so all the citizens could hear him. "SPRINT FOR THE CHURCH, STOP FOR NOTHING!" The formation broke, and both the civilians and the knights ran for the church.

More creatures stepped from behind buildings and out of doorways, but were too slow as the crowd flowed through the church's large, heavy doors. William was the last one through, and he pulled the doors shut behind him. Soon, pounding and moaning could be heard from around the whole building, the demons slamming on the doors. One of the women in the crowd spoke up. "This isn't right! They shouldn't be able to even touch the church without bursting into flames!"

Richard shook his head. "The outside of the church is not consecrated ground. As long as they're out there, nothing will harm them."

"So open the doors!" The voice came from the front of the church. Everyone turned towards the sound, and saw the city's Bishop standing on the large stone alter, arms raised. "Let them enter and face God's wrath!" Christopher and Zachery stood by the door and pushed. It didn't budge.

"It's no good," Zachery said. "The doors open outwards, and with so many of them out there, we're trapped." Christopher mouthed a curse, and fell onto one of the wooden pews. The rest of the knights and citizens followed suit, many of them holding their hands together and praying quietly. However, Christopher quickly stood up and took a place in front of the alter.

"Listen up. We may be safe from the demons here, but we have no food or water. And we need medicine for the people who were bitten. We need to inform the other knights and city guardsmen that we're here. Richard, William, take shifts ringing the churchbell. It will draw more demons but it will also gain the attention of the other soldiers." The two men nodded and retreated through a small door behind the alter. A minute later, the large bell could be heard ringing overhead. Impossibly, the moans of the demons increased in volume.

The doors shook but held strong, made of impenetrable oak and steel long ago, before the walls were built and when raids from the Northern heathens were common. Christopher sat again and shut his eyes. There was nothing they could do but wait.

*****

Bayard sat in the wooden chair inside the home he and Jacob took shelter in. He had remained awake for a long time, but he eventually drifted off. He dreamt of his time as a doctor, healing the people of Valdus.

"She cannot be saved, Bayard. The infection is too deep, and it was left too long. We are wasting resources that could be used far more successfully," Sefu said as he held the bandage over the young red-haired girl's left side.

"That doesn't matter, Sef. As a doctor, I cannot *let* someone die. Go do what you want, I will treat her myself."

Sefu nodded and held the bandage as Bayard took his place, then he moved over to the sixteen year old boy in the next bed. He was awake but shaken, having taken a dagger through his hand in a drunken brawl. The two men quietly worked on their patients, Bayard continuously applying various disinfectants and herbs to the little girl's ruined, dark-red side. No older than four, she had been attacked by a stray dog while she was out collecting water and her father had waited days to bring her to a doctor, as they had no money. Finally someone heard the girl's crying, and when the situation was explained, he told her father of the Travers family, who asked no gold for their services. Sefu finished treating and bandaging the drunken boy quickly and sent him on his way, with instructions to return every other day for new bandages. He then left the room for the other side of the clinic, where their parents were trying quite unsuccessfully to explain to a very old, very senile man that yes, it was a bad idea to go bear hunting at his age, and no, he was not thirty, or a knight.

Bayard sat where he was all through the day and into the night as Sefu and their parents went through dozens of patients, treating the infected dog bite, wiping her sweat, forcing her to drink, and cleaning up after her. Sefu, and even his parents repeatedly told him that the girl would die, but he would not leave her. She soon lost consciousness entirely. Bayard put his disinfecting mush over her wound once more and bandaged it, and then he waited.

When this had really happened he had fallen asleep, but in the dream world, time just seemed to bend how it needed to. He was awake and looking over the girl, his face held in a huge smile as she sat beside the bed and ate the salted duck eggs he had given her. Her name was long gone from his memory, but the sight of her smiling and eating after coming so close to death would stay with him forever. "How are you feeling?" he asked.

"My side hurts," she said, shaking her head. Her red hair bounced about with her movements.

"Well, that's to be expected. It will hurt for a long time, and the scars will never fully heal. I'm just glad you are alright." He stood and moved to get more bandages, and suddenly he heard the clang of churchbells.

Bayard coughed himself awake at the sound. "What kind of idiots are they? Every infected person in the city will go right to them."

"It is foolish," Jacob agreed. "But you do know we have to go, right? My siblings could be there. Even if they aren't, the church will be full of survivors, maybe guards. Surely some are bitten. If we don't go, every one of them will die."

"Sefu would have let them. We don't have the weapons or resources to get through whatever is out th-" Bayard fell, following a strong punch from Jacob.

"YOU ARE NOT SEFU!" Jacob shouted. "Two nights ago, you did everything you could to talk him out of leaving the city to die. Sefu was a smart man, but he was cruel. You are not like him, and you will NOT stand by while the church falls."

Bayard stayed on the ground, staring up at the ceiling. "He was like my brother. But I would be lying if I said there wasn't always *something* dark about him. I remember, as a child, he didn't cry when his father was killed, or when my own parents died, even though we were adults by then. As a doctor, his thinking was never 'how can we stop anyone from dying,' and always 'how can we stop the most useful people from dying.' He would always prioritize healing fit men, and women of childbearing age. Always for the greater good, sickly children and elderly who would die soon anyway could give nothing back to the city or its people. I never thought about it, or cared, because I was there to help everyone who he would not."

"There is always a place for that kind of thinking," Jacob said. "If everyone lived off sentiment, nothing would ever get done. However, for every cold, logical man there must be an equal but opposite heroic, understanding man. That's you, Bayard. Sefu's last action may have saved all of England, but there are many people here, alive and healthy, whose fates rest with you."

Bayard stood up, gripping the handle of his small dagger. "You are right. I don't know what we'll be able to do, but the church door won't hold forever. More and more infected will gather there the longer we wait. It seems like all the infected here have cleared out, I don't see any," he said, looking out the small window again. "And hopefully we can find better weapons on the way."

*****

"Yessss," Gendrina spilled, hefting the massive claymore above her head. "I've always wanted one of these."

"Play with the swords later, Gen, and help me get this damn chainmail on." She dropped the heavy blade and jogged over to Thomas, who was struggling to shake the steel coat over his missing arm. She lifted it over his shoulder and it settled onto the thick, quilted undercoat. She tied the sleeve up with a length of rope, and buckled the straps across the front. Lastly, she removed three gauntlets from the armor chest. She strapped one onto Thomas's remaining hand, and equipped the remaining two herself. They fit well, she had large hands. "Thanks," Thomas said. I found the smallest coat there was, but the chainmail is only one size so it's going to take some work to fit you right. I left it on the bench there," he finished, pointing over his shoulder. Gendrina went over to it and held up the undercoat.

"I'll probably need to tie it up in some places, but it should work." She stripped her leather cuirass and thin shirt off, replacing it with the heavier undercoat and tightening the straps as far as they would go. After applying some rope around her waist, chest, and arms, it fit well enough. The chainmail itself was much harder to fit, hanging down to her knees, and the sleeves a foot below her hands. Even tying it into place, she was unbalanced and slow. She ended up laying it on a bench and taking a large battleaxe to the bottom half and the sleeves until she broke off enough to fit her properly. The repeated crashes had attracted more infected to the barracks gate, but Thomas easily shut them up with the hawk axe.

Just as Gendrina walked back to the massive rack of swords, churchbells rang out across the city. Thomas let out a relieved breath. "That has to be the knights, finally!"

Gendrina shook her head. "That's not good. You know how the infected react to sound. There will be dozens of them there."

"Shite, you're right. And we're right in their path. Enough of them could topple our fence. We need to get to the church before they gather around it, the doors are massive, we can hole up in there for a long time. And it's much closer than the castle."

"Sounds like a plan," Gendrina agreed. She picked the claymore back up and rested it on her shoulder. Thomas tossed his battered hawk axe and picked up a new one from the rack, sliding it into his belt. He also took a hand-and-a-half sword, strapping it to his side. He would have liked a greatsword like Gendrina's, but his one arm wouldn't allow it. He also took a couple of daggers for a sidearm, tossing one to Gendrina.

Quietly sneaking to the fence, he stared out into the night. "There are a lot of them, all heading for the church. The bells will block out any sound we make. If we stay off the main street, we may be able to get there without being spotted by too many."

Gendrina nodded, gripping her weapon in both hands. "I'm ready."

Chapter Seven
Summer of 1513 A.D
City of Valdus
Early Morning

"Look, that's the blacksmith's shop," Jacob whispered, pointing to a dark building twelve meters in front of them. "The city guards get their weapons crafted at the castle, but I've dealt with him before, he made my personal weapons. Goes by the nickname 'Helmet', for whatever reason. The weapon racks outside have been looted, but see there; the door is battered and cut up, but it seems to have held. That probably means he's inside, hopefully healthy."

"Hopefully sane, is what's most important," Bayard interjected. "I'm having a hard time trusting the living after those zealots with the cannon." They walked to the shop, and could see very faint candlelight behind the dark curtains. Bayard tightened his lips, and knocked softly. A sliding chair could be heard inside, and the curtain in the window slid aside and a large bearded man could be seen looking out at them. Seconds later, the sound of the door being unlocked, and it slid open. The smith stood back, a large crossbow aimed directly at Bayard's head.

"What is it yeh're doin' here, tiny?" he asked suspiciously.

Jacob stepped into view, and the crossbow moved to him instead. "It's alright, Sir. I am Jacob Carter of the City Guard. You crafted two shortswords, two crossbows, a hawk axe, and a dagger for my family a few years ago. See here," he said, holding out the battered shortsword. Bayard followed suit, displaying the dagger. "We're simply here to buy a couple of weapons."

'Helmet' grinned and nodded. "Yeah, I remember you. Good with a weapon, but a little on the scrawny side. Judgin' by the look of that blade though, you've seen yer fair share of action since."

"Mostly the past twelve hours, honestly," Jacob sighed. Helmet nodded again, and gestured them inside, bolting the door behind them.

"Have a seat wherever," Helmet said, motioning aimlessly around the dimly lit room. Jacob and Bayard propped themselves up on the low counter, as 'wherever' didn't seem to include any chairs or benches. Helmet leaned on a wall, looking them over. "You've been through some serious shit gettin' here, haven't you? Prob'ly on your way to that damn loud church?" They both nodded. "Best hurry you along then, before the dead grow too many."

Bayard squinted, looking over at him. "Dead? You've realized what they are?"

"What else could they be? Seen dismembered torsos draggin' themselves along the ground, severed heads chewin' on chunks of meat, seen 'em get stabbed through the heart and keep on walkin'."

"You're the smartest man I've seen yet, then," Bayard said. "Everyone in this city thinks they're living humans, possessed by demons. That they can simply be exorcised and healed if brought to a church. They're much further gone than that, there's nothing that can be done for them besides ending them and sending them onwards to whatever awaits."

"It's because this whole city is Christian," Helmet said. "A foolish religion. Where I'm from, Christianity 'as taken over as well. There are very few of us who remain, who still worship the true Gods. This is not the work of the Christian devil, these creatures are Draugr. This city is corrupt and failing, the taxes are criminal, many of the guards steal and rape. The citizens were wronged enough times where even after death, their spirits hold rage towards this city, and their bodies have risen to claim it."

Bayard slowly glanced at Jacob, his look confused, but content. Turning back to Helmet, he said; "Either way, your belief is far closer to the truth. The creatures are dead, and deserve no remorse. As long as you realize that, your reasons for doing so matter not. However, both of our blades are small and ineffective. As a blacksmith, I assume you have weapons you can sell or trade us?"

"Aye," Helmet said. "Come in back with me, and have yer pick." He walked behind the counter and pushed a door open, and Bayard and Jacob followed. They entered a brighter, smaller room, a large bed and many weapon racks lined against the walls. A pale younger woman with blonde hair and a badly scarred face sat in a chair beside the bed, looking tentatively at them over a large book. "My wife," Helmet explained. "It's alright, Jess," he said to her. "Just some late-night customers. They're perfectly alive, and I know one of them." She nodded quietly and returned to her book. "Anyway, find yer pick of weapons. Shortswords for five silver pieces, longswords for eight, axes for seven, spears for six, greatswords and bastards for one gold piece or ten silver...," he trailed off.

Jacob quickly grabbed a wide bastard sword, giving it a couple of practice swings, with one hand, and then both. Bayard felt up a number of longswords before moving to the greatsword rack. His eyes scanned the large weapons, and widened as they settled on it. Starting with a long handle wrapped in red-dyed cotton, his eyes moved up to the circular steel handguard, then onto the long, curved blade. Tapering off into a deadly-looking point, the whole sword was about six feet long and looked like the crescent moon brought to Earth. Helmet stepped up behind Bayard as he reached out for it.

"The Great Scimitar. An old Eastern weapon, designed to cut the legs right off of charging cavalry. Nothing cuts through bone better. Won it off a game of liar's dice with a band of Persian mercenaries months ago. Been trying to sell it since, but nobody will pay the price I ask."

"You really care about gold at a time like this?" Bayard asked.

"I am just a smith. This problem will not last forever, and at some point this city will get itself together or I'll leave it for another town. So yes, I want gold. Ten coins of it."

Bayard sighed. "I can see why nobody's bought it, then. But it isn't like there's much else to do with my money at this point. I don't quite have that much, but I can do five gold pieces and thirty silver pieces."

"I can supply the remaining two gold pieces. And eight silver pieces for this bastard sword," Jacob finished. Two silver pieces short for the bastard sword, but Helmet nodded.

"Thank you, Jacob," Bayard grinned. He extracted a surprisingly large cloth sack from his greaves and upended it onto Helmet's table. Jacob did the same, and they held their new weapons. Jacob got a sheath and carried the bastard sword at his side, and Bayard rested the handle of the moon-shaped, monstrous blade on his shoulder, then looked over to Helmet. "Come with us. We could use your help rescuing the people in the church."

Helmet shook his head. "Want to know how I got this nickname? Five years ago, I volunteered for the City Guard. On my first day, I had to kill a thief who was trying to make off with some noble's necklace. I immediately vomited in my helmet. It stuck. Anyway, I don't have the stomach for killin'. Much rather make the weapons than use them. I'll do what I need to in order to protect me and my wife, but I won't go lookin' for a fight. Good luck to both of you.

Odin guide your blades.

Bayard smiled and nodded. "Yours too. Just make sure it is guided through their necks."

*****

The sun was finally showing itself as Gendrina and Thomas crouched through the bushes behind the church's graveyard. The moans were deafening, and above the shrubbery they could see an ocean of infected surrounding the church. They were too late.

"What now?" Gendrina whispered.

"There's nothing we can do. There are just too many. If we had more warriors we could probably lure them away and cut them down, but with just the two of us, we'd be overrun."

"Then we have to retreat and go to the castle like we planned earlier. Find more guards or knights and bring them-" She cut herself off as the moans of the infected changed, growing louder and more agitated. They chanced standing up, and saw the plagued army circling around to the front of the church. They sneaked through the bushes, and saw the cause of the commotion. Two men, both equipped with very large swords, had charged the massive group of infected, cleaving them down in multitudes. They fell like wheat to a scythe, the two men spiraling through the horde. One of them was a city guard. Small, with a short beard- "Jacob!" Gendrina hissed into Thomas's ear.

They sprinted from their cover and engaged the horde from behind, each taking a side as they cut through the infected. Thomas showed great skill with the hand-and-a-half sword, slashing it at arm's length, quickly decapitating several infected. Gendrina showed much less finesse, but was equally effective, as she simply dismembered everything in her path. It was a difficult fight, but within minutes, the ground around the church was littered with infected bodies. The four stood in a circle, breathing heavily, before Jacob ran forward and embraced Thomas and Gendrina.

"What the shite happened to your arm, Tom?" Jacob said, staring at the stump with eyes wide.

"Gendrina happened. I'm pretty sure she saved my life, though. I'll explain later..."

The churchbells had finally stopped ringing, and Thomas looked over Jacob's shoulder and called out as a young infected woman stumbled out from behind a nearby tree. Gendrina started towards her, sword raised, but the other man whom Thomas didn't recognize held his hand out. "Leave this one to me." He walked to the woman, who reached out for him with hands clawed. He sidestepped, bringing his strange, curved sword around and severing both of her arms. He grabbed her by the back of her hair, dragged her to the church doors, and began to knock.

*****

Christopher stood up as the moans of the demons changed in volume and pitch. They could be heard gathering around the front of the church, and the endless pounding ceased. There were human shouts, and very slowly the moans decreased and finally fell quiet. A minute later, there was a knock on the church door. A steady, human knock.

Christopher motioned to Zachery, who nodded and walked to the door. He hefted the heavy bar out of place and reached for the handle- *CRASH.*

The door flew open following a powerful kick from a dirty, brown-haired man wearing simple burlap clothing. He stormed into the church and, impossibly, he was dragging an armless possessed woman into the church by her hair. He walked tall through the church aisle, stopped in the middle, and raised the demon up for all to see. "LOOK!" he shouted. "This is no demon, this is no creation of Hell, it is no angry spirit, or the work of any deity of any faith!" He stepped up and slammed the demon's head into the basin of holy water in the middle of the church. "She does not burn, or recoil, or become human once again!"

Zachery, William, and Alexander drew their swords, angered by the display of violent blasphemy unfolding before them. They stepped towards Bayard, but stopped as Christopher held out his arm. "Bayard, is that you? What is the meaning of this? Why are you in this city?"

"I'm here to save you fools from yourselves," he sighed, tossing the woman to the ground and decapitating her with his large blade. The citizens screamed and pressed against the church walls as her head began to move and chew uselessly at the air. "This," he said, pointing at the head, "is the victim of a plague. Just like the Black Death. The effects, spread, and control couldn't be more different, but the basic nature of it is the same. These people are-"

"You know this sinner?" Alexander interrupted.

"Yes," Christopher said. "Bayard is his name, he used to be a doctor and alchemist here, long ago, as were his parents. His mother helped deliver my sister, his father saved my leg when I broke it as a child, and he himself helped many knights who have now retired or died. He deserves our attention, if not our respect." The other knights lowered their weapons, but still stared at Bayard with disapproval in their eyes. "Please continue, Bayard."

"Of course, My Lord. As I was saying, these people are dead, not possessed. A rare infection causes their brains to change, altered into a state that cares nothing for any cause besides consuming living creatures. It is indeed a terrifying sickness, but it is earthly, and it can be defeated with some intelligence and precaution." Bayard looked over to the citizens. "Have any of you been bitten or scratched by the infected?" None of them came forward. Many of them looked to each other and shook their heads at him. Bayard turned to Christopher. "Has anyone been growing sick? Skin becoming discolored, or limbs becoming partially paralyzed?"

Christopher nodded. "Two of the citizens we brought here were bitten. They fell very ill and died during the night, only about half an hour ago. Everyone else seems healthy enough."

Bayard bowed his head. "I'm sorry for the loss. Where are the bodies, though?"

"We moved them into a back room," Christopher answered, gesturing to a small door behind the alter. Bayard thanked him and walked over to the door, disappearing behind it. He returned a short time later, his face solemn.

"We seem to be alright here, now," he said. "However, I must explain that if you get bitten or scratched, you will grow sick and die within one day, and you will return as one of the infected. If you are killed by other means after being infected, you will rise very soon after that. The only way to stop someone from becoming one, is to destroy their brain."

"Explain yourself, Bayard," Christopher said, his voice growing with authority. "Why are you in this city? How do you know of this 'sickness'?"

Bayard sighed. "You probably remember my old partner, Sefu." Christopher nodded. "He left for his home country years ago. Two days ago he returned, carrying a flower he took from an oasis in Egypt. This flower is the origin of the plague. We were running tests on the flower to try to figure out a way to prevent it, when my home was broken into by two burglars. One of them contacted the flower and escaped to this city. We followed him here, but it was too late."

"So Sefu is the cause of this? Where is he now?"

"I'm afraid he's already paid the price. He died, his last act was defending the city gates from getting blown up by that insane cannon one of your ancestors brought here. If the gates fall, the sickness will escape and it would spread further than you can imagine."

Christopher cursed. "Yes, we heard the blast yesterday morning. That's when we realized something was happening down here. The plague bars are down on every gate out of this city, I assume that was your doing as well. You do realize that I should have my men behead you on the spot?"

Bayard simply stared at him. "Do what you will. Just remember that these are not demons, and that they can only be stopped by destroying the brain or severing their head. Spread the word to every living person you see, it will mean more coming from a Prince than it would from me."

Alexander stepped forward, grasping his sword in both hands. "Should I, Sir?" he said to Christopher.

Christopher looked Bayard over. "I am sorry, Bayard. Duty binds me to this. By the laws of this city, you are to be executed for the crimes of unlawful imprisonment of citizens, aiding a mass murderer, and high blasphemy. In correct procedure, you would be hung by the neck until dead, however due to the limited time and resources we possess, Knight Alexander Hayes is to execute you on my command." Richard and Morgan circled around Bayard and held him tightly by his arms, forcing him to drop his large blade, as Alexander raised his sword above Bayard's head. Christopher looked away. "Do it."

*****

Bayard closed his eyes and waited. Instead of the quick death he anticipated, there was a soft *thunk*, a loud shout and a crash, a short silence, and then an explosion of panic. Opening his eyes, he saw Alexander laying on the ground in front of him, a crossbow bolt protruding from his shoulder. The other knights dropped Bayard, turning to the door. Looking back, Bayard saw the woman in the battered guard uniform who had helped him and Jacob battle the horde outside the church, a small crossbow held to her shoulder. The one-armed man stood beside her, a horrified expression on his face, and Jacob stood behind them, violently shaking his head.

The citizens were hysterical, rushing to the back of the church and hiding behind pews and pillars. The Prince and the knights were all sprinting to the door, and Jacob and the two people who Bayard assumed were his siblings bolted, outrunning the heavily armored knights with ease. He stood, grabbing his sword, and sprinted for the front door. The other two knights turned, raising their shields and swords into a defensive stance. He knew he wouldn't be able to fight through two fully-geared knights, and even if he could he didn't want to hurt them. Quickly glancing around, he stepped up on a pew and ran, then jumped, kicking off the back of the long bench for extra power. He crashed through a stained glass window, gasping as the glass cut into his arms and back. Toppling to the ground, he looked around and saw the woman crouched in a patch of thick bushes, waving frantically at him. He dove into cover with her and waited.

For a few minutes, the knights could be seen running around the church, killing new infected who wandered near, following the panicked screams. Eventually they retreated inside, slamming the large doors once more. "Thank you," Bayard exhaled in relief. The woman nodded and grinned.

"Follow me," she whispered. "My brothers are probably heading back to the barracks." They could have just followed the road from the church, but for safety they took the long way around, avoiding a number of infected approaching from the west as well as any search attempts from the knights. Introducing themselves as they moved, they slowly crouched through the trees and passed various homes and shops.

Chapter Eight
Summer of 1513 A.D
City of Valdus
Morning

"FIND THEM!" Christopher roared, helping Alexander to his feet. The other knights ran outside and circled the building, but could not branch out too far due to the increasing number of infected approaching the church. Finding nothing, they returned to the large building and pulled the doors shut behind them. Alexander was laying on a pew, Christopher slowly sawing through the shaft of the bolt with a serrated dagger. The fletching fell free, and Christopher looked at Alexander, putting a facade of humor on his face. "I assume you know how broadheads work. This is going to hurt. Try not to complain too loudly."

Alexander grimaced and nodded, clenching his teeth. "Have at it, then." He was a veteran knight, and managed to stay completely silent as Christopher pushed the bolt through his shoulder and pulled it from the other side. He disinfected it with some whiskey from a flask that William had produced, and tied his arm with the shirt of one of the cleaner citizens. Finally, Christopher sat down, his head in his hands.

Richard was circling the walls of the church, scanning the crowd of scared citizens. "Christopher," he called out. "Where's the Bishop been through this whole mess?"

Christopher sat up and glanced around. The tall man in his extravagant robes was nowhere to be seen. He thought for a few seconds, then his face fell with realization. "He went in the back rooms to say the final prayers for the citizens who died last night. If what Bayard said is true-" The knights didn't need him to finish, they were already running for the door behind the alter. Zachery entered, sword raised. Christopher approached the other knights, and as he reached them, Zachery reappeared from behind the door.

"It's bad, Chris. Come, look." Christopher entered the door behind Zachery and immediately saw a thick trail of blood leading up the stairs to the bell tower. He looked into the small room to the left, and saw the bodies of the two citizens, thrown about the floor, both of them beheaded. In the back of the room was a large crate, likely made as a cheap coffin. The lid was tossed aside, bloody handprints covering the edge of the crate.

"The Bishop came back here to send off the dead, but they had already resurrected. They bit the Bishop, and he hid in the crate. Bayard came back here and killed them, and after he left, the Bishop left the crate and retreated to the bell tower, presumably fleeing the sounds of combat. There's too much blood, he cannot survive long if he isn't already dead."

Morgan stepped forward. "It could have been that bastard Bayard who cut him." The other knights nodded their agreement. "He's probably a demon himself, that blasphemer has already-" Christopher cut him off with a stare.

"I cannot believe that. Bayard is...he's never believed what we're told to believe. From the start, his family threw away the laws of our religion and forced themselves down a path they chose to take. He's created medicines and elixirs that cure what the Pope himself has been unable to, and never once has he used his abilities in the aid of evil. I said to execute him solely on my absolute duty to uphold the laws of this Kingdom, but I would call him an angel before I would call him a demon." The knights held their heads down, shamed at being told off as such by their leader. "We will find Bayard and learn the truths we need at another time. For now, we either have a seriously wounded Bishop...or one of those..." He fell silent for a few seconds. "I can't call them demons anymore. We've seen one in the church, seen it contact holy water. Bayard is right, this is a plague, not any Hellish uprising. We'll figure out what to call them later, let's get upstairs. William, Morgan, with me. The rest of you, stay here and look after the citizens," he finished, pointing to Richard, Zachery, and Alexander with three fingers.

Christopher took point, leading with his sword as he ascended the spiral staircase. He soon reached the trapdoor, more bloody handprints pressing against it. He exhaled slowly, and tapped on the wood with the tip of his sword. Immediately, there was a crash, and a gurgling moan could be heard above. "Shit," Morgan hissed.

"Be ready," Christopher warned, and he pushed up hard, flipping the trapdoor open. Rushing up into the belfry, the Bishop could be seen laying on the floor, reaching hungrily towards the knights, obvious bite marks in his arms and neck. His foot was jammed, held by a gap in the rotting wood floor. The bone in his ankle was showing, badly broken, but the moving corpse showed no pain, only anger and hunger. "God forgive me," Christopher whispered, as he plunged his sword through the Bishop's temple. As he stood back, the sound of screams and combat erupted below them.

The knights turned, sprinting for the trapdoor. It slammed shut in front of them. Morgan dove forward and pulled at the iron handle, but it was stuck fast. "Someone must have tied it from the other side," he blustered. Christopher screamed, kicking down onto the wood with his heavy steel boot. He slammed on the trapdoor over and over, the old wood holding surprisingly well. After a number of minutes, the trapdoor finally buckled and a heavy thump could be heard below. Pulling apart the remaining wood, Christopher jumped down into the hall, looked down, and choked back a moan. Alexander lay below the belfry, one end of a thick rope wrapped around his neck, the other end tied to the outer handle of the trapdoor. He was dead, his face blue and his hands hanging limply at his sides.

"He couldn't take it," Morgan whispered. "Nobody can. But for a knight to end his own life..."

Christopher pushed aside his grief and bolted down the stairs, dragging Morgan behind him. They burst from the back rooms to a complete bloodbath. Zachery and Richard were both dead, brutally dismembered. Nearly all of the citizens were gone, only two civilian bodies remained. Christopher fell to his knees, staring at the corpses of his knights. His friends. Slamming his fist to the stone floor, he screamed in rage and anguish, furious at the suicide of Alexander and at the actions of the dead. He stood and started tearing his armor off, ready to chase after the citizens and cut down every one of the infected who followed them, when one of the bodies began to move. A civilian woman, stirring and moaning. He gripped his sword, raised it over her, and-

"No, waaait," she gasped. Still alive, still *truly* alive.

Christopher lowered his blade and knelt beside her. "What has happened here? Your wound was not caused by a bite."

Her eyes were glazed over, her stomach was mutilated, torn open by some serrated blade. She was obviously very close to death. "It was not the demons," she coughed out. "Four men... They entered the church wearing black cloaks and red masks. They murdered the knights with bone daggers, and led the citizens out of the church. My husband tried to fight, and they attacked us too. Why is this..." She trailed off, closed her eyes, and she was dead.

"They've come." The small voice rose from Morgan. "Our great walls and skilled soldiers have kept them at bay until now, but with this plague, we're vulnerable. Alexander did not kill himself, they tied him there to keep us out while they did this."

William looked between Morgan and Christopher. "What is it? Do you know who's responsible for this?"

Christopher nodded. "Their last attack was long before any of us were knights. Today, there isn't much left to them but myth and legend. The Northern city of Sinead has held quiet hatred for us for generations, but none more than the Dryden Brothers. Twenty five years ago, my father burned their parents and their sister in front of them, their crime was alleged sorcery. As children, they joined the Fogwalkers, a clan of assassins who are lored as wraiths of smoke and shadow. Ten years ago, the body of a knight who was out on border patrol was somehow thrown *into* a castle window in the dead of night, a message carved into his back."

"What did it say?" William asked.

"We will sever your royal bloodline with the bones of our family."

*****

An hour later, Gendrina and Bayard came back onto the main road leading to the barracks. There were some infected here, slowly shambling their way along. Bayard took the lead, cutting down the ones that turned towards them as Gendrina shot the ones further away. "They're probably following Jacob and Thomas," Gendrina said. "Those two never could be very quiet."

Bayard stopped and held Gendrina back, looking down the road. It was red with blood, marking the rest of the way down to the barracks gate in the distance. There was smoke rising above it. There was also a smell in the air, beyond the smell of death that they'd long since grown used to. "Something's happened," he said to Gendrina. "The infected don't bleed. Be ready, and stick to cover." She nodded, gripping the crossbow, and they continued to sneak forwards. The pools of blood grew larger and the smell grew stronger as they approached the barracks, and they finally turned the corner to the entrance of the large compound.

"No..." Bayard leaned on the gate, staring in at the nightmare in front of them. He heard a retch as Gendrina vomited, jabbing the tip of her large blade into the ground for support. Dozens of bodies littered the ground within the barracks, stripped and butchered. Some were tied to training posts and burned, smoke still rising from their corpses. Bayard recognized them as the citizens from the church. Messages written in blood covered nearly every inch of the stone walls.

Sins of the King
Fear the Smoke
Your Plague is our Shroud
The Bloodline Ends Now

"Bayard..." It was Christopher. Bayard turned and saw him and two other knights circling around the other side of the barracks gate.

"You seem to have bigger problems than me, My Lord," Bayard said softly.

Christopher nodded. "They attacked the church minutes after you escaped. Assassins from the north, coming after me and my father. They're attacking the most important and the most defensible locations in the city. They took all the weapons and armor and hid them God knows where, so citizens and guards can't further arm themselves. We've been trying to figure out where they are going next, see if we can set up an ambush-"

"Gen!" A voice that Bayard didn't recognize came from a nearby alley, and the one-armed man (Thomas, as Gendrina had told him on their way to the barracks) limped out from behind a decrepit home. Jacob followed, his armor torn up and his side bloody. Gendrina jumped to her feet and ran to Jacob.

"What happened to you? You weren't bit-"

"No, I'm okay. We got here a while ago, just as the four murderers were leaving. One of them spotted me and came after me, ripping up my armor and trying to gut me with some bone dagger, but he didn't see Thomas because he was off pissin' in an alley. Got the jump on the bastard and saved my life."

"I axed him full-on in the back of his head," Thomas spoke up. "His skull should have split, but there was some helmet under his hood. Smoke flew from under his cloak, blinding me, and he ran off.

We hid in a hay cart as he came back with his partners, but they gave up and left about fifteen minutes ago. Who on earth are they?"

"Four brothers with a vendetta against my family," Christopher said. "I know not how they learned of this plague, perhaps they have a spy here, who sent a message by bird-"

"Helmet," Bayard gasped suddenly.

"What?" Christopher inquired.

"They're going for Helmet's."

"Why do they want more helmets?"

"The bloody blacksmith, you-" Bayard cut himself off. Verbally abusing the Prince probably wouldn't be amazing for his health. "The blacksmith, he has a huge stash of weapons and armor. If they're trying to disarm the city, that's where they're heading next. He and his wife are alive in there, we have to go, *now*."

"He used to be in the Lower Ring, but moved here only recently," William said from behind Christopher. "I don't know where he lives now."

"We were there just hours ago," Jacob assured. "Follow us." Christopher nodded, and let Bayard lead the way through the bright, winding roads. Dozens of infected stumbled after them, attracted by the knights' loud armor, and William and Morgan branched out to take down any that got too close. They reached the market street where Helmet had his home, and slid into cover to check around the corner. Bayard peered out down the road and quickly recoiled back.

"I see two of them," he mouthed to Christopher, gesturing to the left side of the street. Christopher crouched down and looked, trying to keep his reflective armor behind the wooden wall. On the roof of the potter shop across from the blacksmith, two shadowy figures stood tall, black cloaks flowing in the light wind and thick smoke rising from their hoods.

"The flame of Hell burns within their eyes," Morgan whispered in a terrified tone.

Bayard sighed. "They have tobacco pipes built into the chin of their masks. It makes for an intimidating effect, but it started out as an invention by a King who was particularly fond of the leaf a few decades ago. Could barely get through a battle without it. He unwittingly became known and feared as 'The Mist King', and since then, some others took up the idea in an attempt to frighten their enemies."

"How in God's name do you know all these things?" William whispered from behind Morgan.

"How about you pick up a book someday?" Bayard shot back.

"Don't you speak to me that-"

Christopher shushed the both of them. "Enough. There are supposed to be four of them. The other two must be inside the smithy."

Jacob leaned back to where Thomas and Gendrina were standing. "Tom, Gen, can you see anything from the other side of the house here?" he asked, turning towards them. They were both gone.

Chapter Nine
Summer of 1513 A.D
City of Valdus
Midday

"But I don't *want* to," Gendrina cried as Thomas finished tying up the light blue laces that held together the back of her dress. "I don't love him. I don't like any of them."

"Please, Gen," Thomas sighed. "You've barely met him, and Garret is a great man, on a clear path to Captain of the Guard. He is strong and honorable, and good to his friends."

"That doesn't matter, I don't want to marry, I just want you to leave me alone about it and mind your own life," she spat, pulling away from Thomas.

"I do not want to force you into this. You are sixteen now, there has to be some man from the Center Ring who you fancy, doesn't there?"

"No."

"Then please at least give Garret a chance. You can't know if you never spend time with him."

"I do know."

"How do you know?"

She was silent. Standing, she walked to the open window and closed the shutters, then the glass itself and stared into it like a mirror, frowning at herself. Looking defeated, she made for the stairs. "If it will make you happy, I will meet him for one night. But when I refuse him, I want you to stop trying to find arrangements for me."

"Alright," Thomas said. "If you do this tonight, I promise not to bother you about this anymore after. You can find someone in your own time." He watched Gendrina proceed down the stairs and he felt bad for doing this to her, swearing to himself that he would keep his promise.

Hours later, he was walking home from the market district, his arms full of breads, cheeses, and sweetrolls as the sun lowered behind him. Gendrina would arrive late at night or, and he dreaded the possibility, in the morning. He knew what could happen with her and Garret, but he trusted the man enough. He clumsily unlocked the door to their small home and pushed it open with his boot, stumbling inside. Placing the foodstuff on the entrance table, he turned to the living room, where Gendrina and a brown-haired woman whom he did not recognize were sitting on the sofa. Gendrina was wearing her nightclothes and there were tears in her eyes, and the brown-haired woman was holding her hand, trying to comfort her.

"Hello," Thomas said tentatively. "What happened? And who's this?"

Gendrina turned to Thomas, looking very distraught. "Garret proposed to me not two hours after I arrived at his home."

"And what did you say?" Thomas asked, afraid of her answer.

"I didn't say anything. I ran."

Thomas sighed, something he had done a whole lot recently. "Worry about that later. Again, who is this?" he said, motioning towards the silent brunette.

"This is Eileen. She is...a friend."

"I've never met her."

"You haven't met a lot of people," Gendrina sniffed.

"Fair enough," Thomas said, walking up to the woman and extending his hand. She quickly stood and took it awkwardly, as though she had never shaken hands before, pinching his palm with her thumb and pointer finger. "Thank you for being here for my sister. I should have known something would go wrong. You should head home, before it gets darker. Would you like me to escort you?"

"It is alright," she piped up, her voice small. "I live nearby, I will go alone."

Thomas nodded and watched the girl leave, then turned back to Gen. "It seems you really didn't like him, then."

"I told you."

"Yes, I suppose you did. Do not feel bad, I will keep my promise. Find someone when you are ready."

"Thank you, brother. I will," she said, looking out the window at Eileen walking down the street. "I'm sorry to have troubled you like this."

"Please, it's alright. I love you and your comfort and freedom is what matters most to me." She smiled and leaned back in the sofa she sat on, and Thomas stood to begin putting the food in the pantry, and then there was a lurch.

Thomas opened his eyes and struggled, but it was futile. Tied tight around his chest to the support beam of some basement, he couldn't gain even an inch beneath his bonds. As he and Gendrina stood back from the knights, they were grabbed from behind and had quickly lost consciousness. His neck didn't hurt, so he figured they must have used some non-lethal toxin rather than choked him out. He heard a groan from somewhere ahead of him and squinted through the darkness. "Gen?"

"Yes, I'm here," she said. "My mouth tastes like I bit a live chicken and I can't feel my arse."

Thomas let out a soft chuckle. "You are smaller than me, so the poison they used is taking longer to wear off on you. I can't see anything, are you tied to a post as well?"

"Indeed I am, but they cocked up this one. I'm a lot smaller than my armor and I think I can wriggle my way out of here with a bit of time."

"Do it," Thomas whispered. "But try to hurry, they could be back at any time."

Gendrina writhed and squirmed, managing to kick herself upwards along the support beam until her right arm slid free from the chainmail. She leaned over and did the same to her left, then let her legs drop. She roughly collapsed out of the quantity of rope and toppled into Thomas's view, painfully clutching at her arms and chest. "Ow ow ow ow..."

"Man up and get me out of here," he hissed, and she pushed herself up and quickly pulled her chainmail back on before working on Thomas's binds. He fell free just as the door above the staircase creaked open, blinding light flowing over him. Two black figures stood there, and then practically flew down the stairs. Thomas threw a punch, but could not even keep track of how many things were hurting him at once as he quickly found himself face-down in the dirt, his hand held behind his back. He looked to his left and saw Gendrina in the same position.

"So much for that, then," she mouthed at him. They were pulled to their feet, and stared into the smoking red masks of their captors.

"You will gain us entrance to the castle," one of them said with a heavy Northern accent.

"And what makes you think that?" Thomas spat, staring into the dark slits in the mask. The man was silent, but forcefully shoved Thomas up the wooden stairs, with Gendrina coming up behind them. They came out of a cellar door onto a stone road, the sun high above them. There were dead infected bodies littering the road, but all was silent. Two more of the cloaked men appeared from behind a nearby house, one of them limping and his right arm heavily bandaged. The other pulled a bone dagger from beneath his cloak and pressed it against Thomas's back, forcing him down the path. He soon recognized where they were, a high-class housing district very close to a gate to the Upper Ring. Minutes later, they approached the shining steel portcullis with a clean, white staircase beyond. To the right, a tall drop to the Lower Ring. Countless moans could be heard below, and smoke could be seen rising even at this height. He shuddered at the complete chaos he knew flourished in the Lower Ring. He was quickly pulled away from the edge, and slammed into the gate.

"In less than five minutes, a knight will arrive at the gate for the midday shift change. You will convince him to open the gate, or we will throw your wife into the Lower Ring."

Thomas had to stop himself from laughing. *If they don't even know she's my sister, they definitely don't know what she's capable of.* He stood by the gate and waited as he was told, and the four men lined up against the wall beside the gate. The injured one held Gendrina, his left hand tight over her mouth and his bandaged right arm around her neck. As they said, a couple minutes later the clunking of armored footsteps could be heard descending the ornate staircase. The knight approached, and a grin spread over his face.

"Am I glad to see a human face," he said. He quickly reached for the lock on the gate, but Thomas quickly shook his head to stop the knight.

Praying he wouldn't miscalculate, and that Gendrina would be able to do what she had to, he inhaled and steeled himself. "Protect the King." The reaction from the assassins was instant. The two closest lunged forward with their daggers, but Thomas was able to dodge one of them, the other's dagger sliding uselessly off his chainmail. He charged towards the remaining two, grabbing Gendrina by the neck of her undercoat and wrenching her away from the assassins with all his strength. "RUN!" he roared, and was glad to see her bolt down the street.

She was hot-headed, but never stupid about the fights she picked, and he knew that she trusted him. One of the assassins took off after her, but his immediate threat was the injured assassin who had grabbed him around the neck, dagger cutting into his cheek and forehead. Thomas used his superior size to stumble backwards, kicking off the ground, and he felt momentarily weightless as they both fell into the Lower Ring.

*****

Gendrina jumped backwards, narrowly avoiding a thrust from the assassin's bone dagger, and swung a chipped shortsword she had found while running. He easily parried it, and lunged in again, catching her in the stomach. The chainmail held, and she turned away, bringing the sword around and slamming it into the assassin's back. There was a loud thunk and he stumbled, but the lack of blood showed that he was wearing full armor under his cloak, not just a helmet. He quickly recovered, rolling forward and gaining his footing before turning and striking at her with a series of rapid jabs and cuts. She guarded her head with the sword, letting her armor do the rest of the work, but she felt multiple ripping pains in her arms and legs. She ducked, then brought the sword upwards, striking the assassin under his arm. He grunted, and she was glad to see a thin stream of blood fall from the wound. It didn't seem to slow him any as he sprinted at her, pressing his forearm against her neck and slamming her into the wall of a house.

She lost her grip of the blade and shoved her right hand against his mask, and her left on his arm to block the dagger. He kept trying to shove it under her armor, but he had no line of sight and couldn't find his mark. Meanwhile, her right thumb found the left eye hole of his mask. She squeezed hard, gouging in as far as she could, and felt the soft organ give. He screamed and toppled backwards, and the mask fell free, taking his helmet with it. She only had time to see a short beard and pale skin beneath the stream of blood, before she threw herself away from the wall and wrapped her arms around his shoulders, locking them across his back. His neck was open, and she leaned forwards and viciously bit into it. The flesh broke with surprising ease and warm blood filled her mouth, but she did not release her grip as they both fell sideways. The assassin took the brunt of the fall, his head striking the front step of a herbalist's shop. He threw his left arm backwards and finally broke her grip, then he pulled himself to his feet and tried to kick open the door to the shop.

Gendrina leaned backwards and retook her sword, then stood up and ran for the assassin. His second kick broke the lock, but Gendrina was on him before he could get through the door. She thrust out, stabbing the thin blade through the back of his right leg and he fell to his knees. She tore the blade free, and he toppled forwards, his head falling in the doorway. Gendrina spun the sword and slammed it through his other leg and into the wooden step, pinning him in place. The assassin was barely able to move, loss of blood and accumulated injuries keeping him from struggling as she placed her foot in the center of his back.

"If my brother is dead, I swear to you that he'll give you three times this when you meet in Purgatory." And she slammed the heavy wooden door, once, twice, and many more, until his only movement was the pool of blood slowly spreading beneath them. For good measure, she withdrew the sword and cut his throat.

*****

"Jacob, *shut it,*" Bayard hissed, grabbing the smaller man around the mouth as he struggled. "We'll find them, just after we handle these two. They probably know where your siblings have been taken." Jacob went limp, and Bayard lowered him against the wall. Bayard stood and looked back around the corner. The two assassins stood in the same place, peering down towards the smithy. Bayard quickly circled around to Christopher. "I'm almost sure they're wearing armor under their cloaks. No matter how fast, four unarmored men can't bring down three fully equipped knights."

"I guessed the same," Christopher assured. "But as with any armor, there will be gaps in the eyes, neck, waist, and under the arm. I don't know how long they plan to stand there, but I'm going to send William and Morgan around behind them and then take one out with my crossbow. When the other jumps down, they'll kill him together."

Bayard nodded, and Christopher performed a series of complicated hand motions which the other knights seemed to understand, as they removed their steel boots and quietly sneaked into the back alley. As soon as they were out of sight, Christopher removed his rucksack and began rifling through it. He removed a large and heavy disassembled crossbow and began putting it together. Once it was whole, he mounted a wide, blackened-steel broadhead and took aim. He slowly exhaled as his finger slid down the trigger wire, and then there was the click as the bolt flew free. A direct hit, Bayard watched as the bolt buried itself into the taller assassin's neck. He instantly exploded in a ball of fire.

Christopher and Bayard fell back, barely avoiding a flying chunk of stone, and watched as the potter's shop collapsed from the blast. Jacob and Christopher were dumbfounded, their mouths opening and closing wordlessly, and Bayard had to physically pull them to their feet. "Blasting powder!" Bayard yelled into Christopher's face, his ears ringing. "They put cloaks and masks on scarecrows and filled them with flint and black powder! A bolt or arrow would spark and set them off! Be on guard, the assassins could be anywhere now, and the blast will attract infected!"

Christopher blinked away the explosion that was burned into his retinas and nodded. "We have to get to William and Morgan, they were right under there," he grunted out. He loaded another bolt and began running for the collapsed building, Bayard and Jacob right behind him. Fire was spreading, easily setting the straw roofs alight. There was a shout from an alley to their left and Christopher turned, seeing one of the knights prone on the floor, the shadowy figure of an assassin kneeling over him. Christopher raised the crossbow and fired, the bolt slamming into the assassin's back. He fell sideways but quickly rolled to his feet, breaking the bolt off on the ground. With amazing speed, he jumped and grabbed the roof of a house, pulling himself up through the flames and vanishing from sight.

Christopher ran to the fallen knight, turning him over. It was William, and he was dead, his throat gouged out. Christopher didn't have it in him to scream, and he simply closed the man's eyes and stood. "We need to find Mor-"

"Christopher?" a weak voice called from further down the alley. Christopher sprinted in, and saw Morgan laying under a flaming wooden beam, his left arm and leg pinned. Bayard tried to grab at the beam as Christopher pulled at Morgan's right arm, but he wouldn't budge. Jacob looked the situation over and turned to Christopher.

"Give me your dagger, quickly!" Jacob said, and Christopher pulled the short blade from his belt and tossed it to him. Jacob fell to his stomach and reached under the searing wood, finding Morgan's arm. Feeling around the gauntlets, he slid the blade under the straps and pulled, cutting the gauntlet free. He did the same to the bracers, and Morgan's arm pulled loose. Jacob rolled backwards, his right hand badly burned. Taking the blade in his left, he spun to do the same with Morgan's leg, but now Christopher, Morgan, and Bayard were all pushing on the beam and managed to shift it enough for Morgan to crawl his way out. They all stood, breathing heavily.

Bayard's right hand and forearm were burned and bleeding, and Morgan's leg was a complete mess, the cloth under the greaves had burned away, revealing red, blistering skin. "Have you found William?" Morgan choked out.

Christopher shook his head. "One of the Drydens killed him right in front of me, then escaped through the fire." Morgan cursed, and tried to take a step, but his leg buckled and Christopher barely caught him.

The explosion had faded from their ears, and now the moans of countless infected grew closer with each second. "We need medicines," Bayard said. "Aloe, mostly. When I lived here, there was an herbalist's shop nearby, close to the gate to the Upper Ring. My father was always feuding with her over the best herbs, and I had a...oh, never mind. Is it still there?"

"I think so. Bought some pipeweed from the witch a month ago, but she would have been nearly a child when your father was around," Morgan said. Christopher slowly turned a glare of disapproval over him, but Bayard just thanked him and grabbed him under the arm. Jacob joined in, helping Bayard move Morgan.

"We need to check on Helmet and his wife, then we can head over there," Bayard grunted. "My Prince, we'll help Sir Morgan along, please keep the infected off of us."

"You can drop the 'My Prince' and 'Sir Morgan' about now," Christopher said exasperatedly. "It doesn't work if you're all sarcastic about it, anyway." Bayard nodded and led the way onto the market road. The infected were everywhere, lurching for the burning building, but quickly turned to the trio as they emerged from the alley. Christopher kept an eye on the three limping men, but ran out and cut down the infected before they could gather together. He cleared a path to the front of Helmet's shop, and Bayard pulled Morgan up the stairs.

As Christopher continued decapitating the encroaching infected,

Jacob banged on the door. It creaked open with ease, and Bayard stepped in. There was no sign of Helmet or his wife Jessica, and the door into the back room was open. Bayard set Morgan down on the counter, then circled around and peered into the bedroom-armory. Every weapon and piece of armor was gone, as was any sign of the smithy or his wife. No blood, no signs of a struggle. Everything was just gone.

"They escaped or were captured," Bayard said. "Either way, we need to get to the herbalist, quickly." Christopher silently led the way back out of the smithy, cracking the skull of a carrier with his shield. After fifteen minutes of winding alleys and battling the dead, Christopher spotted the alley with the flowery, green sign posted on an archway. He could see three infected pounding on the door, which meant the herbalist was likely alive inside. As he sneaked closer, he saw a body laying on the ground outside. A body covered in a black cloak, and surrounded by blood. He quickly found himself grinning.

"They got one of the bastards," Christopher whispered excitedly. Bayard left Morgan to Jacob and ran forwards, quickly dispatching the three infected, then turned the body of the assassin. "Looks like he got in a fight with both humans and infected. Swords wounds, but also a bite on his neck and scratches on his face, not to mention the missing eye...his head is also pretty well crushed, I don't think he'll be coming back."

There was a thump from behind the herbalist's door, and it slowly opened. A black-haired woman of around thirty stood there, her hands and her white apron smeared with blood. She looked over the group, and saw their grinning faces. "I assume this mess isn't one of your people then," she said, gesturing at the assassin's body. Then she glared at Bayard. "What are *you* doing back here?"

"Good day to you too, Lilith," Bayard said simply. "Is your mother here? Three of us are badly burned, we need her help."

She sighed and waved them in. "My mother died six years ago. I handle the shop now. And get that sack of iron off my step while you're at it," she called to Christopher. He grabbed the dead assassin by the hand and heaved him away from the door, and he fell with a loud crash. After they all piled into the small entrance hall, she shut the door and placed a hastily-installed bar lock over the deadbolt, which had been broken at some point. She led them into the main room of the shop, which seemed to have been originally built as an upscale home. "Come into the bedroom and I'll put together medicines for you. Hope you don't mind some company, I've got an injured girl in there as well."

"Girl?" Jacob ran to the front of the group. "Large build, red hair. Named Gendrina?"

"Well, she's a large redhead," Lilith confirmed. "Don't know her name, though." She walked through a door into a short hallway, and opened the door at the end. The men squeezed through, and saw Gendrina laying on a clean straw bed. She was naked aside from the bandages covering her arms, legs, and stomach. Christopher and Morgan quickly turned away, their faces stoic, and Jacob ran to her.

"Gen?" Jacob lightly pressed on her cheek. "Wake up, come on..."

"You won't get anything out of her for at least an hour," Lilith said. "She was screaming about her brother and struggling with me as I tried to drag her in here, bleeding all over the place. I gave her some of my 'special' tea to keep her still so I could properly treat her injuries. Would you be that brother?"

"One of two," Jacob nodded. "But I don't think I'm the one she was talking about. A large one-armed man named Thomas, did you see him? Was he the man who killed the one outside?"

Lilith laughed. "Man? No. This girl here is the one who did that."

Bayard blinked. "That's impossible, that man is a trained assassin."

"Don't ask me," Lilith sighed. "I'm just tellin' what I saw from the upstairs window. He chased her into this alley and she tore him down like a wild animal. She has a lot of minor cuts on her, but my door is in worse condition than she is."

"Thank God," Jacob whispered, covering Gendrina with a folded sheet he found nearby. "But...where is Thomas?"

Thomas hurt all over. Even in his dream about the day Jacob joined the city guard, the pain nagged at him, but he was unable to wake up to face it.

"I like Cub. It suits the little one," Garret said as he, Thomas, and four other guards-in-training looked over Jacob.

"Why won't you just call me Jacob, it's my name!" Jacob moaned, pushing his much too large helmet away from his eyes.

"It doesn't fit the rest of the team, is all. All you trainees call me Sir, then we have Tom, Vic, Pete, and Sam. We can't have 'Sir, Tom, Vic, Pete, Sam, and Jacob.' You need a one-syllable name. Since you're the smallest and youngest, I think we should call you Cub."

"What's a 'sybilalle'?" Jacob asked.

Garret and Thomas laughed, but the other trainees didn't seem to know the word either. "Syllable. It's, er, I guess it's the number of noises that make up a word," Thomas explained. "Like 'Tom' is one syllable, but 'Thom-as' is two. See? And Jac-ob is two, while everyone else here can be called with one."

Jacob nodded. "Why not just call me Jake, then? Or Jay, even?"

"Because that wouldn't be making fun of you, and what's the point in that?" Garret laughed. "Until we get an even younger trainee, you'll be the butt of our jokes."

"Oh, be nice," Thomas said. "Jake it is, brother." Garret sighed and agreed. And then they were in the yard, striking training dummies with blunted longswords. Thomas was the sight to see, wielding the weapon in one hand and holding a hunk of wood to simulate the weight of a shield in his left. Everyone else was struggling to swing their blades in two hands, and Jacob had thrown his sword from a swing four times already, much to the terror of everyone else. While the blades were dull, they still had points, and weighed of solid steel. Eventually Garret lost his patience and tied the hilt to Jacob's hand with about twenty feet of twine.

"You can remove the rope when you can behead a training dummy," Garret shouted. "Until then, you can sleep with the fucking thing."

"How the hell am I supposed to behead anything with a blunt blade!" Jacob complained.

"FIGURE IT OUT!" Garret roared, and he stormed off, leaving the trainees to their business. Thomas could not deny that he felt safer with the blade secured to his brother's body, but he did feel bad watching the child repeatedly and uselessly bash the steel upside the dummy's head.

Thomas strode up behind Jacob, keeping clear of his wild swings, and placed a hand on his left shoulder. Jacob stopped swinging and looked to Thomas, his eyes wet. "What?" he squeaked.

"You aren't strong, Jacob," Thomas explained, as if this were new, critical information.

"You think I don't know that?" Jacob snapped, swinging the weapon half-heartedly at Thomas, who moved to counter it. He caught the blunt blade with his left hand and and gave it a tug, which dragged Jacob onto his knees.

"What I mean," Thomas said patiently, "is that you are not strong *yet*. You are young, your muscles have yet to develop. You need time."

"Gen is stronger than I am and she's a girl!" Jacob cried, collapsing forwards and pounding his fist on the dirt.

"Gendrina has been training every single day since father died. She carries pails of water over her head, one in each hand, and lifts them over and over, for hours. She's outside every night, swinging her wooden sword until her fingers blister and her legs buckle. She hunts birds and squirrels using a bow with a draw weight heavier than her own body. All you do is climb trees and read, when you're not forced to train here."

"Everyone just makes fun of me. Look at this shite," he said, lifting his bound hand, the sword hanging limp. "What's the point?"

"The point, brother," Thomas said, grabbing Jacob's sword arm tightly, "is to become better than them. Garret insults you now, but will he do so the first time you bring him to the ground? Or when you split one of his arrows? Now get up!" Thomas pulled Jacob to his feet and dragged him in front of the training dummy. "You do not yet have strength, but you have agility, and you need to think about your fights. Look at this dummy. Inside is a thin wooden pole, surrounded by tightly-bound straw. You cannot cut through it with a blunt blade, but you can *think* your way in. Look at it."

Jacob stood and stared at the dummy. "I can stab it, but that would not take its head off."

"Yes, but...?"

"The wood inside is thin, yes? If I can thrust the sword in at an angle, accurately enough, I might be able to twist it apart. He never said I have to *cut* its head off, just behead it."

"That's thinking," Thomas said, smiling. Jacob took his place and thrust his sword, missing the target entirely. Thomas sat on a nearby bench and watched. It was three days later that he watched Jacob toss the head of the dummy at Garret's feet to the cheers of the other trainees, and three years later that he saw Jacob first knock Garret on his ass in front of the whole city guard during his swearing-in ceremony.

Garret stood, his right hand bloody, his leathers battered, and his helmet bent. "I have to say," he shouted over the noise, "never would I have thought this day would come. Your strikes are still weak, but strength will come with age. I move to block to my left, and I get hit on the right. I go to parry a thrust, I take your hilt to my shoulder. Your attacks are precise, unpredictable, and when not used with a blunted sword, plenty lethal. I am glad to welcome you as a true member of the city guard." The crowd exploded into applause, and Thomas could not have been more proud.

Thomas coughed and blinked, squinting against the bright sunlight above him. He didn't know where he was, only that it was wet, smelly, and that the moans of the dead were everywhere. He pushed himself up against a stone wall and blinked, trying to gain his senses back. His head throbbed horribly, and his ribs were either badly bruised or broken. There was no sign of the assassin who fell with him. He soon realized he was in a drainage pit, the muddy ground and metal grates made it obvious, though he'd never seen one from the inside. By the moans, he knew the opening above must be completely surrounded by the infected. Even if it wasn't, he would have no chance of climbing out with one arm, hurt ribs, and a still-sore leg.

He walked to one of the two drainage gates and kicked at it. It shook, but it wasn't rusted or loose. It would take him a pickaxe and half a day to get through it, neither of which he had. Trying the other grate, he was pleased to see that three out of the six bars were rusted out. Laying on the muddy ground and pushing on it with his foot, he could make a space underneath about ten inches tall. *Gen might be able to squeeze her way through this, but not me.* Sighing, he plopped down against one of the stone walls, staring into a pile of branches and leaves gathered against the opposite side of the drainage ditch.

Wait. The assassin had an injured arm and leg, how the hell did he get out of here? Checking the damaged grate again, there was no way an adult man could fit under it, not even Jacob. So there had to be *something.* Thomas walked to the pile of branches and gave it a good kick, but it just crumpled uselessly. He stomped around the ditch, pushing on stones and bricks, until he finally and seriously stubbed his toe on something sticking out of the mud. His eyes nearly watering, he bent over and pulled on it. After some tugging it came loose, and he stumbled back holding a blackened steel helmet. After a little more digging, he found a chestplate. *Shite. I guess he left his armor to save the weight and managed to climb out before the infected gathered.*

He grasped the helmet, an idea forming in his head. It would take a while with one arm, but at least it was a way out. He knelt down beside the damaged grate, and began digging out mud with the helmet. It acted as an effective shovel, and within ten minutes he could squeeze himself through the hole. After a minute of wiggling and kicking, he stood up on the other side of the grate. It was a long tunnel, barely tall enough to stand in, and it trailed off into deep darkness. *No other choice, I guess. The drain has a lot of entrances, I'll have to stumble on one of them eventually if I just follow the left wall.* Keeping his stump to the wall, he walked slowly, checking the ground in front of his feet before taking any steps. He quickly found a hall leading to the left and followed it, knowing that it would lead under the Center Ring. He would rather come up there than the Lower Ring. As expected, he soon felt the ground slope upwards. *If I'm lucky, I'll get out near where I fell, maybe find Gen-*

Crash! He was impacted from his right and he toppled, the weight of a person laying on him in the dark. He felt soft, muddy flesh and thought for sure that he was about to feel the bite of an infected. However, last time he checked, the infected didn't punch people. He was taking light hits in his neck and head, and he rolled, throwing out one of his legs. His attack landed and he felt a rush of hot breath and caught the scent of tobacco. *The assassin! Small enough to get under the grate, or did he come down here after me? His attacks are weak, must be badly injured...* His thoughts were interrupted by a kick to his gut, and he jumped back, his eyes wide and searching. *He had enough time in this darkness for his eyes to adjust, but I can't see anything.* Thomas closed his eyes and let his ears do the work, hearing footsteps retreating and circling him.

Step...step...step... *Coming, left!* Thomas spun, bringing his arm around in a mighty backhand, feeling the solid impact and hearing a feminine gasp. *What in the- it's a woman?* Distracted, he took a kick in the knee and he fell, and then she was on him, her forearm held against his throat with her full weight, her other fist pummeling his head. He couldn't block her strikes with one arm, and her legs were positioned on each side to stop him from using his weight to roll away. He managed to slide his arm under her elbow and grabbed her hard around the neck, pushing her back enough to get leverage. He pulled his left leg under her stomach and pushed, kicking her off of him. He heard a soft thud and a scrambling, and then nothing as he stood up. Fearing another ambush from the side, he found the corner of the hall she had come from and backed against it, his arm held out defensively. *Maybe I can provoke her. If she's talking, at least I'll know where she is...*

"I thought you were supposed to be four brothers. Why have they got a little girl with them?" Silence for a moment, and then;

"You thought wrong," she called from somewhere to his right. Her voice was somewhat deep for a woman, with a heavy northern accent.

"I guess this explains how you got through that grate, then. And how come you didn't just kill me while I was knocked out? Some secret assassin code of honor?"

"Not so much," she replied again, now somewhere to his left. She was pacing in the darkness in front of him, trying to see an opening. "Lost my dagger when I fell, and you might have woken up if I tried strangling you or bashing your head in with my helmet."

"So you lure me in here, where I can't see and where my size doesn't matter much if I can't hit anything," Thomas responded. His eyes were starting to adjust, he could see the textures in the walls he was leaning between, but not much else.

"Right," she called, from directly in front of him. He could barely react as a dark form appeared before him, flying from the shadows and landing a surprisingly powerful kick to his chest, knocking the wind out of him. He stumbled forward and caught her leg, but it was slick with mud and there were no clothes to grab onto, and she slipped away.

"Are you not wearing anything?" Thomas chuckled. "Good method for escaping grabs, I suppose. I'll happily get naked too if you'd like to wait a minute. Maybe we can turn this into a different sort of wrestling." He knew his tactic was working as she ran from the darkness again and threw another, even more powerful kick. He dodged it and she slammed her foot into the stone wall, coughing out in pain. He punched at her, but she had already rolled back into the darkness. She had obviously hurt her foot badly, her limping well audible from outside his field of vision. "You're going to hurt your feet like that, girl. Why don't you sew yourself some boots first?"

He heard her growl, heard her approach from the right, and he knew he had her. Just as she appeared from the shadows, he slid to his left and spun his arm around, catching her matted hair. She stopped short and tried to stomp on his foot, but she was too light to cause any real damage. He leaned forward, slamming her into the stone wall. He heard a quick exhale and saw a spot of blood where her head had struck, and she toppled and lay still. He could hear her breathing heavily, unconscious but alive. He knelt next to her, arguing with himself whether or not he should finish her off. Seeing her up close, he could make out severe but long-healed burns covering her legs and waist. Her face was equally as damaged. Just as he decided it was probably for the best and stupid to think otherwise, she woke up and kicked herself away from the wall with surprising speed. She rolled into the darkness and he heard footsteps retreating down the path, then silence. He waited where he was for nearly half an hour, calling out and taunting her further, but there was no response. She had escaped.

*****

"Gah, you really are a witch!" Morgan gasped as Lilith poured half a bottle of whiskey onto his burned leg.

"Oh shush," she answered, and pushed him back down onto his

bench. She pulled a fluffy, light green wad off a nearby plant and stuffed it into Morgan's mouth, and he chewed happily at it. "That will help with the pain, now wait here while I get some more aloe." She walked out as Bayard and Jacob sat in wooden chairs next to Gendrina's bed, their burns already treated and bandaged. Lilith had saved Morgan for last despite his much more serious burns, likely due to his continuous use of the term 'Witch'. She returned shortly with the long, fat, green leaf and began stripping it with a short knife.

If she was feeling spiteful towards Morgan, it didn't show as she slapped the plant onto his leg and sweetly rubbed it in. They waited as she finished treating him, and he plopped down on the second straw bed, giggling merrily, now more bandage than man. Lilith leaned on the window sill, her sleek hair glowing in the afternoon's sun. "I would like you to all stay the night," she said. Let me be sure the burns won't lead to infection at least. You can do what you like afterward."

Jacob shook his head. "We have to find Thomas. Alive or otherwise, if Gendrina is here, he has to be nearby."

"The upstairs lanterns are all on," Lilith said. If he's around, hopefully he'll be smart enough to check in here. You really should stay here for a while. With the fresh burns, any contact with the infected will likely result in your own-"

"Wahpenned?" Everyone turned to Gendrina, who had finally woken up, her face dazed. "Whare Tohms is?"

Jacob stood and knelt next to her. "Gen, it's me. You're in a herbalist's shop, she treated your injuries. Are you alright?"

Gendrina blinked and groaned. "I...think. Thomas, he helped me escape, and I didn't see what happened to him after..."

"Come on everyone, let them alone," Lilith commanded, motioning at Bayard and the knights. The trio limped after her and she shut the door behind them. She led them back to the main room and turned to Bayard. "I need to talk to you alone," she said.

"What should we do?" Christopher asked.

"Like I know. Sit there and talk about swords or something," Lilith quipped, and she pulled Bayard behind the counter and through a small panel leading into the storage room.

*****

"You know what they are, then?" Bayard asked.

"Of course. You know it's in our nature to learn all we can about the unknown. As soon as I learned of the problem, I had a guard help me autopsy one of the infected. He shot her with a crossbow and dragged her into my basement, where I found the deformed brain. I have no idea what causes it, but at least I know what they are and how to kill them."

"The infection only fades from corpses two days after they're properly killed," Bayard said worriedly. "How long ago did you do this?"

"Well over a day ago," she answered. "It seems that unless you have opened wounds, you won't get infected from contact with their skin or blood. How about you? How did you learn of this?" Bayard spent fifteen minutes explaining what had brought him here, starting with Sefu and the flower and ending with the explosion at the potter. Lilith sighed again. "Sefu didn't make it then...I'm sorry, he was a brave man." Bayard nodded but remained silent. "And that flower, what became of it?"

"Burned along with everything I own as we chased the thief to this city."

"That's too bad. I would have liked a chance to study it."

"Trust me; no you wouldn't. Look at the infected...there can be no cure, no protection. This is beyond us. All I could do was destroy the source and try to stop the plague here. I murdered my own city."

Lilith stepped forward and wrapped her arms around Bayard's shoulders. "This is not your fault. I know how plagues work, and despite the extreme nature of this one, you did the right thing." Then she leaned in and kissed him. "I missed you so much, Bayard. Why did you have to leave?"

"I had to get out of the city, Lily," Bayard said as he held her by her waist. "I didn't want to leave you, but my old home held nothing but memories of my parents. I always planned to come back here, but every time I approached the city, I couldn't bring myself to enter it. I am so sorry."

There were tears in her eyes now. "You could have sent a messenger, something to let me know where you were or what you were doing. You could have asked me to come with you."

"I know you wanted to stay with your mother and with the shop. I wanted you to move on, to find someone else who would stay here with you."

"Damn you, Bayard. You know that there is nobody else for me."

*****

Bayard emerged from the storage room nearly an hour later, looking extremely disheveled. Christopher and Morgan were right where Lilith left them, joined by Jacob and Gendrina, who was fully awake and back in her chainmail. They were all grinning stupidly at him.

"What?" Bayard snapped.

Jacob stood and leaned into Bayard's ear. "This store has thin walls, mate."

Bayard sighed as Lilith extracted herself from the small door behind him, peering at the group with an uncaring gaze. "It's getting late in the day," she said. "I can't force you to stay, but if any of you insist on leaving before you've healed better, it is on your heads. I have enough beds for everyone if you choose to stay." She sat behind the counter and buried herself in a book.

Bayard sat next to Christopher and looked Gendrina over. "You did that to the arsehole outside, eh? Seems I've finally found someone more terrifying than Sefu. Shame you never got to meet him."

Gendrina smiled weakly. "I know him. Thomas told me who he was and what he did, and I met him as a child. He helped reconstruct many homes after the fire, right?"

Bayard nodded. "He's not an easy man to forget."

"So, what are we going to do?" Morgan asked to nobody in particular.

"I think it would be best to stay here," Jacob said. "I know we need to find Thomas, but it's getting dark. We'll start a search first thing in the morning."

Christopher shook his head. "I wish I could help you, but me and Morgan need to get back to the castle. The Drydens will go after my father and sister if they cannot find me."

"I understand," Bayard said. "When we find Thomas, can we come to the castle? I don't know how many knights are left or how many citizens they've saved, but I'm sure you could use our help to retake the city."

"Of course," Christopher said. "I'll have to withhold some information about how you got here, but I won't turn down your help. I know there are at least two hundred citizens being kept on the castle grounds, and there were thirty knights when we were dispatched in groups of five. All as well trained as my own team. None of us were touched by the infected, so I see no reason why the others should have a problem. At least I can hope for-"

Knock, knock, knock.

Everyone stood and faced the door. Christopher walked forwards, drawing his blade. He flipped the bar out of its slot with the tip of his sword, and the door creaked inwards. The abhorrently dirty one-armed man stumbled into the store, glancing tiredly at the group. He saw Gendrina and smiled, then choked out two simple words; "Bath, please."

Chapter Eleven
Summer of 1513 A.D
City of Valdus
Early Morning

Bayard was buried in the deepest sleep of his life. Visions and memories filled his head, but one always pushed itself to the front of his mind.

"I have to go, Bayard. I've stayed here as long as I can, but I need to find my mother and tell her what has become of me and my true father," Sefu said as he piled dozens of vials, oils, and herbs into his large wooden trunk.

"I cannot believe this, Sefu. You could have told me you planned of this a year ago, not wake me up one morning saying you're going to cross an ocean. You are my brother, I do not want to lose you like this."

Sefu turned to him. "Come with me, Bayard. There is nothing here for you."

"We have the clinic. I have Lilith."

"The clinic is a charred husk and Lilith is using you for your family's secrets. I would not be surprised if her own mother told her to bed you for them."

Bayard shoved Sefu, hard. It was like shoving a stone wall. "She's never asked me about anything my parents have ever done. For all I know, she does not even know their names. You will not speak of her that way."

Sefu stepped forwards, and Bayard almost thought he was about to be attacked, but then he was being hugged and lifted off the ground. "Please, brother, let us not fight on the day that I leave." Bayard grimaced, then returned the embrace. "Thank you, and your family, for everything. I will return someday, to rejoin you at your clinic."

"It is as you say, the clinic is rubble. I do not think I will stay in the city, I will likely move to a nearby town. Houses are cheaper to build or buy, and the quiet appeals to me. Peydenal, or Kaden."

Sefu shook his head. "*Come with me,* brother. We could do so much good in Egypt, help more people than we ever could here. You will learn the language quickly when you live with it."

"I cannot, Sef. England is my home, and I am afraid that someone of my skin would not be welcome there."

Sefu looked down at his feet, frowning. "I will miss you, Bayard. Good luck, wherever you go." Bayard unwillingly helped Sefu carry the trunk and load it into the cart awaiting them outside. He watched as the horses began to trot along the stone road, and Sefu disappeared behind a corner. The next day, Bayard tied a sack containing every gold piece he owned to his horse, burst out of the city gates, and he rode.

"Wake up, you bloody sack of potatoes," Lilith shouted, smacking Bayard across the forehead. He started and coughed, sitting up from the wooden bench.

"G'morning," Bayard moaned. "Where is everyone?"

"Prince Christopher and Sir Morgan left about an hour ago for the castle, Jacob and Thomas are taking breakfast in the bedroom, and Gendrina is upstairs doing morning things. You, on the other hand, haven't moved since Thomas got here last night."

"Sorry, Lily. Haven't slept in a while," Bayard explained. "Breakfast sounds good." He stood and proceeded to the bedroom where Jacob and Thomas were sitting, enthusiastically devouring cheeses and wild rice that Lilith had fancied up with some of her herbs. He took a seat and had at the food, and they were soon joined by Gendrina and Lilith. Thomas was looking as good as could be expected. Lilith had been unable to supply his bath, what with the town's wells being either dry or tainted by a corpse or two. He had washed off as best he could with Lilith's surprisingly large stash of alcohol (which she had made perfectly clear that Thomas would have to pay for if they lived to see any semblance of civilization) and some sponges, and Lilith had rewrapped the bandages on his arm. Bayard finished chewing his mouthful of cheese and turned to Thomas. "So what happened last night? I'm sure you've already explained but I seem to have been out cold."

Thomas just looked annoyed at his breakfast being interrupted, so Gendrina stepped in. "He fell into the Lower Ring with one of the assassins. He was trapped in a drainage tunnel and while he was escaping, he was attacked by the assassin. It was a woman, apparently. Christopher was very surprised, saying they were only four brothers. He guessed that one had died or become disabled elsewhere, and they replaced him to keep a four-man party. Thomas overpowered her but she escaped into the darkness."

"Going by what Christopher told me," Bayard interjected, "they had a sister but she was killed along with their parents. Burned."

Thomas looked up from his food. "She was burned. Badly. All her legs and waist, and her face."

Bayard was staring at a wall, his eyes squinted in thought. "She'd be wrapped around the stomach and chest if she were tied to a stake. If they tied her with a less flame-vulnerable rope, it would have helped protect her vital organs. It's unlikely, but possible that she survived it, if the murderers were less than vigilant with the oil. It makes the most sense as to who she is, anyway."

"Christopher said that the Dryden's parents and sister were burned for witchcraft," Thomas said. "You don't think tha-"

"Quiet with that," Lilith snapped. "No witch, but chances are she knew of herbalogy and advanced medicine just like me if she were accused as such. If she did manage to survive the burning, she would have known the best way to treat it. We need to get to the castle immediately, seems most of us haven't had much to drink b'sides booze the past three days. That may be my own normal state, but it's not exactly good for you. Prince Christopher said they have plentiful untainted water up there. We'll meet with the Prince, he should be able to gain us an audience with the King. We'll tell him all we know and then we'll figure things out from there."

"We?" Bayard asked. "You're coming with us, then?"

"As if I would let you out of my sight again," Lilith said, agitated. "Besides, I'm sure they need as many healers as they can get."

Bayard nodded. "That's definitely right. Finish your breakfasts, I'll fill a medicine chest to bring to the castle." He stood and retreated into the main room, finding one of the handled wooden chests behind the counter. He wandered the building, gathering every useful herb there was. Yarrow to stop bleeding, aloe to treat burns, pipeweed for pain, and many other herbs to relieve everything from headaches to a severe infection. Once the chest was full to bursting, he squished it shut and hauled it to the bedroom, where the group was done eating and were discussing their stories in getting here. Bayard jammed another wedge of cheese into his mouth and showed Lilith the chest, which Lilith approved of.

"Good choices," she said. "Heavy, but the castle is only a few minutes from here. Is everybody ready?" The group nodded and stood. They took a minute to get their armor on and find their weapons, then gathered at the front door. Lilith stared out the window and glanced around suspiciously. "No infected, but there are muddy footprints all through my alley."

"Oh no," Thomas said, running to the door. He pushed it open and stepped out, staring at the side of the steps. "She was here, look." Everyone piled out of the door and looked where Thomas was pointing. The dead assassin had been stripped to his underclothes, his coat, cloak, helmet, and mask gone. The cuirass remained next to him. Small, muddy footprints marked the path right to him, then disappeared. "She came here and took what equipment she could salvage. The armor wouldn't fit her so she left that, but now she has probably returned to her remaining brothers. If they know one of them has died, they will likely hasten their assault. And they may come here to recover the body. We have to leave, now."

With no plans to argue, Thomas and Gendrina led the way with Lilith in the middle, and Bayard and Jacob lugged the medicine chest between them in the rear. A group of infected shambled towards them from the morning shadows, their moans soon attracting more. Gendrina and Thomas had borrowed Bayard and Jacob's weapons since their own were stolen by the assassins, and they broke off from the group to clear the attackers. Thomas was effectively wielding the bastard sword in his one hand, but Gendrina, despite her considerable strength, looked uncomfortable and awkward wielding the massive scimitar which was longer than she was tall. Bayard called her over, and she took his side of the chest while he reclaimed his weapon and finished escorting the group to the large, shining gate. There were many bodies laying scattered outside the gate, some of them still moving, their spines severed but their brains intact. Bayard put them down, and afterward, heavy footsteps could be heard approaching from behind the gate.

A heavily armed and armored knight clanked into view, wearing full steel plate over chainmail and carrying a spiked war hammer and tower shield. In Bayard's knowledge, knights only geared up like this when expecting open warfare at any moment. The knight lifted his massive great helm and peered at them, revealing short greying hair and an aged face. "The witch, the wolf girl, two guards, one with a missing arm, and one man who looks extremely homeless. You must be 'Bayard's group'. Prince Christopher told me to expect you."

Bayard sighed at his being labeled a vagrant, but couldn't argue that the term fit his current appearance. Subconsciously pulling back his long, dirty hair and brushing off his bloody burlap clothes, he stepped forward. "I would be Bayard, and forgive me for not being able to find a mountain of pots and pans to wear. Besides, this is better for avoiding the dead."

The knight grinned and nodded. "True indeed. I certainly wouldn't choose this getup here either, but every knight has been ordered into full kit with the news of the Drydens' return. Sir Uriel Westlake, at your service," he said, bowing. "I've been instructed to escort you to the survivor camp where you'll meet with Sir Morgan. The Prince is in the castle explaining the situation to the King, but he'll want to talk to you later on as well." He stepped forward and unlocked the multiple mechanisms on the other side of the gate.

The group followed him through and they began to ascend the long stone staircase to the castle grounds. "I'm wondering," Bayard called up to Uriel. "Has the Center Ring's blacksmith shown up here? A man who goes by the nickname 'Helmet'?"

Uriel stopped and thought for a few seconds, then tilted his head. "Probably. I don't know where he's from or what he's named, but a blacksmith carrying a number of brand new weapons arrived here very early this morning. He was with a woman and two other men, who were also loaded with weapons. Said he didn't want civilians to misuse his blades, so we stashed them all in the castle.

"Big beard and hair like my sister's?" Jacob asked.

"Aye," Uriel answered with a laugh.

Jacob sighed in relief. "Great, they got out before the assassins showed up. They must have been found by other survivors who convinced them to come to the castle."

Bayard nodded. "Glad to hear it. I want to talk to him first. I'm sure he saw the flames from the explosion, he should know that his home is alright."

"Very well," Uriel said, and continued up the steps. As they ascended, the sounds of talking and movement grew louder and louder. They soon reached the top and stepped into a flurry of activity, people moving wood, stone, and weapons. There were dozens of tents set up in rows, and wooden shacks presumably built as latrines. Groups of shining knights ordered around the citizens, and city guards were running about to help with construction.

Bayard scanned the area and spotted him quickly, taller than most anyone there and walking beside his wife, who was now wearing a dark emerald green dress. She was limping badly, and had bandages tied around her forehead and arm.

Bayard smiled and started towards them, the rest of the group following him. Ten meters away, he was stopped short by Thomas grabbing him hard around the chest and pulling him behind a tent. "What the hell, Thomas?" Bayard coughed.

"That woman," Thomas gasped. "She is the assassin I fought in the tunnels."

*****

"Yes, our doctors figured out the connection to the bites very quickly. Every civilian was thoroughly searched, and anyone who was bitten or showed signs of severe sickness was banished from the Upper Ring. Their family members fought back, of course, but the knights managed to push out anyone who was a threat. No one still here is bitten, and everyone seems mostly healthy," King Drake Alento explained to Christopher.

The young man smiled. "I trusted our doctors to do as much," he said. "Two civilian healers I met in the city also figured it out. I'm sure you remember Marina Travers, who brought Jenara into the world? And Baeden, who fixed my leg as a child." The King nodded. "Their son, Bayard, is here in the city. He saw smoke rising over the city from his home in Peydenal, and rushed here to lend his aid. He should be arriving in the Upper Ring some time this morning, unless something stops him. Sir Uriel has been notified of his group's appearance and should escort them to the camp upon their arrival. He's accompanied by two city guards and two women, one of whom is an...alternative but effective healer, and the other is a startlingly good combatant, the wolf girl I told you about, years ago. You would never believe it, but she killed one of the Drydens in single combat."

"One is dead? That is good to hear," King Drake mumbled. "And Bayard, that is great news. Our doctors are skilled, but none of them can hold a candle to the Travers family, and in this situation I would never turn away a hand willing to hold a sword, be it man or woman."

"Indeed," Christopher affirmed. "Where is Jenara now, by the way?"

"She's taken it upon herself to convert the treasury into a sanctuary for the children and the frailer women. She had guards carry beds, food, and medicine. They're shut in with enough smoked meat, grain, corn, and water to last a month, even without rationing."

"Brilliant." Christopher smiled. "I apologize, father, but may I leave for the camp to find Bayard and his group?"

"Yes, but I will come with you. The citizens are afraid and demoralized, seeing their King may do them some good." Christopher nodded and stood still as King Drake retreated to his chambers, and returned soon after wearing the shining, golden ceremonial armor of the Valdus Kings. He smiled at his son. "Let us go."

*****

"Are you positive, Thomas? This accusation cannot be taken lightly." The warning came from Sir Morgan, who had spotted the group sneaking into a tent and came in behind them.

"As positive as it is possible to be," Thomas assured, anger in his eyes. "Her face, her hair, her frame, her injuries, it all matches. Apprehend her, check her body, you'll see that the burns match as well."

"I cannot simply arrest a woman and pull up her skirt, especially not with her husband right next to her. I will gather a number of knights, and we will do this properly. Until then-" He was interrupted by the bellow of a Royal horn, the sound echoing throughout the open field. Gendrina peered out the tent's flap, her eyes wide. "Oh, no."

*****

The survivors of Valdus fell silent as the horn sounded from somewhere above them. They all turned towards the castle gates, every one of them staring at the two men walking towards the entrance steps. Some looked on in amazement, others in disdain, fascination, fear, curiosity, and hope. Prince Christopher and King Drake Alento began to descend the stone steps. They walked unaccompanied, the usual procession of knights, servants, and handmaidens busy with more important duties than ceremony, despite the King's choice of armor. No one cheered or applauded, either from their tiredness and depression or from dislike of the Kingdom's royalty. Many of the citizens smiled at the father and son, but just as many recoiled or scowled.

Soon, both men were walking through the citizens, towards a congregation of knights gathered on the other end of the courtyard. Christopher apologized quietly to a woman he bumped into, noticing too late the scars on her face. The instinct hit him before realization did, and his right hand began to cross to his longsword just as Sir Morgan's voice roared out over the silent citizens, issuing the warning seconds after it would have mattered. Christopher felt the pain in his lower back just as his hand wrapped around the hilt of his sword, and he stumbled. The King noticed something was wrong quite quickly, his own hand reaching for his blade while Christopher still fell. It mattered not, as the two tents on either side of the King erupted, shadows bursting forth from their openings and flying towards him with inhuman speed. His sword came loose from his sheath just as the two bone daggers plunged into his body, one in the center of his chest and the other in the left side of his back.

Two beings of shadow and smoke standing above him. A group of men and women charging the figures, who were fleeing. His son, still alive, deep red blood pouring from under his light armor. These were some of the last things King Drake Alento saw as he lay dying. Christopher was somehow still on his feet, ignoring the bloodfall, his hands wrapped around the throat of a small blonde woman. The two shadows stood as if desperate to fight, but finally they were run out by a large group of warriors, none of whom the King recognized. He heard a crack and the woman fell from his son's hands, dead. His last sight was Christopher being tackled by a giant of a man, bearded, roaring, and rippling with muscle, and two city guards attempting to pull him off. He closed his eyes, and he was gone.

Chapter Twelve
Summer of 1513 A.D
Valdus Castle
Midday

If you are currently alive, chances are you have never had the full wrath of a Northern man directed towards you. This was the thought in Bayard's head as the six-foot-five bearded giant called Helmet who had once behaved so peacefully rampaged about the castle grounds. Bastard sword in hand, he sprinted after the bleeding, disarmed, and fully-routed Christopher. Jacob and Thomas were unconscious, Helmet having easily knocked them out with two thunderous punches. Helmet had taken Jacob's blade and made after Christopher. Bayard and Gendrina were following, accompanied by unrecognized castle guards, keeping their distance. The other knights were too burdened by armor to keep up, and so they began to circle around in an attempt to corner Helmet.

Christopher was being smart, leading the fury-blind man in circles so as to avoid sharp turns that would let him shorten the gap between them. Christopher was losing blood fast, though, and soon he stumbled and collapsed forward into the thick grass. Helmet was on him instantly, sword raised above his head for an executioner's strike. He brought the blade down, and Christopher was only saved by the heavily armored Uriel diving on top of him. The blade clanked uselessly off Uriel's great helm and Helmet roared, falling to one knee as he took a crossbow bolt to the back of the leg. It took Uriel, Bayard, Morgan, Gendrina, and three other knights to bring the man fully to ground. Finally, hog-tied, bloodied, and hopeless, Helmet went limp and began to sob.

*****

"I do not think he is one of them," Bayard said as he began to sew up the gash in Christopher's lower back. The lady assassin's blade had missed his kidney by mere centimeters, but it was still a dangerous wound. Christopher would be unable to run or fight for weeks. "An assassin would be prepared to leave someone behind to complete his mission, family or otherwise, just as the other two men did. He is just a blacksmith who was fooled into loving a spy."

"The knights are calling for his execution," Christopher answered. He was laying in his own large bed, red blankets gathered around him, covering his backside, and red curtains flowed in the wind that blew through the open windows.

"But you are the King. Your word is what matters."

Christopher closed his eyes. *I am the King.* It was as simple as that. There was no time or resources for a coronation. No surplus for a feast. They could not even have the gold-embroidered burial robes tailored for his father, as the artisan tailor was somewhere in the Upper Ring, dead and shambling around. "I think you are right about him. However, the citizens must be appeased. Their King has been killed and they believe we have one of the attackers in our custody. What am I to do?"

"You retaliate." The voice came from behind the bed curtains, and it was Gendrina's. "You gather every one of your knights and you have them tear the city apart. You find the real assassins, and you personally behead them in front of everyone."

"As much as that would amuse me," Christopher sighed, "this city is huge. Two men could remain hidden here for years, even if we had a full battalion searching for them, and even if the streets were not taken by the dead. And we cannot rule out the possibility of a third. If that woman was truly their sister as you say, there may still be three living brothers. If Ulfberht is not one of them, that means another is in hiding somewhere. If one was deep enough undercover to legally marry into the city, the other could be anyone."

"Ulfberht?" Jacob's voice piped up from somewhere behind the curtains.

"Helmet's true name," Christopher explained.

"I like Helmet better," Jacob mumbled, to a soft laugh from Gendrina and Bayard.

"Lily, get some yarrow from the chest and prepare it, please," Bayard said. "He's still bleeding pretty badly." There was a grunt of confirmation and light footsteps retreated to the other side of the room, soon followed by the sounds of the chest opening and closing and some chopping. A small hand poked through the curtain, containing a handful of green paste with some yellow flecks in it. Bayard took some and rubbed it into Christopher's wound. He then placed a thick bandage and a heavy book over it. "The bleeding should cease in a little while, and I'll finish the stitching then. For now, we need to come up with a plan to find the rest of the assassins. We cannot stay on the defensive while they pick us off."

Christopher was silent as he thought for a long time. And then he smiled.

*****

Two Days Later
Morning

Tory Dryden scowled as he watched the two through his spyglass. Prince; now King Christopher Alento sat stiffly on the saddle of his large warhorse, obviously in pain, squinting and grimacing with each step the beast took. Behind him, the massive, gilded coffin was rolling on the steel wheels of the cart it was set in. Behind the cart, Princess Jenara Alento walked slowly, her flowing black funeral dress and veil covering her completely. For two hundred years, it has been tradition in the Alento family for deceased royalty to be brought to their resting place by family alone.

Their ancestors believed that the lesser blood of servants and civilians, and even knights, corrupted the spirits of the dead with their presence at the burials. It was a long-done and far-known tradition, common knowledge among the nearby towns and cities. *A superstitious and stupid tradition for a superstitious and stupid city,* Tory thought. Alone, the injured man and the small woman walked down the path behind the castle, descending the walkway that led to the castle's burial grounds.

Tory was prone on top of an abandoned castle turret, and next to him, his brother Kane watched the two as well. "Poetic, is it not?" Kane whispered in their own tongue. "That the last three of our family kill the last three of theirs."

"It is," Tory responded. "It is too bad that Adam cannot be here to land the final strike himself, with all the work he did to remain hidden, but his task is just as important."

Kane nodded slightly, but the gesture was not seen beneath his hood, helmet, and mask. "When do we strike?"

"When they pass by us, we will drop and attack from behind. I will silence the Princess, you can have the honor of taking down the new King," Tory instructed.

"Thank you, brother," Kane grinned. And so they waited in silence as the two vulnerable siblings passed by them. Slowly, quietly, they climbed off each side of the turret and dropped into the grass. For complete silence, they had removed their boots and armor. The kills would be swift, there would be no need for the armor. They calmly approached the grieving woman, and Tory stepped forwards, drawing the bone dagger from his belt and gripping it tightly. He saw her slow gait, her lowered head, he saw the gems encrusting her veil and the dead King's coffin, he saw the new King riding with pained dignity, he saw the trees blowing, the wind in his direction to mask his sound or any scent.

What he did not see was the small, polished gold mirror that sat at the base of the coffin. He did not see the grin that King Christopher wore like a crown. As he reached the Princess and went to plunge the dagger into her heart, he was met with the solid impact of steel armor and the feel of his bone dagger shattering. Then his arm was held with the strength of a man, and he felt the pain of a blade piercing through the front of his leg. Tory shouted, trying to tear his arm away. It came loose, taking the Princess's veil with it. He stumbled backwards and saw an angry, male face with a small beard underneath the feminine garb.

Glancing down to his brother, who had turned back to him while beside the coffin, he saw the coffin's lid fly off and three armored men pile out of it, swarming his brother with shortswords and axes. Tory tried to run, but his injured leg would not allow it, and he fell forwards. He expected death at any second, but it did not come. Instead, he felt his helmet get violently torn off, and he felt a familiarly-scented cloth pull tightly around his mouth and nose. He choked and coughed through it, realized it was the same toxin he had used to knock out the red-haired woman and the one-armed man, and everything quickly went black.

*****

"I still don't see why I had to wear the fucking dress," Jacob moaned.

"You're the only one it would fit," Bayard said, humor in his voice.

"It would fit Gen, she is just as strong as I am," Jacob retorted.

"You know we tried. The plate cuirass and gorget would not fit right on her chest," Christopher weighed in. "It wasn't safe. The decoy needed full, reliable protection."

Lilith cut them off. "Either way, it is done. The toxin will be wearing off soon. Are Sirs Morgan and Uriel ready for the interrogation?"

Christopher nodded. "They should be on their way now, with the tools." The group sat in silence then, until heavy feet could be heard descending the steps to the dungeon. The door creaked open and the two knights entered, dragging a heavy-looking chest between them. They placed it in the center of the large cell and looked grimly at Christopher, who then turned to the group of civilians. "I thank you all for your aid in capturing this man, but I won't ask you to remain here for this. The other knights are all in the Center Ring, searching for survivors and food, and the camp is being run by only a few castle guards. I ask you all to return to the camp and lend aid where it is needed."

Bayard stepped forwards. "I should stay. This man has probably been trained to withstand torture of every sort. If we are to make him spill his guts, he will be brought to a fine line between life and death. Someone with medical knowledge should be here to make sure it is not taken too far."

Christopher nodded. "Indeed. I was going to call on one of the castle doctors, but if you are willing, you may stay." Bayard took a place in a corner of the cell, and the rest of the group slowly moved out and retreated up the stairs. When their sounds had faded, Christopher stepped over to the unconscious assassin and slapped him hard across the face.

*****

Tory Dryden snapped awake, stiff and pained, finding himself in a deep dungeon cell and surrounded by armored knights. As his vision grew stronger, he saw King Christopher standing above him, and two more knights who he knew by sight but not name. In the corner behind him was a civilian who he thought was with the Prince and his knights when he and Kane had taken the redhead and one-arm. Blinking, he looked up to his captors. Remaining silent, he watched as one of the unknown knights stepped to a large chest in the center of the cell and kicked it open, revealing rows of bright steel knives, screws, nails, hammers, and vials. Tory grinned at the chest and asked, "What time is it?"

"And why should we tell you that?" the tallest knight asked, lifting a small hammer from the chest and waving it threateningly.

"Because it will determine how much of your time I have to waste before I tell you what you wish to know."

The knights looked confused, and Christopher shrugged. "It is about an hour before noon," he announced slowly.

Tory smiled. "Ah, in that case there will be no need to use any of those shiny things," he motioned towards the torture chest with his nose. "I will tell you anything you like. It will not change anything."

"Are there more of you?" was the first question, coming from the shorter knight.

"Yes. My last living sibling, by the name of Adam."

"And where is he? What is he doing?

Tory began to laugh. It was an insane sound, an utterly mad cackle, and it only ceased when the tall knight took his hammer to Tory's knee. He coughed and steadied himself. "Adam is in the city of Sinead, sitting in our home, possibly sipping mead and enjoying some fine tobacco." Another hammering, this time on the center of his hand. Tory barely flinched as he glared up at the tall knight. "I am serious," he whispered. "He should have gotten there about four days ago."

The peasant man standing in the corner of the cell seemed to understand first. "A message," he gasped, his eyes wide with horror, to Tory's delight. "Sinead is going to use this plague to finally take this city. You've always had the defenses to repel any army, but now we have nothing."

Tory smiled and began to ramble off. "Six days since this whole thing started. Two days for my brother to ride to Sinead and inform our King that your city is weakened, one day to prepare the soldiers and horses, three days for our army to reach your gates, due to the slowness of riding in a group that size. That makes six! And I do believe that your people never bothered to lower the bars on the *inside* of your gates, did you? Nobody in their right mind would go within a mile of a city that had their plague bars down. Not unless they were given information as to the nature of the plague, how it spreads and how to counter it. A disease that requires you to be bitten by a loud, slow peasant seems pretty easy to handle, to a group of soldiers anyway. This is proven by the fact that none of your knights have fallen to it. Even if you do lock the gates from the inside, their siege ram would break through in minutes, without archers raining down on them." Tory finally fell silent as the group stared at him.

The King, fury glowing in his eyes, turned to the short knight. "Get to the surface, sound the horn for the knights to return to the castle. One short blast to avoid attracting too many infected. Place lookouts on top of the castle, and tell every knight, guard, and able-bodied man to prepare for war."

Tory watched the short knight retreat up the stairs, then flew into his mad laughter again. "Prepare with *what?*" he spat. "When is the last time anyone has checked your castle's armory? Is it that you have not noticed that we broke in last night and tossed every blade and bit of armor into the fires of the Lower Ring? Before you killed her, my sister got a little showy for a knight, a good enough distraction for my brother to acquire his key ring. You have no protection besides the armor and weapons you wear on your bodies as we speak."

The King closed his eyes. He was obviously trying hard not to fly into a rage, to give lucid and logical commands. "Bayard, go to the castle forge. Create as many simple weapons and scale chestplates as you can. Spend no time on chain or ornaments, just tie steel plates together in a way that will sit on a man's shoulders. For weapons, make spiked axes and hammers. They are quicker and more effective against the Northern leathers and chain, as well as the infected. On your way there, tell a castle guard to gather every civilian tool that can be used as a weapon. Woodcutting axes, picks, scythes, anything. And tell them to strap some leather to wood for shields. The guards have been told to follow your orders. Go, now."

The peasant man nodded and quickly bolted through the cell door. The King then turned to the tall knight. "Uriel, gather your squires and your knight's Seal. Bring six castle guards, and go to the barracks. There you will construct a ladder in as little time as you can, and use it to escape from the south side of the city. If any of your men are bitten on the way, behead them on my orders, and tell them to do the same to you. Let no infection out of the city. Travel south to the Kingdom of Haarn. When you arrive, offer Jenara's hand in marriage to their Prince Zane should their King lend his army to our aid. They were fine friends as children and I see no reason why Jenara nor their Prince would protest." The new King thought for a moment. "And send Helmet down, too."

The tall knight, Uriel, saluted the King and clanked his way to the surface. Tory looked to the new King. "A decent plan, my *King.*" The last word was hissed with hatred. "I would wish to see the outcome of the events, but I'm sure you'll have killed me long before they are settled."

"You will be dead," Christopher agreed. "But not by my hand." Just then, the cell door opened, and in stepped the bear of a man. The man that Jessica had used to infiltrate the city. His eyes were dark with sleeplessness, his hair dirty and ragged, and he was holding a hawk axe in one hand and a length of rope in the other. "You murdered my father and my friends, but royalty and knights are always prepared for loss. The true pain was felt by this man, who your family deceived for years. You belong to him."

*****

Christopher left the cell, closing the door behind him. Through the thick wood, up the great length of stairs, and all through the camp, the assassin's screams could be heard for six hours, soon mixed with the sound of war drums that blew in on the Northern wind.

Chapter Thirteen
Summer of 1513 A.D
Valdus Castle Smithy
Evening

Minutes after the assassin had fallen quiet, the door to the forge opened and Helmet walked in. His arms were covered in dried blood that went up to his elbows, and he carried the hawk axe in his right hand and the head of the assassin in his left. The severed head still wore the mask of the Fogwalkers, Helmet had apparently decided to dishonor the clan of assassins beyond just executing one of its members. Bayard remained silent as Helmet tossed the head into the flames of the forge and cleaned his arms in the quenching trough. And then he began to work, taking the other side of the smithy.

After a long time, Bayard spoke. "I guess you've found your stomach for killing."

Helmet glanced at him. "I suppose I just needed the right target," he answered. "I still do not think I could handle slaying another innocent man, like I did as a guard."

"Many would say that a thief is not innocent," Bayard offered.

"Some thieves are not. But the first man I killed was homeless, he had a family. I shouldn't have done it, I could have faked a fall, or pretended I could not run fast enough. But I got caught up in my 'duty' and went too far."

"Do not blame yourself, Helmet. The sword is not to blame for the wielder's actions. You followed orders, the thief's murderer was the old King. Christopher almost had me killed the same way, just days ago. King Drake's idiotic actions also led to the actions of your false wife, and her brothers. Burning a family for witchcraft. You are the only man I can say this to, but Drake Alento deserved the death that he received. However his son Christopher, he has proven himself to be a good man when under his own command. You would be dead if he was not. Power can corrupt, and the future is uncertain, but for now I ask that you not butt heads with him."

Helmet gave Bayard a slight nod, and returned to his work. Together they hammered away through the night, producing two dozen quality weapons, enough to supply about a quarter of the castle guards. They also produced three scale coats each, which would be traded about as needed.

Just as the sun began to shine through the barred windows of the smithy, a squire knocked on the heavy door. "I bring good news, sirs," the little man chirped after Bayard let him in. He continued speaking in a manner as though he could have been reading off a script. "The castle guards have scavenged an incredible number of tools from the civilians here and nearby homes. Ulfberht is to remain here and continue making armor, and Bayard is instructed to return to the camp and examine the health of drafted men along with the castle doctors to be sure they are capable of combat."

"Do not call me that," Helmet growled from his corner. The squire recoiled.

Bayard allowed himself a chuckle. "No need to worry. He is more bark than bite, unless you're that prick," he explained, pointing to the charred skull that ornamented the center of the forge. The squire yelped and bolted. Even Helmet wore a small grin as the little man ran. Bayard gave Helmet a friendly salute and retreated after the squire. They soon came to the front gate and walked into the camp, which was buzzing with action. The tents had been moved to the sides, creating a large empty square in which around forty civilian men stood, holding pickaxes, sickles, rakes, and scythes. A row of knights stood before them, showing them the proper way to swing their various tool-weapons.

Christopher rested on a stable pole nearby, watching the training. "We do not have enough," he whispered, upon seeing Bayard's arrival. "The city of Sinead is very small compared to Valdus, but every one of their men are warriors who have been trained since birth. They will wield greatswords and battleaxes, ride well-fed warhorses and wear armor made from the thickest leathers known to man."

Bayard did not argue. He knew what way this battle would go. Even if every man in the castle were a soldier, they would still likely be outnumbered three to one. "That is why we need to win this battle with our heads, not our arms. I did more than smith all night, Christopher. I planned. As we speak, they are likely breaking camp and preparing for the final approach. They come from the north."

"What does it matter which way they come from?" Christopher asked sullenly.

"Because we need them to approach from the west," Bayard answered.

*****

King Alvor the Wolf grinned wide, displaying his yellow teeth, as the five horn bleats that signaled surrender sounded from the city of Valdus. "Smart one, this King," he said in his own tongue to his two squires, who were busy strapping on his thick coat of chain and leather. "But a coward, to allow me to claim his city without even a hint of battle."

"Indeed, Sire," one of the squires agreed. Minutes later, Alvor was equipped. He stepped from his tent into the war camp, nodding at his men as they bowed to him.

"Stand up, stand up," he shouted. "You know you are not to bow to me on the battlefield. Here we are shieldbrothers, equals. Although, it seems this field shall not see battle. Valdus has surrendered. Keep your armor and weapons, in case we need to battle the plaguewalkers. Remember, if you are bitten or scratched, you will be executed where you stand." There was a yell of confirmation from his soldiers. Alvor grasped a large leg of goose and ate it to the bone, tossing the refuse into the grass. After his soldiers had finished their own food, they stood and looked to him for orders. "Well, what are you waiting for? To their gate, and wait for their envoy!"

The camp quickly broke, and the five hundred men rode for the castle walls. Two hours later, Alvor stared up at the fifteen foot tall gate that blocked his way into his new Kingdom. One hour later, he was losing patience. Just as he was about to remove the plague barrier and enter the city himself, a blonde head poked out from the top of the wall. "Hello!" it called.

Alvor looked up at it. "And who are you?" he asked.

"I am Prince- er, King Christopher Alento of Valdus," the head answered.

"The King comes to greet us himself? Perhaps you are not as much a coward as I thought," Alvor yelled up at him. "I am King Alvor the Wolf of Sinead. Now let us in, and we will negotiate the surrender of your Kingdom."

"All I want is for your soldiers to clear out the infected and protect my citizens. My crown be damned. But there is a slight problem with that," King Christopher said. "The whole northern district is overtaken by the plague. Listen." He let out a loud scream over his city, and it was answered by countless hellish moans. King Alvor shivered. "You will surely lose men if you enter this way. Follow the wall to the western gate, if you will. There, fires have burned away most of the infected, and there is a road which leads directly to the castle, where I will hand over the crown and my knights. Then we can plan our retaking of the city, if you would allow me to serve under you, as a knight."

King Alvor thought for a few moments, then nodded. "Very well," he called up. "We will meet you at the west." And they marched west, following the wall for some time until the gate towers rose up above the wall. "Are you up there?" Alvor shouted.

Out came King Christopher's head again. "Indeed. Come on in." Alvor stepped forwards and lifted out the heavy plague barrier, then pushed on the gate. It did not budge.

"What game is this?" King Alvor shouted up at him.

Christopher looked taken aback. "The bar is still up, so some civilian must have bolted it from the inside. Please be patient, I will drop you down a key. I cannot get down there myself to open it, as the fires burned away the stairs." And Alvor waited, his irritation growing, until finally King Christopher's voice returned. "Got it! I do apologize for the trouble." A flat, square wooden box landed at Alvor's feet. He picked it up. It wasn't the right size or weight for a city key and, suspicious, he unlatched it and flipped the lid open. Inside was the charred mask of Tory Dryden.

"ENOUGH OF THIS!" Alvor roared, violently throwing the mask to the ground. "Prepare the battering ram, this was nothing but a pathetic attempt to buy time." Soon after, the ram was positioned at the gate. A massive construction of wood and iron, a wolf's head carved into the business end of the ram, pulled by fifteen horses and a hundred men. Five more horses pulled the thick rope, and at their maximum pull, King Alvor cut the rope. The three-ton monster slammed into the gate, splintering wood and buckling it inwards. "AGAIN!" he called. And so the ram was pulled back once more, and loosed on the gate a second time. Daylight could be seen through the gate now, one more strike would do it.

As the horses pulled the ram back for the last time, Alvor heard Christopher's voice roar, for the first time with power and authority. "FIRE NOW!"

Six seconds later, it was as though the world ended. The gate blew outward and the battering ram exploded, and Alvor the Wolf fell, deaf, broken, and bleeding with a piece of iron jutting from his chest.

*****

"FIRE NOW!" Christopher commanded, and Morgan lit the fuse on the Bombard, watched the flame get pulled into the black iron, and he ran backwards and shoved his hands over his ears. After what seemed an age, the cannon fired, and the city's western gate ceased to exist. Morgan was almost knocked off his feet, even at this range, but he steadied himself. Taking the war horn off his back, he blew into it with all his power, sounding the charge.

Behind him, the shield wall of knights broke and they ran towards the gates, backed by two rows of castle and city guards and a large group of armed civilians. Morgan joined the group and spotted most of Bayard's people together near the center of the crowd. Only Lilith and Bayard himself had stayed at the castle, in order to prepare to treat the inevitable injuries.

Sprinting out of the gate, Morgan scanned the battlefield. At least a hundred men were dead or crippled beyond any hope to fight, the men who were controlling the battering ram. Many more were on the ground, their legs splintered. Even more were being dragged behind their routed, terrified horses as they galloped away from the gate.

Even the three hundred or so soldiers who remained on their feet were now temporarily deaf and stunned, many of them having dropped their weapons, and they could not reform before the militia of Valdus charged them. The first two rows of Sinead's soldiers were overrun, quickly hacked to pieces by axes, sickles, and knight's swords. The majority of Valdus's warriors were armed with spiked weapons, which easily pierced the Sinead men's leather and chain. Still, the northerners were great warriors, and they soon took full to battle, shields, axes, and swords clashing back. The tide of the battle quickly changed, with many civilian men, and even a few guards and knights laying dead on the ground.

A horn sounded from atop the wall, and the knights of Valdus knew the signal. Each one of them finished off the opponent they were battling and sprinted for the outside of the battlefield, and took up a scattered shield formation that surrounded the rest of the combatants. Guards and civilians ran behind them as they got the chance, and the knights cut down any Sinead man who approached the line. Trapped in the center of the knight's circle, and with apparently no man to lead them, they did the only thing they could do.

One of them shouted in the Northern language that Morgan did not understand, and the remaining soldiers ran for the castle gates. The knights ran forwards, pushing them into the city. The screams soon started as the infected, drawn by the cannon, closed in on the group of northerners. They were obviously prepared to fight the infected, cutting for their heads and necks, but not while being chased by a group of armed living through an unfamiliar city. Those who remained soon scattered, breaking off into small groups or individuals, and the battle was won. The knights led the way back into the city, cutting down the infected that went after them rather than the northerners.

Soon, Christopher had rejoined the group. "Knights, you are to set up camp outside the gate. Half of you are to be awake and attentive at any given time, the rest are to build a blockade from any rubble and equipment you can scavenge from this district. Allow no men or infected to escape. Guards, go out there and gather our injured, and put down their injured. We have no surplus food for prisoners. Be wary of infected. You know what to do if someone gets bitten."

He then turned to Morgan. "You, gather all the civilians, and make haste back to the castle. Put the best combatants on the outside of the group to protect against the infected and any Sinead soldiers you may encounter. At the castle, place two guards at every entrance, even the sewers. No survivors are to be allowed in unless you or someone you know is familiar with them. Some of the northerners may be able to pass for our citizens if they find new clothes." Christopher motioned Morgan away, and he ran off.

After gathering the remaining healthy civilians, Morgan started leading the troop back to the castle. Among them was Gendrina and Helmet, both of whom were placed on the outside of the group and given the best weapons. Morgan made his way over to Gendrina. "Are your brothers alright?" he asked her.

"Jacob was struck in the leg by an axe. He has a deep wound and cannot walk yet, but is otherwise alright. I saw Thomas standing there too, he was fine but I think there were a couple of guards who thought the missing arm was new."

Morgan laughed at this. "That is good. Bayard or Lilith will fix up Jacob when they get back to the castle." The rest of the walk was uneventful, save for a few infected who periodically stumbled towards the noise of the group. Soon, the gate to the Upper Ring was in sight. Three hours later, the second group of guards and injured arrived safely.

Making his way to the knight's tower once the sun had fallen, Morgan yawned and peered out of a stairway window over the city. In the moonlight, he could only see the outlines of the buildings spanning out to the south. All fires had died out, and he could hear no sound from his place in the tower. Turning away from the view, he continued to the top of the tower where he found Christopher sitting in an armchair next to his bed. "My King. What are you doing coming up here with your injuries? You should be with Bayard."

"As your King, I hereby decree you should shut up," Christopher said with a small grin, which Morgan returned. "You are the last of my elite knights, Morgan. The second in command of what is left of my armies. You need to know what comes next."

Morgan looked solemn as he began to remove his armor. "War is what comes next. We have killed the majority of Sinead's soldiers, but we cannot forget their allies. If Sinead spreads word of our weakness, the other Northern holds will not hesitate to break our treaty. When they learn that their King is not coming back, his heir will take his place and he will lead thousands against us, and their offer to integrate us rather than exterminate us will likely not still be on the table. And we cannot forget about the Fogwalkers either."

"They are not an issue, they do not take it upon themselves to avenge their fallen members," Christopher said.

"Have your injuries robbed you of your senses? They may not seek vengeance, but the contract for you and your sister's heads still exists. If war breaks out, they will use it as a shroud to get to you."

Christopher cursed. "You are right. Their mission may have been personal, but they could have easily made the contract official. Another enemy to worry about. For now, we have no choice but to hold the city. God willing, Uriel will return with an army from the south, and we can gather more allies as well. All we can do now is survive, and try to take back the streets from the dead. In the morning, we will have Helmet write a false message back to Sinead in their own language, telling them of our surrender and their occupation of this city. The farce will not last long, when they see that no trade routes are opening and no soldiers are writing to their families. But it will buy us enough time to gather an army, and with luck, to march on them first. If we can attack Sinead before they grow suspicious, it will fall easily to us."

Morgan was out of his armor and into his expensive silk nightclothes. "This is rather wild speculation. What if Sinead had scouts watching from a distance? Word could be reaching their city by tomorrow night, at the latest."

"Then we are dead," Christopher said simply. "Wars are won and lost, Kingdoms through ages rise and fall. There is no garrison we can signal, no army of wolves we can set on our enemies, no mystical sorcerer who can summon a rain of fire. We are on our own here, with not two hundred men, until aid arrives from the south. And that may not even come if Uriel does not complete his journey, or if Haarn's Prince refuses Jenara's hand in marriage."

Morgan looked down, his face pained. "You say we have no army. But we do. Nearly two thousand men, women, and children who know nothing but murder."

Christopher stood up. "You cannot be serious. You would further defile our dead, set this plague on a city full of civilians, and risk all of England?"

"England would be safe," Morgan whispered. "We would corral a few hundred into each siege tower and spill them over Sinead's walls. Close their plague bars and wait as the city destroys itself as ours has. It is-" Morgan fell bleeding: Christopher had slammed his gauntlet-wearing fist across his face.

"WHAT DO YOU TAKE ME FOR?!" Christopher roared, advancing on Morgan as he scrambled backwards against a wall. "We are not murderers, we are not demons, or brigands, or genocidal barbarians. I am the one true King of England, and when Sinead falls to me, it will be a new province of Valdus, a new place for my people to live and grow. This plague is our enemy, not our weapon. Leave my sight, and prepare parties of knights and guards to combat the dead. You are not to sleep until the western gate is rebuilt and the district is clear of the infected, and never speak this madness to me again."

Morgan stood, startled and nearly shaking. He saluted Christopher. "Yes, my King. I am sorry." He quickly left the tower chambers, and Christopher closed his eyes. There was much to be done. War was coming. And so, time passed.

Chapter Fourteen
Autumn of 1513 A.D
Valdus Castle
Early Morning

"Where is Luke?" Jacob asked, looking over the unrecognized guardsman who stood beside him at the castle gate. The man was obviously a veteran guard, at least forty in age with long, greying hair visible beneath his helm. However, he was strapped with muscle and carried his sword sheathed but held in his left hand rather than in a baldric, the sign of a man who had grown paranoid from years of unwanted surprises.

"His wife is giving birth today," the guard explained. "So I was told to take his place. I hope the child comes out alright. Ever since the Travers family disappeared, there have been many more stillborn in the lower and center rings."

"Who were they?" Jacob asked.

"Oh yes, you were probably quite young when they were active. A doctor couple and their son, and a strange dark boy they had adopted long ago. Nobody knows what truly happened to them, but most think they all perished in the great fire, even though some claim to have seen their son and the dark boy after the fires died."

Jacob looked down at his boots. "I might know who you mean...after my brother joined the Guard, he would always bring home ointments and bandages for my sister. They stopped coming soon before I turned thirteen, and could join the guard myself. He told me they came from an Eastern man, but if I was ever told his name, I cannot remember it."

The old guardsman nodded and looked over the land to the south. "This is my first time on the southern gate. They normally have me in the north. This is a beautiful landscape."

Jacob gazed out at the forests and plains that expanded infinitely into the distance. For the first time, he truly noticed the wild patterns in the swirling patches of trees, the way they circled the plains and waved in the wind like a green ocean. For a second, he was overcome with a sense of smallness, but he soon shook it off. "You are right, it is beautiful. I am out here every day, so I guess I never really thought about it too much."

The old guard smiled. "You should climb up on the northern wall sometime. At ground level, all you see is trees. But on the wall, you can see the mountains in the distance. When the sun rises, it casts shadows that travel across the horizon. I have grown used to it, but many years ago when I first stood and gazed over it, I had never felt so alive."

Jacob leaned against the gate and looked up into the sky. "I might just do that. I'll bring my brother with me as well. And my sister, if the other guards will let her up."

"If they complain about it, let me know and I will get you all up there. I may officially be the same rank as you, but they respect me like a captain up there."

"What is your name, Sir?" Jacob asked.

He sighed. "I just said we are the same rank, don't you 'Sir' me, kid. I am Pierre Lucerne. It is good to meet you."

Jacob shook his hand. "I am Jacob Carter. Er, Pierre? You are a Frenchman?"

Pierre tilted his head. "Not quite. I am nearly as much an Englishman as you are. My mother and her husband were French merchants who were staying here on their way to Ireland. A Valdus guardsman had his way with my mother, resulting in me, and her husband left her here because of it. As a child, it was my dream to hunt him down and kill him for leaving us. However, when I grew old enough to understand that travel took far more money than I could ever hope to have, I settled for the guard who raped my mother instead. I was caught with my blade through his hand by four other guards, who were about to kill me when I told him that I would let him live if he spilled all he had ever done. He immediately vomited out confessions for dozens of rapes, thefts, and murders. I kept my end of the bargain and removed my blade, and watched as he was beheaded a week later for his crimes. Then they adopted me into the guard to take his place."

"I joined so I could have money to eat," Jacob said.

The older man laughed heartily at this, leaning against the gate and heaving. "Yes, that's what most are here for," he chuckled. "In the end, it does not matter. We are all here as guards, doing what we do for ourselves or our families. It is not a draft, any guard can quit the job at any time, this is how we keep true loyalty rather than forced loyalty. It would not work in smaller cities, but here we never hurt for numbers."

Jacob found himself wishing that the same stood true now in the present day, as he and Pierre stood on the northern wall, staring across the trees into the mountains. "I am so glad you are alive, Pierre," he told the man who stood beside him. "How did you survive down there for so long?"

"It was easy enough," Pierre said, leaning back on the stone fence that spanned the top of the wall. "Once I figured out how to kill them, they became no threat at all, and everyone else was already dead. I tried to come to the castle first thing, but the gate to the Center Ring from the northern district was blocked by something, and the stairs up to the wall were burned away. I was trapped in there, but all the food and drink was mine to keep. It was not pleasant living on nothing but smoked food and dirty water for three months, but it did the job until the knights came down to clear the district. Obviously they were happy to see I had already done their job for them, and they threw me quite the party."

"Only a week after this all started, Christopher was on the wall in the northern district, why did you not call to him, tell him you were there?"

Pierre cursed. "I tried. I was on the other side of the district when I heard his voice. It was still overrun by the dead at that time. If I yelled out, they all would have come to me. I tried to sneak my way over to him, but he was gone by the time I reached the wall."

"Well, you made it out in the end," Jacob said, clapping Pierre on the shoulder. "It is a great feeling to see a familiar face turn up after this long." After that, both stayed silent for a time while they enjoyed the view. Soon the sun was getting higher in the sky, and Jacob glanced around. "About time. Here they come now."

Pierre turned and walked to the ladder that had been constructed and placed against the Northern wall, and saw the approaching group. Bayard, Thomas, Gendrina, Lilith, and Helmet each made their way up the ladder and onto the wall. Each of them introduced themselves to Pierre and took places along the stone, staring off into the distance. Minutes passed, and slowly the shadows began to form, expanding over the mountains and blackening the earth around them. The shadows flickered through the trees and their silhouettes spanned across the landscape, painting a picture of great oppression and vastness.

They stayed here for an hour, talking of the past, drinking and joking, when the wonderful reprieve was shattered by the blast of a massive horn from the south side of the city. The group turned, startled, and looked to Pierre. "What? I don't know any more than any of you do," he said, and so they started back for the castle. Now that the infected and Sinead's remaining soldiers were as good as gone, the only remaining infected trapped in the drainage system, it was quick and simple to navigate the districts. They were back at the castle gate in an hour, but when they entered, the area was abandoned.

Just as Jacob started to feel a little worried, a fat squire squeezed his way out of a tent and stopped, looking at them. "There you are. My King has instructed me to inform you all to report to the southern gate. The Royal Party of Prince Zane of Haarn has been spotted on the horizon. It appears that he chose to accept King Christopher's offer to marry Princess Jenara. Since we have no official welcoming committee anymore, he wants every living person in the city to be there. Please change into your formalwear and make for the southern district with haste."

Everyone broke into cheers at the good news, but it quickly faded and they all glanced at each other, then to the squire. "We haven't got any formalwear," Bayard explained.

The squire sighed. "No matter. Follow me into the castle and you may borrow some clothes of the nobles." And so they followed him, and soon they were all wearing the most ornate and expensive silks and velvets any of them had ever seen. Jacob was wearing an abyssal black silk doublet with golden lace stitched into every lining. Bayard wore a light blue robe with diamond cufflinks and Thomas was in a maroon velvet suit with a shining, polished steel chestplate and pauldron. Pierre and Helmet dressed simply, both wearing dark tailed coats with no ornaments. Lilith looked radiant in a bright emerald-green dress with real emeralds spaced along the shoulders and chestline. Each of them carried a ceremonial saber, with a golden handguard and gemmed hilt. Only Gendrina looked ridiculous, squeezed into an aqua blue and gold half-dress that was much too small for her, stomping about in heeled laced boots that she could not pull all the way on.

Everyone burst into laughter at her. "No, Gen," Thomas choked. "I know I always tried to get you to wear dresses, but not like this.

Just wear a blue doublet and skirt. And wear your own boots, nobody will care." She clomped back out of the room, flustered, and returned minutes later dressed much more practically. She had chosen a white blouse instead, and a deep blue skirt that flowed like the ocean as she walked. Bayard grinned and nodded approvingly, earning a glare from Lilith, Thomas, Jacob, and Gendrina all at once, but they laughed it off and followed the squire out of the mansion and back onto the castle grounds. The day was cool but bearable in the light formalwear, and they quickly made their way down the path to the center ring, then around to the gate to the southern district.

As they approached, they could hear the noises of a crowd, shouting and cheering, and it increased tenfold as the squire pushed open the thick wooden doors. "I'm excited!" Thomas yelled over the din. "This is the first time that Princess Jenara has been outside of the castle for months. I've never seen her before. She must be stunning."

Jacob nodded vigorously, but Bayard stayed stoic. It took them twenty minutes to push their way through the crowd, and finally the gate was visible, and the armor of the knights could be seen gleaming in the sun. Christopher was standing on a shoddily-constructed platform raised ten feet above the ground, and he looked down into the crowd, nodding at Bayard when he spotted them. He then looked forward and raised his arms to the citizens. "I thank you, all of you, for being here today. Over the last three months, we have faced hardships and pain unlike any experienced before. The last twenty years, the fire, and this plague, have brought my city to its knees. But it ends today. As many of you know, Prince Zane of Haarn is coming to our city. He should soon arrive at our gates, and he intends to marry my sister, Princess Jenara Alento!"

The citizens burst into cheers as the woman stepped onto the platform behind Christopher. She was wearing a long, light pink dress with golden lace circling her shoulders and meeting in a twist that marked the middle of her torso, then split into intricate spirals that snaked along either side of her legs. The way the gold caught the sun made it appear is if the lace gave off its own light. However, Jacob found himself startled by her face. She looked exactly like Christopher. He glanced over to Thomas and Gendrina, both of whom were grimacing. The applause faded slightly, as well. She was not unattractive, but Jacob was having a hard time deciding if her face looked like a man's, or if Christopher's face looked like a woman's.

They were both somewhere in between, he decided, and found himself stifling a laugh. Still, the crowd resumed its applause and Christopher had to wave them down. "I ask all of you to show your respect to Prince Zane and his party. Nobody is to discuss the nature of the plague with them except for me, knights, or doctors. We do not need false information spreading to other cities. And with that, we bid them welcome! Open the gate!" Christopher shouted. Two guards stepped forwards and pushed the gate ajar, and the crowd grew even louder as they saw the royal party approaching slowly from a great distance.

*****

Christopher instantly knew that something was wrong. Squinting out at the approaching group, he saw that they bore no flags, played no instruments, pulled no carriages, and had no formation. The crowd had fallen silent, and a shouting could be heard on the wind. Soon, a single man on horseback came hurtling around a large boulder, galloping at full speed towards the city. "Knights!" Christopher yelled, and the eighteen men formed a shield wall along the gate. The horseman arrived quickly, toppling from his mount and stumbling towards the knights. He was old, at least sixty, with long grey hair, crazed eyes, and blood trickling from his nose and mouth.

"Move- Let me through!" Christopher heard from behind him, and turned to see Bayard forcing himself through the wall of knights. He ran over to the old man and helped him to the ground. "What happened? Why are you running from the men of Haarn?" The man coughed and gasped, seemingly unable to breathe. Bayard placed a hand on his chest and cursed. "He's having a heart attack. Stay back," he told the knights as they tried to approach. Bayard pushed the man onto his back and knelt over him, placing both hands on his chest and pumping. The man struggled, grasping for Bayard's arms. He coughed again, pulled Bayard near to his face, and whispered something. And then he closed his eyes and lay still. Bayard stood, shaking his head.

"What did he say?" Christopher called out to Bayard.

Bayard looked up to him, his face worried and unsure. "He told me to close the gates."

"What could be wrong?" Christopher asked nobody in particular. "They wear the colors of Haarn, they bring no siege engines."

"Excuse me, my King," a civilian man in the front of the crowd said loudly. "I have a spyglass. Please, take it." He tossed the small copper tube up to the platform and Christopher snatched it from the air.

"Thank you, good man," he said, and then he turned to the gate. He opened the spyglass and stared into the distance through it, taking time to focus on the approaching party. Even with the spyglass, they were too far off to see in detail. The first thing he noticed was that there were far too many for a royal party. Haarn was one of the largest cities in England, and at least half of its citizens had to be heading their way. Thousands of them. He saw the front of the group passing over a small hill, and blinked as many of them collapsed on their way down, slowly and awkwardly getting back to their feet. They walked slowly but moved directly for the castle. He noticed that they had no horses and carried no packs for food. Their blue and white clothing was obvious, but through the glass Christopher could make out another color. Red. And then he understood.

"*INFECTED!*" he roared, stuffing the spyglass into his belt. "Close the gates! All citizens, return to the castle immediately! Morgan, bring my sister to safety!" Three months ago, the crowd would have panicked, started trampling each other for a chance at escape. But now, each man and woman of the city had fought and killed the infected, and had been trained by knights and guards. They all saluted the King and turned to retreat.

"NO!" Bayard shouted, and the two hundred people stopped in their tracks. Though of no royal blood, Bayard had earned nearly equal respect to a King from each one of them. "There are too many," he said, struggling to maintain his composure. "If we close the gate, even if they cannot break through, they will pile up outside and pour over the walls. With the fences blocking them from falling into the Lower Ring, they will follow the wall right to the castle. We have to abandon the city," he finished, looking desperately up at Christopher.

Christopher stared at him with wild eyes and an angry flare, then slammed his foot on the platform and furiously cursed at the sky. "HOW DID THIS HAPPEN?" he screamed at Bayard, but he did not wait for an answer as he turned to his knights. "Get the civilians to the castle. Gather all the food and water you can carry, tie more to whatever horses are left, then circle around to the eastern gate and make for Peydenal. You will need to make other plans from there."

Morgan turned away from the shield wall and glared at Christopher. "What do you mean 'You will'? What are you planning?"

Christopher looked strangely calm as he smiled down at the worried knight. "Someone has to close the gates after they enter the city. I am the King, it is my true and final duty to seal the infected in the city to allow my subjects time to escape."

"You are being an idiot," Morgan snapped, completely forgetting his formality. "Even if you seal them in, they will break out eventually. The gates are not designed to withstand a siege from the inside. And as Bayard said, even if they cannot get through the gates, they will just climb over each other to get out. You are the last man of your bloodline, you must live for your city."

"My city is gone," Christopher said. "I am nothing but a soldier without my throne, and as long as I draw breath, I will not allow one more man or woman under my command to die. You will do as I say or I will deal with you as a traitor."

Morgan, in a last desperate attempt to protect his friend, looked to Jenara. "My Lady, what is your say in this? You may be the last person alive who can sway your brother." She had been silent so far, but now she walked to the edge of the platform and spoke to Morgan.

"Sir Morgan, just like my brother, I am a member of the Valdus Royal Family. I took the same oaths, serve the same citizens, and follow the same principles. If my brother will fight to protect his subjects, my duty is to obey him, as is yours."

Christopher looked to his sister, and was suddenly overcome with a wave of grief at the dead gaze in her eyes. She had been perfectly groomed, perfectly *brainwashed*, into being the perfect Princess. It was the fate of many women of royalty, and here on his final day, he wished he could have seen her as the child he remembered, before their mother had gotten through with her. But this was good. She would leave the city. She would live. "Sir Morgan, you have our words. You have taken the oath. Evacuate the city."

Morgan stood still. His face had been contorted in anguish for the duration of this conversation, and Christopher frowned as Morgan's eyes suddenly grew angry. He watched as Morgan drew his dagger and cut the straps surrounding his chestplate, and it clattered to the dirt. He tore off his gauntlets and chainmail, and finally reached the red and gold undercoat that bore the sigil of Valdus on its shoulder. He bundled the patch of fabric in his fist and slashed it off of his undercoat, threw it to the ground, and stepped on it. "Fuck my oaths, and fuck your orders. I renounce my loyalty to Valdus, and as such, you must execute me. As a former knight, I pray you allow me to choose the form of my own execution. If you will allow this, I choose them," he said, pointing at the mass of blue and white that approached the gates, growing steadily closer. "They will break through the gate eventually, or just climb over each other and over the wall. The best thing we can do is kill as many of them as we can, give the others less work to do in the future."

Christopher watched, stunned, as every knight performed the same actions. They stood, swords and shields in hand, a great hole missing from each of their shirts. Somehow, Christopher laughed. "FINE! I sentence each and every one of you to death by combat. They will be your opponents!" he commanded, slashing his sword across the landscape occupied by the encroaching infected. The former knights slammed their swords against their shields and shouted their approval. Christopher spun and climbed off of the platform, followed by his sister. He pushed his way through to Bayard, who was still standing next to the dead old man. "My friend, I am so glad to have met you. You have taught me a lot, you have shown me that tradition and faith are not the same as justice and truth. The future of my people rests with you. As King, I hereby declare that the tradition of nobility needed for Knighthood be abolished, and I name you Knight Commander of Valdus."

Bayard shook his head. "I am no knight, Christopher. These people need you to defend them."

"I know how to defend a city," Christopher sighed. "My place is here, holding the line as you lead the rest to safety. Go to Peydenal, form a strategy like you are so good at, and end this plague. Now *kneel.* You will not be alone. Will the guardsmen Pierre Lucerne and Thomas and Jacob Carter all come forward and kneel as well?"

There was a scuffle as two of the three named men came through the shield wall and knelt before the King. Only Thomas stayed standing. "My King, I will not do this without my sister. She is as much of a warrior as any of us, if not better. It is an unneeded prejud-"

"Shut it, Thomas," Christopher interrupted, grinning. "Yes, how could I ever forget about her? Gendrina Carter, come forward and kneel." She did, along with Thomas, and Christopher drew his sword. One by one, he placed the blade on their shoulders and heads, and stood in front of them. He spoke a new oath, one he invented on the spot, and then the time came for them to repeat it.

"As of this moment, I am a Knight of Life. Through war, hunger, thirst, and sickness, I protect the living until the day of my own death, wherever I may travel. My sole duty is to slay every dead man who crosses my path. I no longer serve a Kingdom, I no longer serve a faith, but I serve a higher duty. I am the life that refuses death, and my blade is the cure for those who walk with empty eyes. I accept my calling to live by this code, and I will only stop when all that walks is living. This is now the road before me, and I will follow it to the end."

Christopher lowered his sword, and the four new knights stood up before him. "I have one last thing to ask of you all," Christopher said. "Should you ever see me as a member of the dead, you must kill me. It might be inevitable that I fall to them, but I place my trust in the four of you to end me should you get the chance."

"That's what friends do," Bayard said with a fake smile.

"Thank you," Christopher whispered. "Now go, and save my people."

Three hours later, King Christopher Alento stood in the center of the shield wall with his eighteen men, staring at the gate that shuddered and buckled as thousands of dead men pushed their weight against it. The gate had held far longer than Christopher had anticipated, and he felt good knowing that the citizens and his new knights had plenty of time to escape. After another ten minutes, the gate cracked open at the hinges and collapsed to the ground, the infected pouring into the city. Christopher gave no rousing speech, no roar of motivation, no prayer to whatever awaited him. He stared into the faces of the thousands and he nudged the men at his sides, offering them his final, impossible command.

"Kill every last one of those bastards, my friends."

The ferocious roars of the knights faded into the distance as Bayard led the citizens of Valdus through the thick forest, hacking through brush and branches with his ceremonial saber. He thought the weapon would be brittle, but under the gold and baubles, it was a solidly constructed blade with a hidden hardwood grip. When he commented on this, Helmet said that he had been the one to forge them, years ago. Bayard was glad of this. Low-hanging branches pulled at what was left of his dirty blue robe, as he had cut off the bottom to allow him to travel through the trees. Gendrina and Lilith had been smart enough to change into leathers when they passed through the castle, and had to physically force the Princess to do the same. Bayard was occupied with the collection of food and water along with Thomas and Jacob, and the three men still wore the light silks and velvets. He felt a tug at his shoulder as Lilith approached him from behind, her face dark.

"How did this happen, Bayard? We were all so careful to stop any infection from escaping the city."

Bayard hung his head in defeat and cursed. "It could have been anything. I have theories, but any of them could be true, and any or all could be false."

"Tell me," she said. He knew what she was doing. She had known him for a long time, she knew that there was nothing he hated more than not knowing. He was thankful for the opportunity to lay down his thoughts, even if they could not be confirmed. At the very least, it would make him feel like he *might* be right. The other four Knights of Life plus Helmet had gathered up behind him, obviously intent on listening in.

Bayard feigned a sigh, and began his words. "At first, I believed the most likely explanation to be that one of the guards who accompanied Sir Uriel from the city was bitten, and hid the bite as they exited the city. But he would have turned and been put down long before they reached Haarn."

"Maybe not," Gendrina spoke up. "When Thomas was bitten, I cut his arm off not ten seconds after it happened. If one of the guards was bitten, Uriel may have attempted the same thing rather than beheading him, seeing as it worked on Tom. But if he waited too long, minutes rather than seconds, it might have delayed but not completely stopped the infection."

Bayard nodded. "That is a possibility. Good thinking. Another possibility is that one of Sinead's soldiers who ran into the city was bitten, and managed to climb over the wall with a rope. He would have known that he would be killed if he returned to Sinead defeated, so he might have headed south instead. He would have fallen on the road, and without anyone to stop his turning, he might have just kept following the road in death. He might have attacked a traveler who then returned to Haarn for medicine and turned there, or made it undisturbed to the city and been dragged to a doctor, church, or dungeon.

"One more idea, and I do not like to think of it, is that the infection came straight from the source. Haarn is one of the first cities visited by mercenaries and traders who sail in from the East. Sefu told me that the oasis where the plague flowers grew was burned to the ground, but any number of things could have caused another outbreak. Maybe another patch of the flowers grew underground, maybe somebody hid one to research it, maybe the spores spread when burned. If that's true, Peydenal is fucked, by the way. And that would open up hundreds of other problems, so let us hope that is not-"

"Ahem," Princess Jenara interrupted in her small voice, stepping out from the line of citizens behind them. The knights stopped to look at her. "I am in pain," she said simply.

"Er," Bayard exhaled. "What hurts?"

Pierre sighed. "I think she's trying to say that she really has to piss. That's what all the highborn girls are taught to say when they quickly need out of feasts or jousts." Jenara glared at him, but her uncomfortable shifting determined that Pierre was correct.

Bayard grimaced and turned to Gendrina. "You, handle her. Jacob, Tom, come with me to scout ahead. Pierre, ride about two kilometers out behind the caravan and ensure that we have not been followed. We will camp here for the night and make it into Peydenal tomorrow afternoon." As the group turned away to carry out his orders, he held Gendrina back. "You have to try to get through to her," he whispered, tilting his head towards Jenara. "Try to make her understand that she no longer needs to behave like royalty, just another one of us homeless bastards. Try to have her swing a sword, and do something about her hair. They could grab her so easily as it is." Gendrina nodded and led Jenara into the trees.

*****

"Thank you, Sir Gendrina," Jenara said, as she tied up her leather greaves.

"Don't call me 'Sir'!" Gendrina almost shouted. "Even if I really was a man, or a knight, I wouldn't want that. I am Gendrina. Bayard is Bayard, Thomas is Thomas. You are Jenara. No more titles, get used to it."

"The King declared that the four of you are knights, so the titles remain intact," Jenara explained pointlessly.

Gendrina stepped forward and placed her hand on Jenara's shoulder. "It is alright to grieve, Jenara. Nobody expects you to behave higher than them. Christopher named Bayard the Knight Commander, and with Christopher not here, what he says goes. He hasn't called any of us 'Sir', and hasn't complained that we have not, so I think the titles are out, right?"

"No," Jenara said defiantly.

Gendrina squinted at her. "You know, the wartime hierarchy goes as 'King, Queen, Prince, Knight Commander, Elite Knights.' That last one would be me. I do not remember 'Princess' on that list. These aren't exactly times of peace, so technically, I outrank you."

"Fine," Jenara submitted. Gendrina slapped her across the face, hard. Jenara tripped and fell into the orange and yellow leaves that littered the ground, looking up at Gendrina with tears in her eyes. "Why?"

"You don't have to say 'Fine', you hear me? If you want to call me or anybody else 'Sir', you bloody well do it. You have spent your whole life following orders, kneeling before men, and choking down your own desires and choices. It ends tonight." She drew her saber and stepped behind Jenara, grabbing the braid of her hair and pulling it taut.

"Please do not do that," Jenara whispered, her voice cracking for the first time. "The women in my family have worn their hair like this for generations. It is a sort of symbol of my Kingdom."

"You don't want this? Then do something about it." Gendrina released the braid and shoved the saber in the dirt next to Jenara, taking a step back. "Take the sword, take it and attack me."

"I will not," Jenara complained, turning her head away from the weapon.

"That sword cuts me, or it cuts your hair. Your choice."

Jenara stumbled to her feet, grasping the hilt of the saber and pulling it from the ground, dirt and mud clinging to the tip. "You tell me that I have a choice, but you will attack me either way. What game is this?" Jenara hissed, obviously struggling to maintain her dignified manner.

"I am showing you that even though you *always* have a choice, people will try to take that choice away from you. People will try to hurt you, they will try to rape you, some will try to kill you. It is my job to teach you how to kill them first. You no longer have a personal guard, you no longer have twenty foot stone walls and kilometers of city between you and your enemies. Everyone in our group will fight to protect each other, but the time *will* come that you must protect yourself. Now, I'm not going to hurt you. Not very much, at least. I'm not going rape you or kill you, but I will slash off that pretty blonde braid you have there, unless you physically stop me.

"Bayard gave the order to take it off of you, so you'll have to stop me, Jacob, Thomas, Pierre, and Bayard himself if you want to keep it." Jenara held the blade limp in two hands, bouncing between her feet and glancing repeatedly into the trees, obviously considering the possibility of making a run for it. Gendrina grinned at her. "If you take off, the wolves will get you before dead men or bandits have a chance. And if I decide to chase you, I'll catch you. I've been navigating these woods for years, and I'm sure that you move like a wounded cow when you try to go any faster than your fancy lady walk. Anyway, enough chatter. I'm coming to get your hair, now."

Gendrina stepped purposefully towards Jenara, and she was surprised yet pleased to have to dodge the saber as Jenara shrieked and swung it at her. Jenara was slow, weak, but her technique was startlingly proper. *She probably spent a lot of time watching Christopher and his knights in training,* Gendrina thought. Still, it was easy to avoid her strikes, and deflect them even with the leather armor she wore. *I could force the sword away from her easily, cut the braid, but that might cause her to lose it. Better to train her, try to mature her until she's willing to get rid of the hair on her own.* And so Gendrina dodged, blocked, and danced her way around Jenara's blade until the young girl was breathless and on her knees. "Enough," Gendrina said, without the edge that she had put in her voice earlier. "You're good. Your handling of the blade and the paths of your strikes are dead-on, but you have to use a lot more speed. Are you afraid of hurting me?"

"I just did what I watched my brother do," Jenara said, her face falling.

Her thoughts confirmed, Gendrina pulled the girl to her feet. "You watched Christopher while he was training his men. Obviously he isn't going to fight at full speed or power. When you fight for real, you need to strike as fast and hard as you can without sacrificing your technique for it. Many people say you need to strike *past* your target, that this misdirection of focus will grant you more speed and strength at the true point of impact. However, I believe that this only works when you're trying to behead a target dummy. Against a live opponent, you strike exactly where and when you mean to. You keep your eyes, focus, and blade on the bastard you're trying to kill, not a foot to his left. Now try again."

Jenara stepped in, swinging the blade in an accurate but still slow cut towards Gendrina's helmet. She leaned back to avoid the strike, and was startled as Jenara disappeared underneath her field of vision. She tried to regain her footing to look down, and just managed to see Jenara flip the blade and slam the blunt side into her stomach, under the armor that had ridden up when she leaned back. Her breath was knocked out of her, but she managed to throw her hand out, grabbing Jenara's hair and pulling her to the ground. Jenara screamed as Gendrina pulled on the braid, rolling Jenara onto her front and pressing a knee into her back.

"This is why you need to lose the hair, Jen," she whispered. "Imagine what would happen if I was one of the infected, and could grab you this easily." She leaned in and gave Jenara a soft bite on the side of her neck, and she gasped and struggled. Gendrina slid her arm down Jenara's own and grasped the bottom of the saber's hilt, pushing it out of her hand, then took her knee off the girl's back and stood, still holding the long braid. "Take the sword and do it yourself. You know it has to be done. Some of your brother's last words were used to denounce the old traditions of Valdus. For a very long time, maybe longer than any of us will live, we will be in a different, darker world. Survival is what matters now. Do it yourself."

Jenara took up the saber again, holding it loosely by her side as she knelt in front of Gendrina. "I'm sorry, mother...father..." And then she lifted the sword and slashed her braid off in one quick cut, letting it fall limp in Gendrina's hand. And then she broke down sobbing. Gendrina sat down next to the girl and embraced her, sitting there for a long time while she cried. She took out her dagger and finished the detail work on the mess of hair, cutting it shorter and trying to make it presentable. Soon, they walked back into the trees and came out where the survivors were nearly done setting up camp. Bayard, her brothers, and Pierre were back, and Bayard spotted her with her arm around the crying Princess.

"What did you do to her?" he asked Gendrina as she walked towards an empty tent.

"I handled her," Gendrina answered.

*****

Sir Uriel Westlake tossed and turned as he slept, the fires of Haarn still burning strong in his mind. He dreamt of the outbreak, the screams, the killing. In Valdus, he was safe in the castle, unaware of the horrors until half the city had fallen. Even after, he was placed as a gate guard, he never killed an infected man, or even saw one up close and moving.

This all changed when the Egyptian slaver ship crashed into the docks of Haarn three days after his arrival. Slavery had been abolished in England long ago, but many slavers from other countries still fancied their chances in England's ports. Uriel stood on the dock with Prince Zane himself, discussing the plague and the war with Sinead, as well as his potential marriage, when the massive wooden ark came into view from the heavy fog.

Some of Haarn's ferries sailed out to the ship in an attempt to stop it, but it belonged to the currents and it crashed through them and into the thin wooden jetty, breaking upon the rocks beneath. From the cracked hull poured the most horrible abomination of mankind that Uriel had ever seen. Hundreds of starved, naked dead men and women, all chained together by the neck, swarmed the shores and began feasting upon the citizens who were gathered at the docks. "Behead them! Strike for their skulls, if you have an axe or hammer!" Uriel had called, but in their blind panic, nobody paid him the slightest heed.

Prince Zane was one of the first ones dead, and Uriel mounted his horse and rushed it towards the inland gate. He flew from the city and slammed the gate, reaching for the plague bar; only to find that there was no plague bar. They must have removed it when the threat of the Black Death faded into history. Cursing Heaven, Hell, and anything else he could think of, he smacked his horse out of the city and ran back inside, slamming the gates and locking the inner bar. Haarn was a harbor town, much more prone to large sieges than an inland city like Valdus, and as such the gates were solid, thick iron rather than the wood of his home city, and the walls were much taller.

By the time Uriel had fought his way into the basement of an abandoned smithy, not three hours after the ship arrived, the city had fallen. Fires raged above him but he was safe in the stone basement of the smithy, and the moans of the dead were muffled. Here he stayed for two days until he was dehydrated and starved, and the moans had increased a thousandfold. On that day, he had no choice but to burst forth from the basement and cut his way through with sword and shield. He beheaded the two nearest with one powerful slash, turning to crush the skull of another with the edge of his shield. He ducked, flipping one over himself and crashed his boot into its head, spinning to take the legs off another. For hours, he warred his way through the city, leaving hundreds of limbs and heads in his wake. Halfway to the docks, faint with hunger and thirst, he pulled a living fish from a saltwater fishing trough and ate it alive in seconds, swallowing its blood and tossing the bones aside, all while battling the dead. Somehow, impossibly, he made it to the ocean and he threw himself in, his armor dragging him to the depths below.

For two and a half minutes, he walked along the bottom of the water, drowning, dying. On each side, shadows of the dead lurked on the sea floor, slowly making their way towards him. Finally his head broke free as he stepped up the shoreline outside the walls. He collapsed and coughed, barely conscious, as two dozen infected men lurched out of the surf, clawing their way onto the shore, water and sand pouring from their mouths. He limped around the walls, looking for someone, anyone, but as far as the eye could see he was the only one left alive. And so he turned, and desperately fought the bloated, rotting bodies that followed him. As the last waterlogged skull hit the sand, he passed out.

He woke up hours later, somehow unharmed. He built a shelter from pine and oak, a bow out of a branch and strands from his undercoat that he weaved together, and arrows from twigs and chipped stone. He hunted and gathered, drank rain and vapor-dripped water he created by taking a window from an abandoned carriage, and survived alone outside the city for nearly three months among the moaning. He patrolled the walls, killing any dead man who managed to find his way around the walls through the water and turning away anyone who approached the city. Then, six days ago, the infected managed to dislodge the bar and flowed from the city like water through a broken dam, and Uriel was routed. He sneaked into the treeline, managing to avoid their attention, and followed their aimless path north. He decided that if they did not change direction by the next day, he would draw their attention and lead them away from Valdus, likely giving his life in the attempt.

Just as he was prepared to do so, he heard a human's scream. A group of travelers camped beside the road, likely a family. There was an old man, a younger man and woman, and two children. Only the old man was on horseback, and the animal took off at full speed with the man still on top as the horde overran the four others. They immediately followed the old man, their hellish moans bellowing after him.

Uriel screamed after them, sprinting behind the horde and cutting down the slowest of them, but they had already chosen their target. He followed them all the way to Valdus. Uriel watched from a cliffside as the horde broke through the gate, heard the knights battling in their last war. Standing on the edge of the cliff, he was only stopped from jumping off by the sight of the citizens escaping through the eastern gate. He climbed down the cliff and gave chase, and now, in the present, he was less than one hundred yards from them. He had decided to allow them a quiet night, devoid of his stories of failure and survival. Soon, as he fell into a deeper sleep, the dreams faded.

Chapter Sixteen
Autumn of 1513 A.D
Woods west of Valdus
Early Morning

Gendrina slept like she had fallen from a cliff, her legs splayed out and her face pressed into the corner of her tent. She dreamt of her training, her lifelong quest to become the strongest of her house.

Coated in thick mud to mask her scent and clad in armor she had handmade from wood and twine, Gendrina stayed crouched on the tree branch, her eyes determined and her legs sore. She held the grip of a longbow tightly in her small left hand, and brushed her damp, muddy hair aside with her right. *I can do this. I can kill it. Ten gold pieces... We would have food for a year, we could buy a horse, we could buy real swords, not those iron poles the Guard gives out. I'm not afraid. I can kill it.* Despite her self assurances, her hands shook and her breath was uneven. She placed her hand against her left side, remembering the last time she had encountered a wild dog. This was different though, this time she was the hunter, and the great grey wolf was her prey.

One month ago, a nobleman's young daughter had been torn apart in front of him by the alpha of a wolf pack, a pack that had been terrorizing hunters and travelers for years, since it was driven south by hunters from Sinead. The nobleman had put out a bounty for any man who brought him the wolf's head. Now Gendrina watched from her perch, staring at the trapped fawn that lay in the clearing below her. It screamed and bleated, kicking about her rope trap, desperately trying to escape whatever fate awaited it. Her hair was standing on end, and her instincts bellowed at her to run, but she would not. She would succeed where guards, knights, and lifelong hunters had failed.

Finally, after hours of waiting in her tree, she heard it. A low growl rose from the brush around the clearing, and she pulled her single arrow, a thick, heavy, iron-barbed nightmare that she had traded a chicken for. Attached to the back of the arrow was a long, strong rope, the other end of which was tied securely around the branch she stood on. She nocked the arrow and aimed the bow, steadying her breath and preparing herself for what was to come.

And then it appeared, the size of a young horse, its fur the color of a storm cloud. Two more smaller, lighter wolves stood nearby, staying near the treeline and watching their superior investigate their desired supper. She drew the bow silently, her growing muscles straining with the weight of it, and targeted the chest of the great beast, aiming inches above her actual mark to compensate for the weight of the arrow. It slowly approached the fawn, which had flown into an absolute panic, and began sniffing at the terrified animal. She released the arrow.

She grinned madly as the arrow slammed into the beast, throwing it to the ground and causing the other two wolves to howl their concern. They were not her concern, however, as the grey wolf tried to run into the trees. The rope attached to the arrow pulled taut, the barbs holding tight in the wolf's sinewy muscles. It thrashed and pulled at the rope, causing more damage to itself, as she drew her brother's long carving knife and dove from the tree, landing in a roll. She sprinted towards the massive animal and crashed into it, thrusting the knife into its chest and toppling it to its side. It bit and clawed at her, but her wooden armor protected her torso and limbs, and she thrust the knife in again, higher, near its throat. With each stab, it grew weaker, quieter, and slower, and finally it collapsed and lay still, its breathing labored. She turned to face the other two wolves, who had stepped towards her, and she roared her triumph, waving the bloody knife at them and stomping her feet. They growled softly at her, before turning away and retreating into the woods with a whine.

She placed her hand on the wolf's back and rubbed it, frowning at the dying animal. "We are sort of alike, you and I," she told the wolf. "We're both hunters. We're both warriors. We're both the strongest of our packs. We both take action while the others stand back and follow orders. The difference is, you can lead, and you're respected. My brothers get to make the choices for me, though, for no reason other than that they've got funny dangly bits between their legs. I don't get to join the Guard, I won't get to fight in tournaments and Jousts, I don't get to travel alone or carry a sword. But when I drag your body through the city and drop you outside the gate to the castle, for the first time, everyone who looks down on me will be *forced* to understand that I am better than them." The wolf was dead by the time she finished speaking. Gendrina stood and walked over to the crying fawn, cutting it loose. It bounded into the trees and quickly disappeared from view.

She recovered the bow and pulled it over her shoulder, slid the knife into her belt, and began tying the wolf's limbs. Soon she started dragging the beast through the trees. It was a difficult task, the wolf was nearly twice her own weight, but she did not have to go far. Two hundred meters and she was on the road, her "borrowed" wheelbarrow waiting in the treeline. It took her twenty minutes of struggling, pushing, and lifting, but finally she stumbled back and grinned as the body settled in the wheelbarrow. And so she began her long walk home, alternating between pushing and pulling the wheelbarrow depending on which of her muscles were currently the most sore. She got numerous stares and whispers from travelers, but ignored all of them as she walked on. She knew that if someone saw her who knew of the bounty, they might try to steal the wolf from her. She wished she could keep one hand on her knife as she struggled with the wheelbarrow, but luckily she arrived at the city without incident.

As she came into view of the northern gate, a guardsman ran out to meet her. He approached slowly, staring at the wolf's corpse, his eyes wide. "What in the name of-" He turned to Gendrina, looking down at this little girl wearing the wooden armor of a barbarian, soaked in mud and blood, longbow across her chest and butcher's knife strapped to her side. "You are responsible for this? Who are you?" he asked, with the faintest hint of a French accent.

"I am Gendrina Carter. Sister of the guardsman Thomas Carter and recruit Jacob Carter. I bring the wolf that killed the young girl a month ago, as well as many hunters. I wish to collect the bounty, but I fear of thieves looking to collect for my work. Will you escort me to the Upper Ring?"

The guard just nodded, speechless, and pushed open the gate into Valdus. She had to wait a long time for the evening shift change so he could leave his post, but eventually they were on their way south. The guard led the way through the city, shooing off any citizens who got too close, while Gendrina continued to drag the heavy wheelbarrow. He had offered his help multiple times, but she would not accept it. Once they were in the center ring, Gendrina relaxed a bit. Thieves were practically a non-issue here, as it was where every guard made their home. She was dehydrated, hungry, sore in places she did not know existed, and her skin blistered and bled from wearing the rough armor for so long. Still she walked until they reached the massive shining gate into the Upper Ring. The guardsman pulled the rope of a large bell that hung from a post outside the gate, and soon a younger man descended the steps. "Hello, Sam," the guard said. "Someone has brought the corpse of the grey wolf, the ten gold bounty."

The young guard, Sam, craned his neck to get a look at Gendrina. She wondered if it was the same Sam that her brother had trained with. "Are you serious?" he asked. Her escort shrugged and nodded. Sam unlocked the gate and pushed it open with his foot, and motioned them inside. The guard turned to Gendrina. "Sam will take care of you from here. I need to go home, now. I hope to meet you again someday." Gendrina smiled tiredly and nodded at him, watching as he walked around the corner towards the housing district.

"Follow me, girl," Sam said. She began walking for the gate, then stopped, staring up the long staircase into the Upper Ring.

"I can't get him up there," Gendrina said, trying not to sound as defeated as she felt.

"Hell, I don't think I could either," Sam grumbled. "Wait here, I'll bring them to you..." He turned and jogged up the steps. It seemed like all she had done for hours is wait, but soon enough she heard loud footsteps approaching down the stairs. Sam was back, accompanied by three heavily armored men, knights, Gendrina guessed, and a younger boy, probably around her own age.

The boy approached her. "Greetings. I am Prince Christopher Alento. What is your name?"

"Gendrina Carter, my Prince," she answered, trying not to appear flustered.

"My father sits in a council meeting with the goldkeeper, and sent me in his stead to greet you and pay the bounty. I must admit though, I find this a little hard to believe."

Sam shook his head. "Pierre Lucerne, of the northern district, vouched for her. And just look at her, can there be any other explanation?"

Christopher squinted at her. "How old are you?" he asked.

"Thirteen," she said.

The young Prince turned to the three knights. "You mean to tell me that four royal hunting parties were unable to find and kill this wolf, but a little girl with a kitchen knife and a bunch of twigs managed it in one afternoon?"

"Well, I've actually been out there since this morning, Sir," Gendrina corrected. Christopher grinned at her.

"Very well. I have no evidence in favor of doubt, so the bounty is yours." He reached behind his back and pulled out a small pouch, handing it to Gendrina. She pulled the drawstring and peeked inside, smiling at the gold that glinted in the last minutes of sunlight.

"Thank you, my Prince," she said.

Christopher nodded approvingly at her. "When I am King, remind me of this day, and I will see you are rewarded greater than this small purse. You did well today."

She wouldn't have been able to wipe the stupid grin off her face if she tried. "Thank you-"

"Gen, wake up. Something's happening," she heard Jacob say, and felt him lightly shaking her shoulder.

"What is it?" she grunted, stumbling to her feet and reaching for her cuirass and saber.

"A citizen spotted someone sleeping in the forest when he went to relieve himself, an older man wearing rusty armor. Bayard wants all of us to go, we take no chances."

"Aye," Gendrina agreed as she finished strapping the cuirass. She stepped out of the tent into an uncomfortable silence, the citizens lined outside the trees and staring tentatively into the woods. Bayard, Pierre, and Thomas were standing in the forefront, sabers in hand. Helmet stood beside them, a massive woodcutting axe held lightly in his hand as though it were a camping hatchet. She walked up behind Bayard. "What's the plan?"

"Jason said that the man is straight this way," Bayard explained, pointing into the forest. "I want you and Jacob to take the bows and follow parallel to me and Thomas, with Helmet and Pierre taking the middle. The four of us will approach the man from either side, and you and Jacob stay hidden in the treeline and be ready to fire if he tries anything."

Gendrina nodded and walked away to gather the weapons. She took a longbow and a hunting crossbow from two citizens and returned, passing the longbow to Jacob. Bayard started into the forest, and Gendrina followed Jacob about twenty meters across from him. She could see Helmet and Pierre sneaking along between them. Watching Bayard, she saw him hold up his hand. They stopped and readied their bows, glancing around for the sleeping man. Soon, she spotted him. Laying on his front, he was nearly black with dirt and mud, with long, filthy hair splayed around his head. Gendrina lifted her crossbow towards him and nodded at Bayard. He signaled Pierre, and they began to move in.

Bayard approached the man and gave him a soft kick. Within a second, the dirty man was on his feet, longsword shoved up against Bayard's throat. Gendrina and Jacob loosed their arrows simultaneously, but he raised a shield that had apparently been strapped to his arm through the night and blocked one, and the other glanced off his left pauldron. Jacob was reaching for a new arrow when he heard Bayard yell "NO!" Gendrina lowered the crossbow and stared. Now that he was standing, she could make out the shape of the armor, the same layered plate over mail that Christopher and his knights wore, and the sigil of Valdus rising from the face of his shield.

"I don't believe it. It's Uriel," Gendrina whispered. She followed Jacob into the clearing, slinging the crossbow over her shoulder, and Uriel sheathed his blade as they approached.

Bayard was beaming, and he embraced the old knight. "Your reflexes are sharp for an old man," Bayard joked.

"And you are exceedingly slow for a young one," Uriel retorted.

"Not as young as I would like, these days," Bayard sighed. "It is wonderful to see you here, we were sure you had fallen on the road to Haarn. Where have you been this whole time?"

"I have been at Haarn. Soon after I arrived, a ship crashed into the city, carrying a full cargo of infected. They overran the city in hours, and when I managed to escape, I stayed outside the gates to prevent their spread. Seven days ago, they broke through the gates and I followed them here. I was going to call out to them, lure them away, but they came upon a camping family. One escaped on horseback, and led them to Valdus."

Bayard nodded and cursed. "This ship, do you know where it came from? Were there any markings, any flags or sigils?"

"I know that it was an Eastern slave ship. There was no crew, they must have abandoned ship at sea. The infected were all chained together, starved and filthy. When they swarmed the shore, civilians could not escape as they got trapped in the chains, pulling the infected straight to them. It was..." Uriel choked, placing a hand against his throat. "I've been a knight for a very long time, Bayard. I've killed my enemies, I've executed criminals, I've seen the worst humanity has to offer. But this was something different. These creatures *can't* exist. How can we expect to live in a world that they occupy as well? I was one second away from throwing myself off the cliffs when I saw you escape the city. It could have been over. What God would allow this?"

Bayard saw the defeat and depression in Uriel's eyes. It was understandable, it was human, but despite all of this, Bayard was infuriated. He grasped Uriel's blade and slid it from its sheath, holding the battered longsword out in front of him. "When I got to this city, months ago, Christopher was going to behead me in the name of God. Dozens of civilians were burned to death by the Drydens because they were brought to a church rather than the castle. King Drake Alento is responsible for that, and he is dead because he burned an innocent family of doctors because he believed they used methods shunned by God. My brother is dead because he stopped a group of zealots from blowing open the western gate. In my experience, when humans bring God into their decisions, logic, and actions, it leads to nothing but tragedy and death.

"Your sword is God, now. Your shield is the White Gate. Your companions are the Angels, the hopelessness in your mind is Hell, the fear and doubt you feel is the Purgatory that holds you back from the light. Your will to survive, your will to protect the people who still live, that is the Heaven you must strive for. These things are all that matter. You do not fear the plaguewalkers, you do not fear death, you do not fear God. You fear only yourself. Conquer these feelings, hold the sword in your hand and the sword in your heart, and cut through the dead and your fear with the same merciless power." Bayard shoved the longsword into Uriel's hands, pushing him back. "You fought for your Kingdom. You would have fought to the death to protect the same people who are with us now. Nothing has changed."

Uriel stood shaking, grasping the hilt of the light blade as though it weighed a hundred pounds. "You have changed, Bayard. When I left you, you were a disrespectful doctor who knew how to swing a blade. Now, you speak as a King. I would be honored to serve under you, in the wake of Christopher's death. At least I will have a direction." Uriel dropped to one knee, holding his sword point to the ground in front of him in a pledge of loyalty.

Bayard looked behind him, at Thomas, Gendrina, Pierre, Jacob, and Helmet. Thomas shrugged. Bayard thought for a long moment, then turned to Uriel. "No. You will never serve under me. You are an equal, we all are. You can follow my requests, if you so choose. Or those of anyone else. If you think someone's idea is bad, say so, and we put it to a vote. You have more experience than the five of us put together, except maybe Pierre."

Uriel grinned. "Very well, if that is the way you want to run this thing." Uriel stood and sheathed his blade. "I will fight with you. What is our plan?"

"We will discuss that soon. Let us get back to our camp so everyone can have their comforts." And so they walked back through the trees and into the camp, where Uriel was greeted with a massive cheer. He was handed boiled eggs, vegetables, smoked meats, bottles of whiskey and mead. Bayard and the other knights ate their fill as well. Finally, Bayard stood. "Everyone, hear me!" he called over the crowd. "It is time that I tell everybody the long-term plan here. Where we will go, how we will survive, how we will reclaim our lost land from the dead. Right now, I'm leading everyone to Peydenal, my old home. Many of you have been there, I am sure. They have a large tavern there that can support us for a few nights. We tell everyone about the plague, train them on how to fight it, and offer them a place in our party. From there, we keep traveling from town to town, doing the same. We form a warband, growing all the time, and we take the fight to the dead. When we have enough men, we invade Sinead and take control of the city. Sinead is high in the mountains, it will make a perfect fortress against the dead. If the infected attempt to attack Sinead, they will block the mountain pass, which is why we must attack first. Humans could get through with blasting powder, but the infected could be effectively shut out. If they swarm the blockade before we control the city, nowhere in England will be truly safe. Does this sound like a good course of action to all of you?"

There was a general murmur of confirmation from the citizens, but Uriel shook his head. "I would not like to see war against the living so soon. The men of Sinead are survivors. They may see the only chance they have is to fight the dead alongside us. It does not have to come to war. We must offer them the chance to join us, and only attack if they refuse. Obviously, their new King will betray us in the future, but we can deal with that problem as it comes. We need every fighter we can get, until the threat of the plague has faded. If they decline, then we fight. I know that many people here may seek vengeance on Sinead for killing our men, our King, but it is not the time for that. Everyone knows the saying 'The enemy of your enemy is your friend', and now is the time to exercise that philosophy." The crowd grew louder, agreeing with Uriel's amendment.

Bayard nodded. "We have our plan then. Anyway, the sun is high in the sky and it is time we move on. Pack up the camp, we make it to Peydenal tonight. Jacob, Pierre, ride ahead and inform them of our approach. I'm sure they know that something has happened to Valdus, you don't just go three months without someone trying to travel to a large city, but do not mention the details of the plague. Let me handle that, the people there trust me." Jacob nodded and kicked his horse into a gallop, quickly disappearing around a bend in the road, Pierre close behind. "We cannot stay here for long," Bayard called back to the civilians. "It is a small town, not prepared to sustain a group this size for more than a couple of nights. We will have a hot meal, some strong drinks, work out a plan, and move on. If they haven't already dug through the rubble and sold them all, we may be able to recover some good weapons from the basement of my old smithy."

They walked silently through the trees, listening to the strong winds that blew above. Four uneventful hours passed, when Bayard held up his hand to stop the group as he spotted something in the distance. He squinted, and could make out a horseman galloping towards them at full speed. Another few seconds and he could tell that it was Jacob, hunched over in his saddle, the shafts of three arrows protruding from his back.

"Lay on your front, and try not to move your arms. Breathe shallow, do not let your lungs expand too far, and do not talk." Bayard whispered, helping Jacob from his horse. Jacob knelt down and collapsed onto his chest, letting out a quiet gasp. Gendrina was on her knees beside her brother, staring at his bloodied back. Thomas stood a meter away, his knuckles white from the grip he held on his saber. "I...I think it's going to be okay," Bayard told the two siblings. "The arrows are not near the heart, and I can see the base of the broadheads, meaning that they probably haven't pierced the lungs. Blood loss is minimal, but we need clean bandages and a disinfectant before I can remove the arrows. Obviously I can't push them through, so I'm going to have to cut them out. Does anyone have any alcohol?"

"Who do you think I am?" Lilith mumbled, drawing a small bottle of whiskey from her rucksack and handing it to Bayard. He took it and placed it next to him, then grabbed hold of Jacob's doublet.

"Uriel, dagger," Bayard said, holding his hand out behind him.

"Bad idea, Bayard," Uriel warned. "I've killed dozens of plaguewalkers with this, it could infect him."

"No, the infection dies within two days of leaving its host. The saber is heavy, I won't be able to properly navigate the arrow shafts with it. If I bump one, it could knock the barbs in even worse. Give me the dagger." Uriel obliged, and Bayard cut the blood-soaked doublet away from Jacob's back. "Does anybody have some kind of a bowl?"

"Aye," came the voice of a civilian woman, handing Bayard a clean cooking pot.

"This will do, thank you," Bayard said, pouring the whiskey into the pot. "Now I need a shirt or rag, the cleanest we can find."

"Mine," Thomas said. "I've been wearing this chestplate the whole time, so my jacket hasn't been exposed to the road." He began grasping at the buckle of his chestplate with his one hand, but Bayard waved him down.

"Velvet won't do, it does not bind well. I need cotton or silk."

"I can help," Jenara piped up. "I saved my dress from when these two forced me into this awful thing," she said, gesturing at Gendrina and Lilith, then down at the dusty leather armor she wore. "The body is silk and the underskirts are cotton, and I only wore it for about three hours."

Bayard smiled at the young woman. "Thank you, Jenara. Go get it, quickly now." She nodded and glided off, returning soon with a rectangular wooden box. Bayard took it from her and pulled it open, removing the pink and white fabrics. He separated the underskirts from the outer dress and handed it back to Jenara. "You keep this, the cotton is better anyway." She curtsied at him and stepped back, stowing the dress back into its box. "Alright, now... Sorry Thomas, but can you lay here, next to Jacob? I need to use you as a table." Thomas grimaced but did not complain as he climbed to his knees and lay face-down next to his brother. Bayard lay one of the underskirts on the back of Thomas's cuirass and began cutting it with the dagger, careful to avoid trailing the clean white cotton in the dirt of the forest. It took him fifteen minutes to smoothly cut all the fabric, then he placed the makeshift bandages into the pot of whiskey, as well as the dagger. He let them sit for a minute, then took the blade in his right hand, grasping Jacob's shoulder with his left. "Sorry, friend. I would tell you that this won't hurt much, but knights aren't supposed to lie."

"Do it," Jacob choked out. Bayard tightened his grip on the dagger, grasped the shaft of the highest arrow, and pressed the tip of the dagger into Jacob's flesh. Jacob began to scream and thrash, but Bayard placed a hand on the back of his head and pushed him down.

"Jacob, if you move that much, you *will* die. Think of your family, you cannot afford to die here. For their sakes, you must show no pain." Jacob growled into the dirt, and Bayard went back to the surgery. He held the shaft and cut at the ruined flesh, slicing it away from the barbs on the arrowhead, as Jacob moaned and writhed on the ground, staying as still as he physically could. Finally, the first arrow came free. Bayard wiped the tip on his pants and looked closely at it, anger growing in his eyes. "Human bone. This is the work of Adam Dryden."

*****

"We have to kill them," Thomas hissed an hour later, as Bayard finished bandaging Jacob's wounds. "All of them. What are we waiting here for? We outnumber any force they could keep in a small town."

"Think straight, Thomas," Uriel spat. "We have maybe seven good weapons between us, one suit of plate armor. Not to mention that we are two warriors down, we have no idea if Pierre is still alive. If they have even twenty geared men, they could slaughter every one of us. And if they set up tents, hunted for game, they could sustain over a hundred soldiers in the town. And if Adam Dryden is there, his primary goal will be to kill Christopher and Princess Jenara. Once he finds out that Christopher is dead, he will turn his blade fully at Jenara. We will kill them, but we have to do it right. Scout the town, their defenses, their numbers, and come up with a plan."

"Right," Bayard said. "Every situation can be manipulated in our favor with intelligence and forethought. We must make camp deep in the trees and scout Peydenal tonight. Come now." Bayard led the group into the forest, and they slowly made their way through the trees until the sun began to set.

"We should be safe here," Uriel spoke up. "Someone get Jacob into a tent. Bayard, Gendrina, Thomas, come speak with me. We will work out our approach for tonight." Uriel led the four of them away from the civilians until they were out of earshot. "Alright, the first thing we need to do is find the darkest clothes we can. Stealth will be our friend tonight, and we must blend with the shadows. When darkness falls, we will travel in the treeline until we reach Peydenal, and scout out their defenses. If there is something that can be done, we will do so. However, if we can not guarantee a successful assault, we must not take action. One injured man is not worth risking our civilians."

"That's my *brother*," Gendrina hissed. "And Pierre is still missing. We cannot let this go."

Uriel frowned at her. "If you wish to fight amongst men, you must understand duty. We have to place the civilians above ourselves, that is what a knight does. I will not 'let this go', but we have to find out what has become of Pierre, and if the enemy can be fought here, we will do so. There are tactical risks and then there are stupid risks. Do you understand me?"

Gendrina pursed her lips and nodded. "As you say. I will trust your judgment." Thomas walked past her towards the camp, giving her a light punch in the shoulder. She frowned and followed after him, Bayard and Uriel trailing behind them.

"Get some rest, all of you," Uriel called. "I will wake you when it is time to move."

*****

"Tom, you're getting fat," Garret complained, jabbing Thomas in the gut with the tip of his training sword. "You may have come into some gold, but that's no reason to overeat."

"I seem to have developed an incurable fondness for soft cheese, Sir," Thomas chuckled. "I will work harder, though."

"Good! Now, give me thirty push-ups and get ready for a spar. You'll be fighting Sam and then Pete, then everyone will rotate from there."

Thomas saluted and dropped to the floor. When he finished his push-ups, he stood and walked across the training yard to the weapon racks. "Spear or sword?" he called to Garret.

"You know I prefer swords, but we did swords all day yesterday, so grab six staves and pass them out."

Thomas stepped to the other side of the rack and grabbed a set of the six foot hardwood staves, one end painted black to signify the tip of the spear. He jogged back across the yard and tossed a staff to each of his group, taking his place on the right side of the line. Garret walked around, pushing his trainees about until they were standing in pairs of two, Garret standing before a slightly terrified Victor.

Victor was the worst of the trainees in single combat, but the best with a bow or crossbow. He was severely farsighted, and could barely make out anything closer than ten feet to him. He was set for sentry duty on the top of the wall when he got out of training. "You'll be okay, Vic," Thomas shouted at him from across the yard. "Stay back and strike for the knees, keep his clumsy arse dancing."

Garret grimaced and waved dismissively at him. "Bow to your opponents and get on with it," Garret yelled back.

Thomas grinned and turned to Samuel. "Ready, Sam?" The

younger man nodded and bowed, then took his stance with the spear-staff. Unlike many instructors, Garret encouraged his trainees to put their own strengths and styles into their combat rather than following directly by-the-book. As long as something wasn't a 'bad idea', he would allow it. Samuel stood with the staff held by his side and forward, pointing up towards Thomas's chest. This would allow him powerful and fast jabs as well as quick, whipping attacks and versatile defense. On the other side, Thomas bowed back and stood with the staff held up, beside his shoulder and pointing down. It was a powerful offensive stance that catered to Thomas's height and strength, its thrusts capable of piercing chainmail and wooden shields, and powerful, bone-cracking swings with the shaft. The disadvantage was shorter range and less flexible defense.

The two boys stood still for a number of seconds, and then Thomas lunged forward with a shout, thrusting his staff towards Samuel's leg. Samuel stepped back, lowering his own staff to parry it, when Thomas turned to his left, dropping his arm and raising the tip of his staff above Samuel's block. Thomas straightened out and lunged, slamming the tip of his staff into the center of Samuel's chestplate, flooring him. Thomas ran forwards, bringing the staff above his head and thrusting downwards, stopping inches above Samuel's throat. Thomas smiled and pulled Samuel to his feet, giving him a patronizing pat on the shoulder and looking around at the other recruits. Peter had taken victory, having cracked Jacob's staff and jabbed him in the thigh, and Garret and Victor were still at it. True to Thomas's advice, Victor was jogging backwards while blindly flailing at Garret's legs. Upon seeing the other fights ending, Garret slammed the back end of his staff into the ground, blocking Victor's wild strikes, then stepped in, poking Victor in the center of his forehead.

"Enough. Good job Pete, Tom. You, Jake, I'm surprised at you. What happened?"

"My staff snapped on the first strike. I tried wielding the ends as swords but didn't have the range. When are we going to replace this old shite?"

"As soon as one of you bastards brings me a bunch of sticks," Garret snapped. "The castle supplies swords, spears, and armor. The staves are on our own time. Jake, grab a new staff and pair up with Vic, you'd be able to handle that one with a toothpick."

Rearmed and repositioned, Thomas sized up Peter. The second largest person there, next to Thomas, he was powerful and quick, but also a little slow in the head. He did what he was told and he did it well, but lacked much self-awareness or empathy, regularly getting carried away and hurting his mates during practice. He was not mean-spirited, just overzealous. Thomas had made it known to Garret, who had responded with "It just makes training more realistic." And so Thomas stood, this time in a defensive stance with the staff held across his chest.

Peter moved first, swinging at Thomas with a mighty downward slam. Thomas sidestepped and lifted his staff, knocking Peter's aside, and spun with a short thrust towards Peter's exposed back. Peter turned quickly and shoved Thomas's staff out of the way with his left arm, smacking Thomas hard in the elbow. With the staff-spears, a match was only ended when the tip of the spear made contact, so Thomas jumped backwards and swung out, catching Peter in the side. Peter caught the staff just below the tip and pulled hard. Placing the tip of his staff directly in Thomas's path, Peter grinned. Thomas shouted and released his staff, rolling forwards and avoiding Peter's staff by a hair. Peter was taken by surprise, and he tried to move his thrust down towards Thomas, but he was too slow as Thomas wrapped his arms around Peter's left leg and stood, slamming Peter into the dirt. Thomas scrambled around behind Peter, forcing his arm around Peter's neck and locking in the hold. Six seconds later, Peter was asleep.

Thomas stood up, lightly poking the unconscious man with the staff to officially end the match before raising his arm in proud victory. Then Garret was there, grinning at him. "Unorthodox, but it works," Garret chuckled.

"So who won the other matches?" Thomas asked, bending down to slap Peter awake. He coughed and sniffed, standing up quickly and rubbing his neck.

"Sam actually got the better of me with a throw," Garret admitted. "I never expect it coming from one of the staves, but it counts. Jake downed Vic in three seconds, obviously."

"I could put a bolt in your arse from fifty meters," Victor shot back.

"Try Thomas, his is a bigger target," Jacob snorted.

"Enough, enough," Garret said. "Thomas, with me. Jake, with

Sam. And I don't really want Vic's death on my hands, so the two of you go practice on the dummies, fifty thrusts each," he finished, waving Peter and Victor away.

Thomas reclaimed his staff from the ground and stepped away from the others, waiting for Garret to take his spot in front of him. The two men bowed, and Thomas went back to the offensive stance he used on Samuel. Garret took the same stance, making Thomas grin. "You aren't as strong as I am. That might not be a great idea."

"I am the instructor here, don't you go on like that," Garret barked. "Attack me and see what happens." And so Thomas stepped in, swinging the staff upwards. Garret stepped back and avoided it, but Thomas flipped his grip and brought the staff down towards Garret's helmet. Garret tilted to his left, absorbing the impact with his thick leather pauldron, then charged forwards and slammed the tip of his staff into Thomas's gut, knocking him backwards. Thomas stumbled and managed to keep his footing, but the match was over. Garret dropped his staff and stepped towards Thomas, grabbing his shoulder. "Strength is no substitute for experience, Tom. You could be strong enough to lift a castle, and it would mean nothing if the other guy is better than you. Focus, rely on technique as much as power."

Thomas grimaced and nodded, rubbing his belly. "As you say, Sir."

Garret turned back to the others. "Alright. Jake, spar with your brother. I'll take Pete. Sam, don't hurt Vic too badly..."

"Thomas. It's time. Put these on and meet us by Bayard's tent," Uriel whispered, tossing a set of ragged, dark brown clothes onto Thomas's face.

Thomas cringed and groaned, rubbing his eyes. "Aye, fine. See you there in a minute." He got to his feet and stretched, then stripped and pulled on the dark clothes, tying up the left arm. They were baggy on him, but they were perfect for remaining unseen. He left his tent and headed for Bayard's, where there was a commotion going on in the treeline.

"Stop it, it's disgusting, no," Gendrina was complaining as Bayard tried to wrestle some dark object onto her head as she slapped at him.

"Your hair is absurd, you can see it from a kilometer away,"

Bayard argued. "It's *clean*, just put it on."

Thomas stepped up to see the object was a horrific, ratty hat, seemingly sewn together from a number of socks. "You're acting like a girl, Gen," Thomas warned. "I know how you don't like to be called that."

Gendrina sighed and dropped her arms as Bayard shoved the hat over her short, bright red hair. "There, not so bad."

"Speak for yourself," Gendrina whispered, pouting and adjusting the longbow that was pulled across her chest.

"Anyway," Uriel interrupted, "let's get moving now, we do not know how long it will take to get there, or how long we will need to stay." The others fell silent, and the group of four turned to the trees.

"Oy," a loud voice called from behind. Helmet stomped out from his tent, wearing his dark formal coat, a woodcutting axe resting on his shoulder. "Don't you leave me here. Yeh're two men down, and I plan on giving Adam Dryden a new arsehole."

"Not if I get there first," Thomas boasted.

"Sod off, the both of you," Gendrina interrupted. "I'll choke him to death with this fucking hat."

"Only if he's still alive after I stab him through the heart," Uriel added.

Bayard stayed silent, grinning to himself. *Despite everything, you cannot fault them for their morale. As long as I stay strong as they have, we will win at the end of this.*

"Bayard," another voice whispered from behind him. Lowering his head, he slowly turned to face Lilith. She was wearing a thick nightgown, her eyes tired and her head lowered as well. "I will not ask to come with you, I know you must be focused, and you cannot protect me. If you want to save the world, you must understand that this is not a time for heroes. Dying tonight will destroy any hope we have of defeating this plague. Learn what has become of Pierre, and come back to me."

Bayard reached out and took Lilith's right hand, holding it in front of him. "No Northman could ever get the better of me," he whispered to her, grinning. "I may not the the best sword in the Kingdom, but you well know that I have the best mind. You would not think me good enough if I did not." He leaned down and kissed the wedding ring that circled Lilith's finger, and she smiled sheepishly at him. "I am sorry, but you will have no sleep this night.

You are in charge of the camp until we return. Rouse four others and have them patrol around the camp, and you care for Jacob and prepare what supplies we have left in case any of us return injured." He glanced to the four other warriors. "We have to go now, we only have so much time before the sun begins to rise." Lilith nodded silently as he dropped her hand.

Bayard turned and walked into the trees, his companions on his tail.

An hour went by, and the sun had passed midnight when the orange flicker of firelight could be seen through the trees. Bayard held his arms out, stopping the four others. He crouched down and slowly proceeded forward, squinting from the sudden intake of light. Soon he could see his old town. The tavern sat in the very center, torchlight pouring from the windows. Song and shouting could be faintly heard, and shadows were dancing along the dirt where people moved about in the large building. Other than the tavern there was the stables and the housing row, twenty small, shabby buildings. About twenty meters to their left was the merchant's row, Bayard's old smithy, now just a heap of charred rubble on the ground, as well as a potter's shop, butcher, tailor, logger, and well house.

Suddenly, a man appeared around the side of the tavern. He was dressed in thick heavy leathers and chain, wearing a plate helm and pauldron over his left shoulder. He carried a spear with a shortsword at his side. Uriel tapped Bayard's shoulder. "Guards. There seem to be four of them, look." Bayard peered around, and spotted three other men dressed the same way. They patrolled in patterns, one circling the tavern, two others paced back and forth in front of the housing row, and the fourth sat next to a campfire, close to the opposite trees, drinking from a large tankard. There was nobody else in sight.

"We need to find out where the civilians are," Bayard whispered. "They probably have the women in the tavern to serve them. The men and elderly are either in one of the homes or shops, or dead. We can't do anything until we know for sure. We must circle around the town and capture the man by the fire. He is not visible to the others, if they keep their current patrols." Uriel nodded and led the way through the treeline. They stayed low, crawling through the bushes and pines. It was a slow journey, and ten minutes later they stopped, five meters away from the seated guard. Examining their lines of sight, there was no sign of the other guards. Bayard grabbed Gendrina's arm and pulled her forwards, motioning for her to watch. He pointed to the guard's helmet and imitated the action of tearing it off, then looked at her expectantly. She grinned and nodded, tugging on her hat to confirm it. He patted her shoulder and pointed, then made a 'shoo' gesture towards the guard.

She gingerly stepped out of the treeline and sneaked silently through the grass, her bare feet making no noise in the windy night. Bayard followed, drawing a length of thick cloth from his pocket and bundling it in his right hand. Gendrina reached the guard and waited until Bayard was beside her. He nodded. Gendrina dropped to one knee and slid her saber under the leather strap that connected the helmet to the pauldron, simultaneously wrapping her left arm around the helmet. She slashed the strap and fell backwards, wrenching the helmet off the man's head. He had time for little more than a gasp before Bayard grabbed the guard in a chokehold and forced the bundle of cloth into his mouth. Uriel and Helmet ran from the treeline and the four of them dragged the choking, bug-eyed guard into the forest.

"Helmet, hold him," Bayard commanded after they had dragged the guard a hundred meters through the trees, into a moonlit clearing. Helmet wrapped his right arm around the guard's neck and his left around the torso, holding the guard's arms tightly. Bayard stepped forwards, raising his saber horizontally to the right side of the guard's chest. "Do you know what will happen if I lean forward? My blade will slide right between your ribs and into your heart. My companion behind you there has a chestplate beneath his coat, so he will be perfectly safe. If you shout when we remove that cloth, he will choke you, and I will stab you. Not only that, but the wind is blowing towards us right now. None of your friends would ever hear you. Now, when I remove this, are you going to shout?"

The guard vigorously shook his head. Bayard smiled and nodded, then pulled the cloth out of the guard's mouth. As agreed, he remained silent. Bayard motioned for Uriel to approach. The old knight stepped forward, looking over their captive. "I suppose you're smarter than you look. There is no need for you to die here, just tell us how many of you there are, and where the civilians are."

The guard was exceptionally drunk, his eyes unfocused and his legs limp. Anyone weaker than Helmet wouldn't have been able to hold him straight. "There...s'were fifty of us, a few died when we attacked-ed this town, there are a lot? In the tavern..."

Uriel sighed. "Good enough. Again, where are the civilians?"

"Men and old people are at the potter. Boss said it had good locks. Got the cute girls in the tavern," he finished with a drunken chuckle.

"Dryden. Is he in the tavern as well? And our friend, wearing a coat similar to the big man's here, where is he?"

"Boss is unnerneath tha' burned blahsmith. Lotsa weapons down 'ere, but most're blunt. He's sharpenin' the good ones for us to use. And if yeh mean the old bastard what came with the man tha' Boss shot up, he surren...sren, eh gave up. We have 'im with the other people in the potter."

"And what about the other guards?" Uriel pressed. "Are there more of you in the forests? Will more come out of the tavern any time soon?"

"I...wha?"

Uriel slapped the guard across his face. He coughed and blinked. "Ow, stop'at, guards change out er'ry hour. Just four at a time. Came out few minutes before yeh got me."

Bayard closed his eyes tightly and slowly moved his head around, mumbling to himself. And then he grinned. Thomas glanced at him. "I know that face. That's your 'plan' face. What have you got?"

"Get this bastard out of his armor, we can't bloody it up," Bayard whispered. "Then kill him. Gen, take the sleeves off your undercoat and cut them into four eye patches, and do it quickly."

Chapter Eighteen
Autumn of 1513 A.D
Village of Peydenal
Middle of the Night

Lyanna Sendiil wiped away a tear as she approached a large red-faced bearded man and refilled the tankard that sat on the table in front of him. He gave her a shove, and she stumbled back, careful not to spill the carafe of mead she carried. She looked to the three other girls, her sister Brielle, and the two daughters of the potter, Mary and Sarah, who was only thirteen. She tore her gaze away, knowing that she would be hurt if she delayed. For forty minutes she wandered around the tavern, filling mugs, getting grabbed and prodded, but luckily all of the large red-faced bearded men were too drunk to find motivation to do much worse.

Lyanna was returning to the dining room after refilling her carafe when one of the men stood and hobbled across the floor, shoving a window open. "Eeyyy, shift change, git back in 'ere, the lot of yeh," he shouted out the window. The four guards soon squeezed their way into the crowded tavern, and four others went out to get their equipment and replace them. One of the guards immediately sat down on a wooden chair beside the door, and the other three sat on the floor near the large fireplace that lit the tavern, their helmets still on. The largest of them waved his hand in the air, shouting in their northern accent, "Girls! Bring us a bucket of water, we need to wash the dirt off of us!" The two potter's daughters quickly jogged into the kitchen, returning minutes later with a small tub of water. The guards looked at it, but did not begin washing themselves.

"You there," the guard by the door called, pointing to Lyanna. "Bring mead, right now." She faked a smile and grabbed a tankard from the counter, approaching the man. As soon as she was done filling his mug, he placed it on the floor beside him, then pulled Lyanna onto his lap. He reached around, grabbing her breast and pressing his helmet against her neck.

"I am Bayard Travers," he whispered. She tensed up and stopped struggling. "I bring knights of Valdus to defend this town. The other guards who just entered are with me. I need you to *quietly* instruct the other girls to step behind the counter. When the fire goes out, get on the ground and do not move until I say." Bayard let go of Lyanna and pushed her away. She stumbled against a table, but caught herself and quickly walked to Brielle.

"Get behind the counter. Valdus is here to aid us," she whispered. Brielle went wide-eyed. "How are they supposed to help us? Valdus is burned to the ground."

"I don't know, but Bayard is here. You know he is to be trusted."

Brielle nodded and silently made for the counter. Lyanna circled the tavern, telling the same to Mary and Sarah. "Hey," one of the drunken soldiers called. "What are you all doing back there? Bring me more chicken and mead!" Just then, Lyanna saw the three guards in front of the fire stand, pick up the tub of water, and hurl it into the flames. She grabbed her sister and they hit the floor just as the tavern burst into chaos.

*****

Bayard watched as Helmet, Uriel, and Thomas threw the tub of water onto the fire. As soon as the light faded, Bayard tore his helmet off, followed by the patch that covered his right eye. The room suddenly became visible, his right eye already accustomed to the darkness. There were shouts and grunts, all the blind, drunken soldiers tripping over the tables and chairs. Bayard slammed the lock on the tavern door and unsheathed his stolen shortsword.

It was a complete massacre. The northmen blindly swung fists and chairs as they were cut down, toppling over tables and screaming for help. Any who made it to the door were unable to find the lock and fell to Bayard's blade. Soon, the quantity of bodies on the floor made it impossible to run, and more of them tripped and stumbled, meeting their deaths at the tip of Uriel's spear. Soon, all was quiet save for the soft cries from the women behind the counter.

"It is safe now, Lyanna," Bayard called. "Let's leave through the kitchen, you do not need to see this." She whimpered quietly as Bayard escorted her into the kitchen with Thomas, Helmet, and Uriel bringing the other women behind him. Bayard shoved the large window open and stepped out, helping Lyanna and the others find their way through in the darkness.

"What of the other guards?" Brielle asked.

"Taken care of," Thomas assured her, pointing to his right. Glancing over, Bayard saw the four replacement guards crumpled outside the tavern door, an arrow protruding from each of their necks.

Bayard stopped and pointed into the forest across from the tavern. "Our companion is right there, go to her. She will lead you all to safety."

"Thank you, Bayard," Lyanna sobbed. "We will never be able to repay you for this. But...where will we go after?"

"We'll sort that out later, now *go there,*" Bayard ordered, nudging her towards Gendrina. The women ran into the trees, and Bayard turned to the ruins of his old home.

"Why didn't he come out of there?" Thomas asked. "Think he barricaded himself in?"

"No," Bayard answered. "The foundation of the house is thick, as is the cellar door. You couldn't hear a cannon fire out here if you were in the smithy. He has no idea that something has happened."

"So how do you want to handle this?" Uriel asked.

"We could block the door with wood and brick, let him starve," Helmet offered.

"I thought of that too," Bayard sighed. "However, we cannot underestimate the Drydens. They've used explosives before, and if he uses the forge as cover, he could blow his way out. Also, with the infected spreading out from Valdus, we must not waste time here. Until we watch the life leave his eyes, we cannot leave him. We will wait for him to come out, and we will defeat him head-on. The Drydens are great warriors, but we have all seen that they can be killed as easily as any other man."

"Works for me," Thomas agreed.

"Wouldn't want it any other way," Uriel snarled.

*****

"Bugger off, Garret, I paid for it and I'm not going to let you chip the blade first thing," Jacob complained as Garret reached for the brand new shortsword that hung from Jacob's hip.

"What's the point of buying a sword if you aren't going to test it out? And I'm your superior, give it here, Carter," Garret insisted.

"That doesn't count for shite when it's *my* sword on *my* property," Jacob retorted, retreating to the other side of the long table.

Garret sighed and sat back down, staring into the face of the roast pig that rested in front of him. "Where did you three get the money for all this anyway? Am I training a couple of jewel thieves?"

"Not quite," Thomas chuckled. "Gendrina brought a bounty to the castle a few days ago. She had been missing all day, our longbow was gone, we were worried sick. Then she comes stumbling in an hour after dark, covered in blood, drops a sack of gold on the table, fills the chamberpot, and passes out on the floor."

"*Shut up, Tom,*" Gendrina hissed, throwing a spoon at his head. Thomas caught it and went at the large bowl of pheasant stew in front of him.

"Bounty, eh?" Garret questioned, looking across at the young red-faced girl. "Who did you kill?"

"Not a who," Gendrina explained, glaring at him. "The grey wolf."

Garret blinked. "Well, then. If they paid out, I guess there must have been proof. Who am I to argue? You did well. Anyway, Jacob, what else have you got?"

"We bought a shortsword for me and Tom, a hawk axe, a dagger for Gen, and two crossbows. She wanted a sword but the smith wouldn't sell her one. Said he had no problem arming women, but she needed a few more years."

"Wise smith," Garret said. "There are exceptions, apparently, but most girls her age would throw the sword every time they swung it," he finished, with a smirk at Jacob.

"It's been a year, you really won't let that go, will you?" Jacob sighed.

"Not like you let that sword go," Garret coughed out behind his laughter. He took a moment to regain his composure, then grinned over at Jacob. "In all honesty, Jake, you are improving well, particularly with a longsword. You have the speed, you can gain the power, and your technique improves every day. You'll be a castle guard by the time you're twenty."

"I wouldn't want to be a castle guard," Jacob said. "Staring at a gate all day. I want to be on the wall, or outside the gates, with the wind and the open sky."

"Respectable," Garret nodded. "I will keep that in mind when you finish your training, but in the end you will go where you are needed."

"I understand that," Jacob mumbled through the pork rib that poked out of his mouth. "I just hope for the best." Jacob stood to reach for a bowl of stew, and then his back began to throb.

"Bayard?" Jacob coughed, blinking into the darkness. He was laying face down on a soft surface, his head held up by a wooden block. His back was a solid mass of pain. "Bayard!?"

"You'll have to settle for me," Lilith's voice whispered from beside him.

"Lily...what happened? Where am I?" he asked, struggling to push himself up. He felt a small hand on his shoulder, holding him down.

"Please do not move, your injuries must settle. You're in my tent, and I won't lie to you, you are barely alive. If not for Bayard's skills, you would not be."

"Am I going to be alright?"

"We think you will be. The arrows missed your backbone and did not pierce far enough to hit your lungs. The only thing that saved you is the Dryden's insistence on using bone as their weapons. A steel-tipped arrow would have gone straight through you."

"I guess I should thank Adam then. How long until I can swing a sword?"

"You've got a couple of months at least," Lilith explained. "I know it seems a long time, but it is better than being dead or paralyzed, right?"

"Besides," Gendrina's voice called from outside the tent, "Adam Dryden will be dead by sunrise."

Lilith gasped and stood, leaving Jacob alone in the tent. "Where is Bayard? Who are these women?"

"Bayard and the rest are fine. The women are citizens of Peydenal. We cleared the town of Sinead soldiers, only Dryden is left alive, locked in the basement of Bayard's old smithy. When he comes out, they will kill him. I must go back quickly, or I'll miss my own chance at him. How are you doing in there, Jacob?"

"Better than ever," Jacob moaned.

"Glad to see you admit you were always useless," Gendrina replied with a grin that went unseen by Jacob. "You just rest, we will be back soon with Adam's head." She turned to the four Peydenal women. "If any of you are hurt, talk to Lilith here, she will help you. Otherwise, get some food and water and try to sleep." They all nodded, thanking her, and Gendrina spun and sprinted back into the trees.

*****

"How long do you think he's going to stay in there?" Thomas growled.

"I had dozens of blades in there when I left," Bayard explained. "If he's sharpening all of them, it could be-" There was a massive crash and the sound of breaking glass from a second floor window of the potter's shop. Bayard jumped and turned, seeing a heavy wooden chair smash on the ground below the window. Pierre stood in the window frame, breathing heavily and glaring at them.

"Thanks for letting me out, you bastards," he shouted down at them. He vaulted out of the window and landed with a roll, stumbling to his feet. Muffled yelling could be heard from the window above him. "How long have you all been out here?"

Bayard clapped a hand on Pierre's shoulder and gave him a shake. "I apologize, friend. We are sort of on the attacking side of a miniature siege here, Adam Dryden is in there," he said, pointing at the cellar door set in the ground in front of them. "Didn't send anyone after you because we couldn't chance him coming out while we were down a man."

"Aye, the cloaked bastard who captured me," Pierre spat. "I've never been so humiliated. You or that witch wife of yours had better have some good pain medicine back at camp, I had to dislocate my arm to get out of the ropes he tied me up in." He turned, displaying a limp right arm.

"I can fix that," Bayard said, quickly grabbing for Pierre's arm and wrenching it up with great force.

"FUCK, WARN ME," Pierre shouted, shaking out the arm. "Gah, just give me a weapon so I can have a go at him." Uriel drew his shortsword and handed it to Pierre.

"What about the other civilians? They're in there too, yes?" Helmet asked.

"Yes, tied up like me," Pierre confirmed. "It would have taken hours to get them out with no blade, and we were locked in, so I just jumped down here."

"Pierre!" Gendrina had come back, jogging from the treeline and joining the group. "This makes six. Adam doesn't stand a chance."

"Again, do not underestimate him," Bayard warned the lot of them. "Gen, the moment he appears, put an arrow in him."

"I'm not underestimating him," Gendrina whispered, tightening her grip on the bow. "Just no point in fighting on if you can't enjoy it." She grinned at Thomas. "It's funny seeing you with two arms again."

Thomas glanced down and smiled. "Guess I haven't thought about it like that." The left sleeve and gauntlet of the stolen guard armor hung at his side, creating the convincing illusion of his arm having regrown. He bounced on the balls of his feet and it flapped uselessly, making Uriel chuckle uncharacteristically. Their banter was then interrupted by a loud, metallic thud.

The six of them immediately tensed up, raising their weapons and staring at the thick cellar door. It creaked open, and the assassin strode up the stairs wearing the signature flowing black cloak, smoke rising from the black mask, carrying a smooth steel longsword. Upon reaching the surface, he stopped and tilted his head, staring towards the dark tavern. Gendrina released her arrow. Impossibly, he heard the bow string or *sensed* the danger, and he threw himself forwards, the arrow slamming into his left shoulder right where his neck had been less than a second ago. It shattered against the steel armor under the cloak, but he stumbled and gasped as the group charged at him.

He recovered quickly, sprinting forwards to create distance, then spun and raised his blade above his head just as Thomas crashed into him, taking him to the floor. Adam Dryden kicked and punched at Thomas as he tried to lock in a chokehold, forcing his way free but suffering a kick to the ribs from Pierre, between the front and back plates of his armor. Thomas leaned forwards and grabbed the cloak, trying to hold him in place, but Adam stood and pulled back, the cloak and mask falling to the ground. He stumbled backwards, slashing at Gendrina, who blocked the strike with her bow. The weapon fell in two pieces, and she jumped back as Uriel thrust in with his spear. Adam sidestepped and danced out of range, his blade held up defensively.

"Stop..." Uriel paused at the voice, originating from Thomas. "It's impossible. This is *not possible.*"

Gendrina stared madly at him, then turned back to their enemy.

She looked him over and froze, her own eyes growing wide.

It was Pierre who noticed next, his face contorting into pure rage. "You fucking *animal.*"

"What's *wrong* with all of you," Bayard hissed, his sword still raised towards Adam.

Thomas shook his head at the assassin, his face a painting of absolute, utter disbelief. "All this time?"

"You can't choke somebody with one arm, Tom," Garret said. "I taught you better than that."

Chapter Nineteen
Autumn of 1513 A.D
Village of Peydenal
Early Morning

"Are my siblings dead?" Adam asked, looking to Thomas.

"Slaughtered like animals," Gendrina answered for him. "I still remember what your brother's skull sounded like as I crushed it in a door."

Adam just nodded. "And I assume Drake and Christopher Alento are dead as well, or they would be here with you. Does the Princess still live?"

"She is dead," Thomas said quickly. "She was bitten as we tried to escape Valdus."

"That is funny," Adam chuckled, "since one of my scouts saw her and your sister having a bit of a row in the woods the day before yesterday."

"We did not know she was bitten yet," Bayard interjected. "She hid the bite, we were not aware until she began getting sick late at night. We had no choice but to put her down then."

"That's even funnier, because I was told she was wearing thick leather armor," Adam said. "No Princess would know how to get armor on without help, so whoever did help her would have seen the bite, no? And once it was on, she could not have been bitten anywhere besides her face, no? And that would be pretty obvious. See, I think that the Princess is sleeping peacefully at your camp, waiting for my dagger to end the Alento bloodline."

"Stop this, Garret," Thomas spat. "You were a soldier of Valdus. Whatever Drake Alento did to your family, it has nothing to do with Jenara, it has nothing to do with you."

"My name is Adam Dryden," he whispered at Thomas. "And it has everything to do with me. I took an oath when I joined the Fogwalkers. Either my target dies, or I do. This is beyond a personal vendetta."

"THEN YOU DIE," Uriel roared, charging towards Adam with a mighty spear thrust. Adam stood his ground and raised his left hand, catching the spear and dragging it backwards, forcing Uriel to one knee. Thomas and Pierre ran in and tried to force Adam away from Uriel, but Adam jumped sideways, tearing the spear from Uriel's hand. He swung the heavy polearm into Thomas's ribs, and he toppled over, taking Pierre with him. Helmet ran in, swinging his axe towards Adam's neck, but Adam dropped to the floor and rolled backwards, landing a powerful upwards kick into Helmet's knee. Helmet toppled and Adam scrambled to a kneel, slashing his sword across Helmet's shoulder and bicep as he fell. Uriel, now unarmed, slammed his heavy leather boot into Adam's back, but Adam just rolled with it and stood, spinning around and trusting the spear through the armor gap at Uriel's thigh. Uriel shouted and crashed into the ground hard, and Adam raised the spear above his head. Gendrina, armed with nothing but a broken bow, dove forwards and grabbed Adam's arm, pulling the spear away from Uriel. Adam tore his arm free and slammed the spear shaft against Gendrina's left arm with a sickening crack. She screamed and fell sideways, grasping her arm.

Adam spun the spear and kicked Uriel into the dirt, then turned and looked to Bayard. "My brothers were far older than I am. They had both suffered from famine and disease growing up, but not me. I am at my peak. I am what a Fogwalker truly is. If you insist on fighting me here, at least three of you will die before you take me down. You are all experienced fighters, you can tell that I speak the truth. I will make you this one offer: Leave now, and you will all survive this encounter. Or fight me, lose half of your best warriors, but defeat one insignificant nemesis. Of course, I cannot leave this land until Jenara is dead, but that battle can take place at another time, with less casualties for you."

"Kill him, Bayard," Uriel coughed. "Everyone here is prepared to fight and die on your orders. Jenara must live."

Bayard stared at Adam, then at the others who circled the assassin, all injured and most bleeding. "You may be prepared to die on my orders, but I am not prepared to order you to die."

Adam Dryden grinned and lowered his spear. "You are making the right choice."

"LET ME FINISH!" Bayard roared, stepping towards Adam. "I am not prepared to order them to die, because I trust them more than that. Not one of them would die to someone like you. My men have battled death itself. We defeated an army of five hundred warriors while wielding gardening tools. This woman killed your brother with her bare hands. I don't know who you think we are, but I can assure you, you will meet your death at the edge of one of our blades."

"Then try it," Adam hissed, thrusting the tip of his longsword towards Uriel's neck. The old knight shouted and rolled, grasping the blade of the longsword in both of his hands. Blood poured down the blade and onto his armor as Adam pushed, and Uriel forced the blade aside and it slid through the gap of his armor into his left shoulder. Reaching up, Uriel grasped the handguard and pulled it down, forcing the blade out the back of his body and into the ground. Adam screamed and pulled and kicked and battered Uriel with the tip of his spear, unable to find his way through Uriel's armor.

Uriel would not release the sword, holding it in place as Helmet appeared behind Adam, blood pouring from his shoulder, and he took a mighty swing with his wood axe. Adam shouted and released the sword, dodging forwards. He was too late as the axe sunk straight through the plate armor and into Adam's shoulder blade. Uriel was on his feet in a second, grabbing the shaft of the axe with his right hand and forcing Adam to his knees. Thomas stepped forwards, raising the tip of his shortsword to Adam's throat.

"Enough," Adam choked. "You have me beaten. Take me as your prisoner. I will-" Thomas shoved the blade through Adam's neck and watched the life leave his eyes.

*****

"Who was he?" Bayard asked Thomas as he knelt over the body of the assassin.

"He trained me and Jacob," Thomas whispered. "He was one of my best friends growing up. I once tried to marry Gen off to him."

"It was all a cover," Bayard said. "As a guard, he could always know what defenses the city had, how many guards, how many knights. He probably planned to become a castle guard eventually, where he would have had a clean stab at the royalty as they slept."

"Aye," Thomas agreed. "I cannot see him this way, let's free the civilians and get back to camp." He stood and walked over to Adam's ragged cloak, wrapping the mask up in it and stashing it in his shirt.

Bayard was at the door of the potter's shop, peering into one of the windows. Helmet stepped up and leaned forwards, preparing to kick the door in, but Bayard waved him down. "Look here," Bayard said, feeling the top of the window frame and pulling down a long iron key. "Years ago, he had me forge a spare and put it up here so I could deliver tools to him while he was traveling to Valdus. He completely forgot about it by the time he got back." Bayard unlocked the door and it creaked open. He stepped into the dark room and glanced around, spotting the staircase at the end of the hall. "Helmet, Uriel, Gendrina, you three go back to camp and have Lilith treat your injuries. Thomas, stay here and watch the door. Pierre, with me."

"I'm fine," Helmet, Uriel, and Gendrina chimed in unison. Uriel still had Adam's longsword in his shoulder. Bayard sighed.

"You know I do not like pulling rank, but *go back to camp* before you all bleed to death."

"I'm not even bleeding," Gendrina argued.

"Your arm is wrecked, Gen," Thomas said. "Unless you want to end up like me, get to Lilith quickly." That was enough motivation for Gendrina to pull the door back open and follow Uriel and Helmet outside.

"Let's be quick now," Bayard said, jogging through the hall and up the stairs. Turning the corner of the upstairs hallway, he saw a blockade of furniture barricading a door at the end of the hall. He and Pierre quickly removed the various wardrobes and chairs, and Pierre pushed the door open. They were instantly greeted with muffled groans and shouts. Fifteen people were tied in various spots around the room, mostly adult men but some elderly women as well. Far too few to be the whole town. Bayard spotted the potter, George Crane, and pulled his gag out.

The bearded man coughed and spat, shaking his head. "Bayard, is that you? What the hell has happened out there?"

"You are all free," Bayard said. "We have killed the Sinead men and their leader, saved your daughters and the other women in the tavern, and we will bring you all to our camp. Pierre, cut them loose. Where is everyone else though?"

"Dead," George whispered, staring at the floor. "Anyone who resisted had their throats cut."

Bayard cursed and slammed his fist on a nearby wall. "Damn them. We have bigger problems than some twenty year old vendetta between dead kings."

"What?" George gasped. "The King is dead?"

"Yes," Bayard confirmed. "Christopher became King for about three months, but he is certainly dead as well. Do you know of the plague?"

"Indeed. Saw the plague bars down myself two months ago. I rode to other towns to warn them, guards were posted on roads, nobody has been near Valdus for at least six weeks."

"That is good, but not what I mean. Do you know what the plague does to people?"

"I don't know, it kills them? What else would a plague do?"

"I'll explain back at camp," Bayard said. "Follow-"

"Bayard?" An excited voice rose up from the corner of the room where Pierre was cutting out a small dark-skinned boy of around fourteen. "You, Bayard!"

Bayard turned away from George and walked to the young man. "Do I know you?" Bayard asked. He looked familiar, his dark, long hair covering hard eyes and a long nose.

The boy shook his head. He ran past Bayard, to a pile of clothing and rucksacks, and picked up a ratty leather bag. He dug inside and pulled out a square, wooden box, about a foot tall and wide. "Read," he said, shoving the box into Bayard's hands.

Bayard turned back to George. "Who is this boy?" he asked.

"Damned if I know," George said. "He showed up two weeks ago with a drawing of you, but he can't speak right. I would have pointed him towards Valdus, but obviously I couldn't let him go. He stayed in the tavern since then, he seemed to have no problems paying for food, drink, and bed." Bayard furrowed his brow and stared at the box. It was shut with a brass latch and had foreign writing inscribed down the cover.

"This is Arabic," Bayard whispered. He pulled the latch open and lifted the cover, revealing two pieces of folded parchment. He opened the first to find an exceptionally well-drawn portrait of himself, although the likeness matched Bayard's appearance from ten years ago. His curiosity growing quickly, he opened the second parchment. The English writing jumped out at him, and he began to read.

Bayard Travers,
My name is Albert Hesen. Praying that Sefu Najjar successfully completed his journey, I am sure he told you about me. The boy who

gave you this letter is Sefu Almasi, the first son born to Sefu Najjar's mother to her second husband. Sefu Najjar spoke much of you and your fame in England, so I figured Sefu Almasi would have an easier time finding you than his brother. I send Sefu in my stead, because as I write this, I am infected with the Demon's plague. One week ago, from September the Eighth, a new member to our community found one of the plague flowers underneath a stone. Ignorant of its effects, he picked it up and showed it to me, surprised that a flower would be found there. He was immediately locked up, but in a panic he killed the man we posted to guard him, stole a horse, and rode into the desert. We searched for days, but soon we began encountering dead men wandering the sands. I was bitten hours before I began writing this, and I do not have much time left before I start getting sick. To Sefu Najjar, I am sure your brother told you already, but in case you disbelieve: Your family is gone. The whole town was overrun with infected, I saw it with my own eyes. Almasi escaped on foot and came to us, but we could not help your town. That is where I was bitten. I am sorry for all of this, I am sorry for your family, I am sorry for your home. I have given your brother enough gold to last a lifetime, as well as the instructions needed to reach Valdus. Egypt is falling, the infection spreads quickly across the desert, and the dead do not need water and shelter. Do not come home. Goodbye.

Bayard looked up at the boy, remembering the Sefu of fifteen years ago. Make him taller, add muscle, remove a foot and a half of hair, and it was obvious. "Sefu," Bayard whispered.

The boy nodded. "Where Sefu Najjar?" he asked.

Bayard had no idea how to communicate with the boy. He could only look at his feet and shake his head. Sefu Almasi understood. He dropped the bag and screamed in anguish, throwing a chair across the room and beating his fist on the nearby window sill, cutting his hand on broken glass. Bayard ran forwards and embraced the boy, pulling him away from the window. "It will be alright, Sefu, it's alright. I know the pain, I know the loss. You'll be alright." Bayard's words went unheard by the boy who had lost everyone. Bayard turned to Pierre. "Lead the civilians down into my smithy, along with Thomas. Gather everything you all can carry. I will be down soon."

Pierre nodded and turned, waving at the citizens of Peydenal to follow him.

*****

Pierre led the group back outside and to the ruins of Bayard's smithy, pulling open the heavy door. "Thomas, come." He went down the stairs and smiled at the sight in front of him. Dozens of swords, axes, hammers, and daggers littered the room, almost all of which had just been sharpened to perfection. There were also five chainmail shirts and coifs, and a dozen chestplates stacked up on a chair, as well as various unorganized boots, greave plates, and gauntlets scattered around the forge.

"Thanks for the parting gift, Garret," Thomas mumbled, lifting a hand-and-a-half sword out in front of him and thumbing the edge. "What was Bayard doing making all of these weapons? Helmet and the castle smith supplied Valdus, where were these going?"

"To Haarn," Bayard answered, stepping down the stairs with the dark-skinned boy trailing behind him, his face blank and his gaze unfocused. "Their barracks was located on the waterfront. I received a letter saying the storm last spring had destroyed a garrison's worth of arms and armor, and an order was placed for enough to equip twenty men. Another letter came two days before this all started saying that they bought what they needed from a trade ship. I was out two hundred gold pieces, I was furious, but obviously it never mattered." They ran the equipment up the stairs and loaded up every citizen with as much as they could carry, and began their trek through the trees.

*****

"They're coming!" Lyanna called, pointing into the treeline as Helmet appeared, dressed in dirty cobbled-together armor and soaked with blood. Lilith stood and ran towards him as Gendrina stepped out behind him, followed by Uriel, who had a sword through his shoulder.

"Uriel, what in the- wait, where is Bayard?"

"He is fine, Lilith," Gendrina said. "He's freeing the civilians and then they will come here. He made us leave so you could treat our injuries. Thomas and Pierre are with him."

"Good," Lilith mumbled. "Come into the tent, and Uriel, move carefully please..."

Two hours later, Gendrina and Helmet were both wearing makeshift slings, while Uriel resembled an Egyptian mummy. "Where is Bayard? I am getting very worried," Lilith hissed. "Gendrina, you are the least injured here, will you come with me to find him?"

"Soon," Gendrina said. "It is an hours walk at a regular pace, and the three of them are wearing armor and leading civilians who may be starved or injured. If they do not arrive by the sun's first light, we'll go."

"Fine then," Lilith agreed with a panicked tone that betrayed her relaxed gaze. An hour later, Lilith was already standing at the forest's edge as Pierre emerged from a thick row of pines, and she finally exhaled as Bayard followed him into sight along with numerous civilians. All of them were carrying piles of swords and other weapons, and wore various pieces of armor. Bayard was leading a small, dark man by the shoulder. He stopped and kissed Lilith, then Thomas barged in between them, shoving a dented Fogwalker mask into her arms.

"You look like you've been worrying," Thomas said. "Adam Dryden is dead. Your husband is a true warrior and knight. With these weapons, and with Bayard back in his forge along with Helmet, with Uriel here to train us, Sinead will fall to him the same way."

"No," Bayard said. "The destruction of Sinead will do nothing but weaken England as a whole. For now, we must recover, we must strengthen our defenses, we must gather and preserve food for the winter. For generations, the leaders of Valdus and Sinead have been at each others throats, and it will end with me."

One Month Later

Kerren the Squire jogged up the long staircase, struggling with the weight of the heavy steel scrollbox. Upon reaching the top, he paused and stared out over the expansive, bustling city of Sinead. Women jogged about with armfuls of cloth and smoked meat, men ran logs and crates through the streets, news criers stood on corners, shouting the latest important information. Looking the other way, Kerren stared up at the mountain range that loomed over Sinead, the ever-present symbol of the north. He turned away and pounded on the large wooden door to the King's bedchambers. There was no response. He knocked again, hard enough to hurt his knuckles. Again he was met with silence, so he grasped the iron handle and pushed the door open.

Upon walking in, he found King Alvor the Second, along with his wife Queen Gillian, engaged in a very energetic activity. King Alvor spotted him and gasped, throwing the Queen aside and tossing his blanket over her. "Damn you, Kerren, I should have had you beheaded by now," Alvor roared. "My father would have."

"I suppose I am fortunate that you are not your father, then," Kerren droned. "If you do not wish me to see your wife's effects, answer the bloody door when someone knocks on it."

Alvor growled and tore the scrollbox away from Kerren, pushing him backwards. "It isn't my fault that Barric burst my ear in training," Alvor complained, rubbing the lumpy flesh that used to be his left ear.

"Actually, Sire," Kerren said, "If you had blocked his attack, it would not have happened. Or if you did not spar full-speed to begin with."

Alvor was fuming now. "Get out of here before I behead you with my fucking teeth!" he shouted, pointing towards the door. Kerren gave an overly graceful bow and turned, making for the door.

"Wait," Alvor groaned. "I need you to copy this scroll for the records, you know that. Just get a quill, sit down, and write what I read."

"Maybe you would like me to give the Queen a moment to dress?" Kerren suggested.

"Oh, forget her," Alvor mumbled as he fiddled with the lock on the scrollbox. Queen Gillian let out a huff and stood, striding across the room and hiding herself behind the dressing doors. Kerren settled behind a desk with quill and ink in hand as Alvor finally managed to open the scrollbox. He removed the length of parchment, and began to read slowly.

"To my King Alvor the Second, Son of King Alvor the Wolf, King of Sinead, I regret to report that Adam Dryden is dead. His body was found hung from the rafters of the stables at Peydenal. The scout who found him was run from the town by a group of knights who we believe to be survivors from the fall of Valdus. There are at least thirty knights stationed there as I write this. A makeshift barrier has been constructed around the town, dozens of plague victims bound to trees surrounding Peydenal. They begin moaning if a human or plaguewalker approaches the town, forming a sort of self-ringing alarm bell. An assassination attempt is impossible, even for the Fogwalkers, and more infected are added to their system every day. Scouts also report a group of plaguewalkers numbering in the hundreds slowly moving north, and unless they alter their path, they might reach our outlying villages in as little as a week. As you well know, a majority of our combatants fell in your father's attack on Valdus four months ago, and no civilians will voluntarily fight with winter fast approaching. I suggest a draft, arm every man who can hold a sword before the heavy snows start to fall, and dispatch them to deal with the infected with strict instructions to behead anyone who is bitten. Christopher Alento is proving to be a startlingly competent leader, and it would be wise to fear an attack on our own city or surrounding towns as they attempt to seek shelter and defense against the increasing number of infected. As your war adviser, I believe that it may be in your best interests to bolster the defenses of Sinead, and wait for winter's end to continue your conquests in the south after securing our own lands.
-Barric Eathellen, General of Sinead."

Alvor waited a short while as Kerren finished his writing, then took the parchment and looked it over. "Good job, Kerren. You may botch up half the things you do, but nobody can fault you for your handwriting. Get this to the library with haste and put it in the records with your own hands, do not let anyone see it. If our citizens learn of the plague approaching, they will panic. On your way down, speak to the castle smith, tell him I want as many hawk axes as he can produce in five days, and tell the town smith the same thing. What was his name? Sjarmir, yes? The castle smith knows his place, but tell Sjarmir that he will be paid one gold piece for each axe he produces. It is a hefty fee for some wood and iron, but we do need them fast. Then return here to write up some draft notices. That is all, now go." Kerren gave another bow and turned away, retreating from the chamber.

Kerren breathed in the fresh air, turned for the stairs, and immediately crashed face-first into the broad chest of Barric Eathellen. Kerren stumbled back and sputtered, staring indignantly at the large bald man. "Barric? What the hell are you doing up here after you made me run that scrollbox all through the city?"

"I am sorry, Kerren," Barric said gruffly. "However, I specifically remember giving you that message *last night*."

"Squires need sleep too, Sir," Kerren complained. "I am on my way to deliver the King's orders and bring the message to the library. Really though, what brings you here?"

Barric glanced around, looking uncomfortable. "Five knights arrived at the gates early this morning, flying the sigil of Valdus. They seek an audience with the King. We have them under guard at the barracks, but we do not want to do anything without notifying the King."

"Five knights? Are you sure they do not have more nearby, in hiding?" Kerren asked.

"My men searched up and down the road, in all the known caves, and all around the outer walls. The five are all that are here for at least ten kilometers." Barric looked over the city, out towards the gates. "Why now? They must know that an attacking siege with winter on its way is certain death for them."

"Their King Christopher has outsmarted us at every turn. Whatever they are plotting, it is not as crude as a siege. Go in and see the King, I will wait here for any new instructions. I pray this is not the beginning of open war."

*****

"Bayard, this may be the worst idea you've ever had," Uriel mumbled from his bench in the emptied armory that they were captive in. "The Kings of Sinead are not known for forgiveness and mercy. You underestimate them, we will be executed for this." He tugged at the neck of his thick robe, glancing around the room uncomfortably. "I know this was my idea at first, but that was before we slaughtered their men at Peydenal."

"You are the one who underestimates them, my friend," Bayard said. "Kingdoms always tend to think down on their rivals. You think Sinead stupid and barbaric, they think us weak and greedy. The truth is, we are not so different. The Drydens invaded our home and burned our citizens alive, but only after King Drake did the same to them. We slaughtered their soldiers in the night, but only after they murdered our citizens and took our town. It is an endless cycle of retaliation that never should have had a beginning. I have no desire for vengeance, I have no religious convictions, I have no hatred for their King. If anyone will be able to end this reasonless war before it truly begins, it is me."

"I think Uriel is right," Gendrina whispered. "The northmen are an angry, vengeful people. You may have won over Valdus with your words, but Sinead will only respond to strength."

"Trust him, Gen," Jacob said. "If not for Bayard, every one of us would be long dead. He knows what he is doing."

"I trust Bayard with my life. It is the northerners that I cannot trust."

"They are born and bred warriors," Thomas said. "They will know a good leader and a strong man when they see one. We know nothing of their new King, and if Christopher is anything to go by, sons are not always as unreasonable as their fathers. We are here now, no use arguing about it at this point."

"We should have backup," Uriel complained. "People in hiding outside the walls with spare weapons. If they decide to kill us, we have no way to defend ourselves, no way to get a message out."

"We won't need to," Bayard said. "I'm sure they sent scouts out to check for just that. We are here to negotiate, nothing more. Winter approaches, and they know that our deaths would lead straight to war. Nobody wants to fight in the winter." The group sat in silence for a long while, and then Bayard looked up as he heard the *thud* of a wooden bar lock hitting the ground nearby. Footsteps approached the armory quickly, another *thud,* and the thick iron door creaked open. There stood three men, the one on the left tall and bald, the middle wore ornate, shining chainmail and had his beard and hair to his chest, and on the right a short, thin man with a book and pen in his arms. Bayard stood and smoothed out his robe, taking a powerful posture as he focused on the man in the middle.

The man on the right stepped forward, and began shouting at an unnecessary volume for the small room. "I bring you King Alvor the Second! Son of King Alvor the-"

"Wolf," Bayard interrupted. "I know who you are, and I know your father. There is no need for the formal introductions."

"And you are certainly King Christopher Alento," Alvor growled at Bayard. "We were concerned about your leadership, but if you walked to your death like this, I can see that Barric was mistaken," he finished, nudging the bald man with his elbow.

"You are the mistaken one," Bayard said. "My name is Bayard. Christopher was killed by Tory Dryden over four months ago. I have been leading the forces of Valdus since then."

Alvor squinted. "You are the Knight Commander, then? Which of the Noble Families are you from?"

"That is the title that Christopher bestowed me with some of his last words," Bayard explained. "However, it means nothing to me. When I earned the loyalty of his men and the citizens of Valdus, I was simply a doctor and a blacksmith. I am of the Travers family, of no noble blood. I got where I am with my head and my sword arm, nothing more."

"It was *you,*" Alvor hissed. "You are the one who defeated our attack on Valdus, you are the one who slaughtered my men in Peydenal, you are the one who killed the Drydens. You are the one who killed my fath-"

"Your father," Bayard interrupted again, "attempted to sack a defenseless, plague-riddled city. He attacked without honor, like an assassin from the shadows, no better than the Fogwalkers. That is not how a King should do battle. The fact that my companions and I are not currently burning on stakes already proves that you are better than he was."

"How did he die?" Alvor asked suddenly, clenching his fists and breathing heavily.

"It was a glorious battle," Bayard lied. "Me and your father were some of the last warriors left on the battlefield. He wielded an axe, I wielded a sword that I took from the body of one of your men after my own had been broken. We fought for a long time before I split the shaft of his axe. I allowed him to draw his sword and we fought on still, but in the end it was I who put my blade through him."

Alvor stood silently, staring at Bayard, seemingly in an attempt to figure out his motivations. *Why are you here?"* he finally asked, giving up on his own analysis. "Why would you walk, unarmed and without an army, into the city of your enemy?"

"It is because I do not want to see you as an enemy," Bayard whispered. "For generations, your ancestors have warred with Valdus, and Valdus has always fought back. You've killed our Kings, we've killed your Kings, you've taken our land, we've taken your land. It is endless, and it is so *stupid.* You know the walking death spreads within England, and I can promise you that it is not contained on this continent. We battle each other when the real enemy wanders the Earth, consuming everything. I come here to make peace with you, to join our forces in defense against the plague."

Alvor blinked at him. "Are you serious? You've killed my father, hundreds of my best men, and you come to me seeking peace?"

"IT'S OVER!" Bayard roared, advancing on the King of Sinead. "I killed your father, I stabbed him through the heart because he actively tried to kill the people that I love. It is for the sake of those who have fallen, and for the sake of those yet to be born into this world, that we must throw away our grievances and *wipe out this plague.* You have won the war, Alvor. King Drake and his son both lay dead by the hands of your assassins. The only living Alento blood rests in the body of a fifteen year old girl, and she should mean nothing to you. Valdus has always seen your family as unreasonable and barbaric, and it can be you who proves all of us wrong. Be better than the men who came before you. Let us join under your banner, let us lend you our strength, and together we will protect England from the plague and unite the Kingdoms under one name. This is bigger than a vendetta, this is bigger than a war. I am not asking you to join us. I am asking you to allow us to join you."

"Bayard," Uriel hissed, glaring at Alvor.

"Silence, Uriel," Bayard warned. "You will accept whatever happens here." Uriel closed his eyes and leaned back against the stone wall.

Alvor stepped forwards, nose to nose with Bayard. "How do I even know you speak the truth? You might have no skill at all, no ability to lead. Your King Christopher could be alive and waiting to besiege us, planning every move of this. You are no one."

Bayard stood taller, almost a half foot above Alvor. "You cannot know," he whispered to Alvor. "Everything I said here could be a complete lie, and you would never know. However, you should be smart enough to understand that it *does not matter.* Within weeks, your people will begin to starve and freeze, unable to gather food and firewood due to the plaguewalkers that surround Sinead." Bayard saw Alvor tense. The bearded King slowly shifted his weight onto his right foot, clenching his fist. Bayard's breathing hastened and he loosened his own knees in preparation. "Despite everything, you know *that* is the truth."

"Leave us, Barric." Alvor whispered, glancing back at the bald man. "You too, Kerren."

"My King, you cannot-"

"I said *leave us,"* Alvor hissed, pushing Barric away. The two men gave quick bows and retreated from the armory.

Bayard exhaled slowly. "Jacob, Thomas, you two are the most level-headed here. Make sure Uriel and Gen do nothing to interrupt us."

"What are you-" Jacob started, when Alvor stepped in with a fast, powerful punch towards Bayard's temple. Bayard raised his left arm and absorbed the blow, retaliating with an uppercut that Alvor barely dodged. Bayard pushed his weight forwards and redirected the uppercut into a downwards strike with his elbow, crashing into Alvor's shoulder. The King coughed and stumbled, but quickly found his footing and threw a front kick to Bayard's thigh. Bayard lifted his leg and met the kick halfway, reducing the impact, before twisting his waist and slamming into Alvor's gut with a side kick. Alvor reached out, grasping for the empty weapon racks, but ended up on his back. Bayard was on top of him quickly, landing two fast jabs on Alvor's chin before Alvor managed to pull his legs inward and kick Bayard across the room.

Bayard hit the wall and somehow managed to stay standing, but toppled over a bench as Alvor tackled him. Letting out a gasp as his knee slammed into the stone floor, Bayard threw his arm out, landing a mighty backhand against Alvor's chest. Coughing, Alvor stood and stepped back, and Bayard rolled over, grabbing Alvor's leg and forcing him back to the ground. Still grasping Alvor's leg, Bayard scrambled around and jumped in, smashing his knee against Alvor's ribs, and the King went limp.

Bayard stood, breathing heavily and holding his shoulder. "Are you done?" he asked Alvor, who was clutching his side and squeezing his eyes shut.

"Aye," Alvor moaned through gritted teeth. "I'm done. You are no stooge for a craven King."

"You are young, Alvor," Bayard said. "Eighteen? Nineteen, maybe? You have been trained well, you command strong men, but you have no experience. Accept the aid we offer and become a stronger Kingdom than Sinead has ever been before. You royalty like titles. I am Knight Commander Bayard Travers of the Knights of Life. I took an oath to Christopher, minutes before he died. *'As of this moment, I am a Knight of Life. Through war, hunger, thirst, and sickness, I protect the living until the day of my own death, wherever I may travel. My sole duty is to slay every dead man who crosses my path. I no longer serve a Kingdom, I no longer serve a faith, but I serve a higher duty. I am the life that refuses death, and my blade is the cure for those who walk with empty eyes. I accept my calling to live by this code, and I will only stop when all that walks is living. This is now the road before me, and I will follow it to the end."*
Bayard stepped forwards and bent down, holding his hand out to Alvor. One eye still closed, a grimace of pain plastered across his face, Alvor pushed it away and stumbled to his feet.

"How am I supposed to trust you?" Alvor said, looking to Bayard's companions, all of whom were standing and ready for combat. "Every time we've made peace with Valdus, you are the ones who broke the treaty. What will stop you from cutting my throat as I sleep should I allow you into my city?"

"You want the hard truth, King of Sinead?" Bayard asked, looking solemnly at Alvor.

"Yes. Say what you will."

"I simply do not care enough about you to betray you," Bayard stated. Alvor blinked and opened his mouth, but Bayard held up his hand. "My men have all accepted the past, and are willing to accept a new future in which we are friends. My companions may seem hostile, but they just want to protect me. I say one more time, will you be better than your father, will you allow us to join you against the walking death?" Bayard held out his hand once more, looking down into Alvor's eyes.

Alvor had nobody to look to, nobody to influence him. His breathing steadied, and finally, he slowly nodded his head. Bayard grinned as Alvor reached out, taking Bayard's hand. "Very well, Bayard Travers. I shall give this alliance a chance."

Chapter Twenty-One
Autumn of 1513 A.D
A shack in the forests of northern England
The Next Day
Midnight

"Dirk approaches now," Mace announced, staring through the ratty curtains that covered the windows of the small wooden shack. Seconds later, the door slid open and Dirk stepped in, snuffing out the burning tobacco in his mask.

"I have important news," Dirk said, tearing off his cloak and tossing it in a heap with the others. "The Drydens are dead. Every one of them, killed by the men of Valdus. However, they succeeded in killing King Drake and his son."

"What is your source?" Saber asked. "Jessica, Edward, and Kane I can accept, but Tory and Adam? They could both bring down an army."

"A message from Barric Eathellen," Dirk explained. "Alvor fell into a truce with survivors from Valdus, he sends orders to cease any attacks towards their citizens, including the bloodline of King Drake."

"We may be friendly with Sinead," Sai whispered from behind her longpipe, "but they do not command us. If they expect us to abandon a contract because of this, they will have a rude awakening."

"No," Saber said quickly, turning a long knife between his fingers. "The Drydens are the ones who submitted the contract, before they even joined us. We would have done the deeds many years ago, but they insisted on killing the Alentos themselves. Now that they are dead, the contract no longer has a client. We have no obligation to fulfill it. We should operate in a different region for a time, let things settle here before we return. The soldiers of Valdus have proven to be our equals in combat, and it would be stupid and arrogant to antagonize them further."

"They killed five of our own," Mace argued. "Will we really let that go?"

Saber tilted his head. "The Drydens joined us. We trained them, fed them, raised them from childhood into assassins. And the whole time, all they did was plot their vengeance on Valdus, and then they died. They did nothing for us. I see no reason to risk more of our lives for their sakes." The rest were quiet, unable to disagree with him. "If Sinead has allied with Valdus, they will no longer make use of our services. Not to mention the spreading plague. It is time we move on from here. We'll pick up camp during the day tomorrow and travel by night. For now, we should-"

"Grrruuuuh." A long moan pierced the walls of their thin shack.

"We have company," Sai said, moving the curtains aside and gazing out into the darkness. "Infected. I have eyes on four of them." She released the curtain and strode across the room, taking a dagger from the weapon rack that lined one of the walls. "Should I take care of them?"

"No," Saber said again. "There are likely many more nearby, and they swarm if you attract their attention. Stay low, snuff the candle, and wait for them to pass." Dirk jabbed the candle out with the tip of his shortsword and ducked below the windows, leaning on the rough wood. The others knelt down, breathing slowly. Short, scattered moans could be heard passing them, and some of them bumped into the shack with a thud. It went on for well over twenty minutes, the numbers far greater than Saber would have thought. Their empty voices rang through the night, the voices of dead men, women, and children, as the Fogwalkers hid in the darkness. Soon, everything was quiet. They waited a few minutes, and Dirk sat up and turned, looking out the window under the curtains.

"It looks clear. Wait, no, there's one still out there. Big guy. He's moving around on the ground, like he broke his leg or something. We should put him down before he attracts... Never mind, he's getting up. Wait, WHAT IS-" The window shattered and a thick, dark arm wrapped itself around Dirk's head. Saber charged forwards and slashed his knife at the infected man's arm, cursing as it glanced off of impossibly hard flesh.

"What is it?" Saber hissed, slashing the knife again to the same useless result.

"Help me," Dirk wheezed. "Help..." It was the last thing he ever got to say as his head was ripped from his neck. Saber jumped back as Dirk's bleeding body collapsed, and for the first time in decades, he felt true fear as the abomination began to climb through the window. Missing its left arm and right leg, with blackened, calloused skin, it crawled over the sill and fell onto the floor over Dirk's body.

It wore dirty pauldrons held on only by the leather straps, the left hanging limp over the missing arm, and greaves that were cut off under the right knee. Writhing on the ground, it released an ear-piercing roar that vibrated the walls of the shack, causing dust and dirt to fall from the ceiling. Then it rolled over, locking its solid white eyes on the three Fogwalkers.

"Run," Saber whispered. Sai turned and sprinted for the door on the other side of the shack, and the monster turned its gaze to her. It sat up and spun around, putting its weight on its one leg, and propelled itself through the air. It crashed into her and slammed into the shack wall, opening its mouth impossibly wide to reveal cracked, elongated teeth. And then it bit into her arm, ripping and tearing at her as Saber and Mace dove out of the broken window, her screams chasing them through the darkness.

Dodging trees and roots, they sprinted through the forest. "How... How did it get like that?" Mace panted as they ran. "They're slow, soft, what happen-" Mace fell silent as the earth-shaking roar shattered the air behind him. He felt the impact and hit the ground, and for a split second he felt the teeth sinking into his back before his spine was broken in half. Saber picked up his pace, hurtling through the woods at his maximum speed, throwing himself over fallen trees and tangled roots.

Sinead, I can make it to Sinead. They'll imprison me, they might execute me, but it is better than this, Saber thought desperately. He somehow pushed himself even faster as he heard the scream of the Hellbeast closing in on him. He couldn't help himself, he glanced behind him and he saw it, eyes glowing white in the darkness, charging towards him in a crouched run, bounding through the air on its one leg and pulling itself along with its one arm. It was too fast, it was too bloodthirsty. With one last mighty leap, the monster landed on Saber and tore him limb from limb.

*****

"Have you *really* never had a drink?" Lilith asked incredulously as Jenara stared curiously into her tankard.

"Father would never let me," she explained. "And I was never the sort to sneak around. By the time this all happened, I had sort of stopped caring."

"Drrriiiink!" Jacob cheered over his own pint of mead as he slammed it down on the table. "See what happens."

Jenara shrugged and threw back the mug, performing a decent imitation of Jacob's tankard-slam. She frowned and held it in for a moment, and then opened her mouth with a "muuhh", the drink spilling out and down the front of her dress. The whole table erupted into laughter, drawing looks from the others in the mead hall. "I'm sorry, I'm so sorry, I didn't mean-"

"It's okay, Jen," Gendrina chortled, throwing an arm around the girl. "I vomited my first time, so you have me beat."

"Why would anybody drink *that*," Jenara groaned, angrily eying the tankard of mead as though she had caught it watching her undress.

"While a lot of it tastes good," Gendrina said, "the point of it isn't the flavor. It's about the way it makes you feel after you drink a lot. All warm and wobbly, kind of stupid but pretty fun, too. Forget the mead, try some wine, here." She reached across the table and pulled over a pitcher of white wine, pouring some in her empty tankard and handing it to Jenara.

"I don't want to," Jenara complained.

"Oh, go on. It's completely different," Thomas said.

Jenara sighed and took a small sip of the light drink. She set the tankard down and swallowed, a small grin on her face.

"See? Much better," Gendrina chirped. Jenara nodded and took a longer sip, her face reddening slowly.

"All of you," Bayard called from the next table over. "Come over here. And someone get Helmet." Gendrina took her arm off Jenara and stood, sliding her chair in. She looked around and spotted Helmet, the tallest man in the massive room, in deep conversation with Florin Gaige, the castle's blacksmith. She twisted and turned her way through the many chairs and party-goers, gracefully dodging around serving girls and drunken stumblers until she reached the pair of smiths.

"Oy, Helmet. Bayard wants us," Gendrina shouted over the din.

"But he's tellin' me about his technique for foldin' purified-"

"Helmet..."

Helmet sighed. "Aye, fine." He turned back to Florin. "I'll meet yeh in your forge tomorrow, we have a lot to discuss." The smaller, equally bearded man nodded, looking tired, and went back to his drink. Helmet turned and went after Gendrina, ungracefully barreling through serving girls and drunken stumblers until he reached Bayard's table. "What's goin' on?" Helmet asked, pulling up a chair and shoving his way between Pierre and Jenara. "And when's our food coming? Everyone else is feasting away and we're stuck here drinking on empty stomachs."

"That's the thing," Bayard said. "A squire just came to me and told me that everyone in my, and I quote, 'Inner Circle' is to dine with the King tonight."

"Why is Alvor not attending the feast?" Uriel asked.

"Don't know," Bayard conceded. "We should get up there though, it is probably important."

"Should we get Sefu?" Jacob asked, glancing towards the stairs that led to their temporary lodgings.

"No," Bayard said sadly. "He is getting better by the day, but he is in no shape for politics, and it would be wise to keep him out of our dealings until his English improves." Bayard sighed and chugged the remainder of his mead. They stood and pulled on their coats and cloaks and Bayard started leading the way to the King's chambers, before realizing that he had no clue where the King's chambers were. "Erm..."

"Bayard Travers?" a high voice asked from behind him. Bayard turned to see the short, tired-looking man who had been there the morning the alliance was formed. "I am Kerren, one of King Alvor's squires. Please follow me." Bayard shrugged and started after the small man, following him out of the mead hall and into the open air. They walked through the cold streets, empty aside from a pair of goats in a nearby pen and a drunken couple giggling happily and cuddling in a bale of hay. They walked out of the castle gate and followed Kerren down numerous streets and torchlit alleys, when Bayard reached out to stop the squire.

"Excuse me, Kerren, but where are we going? Does the King not dine in his chambers?"

Kerren turned and glanced around suspiciously, looking into the dark windows of nearby homes. He pulled Bayard closer and whispered into his ear. "We are going to meet the King in the barracks, but you will not be dining. He needs your help." Bayard fell silent and they continued their long walk through the buildings. Finally, the walls of the barracks came into view, the light grey stone glowing in the moonlight. Kerren stepped up to the gate and knocked. They waited for a few moments, and Kerren knocked again, harder. Eventually, Kerren sighed and turned to the group. "Have any of you got an axe or a hammer?"

"Er, here," Helmet said, drawing a small but heavy smithing hammer from his belt. Kerren took it and began continuously pounding on the gate until the inner door slid open and King Alvor stepped out, squinting.

"What's all the fuckin' racket?" Alvor complained, glaring at Kerren.

"You should know how this works by now, my King. I have everyone with me."

"Good, good," Alvor mumbled. "Come with- Wait, why are they here?" he finished, pointing two fingers at Lilith and Jenara.

"I was told to bring all my companions to dine with you," Bayard explained. "They are my companions."

"Things were...badly communicated, then. Warriors only." He turned and strode back inside without another word, his fur cloak trailing behind him.

"What is this about, Alvor?" Bayard asked, following him down the dark hallway towards the armory. The rest of the group squeezed in behind him, Jenara lurking in the back, a confused expression worn over her reddened face. "Looking to imprison us again?"

Alvor let out a humorless laugh. "I wish it was something so easy. Truth is, my scouts have been reporting hundreds of plaguewalkers steadily approaching my lands. According to them, our outermost town, Gattewen, will be under attack by midday tomorrow. Nearly all the proper warriors of Sinead were killed, by you and your men. If you wish us as allies, you will make up our loss with your own arms. We will ride out tonight, along with some of my remaining soldiers, and slay the infected horde before they reach Gattewen. There are also reports of howling in the forests, always near the horde. The scouts think that a pack of wolves may be after them, feeding when one falls. If we could find and kill the wolves, they would make meals for many nights. I trust you will help us without a fuss?"

"It would be my pleasure," Bayard agreed. "It is our duty to slay every plaguewalker that we can. However, Jacob still carries injuries given to him by Adam Dryden. Well, most of us do, but his are the only ones that still need much recovery. I request that he be allowed to stay at the castle. Along with Lilith and Jenara, of course."

Alvor mumbled under his breath as they walked. "Aye, fine. Better a man be missing than a burden, and the Princess and the witch certainly do not belong here."

Bayard turned to look at Jacob. "Tell nobody what we are doing, and take care of Lilith if I do not make it back. You do remember where the gold is?"

"Nothing will happen to you, Bayard," Jacob tried to assure him. "No plaguewalker could touch you."

"It is not the infected that worry me," Bayard whispered, leaning in closer and holding Jacob back. "Alvor may have agreed to this truce, but his men did not. It would be wise to fear betrayal, even assassination from the lower ranks. When you return to the feast, only eat what you take for yourself, accept no food or drink that is handed to you. Lilith already knows this, as well as many other ways they might try to get at us. She is just as wise as I am, remain close to her. You protect her, and she will protect you."

Jacob stared at his feet, looking worried and uncertain. However, he soon hid his fear with a sly smile. "Careful, Bay. I might steal your wife if you keep on like that."

Bayard returned the grin. "You'd have better luck trying to romance a plaguewalker." Bayard gave Jacob a brotherly smack on the shoulder, sending him on his way back towards the mead hall. Lilith hugged Bayard for a long time, whispering something in his ear, before striding away. Jenara glanced between them, then stumbled after Lilith without a word. Seconds later, they reached a door on the left of the absurdly long hallway, and Alvor booted it open. Bayard recognized it as the same room they had been held in when they first arrived, but instead of the grey, empty walls, the room was lined with every weapon known to England. Longswords covered the entire back wall, with lines of shortswords, sabers, daggers, axes, maces, hammers, longbows, and crossbows spread out among the remainder of the armory.

Bayard and Gendrina stared longingly at the swords, but soon every person there had taken a hawk axe, having long since agreed that they were the most effective weapon to use against the infected. Uriel and Pierre each took a shortsword for backup, and Gendrina and Helmet both took a longbow and a quiver with twenty arrows.

Everyone also took a dagger, for a sidearm and utility use. "I hated this room a couple days ago," Gendrina whispered in an astonished tone. "Now I'll hardly be able to walk out."

"I have to ask," Alvor said, staring at Gendrina. "Why do you allow a woman to fight with you? Does she...service you?"

A month ago, Gendrina would have impaled Alvor on the spot, consequences be damned. But after training daily with Bayard and Uriel, her rash nature had been tempered as much as it was likely to be. She stood silently, glaring at the King. She had no need to defend herself, as Bayard was there to do it for her. "Anyone who tried would lose their manhood. I guarantee she could defeat any one of us in single combat, *maybe* excluding Uriel. It would be very wise to remain on her good side."

Alvor responded with a "Hmm," and turned back to the weapon racks. "My squires should be here soon with our armor. I don't know about the woman, but it should fit the rest of you just fine."

"I've learned to manage," Gendrina said coldly. "However, they are likely bringing the wrong armor for the job. Let me guess, scales over chain?"

Alvor blinked at her. "Yes. Why?"

"That works when facing human enemies that fire arrows and wield spears and swords." Gendrina sat on one of the stone benches, looking up to Alvor. "The only weapon that the infected carry is their teeth. Scale and chain needlessly weigh you down, and offer no spare protection over hardened leather. Everyone in our party should be equipped with a leather cuirass, boots, and greaves. The bracers and gauntlets should be plate. Most bites occur on the hands and arms, so those should be the most well-protected while offering the least excess weight."

Alvor looked at her, his face a blend of curiosity and disdain. He shook his head and turned to Bayard. "This is your real test, Bayard Travers. Show me that you people are what you say you are, and you will find a place among us. Show weakness, show any sign of betrayal, and you will wish that you had been consumed along with the rest of-"

Knock, knock, knock.

Alvor cut his threat short and jogged to the door, pulling it open. Three young boys stood there, each no older than ten. A massive trunk sat behind them, so large that Bayard found himself confounded at their ability to move it. "We 'ave yer armors, my King," one of them squeaked.

Alvor looked over his shoulder at Gendrina, letting out a long sigh. "I apologize, but this will not do. Please return it to the other armory and bring leathers. Enough boots, greaves, and chestplates for seven men, and plate gauntlets and bracers for just as many. Be quick now."

"Erm, I will help them," Helmet barked from the corner of the room. He stepped out and grasped the trunk, hauling it after the three boys.

"You know what's a problem?" Alvor said suddenly. "Having two armories. We have the weapon armory here, and then we have the armor armory. But 'Armor Armory' just sounds bloody stupid, does it not? I've tried calling them 'Armory One' and 'Armory Two' but then none of the squires could remember which was which, and it just caused more confusion and wasted time. This has been a continuous issue for my family for as long as anyone can remember."

"Isn't it the *worst*," Uriel moaned. "We had the same problem in Valdus. We had three armories. Weapons, armor, and joust equipment. Just a couple of months before the plague began, one of our other knights, William, came up with the solution. He had a carpenter carve out a wooden sword, wooden shield, and wooden horse, then hung them on the armory doors. Easy to notice, and they went by 'Sword Armory' and 'Shield Armory' and 'Joust armory'. Nobody messed it up after that."

"That is actually brilliant," Alvor said in an astonished monotone, as though he had just been taught the meaning of life. They sat in silence for close to five minutes, and then the sound of dragging wood began slowly approaching the open door. Alvor stood as Helmet appeared in the doorway, the giant trunk and three young squires standing behind him.

"Everythin's here," Helmet said. The group pulled their armor over the heavy furs they already wore, ignoring the lighter undercoats that lined the bottom of the trunk. Soon, they were all armed and armored, and gathered by the door.

Alvor stepped out and began speaking to the three young squires. "Bann, I need you to go to the training yard and tell the soldiers to gather by the front gate as soon as they can. Tell them they should have hawk axes, and armor the same as you just gathered, and at least six of them should have longbows. Ethan, run to the stables and tell Jory to have twenty horses ready to ride. Finn, go back to the feast and find David. You know, the carpenter? Tell him I need an ornate wooden longsword and kite shield, full-size, with the sigil of Sinead on both of them. Three silver pieces each, paid on pickup." The three boys gave dramatic bows and sprinted away towards the door. "Is everyone ready?" Alvor asked, turning back to the others. They all gave a quick nod.

Alvor led the way out of the armory and back down the hallway, soon coming out into the cold night air. "Why only us, Alvor?" Bayard asked. "We have over thirty fighters, all capable and trained by knights, with their own armor and weapons."

"As I said earlier, this is a test," Alvor said gruffly. "A group of infected less than five hundred on open ground should pose no threat to twenty trained soldiers who know how to kill them. You six are the leaders of your party, and I want to see how you lead and how you fight with my own eyes. Besides, we cannot forget the possibility of hunting those wolves. A group too large would scare them off. We need to slay the infected and hide ourselves, wait to see if they come to feed and pick them off with arrows."

Bayard asked no more questions until they reached the front gates, the moon high above their heads. There were shouts rising from the road leading south, the stable boys working hard to get their animals ready. "You should know," Bayard said to Alvor as they leaned on the stone walls. "The infected do not discriminate between human and animal, and horses are known to panic when they are near. We should leave the horses at Gattewen upon our arrival and travel on foot. This will protect the lives of not only the horses, but anyone who may be thrown off."

"Yes, I've already figured as much," Alvor mumbled. "Scouts told me how the horses scream and bolt when the infected get near, and Gattewen has already been informed that they'll have to host twenty-"

"Ho, King Alvor!" The loud voice startled them all, coming from an alley to their left. The large bald man known as Barric Eathellen stepped out of the shadows, leading a number of soldiers geared in the leather and plate armor mix. Bayard did a quick count of everyone present, coming to nineteen soldiers. Figuring it must have been because of Jacob's leave, Bayard ignored it and stepped next to Alvor. "I do not believe we have been officially introduced," Barric said, extending his hand. "I am Sir Barric Eathellen, General of the Forces of Sinead and War Adviser to King Alvor the Second."

Bayard shook Barric's hand with a grin. "I am Bayard Travers, Human Male."

This got a barking laugh from Barric. "Aye, I've never been a big supporter of titles myself, but it helps keep things professional in the battlefield. Anyway, my men are all ready."

"Us too," Alvor said. "We will ride straight to Gattewen and rest until morning, then ride out and engage the plaguewalkers during the day. Barric, remember that Bayard is in command for this task. You are not to interfere with his orders unless he is actively getting us killed. I have a war horn in my bag, we can use it to draw the infected right to us, save ourselves the trouble of hunting them."

"Good plan," Bayard agreed. Barric pushed open the gates and they began the trek down the wide road towards the stables.

Bayard lay sleeping in a comfortable bed within the Gattewen inn. The small town reminded him much of Peydenal, and he found himself dreaming of an incident that disrupted the peace of his old town, years ago. He dreamed of it often, the first time he had taken a human life.

"Mary? MARY!?" Bayard set his parchment down and looked up, squinting. The desperate voice of George Crane pierced the walls of his home. Bayard stood and walked over to the window behind him, pushing it open and leaning his head out. The potter was stumbling down the streets of Peydenal, his face a painting of fear. "MARY!"

Bayard turned and jogged out of his bedroom, grabbing a shortsword from the rack beside his bed. Running down the stairs and out his front door, he saw George on the ground, red-faced and sobbing. "George, what has happened?" Bayard asked. "Where is Mary?"

George looked up to him, helpless. "We were eating breakfast, there was a knock on the door. Thought it was a customer, sent Mary down to deal with it. Heard her scream, and she was gone. He took her, he took my girl." George collapsed forwards, screaming in grief.

"Who took her? Who was it? Get yourself together, Crane, speak to me."

"I do not know," George cried. "It could have been anybody."

"Nobody who lives here would do such a thing," Bayard said. "It has to be someone who was passing through, someone has to have noticed him. Go home, be with Sarah, I will find your daughter."

George nodded and got to his feet, blindly walking away without another word. Bayard bolted to the tavern in a flat-out sprint, pounding on the door until Lyanna Sendiil opened it, still in her nightclothes and looking groggy. "Bayard? What the hell is with all the noise this morning? Who was shouting?"

"Lyanna, I need you to remember very clearly," Bayard said without answering her questions. "Was there anybody unusual in the tavern last night? Any travelers, or mercenaries, or traders?"

"I...yes," she mumbled. "There was a farmer, I don't know from where. He stumbled in last night covered in dirt and already drunk, and tried to..." She shuddered. "He tried to *buy me.* I told him to piss off, obviously, and I have not seen him since."

"Farmer," Bayard whispered to himself. "About how old was he?"

"Probably about your age," Lyanna said. "Why, what is all this about?"

"Only two farms nearby," Bayard murmured, still ignoring Lyanna. "The Valdus farm, and the farmer there is at least fifty. Then there's the farm at Kaden, he has to be from there. Too far to walk." Bayard turned and ran off, leaving Lyanna standing there in confusion. Bayard stopped in at the stables next, grinning slightly when he saw all the usual horses in place. Thanking yesterday's rain for the soft dirt, he crouched down and circled the construct until he spotted deep hoofprints leading off to the east. Bayard mounted his own brown steed and took off along the trail, stopping frequently to check he was still on the right path. He was ten kilometers out of Peydenal when he spotted the large black mare, tied to a tree with a bag of feed strapped to her head. Bayard dismounted his own steed and tied his reins around a thick branch, then he started examining the ground. Bootprints led into the trees, but were quickly lost with the grass and brush that covered the ground.

Bayard cursed and kept up his path for a distance, searching the ground for any other signs. He was about to give up and try another way from where the prints stopped, when he heard a high-pitched scream quietly pass by him on the southern winds. Bayard tore his shortsword from its sheath as he sprinted through the trees, the screams growing more frequent the further south he got. He stepped over a fallen tree and stumbled as Mary Crane crashed into him with a shriek.

"NO, PLEASE- Wait, B...Bayard?" Her whole body was shaking and her nightgown was torn up to the waist, wet blood staining her face and throat. Bayard knelt down and lifted her chin; she looked uninjured. Just then, the man stumbled out of the trees, his right hand dripping blood.

"Ye little *bitch,"* he hissed, stepping over a thick root into Bayard's sight. He stopped upon seeing Bayard, reaching to his hip to pull a small hatchet. "Who the 'ell are yeh?" he snapped, raising his hatchet towards Bayard.

Bayard ignored him and looked to Mary. "Did he rape you?"

She released a huge sob and shook her head. "He tried, but I bit him and ran, just a minute ago..."

Bayard grasped her shoulder and gently pushed her against a tree. "Cover your eyes, do not move until I say." He stepped towards the man and raised his shortsword. "You asked me who I am. My name is Bayard Travers. Remember it in Hell."

"Yeh can't kill me," the man shouted with a slurring voice. "I'm the only farmer Kaden has, they'll starve without me-" Bayard ran forwards, pulling his sword arm back. The farmer swung his hatchet at Bayard's head, but he caught the shaft and tore it from the man's hand, thrusting the shortsword through his chest and pushing him down into the dirt. He coughed twice and lay still, blood dripping from the sides of his mouth. Bayard withdrew the sword and turned, taking Mary by the hand and leading her away from the farmer's body.

"My father has friends in Kaden," she said. Her voice was steady and mechanical, she was obviously in shock. "Will they really starve?"

"They will not, you sweet girl," Bayard whispered. "It is the season for harvest, and it does not take much skill to pull vegetables from the dirt. I fear for their cattle if nobody knows how to handle them properly, but the citizens will easily be able to survive the winter either way. Kaden is also a fief of Valdus. I will send a message to Valdus, I hold some standing there and it is their duty to send someone to replace him." Their return to Peydenal passed silently aside from the hooves of the horses. Mary said she knew how to ride, so he allowed her to follow behind him on the farmer's black mare. She was a strong, well-bred horse, with a thick mane and tail that bounced as she trotted along. She would go to someone in Peydenal, or Bayard would sell her if nobody there wanted her. They finally reached the road that led into town, and ten minutes later Bayard was knocking on the potter's door. It opened almost instantly, and Bayard stepped back as George embraced Mary.

"All this blood, are you-"

"She is fine, George," Bayard said to him. "She bit the kidnapper. He did nothing to harm her."

George stood and looked seriously at Bayard. "What has become of him?" he asked. Bayard drew his shortsword and showed it to George, the blade bloodstained down to the hilt. George nodded, holding Mary close. "There are no words that can tell you how thankful I am to you, Bayard. I will owe you until the day that I die."

"If you want to repay me, buy one of my swords and let me teach you how to use it, and how to defend yourself and your family. It is a dark world."

"Bayard," Mary said, looking up to him.

"What is it?" he asked her.

"Bayard," she said again, loudly this time.

Bayard blinked, and Gendrina was standing over him, nudging his side with her boot. "*Bayard.* Sun's just coming up. Alvor and his men are already outside, ranting about what a lazy leader you are."

"Ah, shite," Bayard groaned, stumbling to his feet. It took him a moment to remember that he slept naked, but Gendrina seemed not to care in the slightest. He quickly pulled on his underclothes, followed by his coat and then the leather and plate. They walked down the creaky wooden staircase of the Gattewen inn, and the voices of many men grew in volume as they descended.

"You deal with them, I'll wake the rest," Gendrina said, jogging back up the steps. Bayard opened the door and walked out into the dim morning sun and strong northern wind.

"About time," Alvor complained, to the scattered agreement of his soldiers. "My scout says the first of the infected are less than three kilometers from here. We leave in fifteen minutes. Are you prepared? Where are your people?"

"My 'people' will be out in a moment. Are we having any breakfast or what?"

"Aye," Alvor said, tossing a lump of cheese at Bayard. He caught it and took a bite, chewing it unenthusiastically.

"Mwhut is dis?" Bayard asked through the mouthful. "It's turrible."

"It's sheep cheese," one of Alvor's men explained. "We have so many sheep in Sinead for the purpose of clothing, so we use them for cheese as well, unusual as it may be. Only thing that was light enough to bring in order to feed everyone here without burdening Gattewen's inn. No need to waste their food with winter approaching."

Bayard swallowed the disgusting lump with a pained gulp. "Well, it's food," he offered. He leaned against his horse, watching the inn door as he finished the chunk of cheese. Uriel was the first one out, his hair tied in a wolf tail that fell past his shoulders. Thomas was next, followed shortly by Pierre. They were all given chunks of the sheep cheese, and all started eating it just as begrudgingly as Bayard did. "Where's Helmet?"

"Erm-" Thomas started, before muffled shouting could be heard from inside the inn. The door flew open and Helmet stomped out, looking exasperated. Gendrina strode out behind him, looking annoyed.

"Yeh *can't* wield a halberd!" Helmet was yelling. "It isn't about strength, I know yeh're strong as an ox, but yeh're too short, it would get jammed in the ground ev'ry time yeh swung it."

"So forge one for Jacob and let me give it a go-"

"JACOB'S SHORTER THAN YOU ARE!" Helmet roared, drawing stares from the stable boys and laughs from the soldiers.

Gendrina shrugged and jogged over to Bayard. "Oy, Bayard, you'll make a halberd when you get back in a forge, right? I've always wanted to train with one, but never had the chance."

Bayard grinned at her. "I'll cut you a deal. I'll pay the carpenter to make you a wooden one to train with. Show me you can handle it properly, and I'll get around to forging a real one."

"Works for me," Gendrina conceded.

"Enough chatter," Alvor shouted over the group. "The infected are approaching steadily. As of now, Bayard Travers is your commander for this mission. You are to obey his orders as though it were I who gave them, understand?" There was a shout of agreement from his men.

Bayard nodded and steeled himself, stepping up on a tree stump to look over the soldiers. "Men of Sinead," Bayard said, raising his voice over the howling wind. "I will not waste time with a long introduction and promises of victory. You must take victory with your own hands. None of you have faced the infected before, and you must understand what they are. More than that, you must understand what they are not. They are not people. They wear the skin of women and children, they call out to you in their tormented voices, but there is *nothing* inside of them. I'm sure that to most of you, the human body is just that. You cut it open, and it dies. But these are not humans, they are siege weapons. The easiest way to stop them is to sink the pike of your hawk axe into the top of their head, though any heavy damage to this whole area will do the job." Bayard gestured all around his head. "If all you have is a dagger or knife, thrust it through here, the softest part of the skull," he said, pointing to his temple. "If you have a shortsword, do not risk cutting into the head, except as a last resort. Skulls are hard and you may fail to cut through, and it will certainly damage your weapon. Instead, try to get around the plaguewalker and swing your blade into the back of their neck. This will instantly disable them. Avoid using blunt weapons against them, unless there is no other choice. They simply are not reliable. If you are unlucky enough to find yourself without a weapon, *do not,* under any circumstances, try to fight them bare-handed. They move very slowly, run away until you can rearm. Do not seek death in an attempt at glory, they have nobody to impress. And if you are bitten, you will be given a choice to either be executed then and there, or be put down after you die to the plague. Those of you who have long hair, take your dagger and cut it all off, right now. That means you too, Alvor."

There was an explosion of protests from the northmen.

"That's an order," Bayard shouted over them. "I will not have good soldiers dying because they like their bloody hairstyles. Off with it all."

Alvor stood beside Bayard, looking furious, but he grudgingly nodded. "Do as he says," Alvor spat. He pulled a long dagger from his belt and bundled up his long, dark hair, twisting it together and slashing through it in one motion. Uriel did so next, tossing his wolf tail aside. The rest of the soldiers followed their lead, and soon they all looked a whole lot less grabbable.

"Good," Bayard said. "There is no reason why we should lose a single person here. Be smart, and follow the advice of me and my own men. If we are forced to split up, be sure that you stay with a member of my group, we all have plenty of experience fighting the dead in a forested environment and will be able to reorganize even when separated. Helmet, I am sorry, but I must leave you here to protect the village should any infected make it through." Helmet just gave a short nod. Bayard jumped off his platform and walked through the soldiers towards the gate. "It is time, follow me."

Despite Bayard's grim and direct speech, the soldiers slammed the flat of their axes on their chests and shouted their northern war cries, stomping their feet as they marched for the town gate. Bayard slowed down and fell behind them, gathering with his own group.

"What do you think?" Uriel asked him. "They appear to be skilled soldiers."

"That's just the problem," Bayard said. "They believe that they are going to war, but that is not the case. This is not battle, it is surgery on a grand scale, and it requires precision and understanding. They're going to charge in with axes swinging wild, hacking and chopping, no matter what I told them against it. They'll learn quickly, same as we did, but I just hope none of them are bitten before they do. The armor will definitely help. Gen, come over here please."

Gendrina stepped around Thomas and walked beside Bayard. "What is it?"

Bayard grimaced and glanced around over the men in front of them. "You have to listen to me, Gen. I know you, but these soldiers do not. They will not listen to anything you say, they will not respect you yet. If you find yourself alone with them, they will likely try to take advantage of you. I know that you can handle yourself, but we cannot get any Sinead blood on our hands. I need you to play it safe here and stay with me or Thomas, or even Alvor. Do you understand why it has to be this way?"

"I am not a simpleton, Bayard," Gendrina whispered. "Because of some sideways trick from God, I grew up as a boy in a girl's body, and I've faced all the difficulties that come with it. I can never explain to you how grateful I am that you allow me to fight as an equal, and taking the back of the horse for a while is the least I can do. I'll stay with Tom."

"Thank you, Gen," Bayard said, clapping her on the shoulder as she turned towards Thomas. "Alvor," Bayard called to the King, who was making his way to the front of the soldiers. "We're far enough away from the village, get the horn out and start making some noise. Everyone else, I need you to follow my orders *exactly*. Do what I say, and we will all go home tonight. Form a circle, and do not move from your spots unless I say. Alvor will stand in the center, drawing the attention of the plaguewalkers. When one approaches the circle, whoever is closest will take it down with one accurate swing of their hawk axe. You will not step out of the circle for any reason. When the bodies get too high, we will move as one to another location. Take your positions."

There was a scramble as everyone formed the circle. Bayard was next to Pierre and a Sinead man who he did not know. Gendrina was with Thomas, and Uriel stood next to Barric. Alvor was digging in his bag, and soon pulled out a short ivory war horn, banded with iron and engraved with old runes. "Ready," Alvor called. Bayard nodded at him, and Alvor drew in a huge breath and blew into the horn, sounding their presence to everything within five kilometers.

They expected to hear moans from the infected.

They did not expect the primal, earth-shattering roar that responded to them, calling its challenge with a fury unequaled even in the darkest reaches of humanity.

Chapter Twenty-Three
Autumn of 1513 A.D
Forest in Northern England
Morning

Bayard was certain that the world was splitting in two. It was as though a cannon blast was prolonged by fifteen seconds, an impossible sound that vibrated his bones and tore at his ears. It faded slowly, echoing across the trees and hills. Bayard spun around, seeing Alvor on one knee, hand pressed against his one good ear. "What the *fuck* was that?" Alvor hissed, his eyes watering.

Bayard noticed that he was breathing heavily, and his hands were shaking. Something alive had made that sound, and Bayard found himself thinking of the illustrations in books he had read, the monstrous elephants of Africa. Obviously there could be no elephant here, but the sound was how he would have imagined it. "I have no possible idea," Bayard choked out. "There is nothing in England that could do that."

"It had to be a bear?" Alvor tried to convince himself.

"There hasn't been a wild bear in England for five-hundred years, Alvor," Bayard whispered. "And even if one was imported for food or entertainment and escaped, it would never be that loud. Something is wrong, we have to get-" Bayard fell silent as the first of the plaguewalkers stumbled out from behind a tree ahead of them, an older woman in a cook's apron. Her left hand was chewed to shreds, and her dress was deformed and plastered to her legs by dried blood. She spotted the party of soldiers and raised one of her arms, opening her mouth with a hoarse groan. As soon as she started moaning, the sound of hundreds more rose over the forest.

"Whatever that roar was, we cannot abandon Gattewen," Alvor said. "Hold the circle, weapons ready." His soldiers raised their axes to rest on their shoulders, ready to strike quickly. Bayard's warriors looked to him.

"Alvor is right," Bayard told them. "Stow your fear, and prepare for anything." They all gave him a determined nod, raising their own weapons. The infected woman was the first to reach them, shambling towards Barric. He stepped forwards and spun his axe, slamming the pike into the crown of her head. She dropped instantly, and he retreated back to his place in the circle. "That's the way," Bayard called. "Do exactly as he did, and not one of them will reach us." A minute passed before more infected began lumbering towards them. The first wave consisted of dozens, singing their monotone song of hunger.

"Mother of God," whispered one of Sinead's soldiers. "This cannot be possible."

"You see it now, with your own eyes!" Bayard called. "That is the fate that awaits us all, should our truce fail. Remember their faces, remember your fear. This is what ties us together now, this common enemy. The age of Kingdoms is over, all that's left is the living and the dead. Now *fight*, not for your Kingdom, not for your faith. Fight for your own life, for your families, for your home, for the people you protect."

Gendrina jumped forwards and spiked a large plaguewalker, and one of the Sinead men did the same. As more infected approached them, the other soldiers showed their understanding of Bayard's tactic. They learned quickly, and it was a slow but simple process as the hours passed by.

"This is wrong," Barric shouted over the combat. "The scouts said there were no more than four-hundred walkers just three days ago, and we've killed six with no end in sight. We will soon be exhausted."

"The wolves they reported," Pierre yelled. "There aren't any. They heard the roars from whatever that was, and reported it as wolf howls because they didn't know how else to explain it. If the sound carried south to Valdus, it could be drawing every infected from Haarn. Thousands of them."

"The wind has been blowing south," Alvor said, his eyes growing wide in anger and fear. "It is possible."

"RETREAT!" Bayard roared. "Back to Gattewen! We must gather the citizens there, and from the other towns between here and Sinead! Break the circle and run, we stand no chance here!"

The soldiers killed what infected were near, then turned and sprinted in the opposite direction. They ran through patches of trees and came into an open field, with Gattewen in the distance ahead of them. Bayard looked over his shoulder, seeing his people close behind him and Sinead's men taking up the rear. They started across the field and were nearly half of the way to Gattewen, when Bayard heard the sound of a person collapse behind him, and the unmistakable sound of a bone breaking. He came to a halt and spun, and his breath caught in his throat as he saw it.

Kneeling over Barric was a being that Bayard could not comprehend. Once again, his mind raced through all the books he'd read, all the knowledge he had on every subject that he had studied. He remembered books on the old Northern religions, he thought of the Frost Giants, and the trolls of Scandinavian lore, but this was just his mind's desperate attempt to rationalize what he was seeing. It had been human, once. Bent scraps of steel armor sunk into its flesh, and rags of a red cloak hung from its back. It got to its feet, and Bayard saw that both its left arm and right leg ended with a single, elongated bone that protruded from the stumps where its limbs used to be. It stood still, looking down at Barric.

The man was alive and screaming, his leg broken and limp as he tried to drag himself away from the monstrosity. It stepped in front of him, and Barric swung his axe into the creature's leg. The spike sunk less than a quarter inch into its flesh, and the weapon fell uselessly to the ground. The deformed *thing* raised its right leg and slammed its bone club of a foot into the back of Barric's head, crushing it into the ground with a gut-wrenching sound. And then it turned towards Alvor.

All the Sinead men gathered in front of their King, screaming their war cries at the monster, swinging their axes through the air. Bayard could have sworn that he saw the abomination grin. With speed unmatched by the crows that soared the sky, it ran forwards and crashed into one of the soldiers, impaling him with the bone spike that took the place of its arm. Three of the warriors slammed their axes into its back, causing no damage, and it grasped one of the soldiers across his face. It lifted the man off the ground and squeezed, tossing the body aside with a growl.

"We have to run!" Uriel shouted. "We cannot hurt it!"

"There's no use, it's too fast," Bayard said. "We have to fight, strike for the eyes and the backbone, we might be able to at least disable it."

Gendrina pulled her longbow off her back and nocked an arrow as Uriel, Pierre, and Thomas ran into the fray. She fired again and again at the creature's face as it slaughtered the Sinead soldiers, the heavy broadheads slamming into its flesh. Its head snapped back with each impact, but the skin would not break, and the arrows fell to the ground. Thomas jumped and swung his axe into the back of its neck, but the shaft cracked and splintered into Thomas's hand. The monster turned and grasped Thomas by his leather cuirass, throwing him back towards Bayard. He crashed into the grass and rolled to his feet, breathing heavily.

Uriel was next, drawing his shortsword and slashing with axe and sword in a fast, brutal combination across its back as it bit through the throat of a Sinead soldier, but all it did was cut the strap that held its pauldrons on. The pieces of armor fell into the grass as the creature grabbed one of the soldiers by his neck. It turned and saw Uriel, and they stood face-to-face for a number of seconds before the creature released another piercing roar, snapping the soldier's neck and landing a mighty front kick to Uriel's armored chest that sent him sprawling. Bayard ran to Uriel and knelt next to him, and the old knight coughed and sat up.

"What is this? WHAT MAGIC IS THIS?" Alvor screamed from behind them, staring at Bayard with hatred filling his eyes.

"What are you talking about, Alvor?" Bayard snapped as he helped Uriel to his feet.

"It tears apart my men, but does not kill yours. You did this, somehow, this is your plan. Your witch wife summoned a demon to destroy us, YOU DID THIS!"

"Get a hold of yourself, Alvor," Bayard shouted. "I am as clueless as you are, we have nothing to do-" Bayard stopped talking as Alvor lurched forwards and collapsed, the creature standing over him.

Alvor rolled over and looked up at his killer, then stared madly at Bayard. "Every one of your people will be executed-" The monster grasped Alvor by his leg and cuirass, lifted him over its head, and tore him in two. All the Sinead men were dead, scattered around the field in bloody heaps. Blood dripped down its body as it lowered its arms, and it stood still as it looked to Bayard. He was unable to see when it fought, but now Bayard could see that the creature was breathing. Vapor blew from its mouth in the cold autumn air.

This is no member of the dead. It is alive, it has flowing blood, intelligent thought. It looked to the sky and a third roar burst forth, somehow louder than the previous two combined. Bayard pressed his hands over his ears and hunched forwards, and out of the corner of his eye, he saw the monster shake its head before it sprinted away towards Sinead.

"Alvor was right," Uriel said suddenly. Bayard looked down. Uriel was holding the scrap of armor that had fallen off of the monster. A steel pauldron, dirtied with blood and grime. "We did not summon it, but..." Uriel spat into his hand and rubbed at the armor, cleaning away the dirt until a worn sigil could be seen in the metal.

"What are you talking about, Uriel? You know this is not our doing."

"I saw him," Uriel whispered. Bayard was startled to see that the knight looked to be on the verge of tears. "I would know his armor anywhere. Somehow...that monster is King Christopher."

*****

One Month Earlier
City of Valdus

Christopher Alento forced the edge of his axe into the skull of a plaguewalker, then spun to pike another. Morgan bumped into him as he backed away from a group of three, slashing at their necks with his longsword. "Are you alright there, Christopher?" Morgan asked, sparing a second to look at the bleeding stump that used to be Christopher's left arm.

"Aye," Christopher groaned. "We need shelter fast, we need to cauterize this."

"I think-" Morgan paused to slam the edge of his shield into the head of an approaching infected woman. "I think that the lamplighter's shack is just a couple hundred meters down this street. There will be oil we can use to start a fast fire." Christopher wordlessly followed Morgan's suggestion, stumbling down the street. Morgan ran ahead, clearing the path for Christopher. Finally Morgan was pushing on the door of the lamplighter's shack, finding it locked. Morgan unlocked it with his boot and helped Christopher inside, slamming the door shut and barricading it by forcing his sword through the gap between the door and shack wall.

Infected soon began pounding on the lamplighter's door, and Morgan looked around, spotting a small barrel with a cork stopper sitting in a corner. He picked it up and grinned at the weight, then began kicking apart the decaying wooden table that took up the center of the room. He placed the shards of the table in the middle of the room and poured a liberal amount of oil in the center. "We have to be fast about this, before the fire starts spreading," Morgan said. He slid his arm out of his shield, placing it at an angle above the firepit. He drew his dagger and smacked it against the shield, and after a few strikes, the spark caught. The fire blazed up quickly, and Morgan held one side of his shield directly in the flames. The steel soon began to redden, and Morgan withdrew it from the flame. "Off with the shirt."

Christopher cursed and began fiddling with his undercoat, pulling it over his head and tossing it aside. "Get on with it," Christopher hissed, squeezing his eyes shut. Morgan walked on his knees to sit beside Christopher, and pressed the shield into the bleeding wound. Christopher gritted his teeth but let no sound of pain escape him, lest they attract even more of the infected.

Three days passed, and Christopher was alone. He had watched every one of his men fall to the infected, and he was somehow still fighting. They could do nothing to reduce the concentration of the dead, and Christopher was just one man with one arm. Despite this, he still fought on. Every day he went outside and fought to exhaustion, and this day his persistence failed him. He had to abandon his boots the day before due to swelling in his feet, and his right ankle was bitten into by a dismembered body hiding beneath an old merchant's cart in the Upper Ring.

Cursing and screaming at anything that might hear him, he stumbled into the castle. He found dark torches still held in their sconces and he was lucky enough to feel oil still dampening one of them, and he lit it and retreated into the dungeons. *Won't give up. Can NOT give up. Have to buy time for them, have to protect Jenara.* He tore open the gates to the dungeon's old torture chamber, a long-forgotten relic of an even darker age than this. He pulled sheets off tall pieces of equipment, finally collapsing on his side as he uncovered what he was looking for.

Standing ten feet tall, the thing that all criminals feared throughout their lives. The guillotine. In the reign of his father, it had taken countless lives, and now it was the only thing that could save his own. With no hesitation, he raised his bitten leg into the circle, locked it in place, and pressed the lever with the tip of his sword. Again he did not scream as it severed his leg as cleanly as a sword through snow.

Alive. Somehow alive. Christopher was laying on the wall of the castle, staring down into the faces of hundreds of plaguewalkers, all of whom wanted nothing more than to devour him. He held a light crossbow, made for a child, in his right hand. He could pull the string with one arm, and it still pierced their skulls at close range. For over a week he stayed on the wall, going through the castle armory's store of bolts. He shot down into the crowd that gathered below, occasionally shouting to draw more to him. On the ninth day, he stood using the crutch he had hammered together in the castle carpenter's workshop. He turned to retrieve more bolts, when the wood of the crutch gave out and he fell backwards into the horde of walkers.

In a fit of adrenaline and desperation, he rolled his way out of the crowd and began crawling towards the nearest home he could see. The infected were slow, but he was slower. One of them reached him and collapsed on top of him, and despite his writhing and his punches, the dead man bit into his thigh, right under his cuirass. Christopher roared his anger before he crushed the man's head in with the stock of his crossbow, and seconds later he rolled into the large home and kicked the door shut, leaning against it. The dead pounded their rotting fists against the thick wood as Christopher sobbed his defeat. This was the end of the Alento name, and the true end of Valdus.

Blood leaked from Christopher's thigh as he thought of anything he could have done differently. *Sinead. They are responsible for this. They killed my father, they killed our knights and guards, they weakened our defenses. I should have attacked them months ago with the full force of Valdus, even if victory seemed impossible. We would have had a chance. Will they try to hunt Jenara and the civilians? Will they try to take over Valdus? I should have killed them. I should have listened to Morgan, and used the infected as a weapon against them. I should have slaughtered them.* Christopher closed his eyes and waited for his death.

Two days. I've been here for two days, and I am still me. I am not thirsty, or hungry, but I cannot move. Is this how it is for all the infected? Do they have their minds, but no control of their bodies?

Christopher tried to move his left arm. It did not respond. He tried again, willing his arm to move with everything he had in him. He gasped as the arm shot forwards, held out in front of him. *What is this? It is not my arm.* He closed his fingers, and the fingers of the deformed, black hand closed as well. *It is me. What is this? What am I?* He tried standing, placing the unfamiliar arm on the wall for support. Again he was surprised with the speed in which this body moved. He stood on his one leg, leaning on the door that still shook with the pounding of the dead.

I do not want to be one of them, but I do not have it in me to end my own life. I will go out there and fight until there is nothing left of me. He grasped the handle of the door and turned the knob, and the door buckled inwards. Twenty plaguewalkers poured into the small room and swarmed Christopher, biting down onto his arm, leg, and body. *I feel...nothing. They should consume me in seconds, but they cannot break my skin. Does God protect me? Or does Lucifer transform me into one of his own?* Christopher reached out and grasped the arm of one of the infected, lifting him off the ground. *He seems nearly weightless. Like when I would lift Jenara when she was a child.*

Christopher dropped the walker and grasped another around her neck, and gave a light squeeze. He felt her neck snap within his hand, like a twig would to the hoof of a war horse. He threw a punch at another and watched as he flew backwards and slammed his head on the opposite wall, six meters away. Christopher ignored the others, using their shoulders to balance as he hopped out of the house. He slowly started for the castle, but soon realized that this body was fast. He could run easily on his one arm and leg, and he could jump. He made his way over the castle wall and circled around to the graveyard that spanned the grounds behind the castle.

He found himself looking at the mausoleum that held his father and all of his ancestors. *I will not be joining you in death today, Father. But I will promise you this. I will destroy your enemies. As long as I keep my mind, I will not stop until they fall before me.* Christopher turned and began making his way back up the long hill, and half way up a scent caught his attention. He stopped and turned, spotting a dark cloth half-buried in the dirt under a nearby tree. He crawled over to it and grasped it, raising it to his nose. *How am I able to smell this? The scent is...familiar. It is them. It is Kane*

Dryden, but there are other scents too. It is the other Fogwalkers.

Days passed as Christopher explored the city with his new form, effortlessly tearing infected limb from limb, but soon he began traveling north, following the scent of the Fogwalkers. With every hour that passed, he could feel his sanity slipping out from under him. His bloodlust was growing, and his thoughts were weakening. Memories of his friends and family faded away to near nothingness, just small footnotes in the back of his mind. His senses of love, morality, and justice were long gone, replaced by one simple thought.

Kill Fogwalkers. Kill Sinead.

*****

"Immunity," Bayard shouted to Uriel as they pushed their horses to their limits back towards Sinead.

"What is that?" Uriel called back. They were only two meters away from each other, but the sound of the horses was deafening.

Bayard glanced behind him, seeing the townspeople on their weak, malnourished horses, some with up to three riders. He pulled on the reigns, slowing down so they could keep up. "You know how when a child gets pox, he never gets them again if he survives it the first time?"

"Yes, but what does that have to do with Christopher?" Uriel asked.

"You saw his arm and leg. I think that he was bitten twice and took off the limbs. This plague is aggressive, more than any other sickness I've ever seen. By taking two bites, but removing the limbs before infection could truly take hold, he built up a resistance to the disease. Since the plague was unable to kill him, it continued evolving unimpeded within his body and turned him into the creature that he is now."

"But he had bones, where his leg and arm used to be. He could not have cut them off."

"I think they...regrew, much like some reptiles and fish, " Bayard explained. "There was no sinew or muscle left on them. I think the plague is trying to force his body into a state more convenient to it.

Since it's *supposed* to kill all of its victims, this change cannot occur normally."

"Are you saying that I'm going to become one of those things?" Thomas yelled from his horse behind them.

"I think you are safe, as long as you're not bitten again," Gendrina offered. "I cut your arm off within seconds, and who knows how long Christopher went after his bites."

"I agree," Bayard said. "We would have seen a change by now."

"So how are we going to kill it?" Pierre asked from atop his dark grey steed.

"Kill it?" Uriel shouted indignantly. "That's Christopher!"

"Uriel, I am sorry," Bayard said solemnly. "That cannot mean anything to us. We are allied with Sinead, and it is obvious that he plans to attack the city. We must protect them, and we must give Christopher mercy. We will get back to Sinead and defend the gates from the horde of infected, and we must lure Christopher into some trap. For now, we have to block off Sinead from the horde, that is what will wipe out the city. Pick up speed, we must prepare the city for the siege."

"Excuse me, Sir?" a loud voice called out from the citizens behind them. An older man with one eye and many scars across his face rode up beside Bayard. "My name is Ringlef, I used to be a guard in Sinead, long ago. There is a path through the mountain that leads right into the castle dungeons. It serves as an escape route should the city fall to a siege. It might be wise to enter the city through there, since that demon will likely be attacking the main gates."

"Thank you," Bayard said. "I agree, that will be the safest thing for us. Lead the way."

Sefu Almasi squirmed in his bed, dreaming of the day he had to abandon his home in Egypt.

He held a heavy, worn stone between his hands. He felt the sands beneath him shift as he stood, his whole body shaking in grief and fear. His mother lay dead beside him, and his father stood outside his room pushing on the rotting wooden door. Sefu could see his eyes through one of the many cracks in the wood. The dead, grey eyes that held no love or mercy. His father screamed his anger at being unable to reach his target, slamming his head against the door and reaching through a hole with strength enough to tear the flesh on his hands. Sefu knelt down again, waiting and waiting. It was all that he could do.

An hour passed, and Sefu felt something brush his arm from behind him. He jumped and turned, seeing his mother alive and reaching for him. And then she raised her head, with her mouth opened wide, emitting the moans that were slowly driving Sefu to insanity. He screamed and jumped backwards, raising his stone above his head. His mother slowly rolled over and toppled off of his bed, getting to her feet and slowly walking towards him. She reached out with her fingers clawed, grasping for his throat, and he brought the stone down. It crashed into her shoulder and sent her toppling backwards, and Sefu ran past her to the one door out of his room.

With the strongest kick his small body could muster, he sent the door crashing open and sprinted past his floored father and into the main of their small home. The door shook from the dozens that were outside, and Sefu threw his stone through the window on the other side of the room. He tumbled out, cutting his leg on the glass, and began running as fast as he possibly could. He remembered what his half-brother had told him, of the people in the East who had weapons, knowledge, and shelter. He ran for miles through the thick sands. He ran until the cold night fell and he knew he would freeze. His foot slipped into a dip of the sand, and he felt himself falling.

Sefu awoke to the loudest sound that he had ever heard. The roars of sandstorms, the screams of dying camels, none of it came close to the sound that split the air over Sinead. He rolled to his feet and stared out the window, but saw nothing other than the cloudy night sky. Soon he heard the shouts of guards and soldiers, followed by warning bells. Heavy footsteps thundered past his room, and shouts could be heard rising from the grounds below. He jumped as there was a hard knock at his door. He jogged across his room and pulled the door open to find Lilith Travers standing there in her nightclothes.

"Sefu, we have to hurry," she whispered. "The gate is under attack. It isn't the infected, they don't know what it is, but the women and children are to take shelter in the dungeons."

"I am not child," Sefu asserted. "I fight."

"You will have your chance, but not right now," Lilith said. "We must do as the guard tells us, until we are more friendly with them. Come with me." She grasped Sefu by the arm and effectively dragged him from the room, leading him down the dim halls that had been hastily lit with far too few torches.

"Where Bayard?" Sefu asked.

"I do not know," Lilith whispered. Sefu felt her hand shaking as she said it. They turned a corner and Sefu stumbled as Lilith bumped into an armored man. He pulled his helmet off and Sefu saw that it was Jacob Carter.

"Oh, Lily," he gasped out. "This hall is blocked off, go down the stairs through the mead hall and then through to the dungeon."

"What is happening, Jacob?" Lilith asked in a panicked tone, finally releasing her grasp on Sefu's arm. "A guard told me there are no infected at the gates. Are we being attacked by another city?"

Jacob glanced around, then leaned in closer. "I do not know what is truly at the gates, but half the men talk of the Devil and the other half of something called a Jotunn, whatever that is. The actual fact is that there is one single *something* that's destroyed all of the road's defenses and is now trying to break into the city. Get Jenara and get to the dungeons, I will come down and tell you as soon as it is safe."

Lilith nodded and turned, leading Sefu further down the hall. They came to another door and Lilith pounded on it, and Jenara answered, already in her leather armor. "What is it?" Jenara asked. "Are there walkers at the gate?"

"Not exactly," Lilith said. "We have to get to the dungeons, I'll explain what I know then."

Jenara nodded and started after Lilith and Sefu. They turned another corner and came to the stairs into the mead hall, and were half way through the large room when a stone the size of a man crashed through one of the hall's windows, splintering tables and chairs.

"Trebuchets," Jenara gasped. "We are under siege from a human enemy?"

"*I don't know what it is,*" Lilith shrieked. Jenara turned away from the window and they kept running for the dungeons, jogging down the stairs and into the dark hall. Voices could be heard in the distance, and they ran towards the sounds. Turning one last corner, they came to a solid stone wall. No doors, no openings.

"What is this? Where are the dungeons?" Jenara shouted.

"Hello?" A voice called from behind the stone wall in front of them. "Is someone out there?"

Lilith pushed past Jenara and pressed against the wall. "How do I get into the dungeons?"

There was a long pause from the other side. "I am truly sorry," the voice finally said. "But the mechanism that raises the wall has broken. Without the proper tools and the people who know how to use them, the wall cannot be moved."

Lilith screamed and slammed her hand against the stone. "THERE ARE KIDS OUT HERE!"

"There is nothing I can do," he said. "I am sorry."

"You sound like an adult man," Lilith shouted. "Only women and children are supposed to be in there! What are you playing at?"

"I am sorry," he said again.

"What do?" Sefu asked her. "We leave city?"

Lilith turned and stormed away from the wall. "No, we have soldiers here, and whatever protection the castle offers us. And we must wait for Bayard, he will know how to handle this. If we cannot get into the dungeons, we should-" She was interrupted by a sudden thunderclap. "Of course the weather chooses *now*... Anyway, we should shut ourselves in the kitchens. They're underground and stone-walled just like the dungeon, and the door should be metal to easily block off a fire."

They took off back up the stairs and were nearly at the mead hall when Sefu tugged at Lilith's nightgown. "Listen," Sefu said. "No sound."

Lilith stopped and shut her eyes, listening to the deep silence that had suddenly taken over the castle. She gasped as another thunderclap shattered that silence, and she shook her head. "We don't have time to think about it. We must get to the kitchens, come now." They proceeded into the mead hall and Lilith glanced around, then pointed towards a small, solid iron door a few meters to the right of the mead hall's hearth. They made for it and Jenara pulled on the handle, but it held fast.

Lilith started cursing loudly and continuously, but the door soon creaked open to reveal the face of a young boy, no older than ten. "Come inside," he said quickly. "Before it sees you." Sefu peered over the boy's shoulder and saw dozens of women and a few children huddled close together inside the large kitchen. Lilith pushed Jenara inside and then stepped in herself, holding the door open for Sefu. Just as he began moving for the door, his ears were battered by the same roar that had woken him up. It was so much louder, so much angrier, and it was right behind him.

Sefu spun around and froze, locking eyes with the creature that stood in the shattered door frame of the mead hall. Sefu thought of the thick, iron-banded wood that made up the city gates. He thought of the stone the size of a man that had been thrown through the window. *The kitchen door won't hold. This monster would break through in seconds.* Jenara reached out and grabbed Sefu's arm, pulling him towards the door to the kitchen. Sefu tore his arm away from her, forcefully shoved her back into the kitchen, and slammed the iron door between them. Sefu inhaled and shook out his legs as he turned to look at the beast that walked slowly towards him, kicking aside heavy tables and chairs as though they were made from straw. In his own language, one he knew that neither the monster nor any man for thousands of miles would understand, he shouted at it. "MY BROTHER DIED A HERO, AND I WILL BE NOTHING LESS!"

The creature roared its acceptance of Sefu's challenge and crouched down, then leaped towards him. Sefu dove forwards, sliding underneath it as it slammed down on the stone floor in front of the kitchen. Sefu jumped to his feet and bolted, screaming the whole way to keep its attention. It took off after him, moving in a combination of quick sprints and jumps as Sefu vaulted over the tables that littered the mead hall. It crashed its way through behind him, and Sefu turned at the last second to dodge a slash from its sharp, boney arm. Sefu ran back across the hall, pushing himself up with a chair and grasping the bottom of the broken window.

Sefu hauled his way through and tumbled onto the wet ground, cold rain pouring over him and soaking through his thin clothes. He got up and ran across the muddy ground, glancing behind him to see the beast climbing through the window. Sefu tore around the corner of the mead hall and down the street, trying to take in his surroundings. There were two bodies slumped outside the entrance to the mead hall, but other than that the city was surprisingly peaceful. There were no panicked civilians or rushing guards, and Sefu had to try hard not to let his mind wander to where they could be.

He twisted and turned down every alley he could find, using small gaps and sharp turns to slow down the demon that was trying to drag him to Hell. He listened to the monster tearing the city apart as it chased him, and he stumbled as he was blinded by a sudden flash of lightning. Blinking away the brightness, he heard a soft thump in front of him as the monster landed in the mud. It ran towards Sefu and threw a merciless punch towards him as another boom of thunder reverberated across the city, and Sefu dodged it within an inch. He ran backwards, then jumped for the window sill of a nearby home. He pulled himself up, grasping the top of the window frame and placing his foot on the sill, and finally he was on the roof, breathing heavily.

He felt the building shake as the creature tried to claw its way up after him, and Sefu rolled to his feet and ran across the roof, leaping over to another and making his way towards the city walls. *If I can escape the city, lure it away, at least I can buy time for Bayard and the others.* It had finally made its way to the rooftops and was bounding after him. Sefu jumped from the edge of the roof he was on and landed on a shorter home with a roll, then vaulted across a gap to another. Another flash of lightning lit the city walls ahead of him. *Close now, just a few more seconds.* Sefu leaned forwards and put everything he had into his speed, and finally he launched himself towards the wall, catching the edge of the wet stone with his fingertips.

Finally he was standing on the top of the wall, and he looked over the edge to the ten meter drop to the ground below. He would never make the drop uninjured enough to run. He turned and sprinted along the wall, looking for anything he could use to descend the wall. *A rope, a ladder, a damn mattress would work at this point.* There was a crash from behind him as the beast threw itself into the wall, trying desperately to reach its prey. Sefu could find nothing, the wall was bare except for some empty crates and racks of hand-held weapons that he knew would do nothing to the creature. Sefu turned a corner onto the southern wall and saw a row of unfamiliar devices lined up on the edge.

They looked like the crossbows that some of Bayard's companions carried, but the size of a merchant's carriage. There was another roar and a crash as it tried once more to scale the wall, and Sefu ran for the massive weapon. There was a handle on one side, protruding from a circle covered in rope and iron bands. Directly behind him was a long crate, and inside he saw a single massive arrow with a spiral broadhead, and a rusty greatsword that was longer than he was tall and had no hilt or handguard. Sefu turned back, grabbing hold of the handle and pulling. The whole back end of the thing started sliding with him. The string began to move, and the tension increased as he leaned back. Soon, he could move the handle no further with his arms alone. He fell back with all of his inconsiderable weight, pushing against the floor with his legs.

Suddenly, the handle slid backwards with a *clunk* and went loose, and Sefu realized that it was a crank. He stood back up and began twisting the heavy steel handle as fast as he could, and with each rotation the string of the weapon moved back another inch. There was a third crash, and the monster finally clawed its way onto the wall and stood. It looked around, and Sefu dropped to the floor, still working the handle. *It can't hear me through the rain.* He saw the top of its head as it wandered the wall, looking around for its target. It leaned over the edge and stared into the distance, then turned and started walking towards Sefu.

He picked up speed on the crank, and finally there was a much louder *clunk* as the string set into place. At the sound, the creature roared and started its sprint along the wall. Sefu stood and turned, running to the long crate that contained the arrow. He struggled to lift it, a five-foot long rod that came to a brutal, twisted point. He slammed it into the weapon and pulled it against the string, grasping the lever to his right. He leaned sideways, and the massive bow turned with him, loudly creaking as he pushed.

He looked up and saw the demon turning the corner towards him, and Sefu slid the weapon directly in its path. It began to run towards him, and Sefu pulled the lever. There was a loud *thud* and an extended groan from the metal, and Sefu looked down to see that the barbs of the arrow had caught on the front of the weapon and bent it into the wood. Sefu screamed a curse and grabbed the crank and it quickly sank back into place, but the arrow was ruined. Sefu tore it out of the weapon and threw it off the wall, and turned to see if he could find another.

He heard the footsteps of the monster behind him, and Sefu ducked and rolled just as the bone spike of an arm slammed into the stone where he had been a moment before. He stood and ran the other way, desperately searching for anything he could use. And then he realized. He ran back and reached into the long crate, grasping the base of the rusty, disassembled greatsword. *What else is an arrow, anyway? Something long and straight.* He turned and shoved the bare blade into the weapon just as the creature reached for him. He tried to dodge, but for the first time, he was too slow. The beast gripped Sefu's face with its giant hand and pushed, sending him off the wall.

He could have sworn he heard someone screaming his name as he fell, and a moment later, everything went dark.

*****

Three Hours Earlier

"This is the entrance," Ringlef said, pointing to an indentation in the stone base of the mountain that loomed over Sinead. Bayard dismounted his horse and stepped into the shadows, seeing a rectangular stone slab that rested against the dark grey mountain.

"This leads directly into Sinead?" Bayard asked incredulously. "How foolish could your kings have been? If one man betrayed the city, an army could come through here and take the city in a heartbeat."

Ringlef cackled and coughed into his elbow. "Not so much,

young one," he mumbled. "The entire path has been set with barrels of oil and blasting powder for a few dozen years now, and is always under watch by spyglass. If an attacking army enters the caverns, *BOOM*, and straight to Hell with all of them. The blast would destroy the castle's dungeon and half the mead hall, but it's better than losing the city."

"How are they to know we are not an attacking army?" Thomas asked.

"Just gotta show 'em a bit o' cooperation," Ringlef grunted. He grabbed a torch out of Gendrina's hand and waved it in the air. Moments later, a flaming arrow flew from the darkness above and landed a dozen meters away from them. "That means we can go in."

"What happens if we can't go in?" Thomas asked inquisitively.

"Well, the arrow would've landed in yer head," Ringlef said matter-of-factly.

Bayard grinned as he followed the old man to the slab. He pressed on the side of it, but it wouldn't budge. "Helmet, give us some help here," Bayard called. The giant man stepped up and leaned against the stone and it toppled sideways with ease, revealing a long, dark hall.

"Get more torches out," Ringlef said. "And do not set them on the ground for any reason." Bayard handed a torch to Helmet, telling him to follow in the rear of the group after he replaced the slab, and gave another to Pierre and a new one to Gendrina, as Ringlef still held her first. Bayard led the way into the tunnel and they walked slowly through the darkness, their visibility fading just a couple meters ahead of them.

"It feels like we've been walking for hours," complained one of the citizens of Bastoc, the second town they had evacuated on their way here. Uriel had feared that the citizens would not listen to them, but Bayard had correctly gauged their collective ignorance. He had scavenged the engraved pauldrons and signet ring off of Barric's body and put them on Helmet, and he played the part convincingly. Only the citizens of Gattewen knew the truth, but they had seen the threat with their own eyes and took no issue with Bayard's orders.

"We'll be in the city soon, quit your whinging," Ringlef shouted back at him. Minutes later, a sound began echoing through the hall. Bells rang continuously, and indistinct shouts passed by them. "Those're the alarm bells," Ringlef whispered. "It is already at the gates. Come now, we are close." They picked up their pace, and soon they were ascending a long staircase. "Just up here," Ringlef had said a total of six times before they finally reached a dirty wooden door. The bells had stopped, and Bayard found himself nearly praying that they had managed to kill Christopher without him having to deal with it. "Hopefully someone is present in the dungeons, or we might have to break our way in. It's happened before, they don't get mad." He stepped up and pounded on the door.

They were instantly greeted by a loud, terrified scream. "GO AWAY!" it shouted. "I cannot open the wall, the...the thing is broken!"

"Open the door here, you fool!" Ringlef shouted through the iron grate that rested in the center of the door.

"NO!"

"Get the big one up here," Ringlef sighed. It took a full minute for Helmet to squeeze his way past the citizens and to the door. Bayard moved everyone back as Helmet crashed his boot into the right side of the door. There was another scream from the man on the other end, but the door held through it and another two kicks after. On the fourth, the door finally crashed inwards and Helmet stumbled into the castle dungeon. Bayard walked in behind him to see a large, rectangular room full of crates and empty prison cells. In the corner, one small, shaking bald man sat huddled.

"Please go away," he cried.

"What is this madness?" Ringlef asked, stunned. "I heard the warning bells, the women and children were to take shelter here." Ringlef looked up, at a square of stone that did not match the rest of the wall. A long lever protruded from the wall beside it. Ringlef stood still, staring at the man in the corner. Slowly, his hands curled into fists. *"You...COWARD,"* Ringlef roared. Faster than Bayard could stop him, and far faster than any old man should be able to move, he pulled a long dagger from under his coat and sprinted for the man in the corner. The man screamed his pleas as Ringlef ran him through to horrified shrieks from many of the civilian women. The man coughed and fell sideways, and Ringlef withdrew the dagger. "Pathetic worms like you have no place in this city, or this world," he whispered to the dying man, seconds before he stopped breathing.

"That was...unnecessary," Bayard said. "We should have locked him in one of the cells and dealt with him properly when we could."

"There is no room for cowards in this city," Ringlef grunted, sliding the dagger back into his coat. "Forget about him, this wall here is the door to the castle. Pull the lever to get it open." Bayard stepped up and grasped the lever, giving it a pull. It slid easily along a slot in the stone wall, and the discolored stone in the center of the wall began to rise smoothly into the ceiling. They ascended some more steps, and soon Bayard walked out into the corner of the mead hall.

"If they couldn't get into the dungeons, where would the women have gone?" Bayard asked Ringlef.

"Anyone with brains would get to the kitchen," Ringlef said. "Large room, solid door, food to last a week at least. It's right there, next to the hearth," he finished, pointing to the flames that still lit the mead hall.

"Stay here," Bayard said firmly to Ringlef. "Watch over the citizens." Ringlef nodded, and Bayard ran for the door and knocked sharply on it. "Hello? Is there someone in there?" The door opened instantly, and Lilith bolted out and into his arms.

"Bayard, I thought you were dead," she cried into his chest.

"It takes a lot more than a giant mythological Hellbeast to kill me," Bayard said with a grin.

"Is that what it is then? Lilith hiccuped. Bayard could smell strong alcohol on her breath. "A true demon?"

"You know that it isn't, Lily. I will explain it to you in full later, but for now we must stop it."

Lilith's eyes suddenly went wide. "Sefu. He shut us in here and lured it away. We had nobody who could go after-" The quiet of the mead hall was broken by the roar that had grown too familiar to Bayard, followed by a bright flash of lightning.

"Lily, I promise you that it will not harm me. Stay here until I get back." He kissed her forehead and led her back into the kitchen, and she just sat down where she was. Bayard pushed the door closed and turned, running for the door of the mead hall. As he stepped out into the cold rain, he heard another roar to the south. "It's near the gates," Bayard said.

"What are we going to do?" Gendrina asked. "We cannot hurt him."

"*It,*" Bayard corrected her. "It is not truly Christopher anymore, and if we think of it as such, we will hesitate when we must not. As for what we will do, I honestly do not know. We must work with the surroundings, wherever it is. Since it won't try to kill us, we won't be able to lure it into a trap. Either way, Lilith said that Sefu is out here, and we must find-"

"Tom, Gen!" Bayard jumped and turned to see Jacob jog out from behind a nearby building. "I'm so glad you're all safe. What the bloody hell *is* that thing?"

Gendrina ran forwards and embraced her brother. "That is not important right now. What is important is the fact that we must kill it. No weapon will pierce its body, and we have no idea how to stop it. It is after Sefu, we think it's near the wall. Where the hell are the guards and soldiers?"

"We had entered the barracks to get weapons," Jacob explained. "The creature broke the door down, and the entrance collapsed. I was the only one small enough to crawl out. They're all sealed in there, it would take an hour to get them out. As for this enemy, you say no weapon can harm it, but how about a siege weapon? There are a dozen ballistae lined on the southern wall. If we can lure it up there and fire one into it, nothing could survive that."

"You are as smart a man as Bayard is sometimes, Jacob," Uriel laughed. "Hurry now, to the top of the wall!" They rushed through the streets, skidding on mud and stumbling over objects in the darkness. Numerous thunderclaps and lightning flashes broke the skies above them as they ran, and the rain got heavier with each passing moment. Soon they reached the base of the wall, and another lightning flash illuminated the beast. The city gates were wide open, the lock bar shattered through the middle as though it had been battered open by a siege ram.

There was a quick human scream, and Bayard looked up at the monster. He recognized Sefu's small frame, held across his face over the stone edge. There was nothing he could do as Christopher threw him off the top of the wall. "*SEFU!*" Bayard roared right before the boy landed in a heap outside the gate.

Uriel stood back as Bayard sprinted to the fallen boy. He knelt over the motionless body and shook Sefu, then pressed his head against his chest. "He is alive," Bayard shouted. "He has a broken leg, ribs too I'm sure, but his head seems uninjured. We have the mud to thank for that. Pierre, carry him to the castle and let Lilith treat him." Bayard stood, gingerly lifting the unconscious boy. He walked towards the six warriors, and passed Sefu to Pierre. "Be gentle, and avoid holding his left leg." Pierre nodded and walked away towards the castle without another word. While he wanted to fight, he did not argue. Bayard was the only reason he was still alive. The only reason any of them were still alive.

"Jacob," Uriel whispered. "That abomination up there is Christopher."

"What? That cannot be possible, how in-"

"Bayard would have to explain that to you. All you need to know is that he must be killed before he destroys this city. An army of infected travels this way as we speak, and the city must be secure before they arrive."

"I understand," Jacob said. "The stairs are this way." Jacob ran to the left, and around the base of a guard tower. A wooden staircase rose from the mud and they all made their way up, standing up to the sight of a low, full moon that shone through the black clouds. The beast still stood where it was, and it turned towards them as they lined up on the wall.

Bayard stepped forward and raised his axe. "Right before we left Valdus, you told us to end you should you ever join the dead. I do not know what it is that you are now, but it is not human. Christopher Alento, I accept your last wish. If you run, we will follow you. If you hide, we will hunt you. Fight us, and meet your death as the true warrior that you were."

The monster that was once a King roared again, louder than it ever had before. It raised its bone arm towards them like a man raising his sword to an enemy, and it charged. The group scattered, but the monster stayed focused on Bayard. He crouched, ready to dodge, but Helmet stepped into his view and grasped it around its right arm. Helmet was likely the only man strong enough to move Christopher in his current form, and Helmet twisted the creature away from Bayard. It quickly tore its arm away from Helmet and spun around, shouldering him to the floor.

Gendrina had been firing her arrows into the beast to no effect, and felt naught but air as she reached for another. "Gen, there!" Jacob shouted, pointing at a thin barrel a few meters to her left. She ran over to it and looked in, seeing countless arrow shafts.

She gave him a nod, reaching in to draw one of them. It was tipped with a sort of point that she had only seen once before, when Thomas had shown her around the barracks of Valdus as a child. *"Siege arrows,"* he had said. *"Very heavy, designed to pierce straight through shields and armor, but with no barbs or blades like are needed for hunting large game."* She held the fletching between her fingers and gave the long, slim spike a glance before she nocked it and pulled her bow. After a quick exhale, she released the arrow to great effect.

It slammed into the monster's back, sinking inches into its body. It lurched forwards with a roar, stumbling over Helmet and nearly slipping off the wall. It caught itself and sidestepped a tackle from Jacob, who then spun away from its reach. Jacob slashed at its face with his sword but the blade just slid across its hard flesh. It turned away from Jacob and grasped Helmet by the arm, lifting him to his feet. Helmet threw a mighty punch that went ignored by the beast as it turned and threw Helmet through the air. Helmet collided with Bayard, and then the creature was standing over Bayard, wrapping its one hand around his neck. Bayard choked, he could *feel* his throat collapsing under the pressure. He swung up, slamming his axe into the monster's head to no effect.

Just as his vision began to fade, Bayard saw Jacob on the beast's back, forcing a dagger into its left eye. It roared in pain and released Bayard, stumbling backwards as Jacob thrust the dagger in again. "Why won't he die?" Jacob hissed. "The dagger is long enough to reach his brain!"

"Up," Bayard coughed out. "You're stabbing too low, you have to twist it up." Jacob readied the dagger for another thrust, but the creature threw itself off its feet, slamming its entire weight on its back. On Jacob. The small man released his grip and lay still, and the monster grasped him by the front of his cuirass. Jacob was lifted off the ground, and another two arrows from Gendrina did nothing to stop it from sinking its teeth into the back of Jacob's neck.

Gendrina's screams combined with a string of thunder rolling over them completely drowned out the metallic crash as Uriel pulled the lever of the ballista. Faster than Bayard's eyes could track it, a greatsword was somehow lodged in the left side of Christopher's chest, protruding two feet out of his back. He dropped Jacob and stumbled backwards, grasping at the bare tang. Under the blackened, tumorous flesh that made up Christopher's face, was the unmistakable stare of disbelief. He fell backwards and hit the ground, the tip of the sword rolling him onto his side.

Bayard fell onto his knees next to Jacob, pressing his hands onto the wound as blood flowed through his fingers. Jacob's mouth was opening and closing silently, but the sickening motion thankfully ceased before Gendrina and Thomas could collapse over him. "He is gone," Bayard whispered to them. He knew that no words of sympathy would help them now, and he stood up to look over Christopher. "What the hell has happened here? Where did this sword come from?"

"That was me," Uriel said solemnly. "It was loaded in the first ballista. That is what took me so long. I never believed it would actually fire, and I was looking for a real bolt. There were none, and when I saw it lift Jacob, I had no choice. If I had fired first thing, this would not have-"

"Uriel, you will not blame yourself," Gendrina cried. "My brother is gone, but in this world, a death like this is the best a warrior can receive. Do not soil his memory with your regret."

Uriel looked to his feet, squeezing his eyes shut and shaking his head. Then he stood straight up, and gave Gendrina a formal salute. "I apologize for my display of weakness. Jacob Carter died as a true knight, and he will be given a place of honor within the Kingdom of Heaven."

Gendrina got on her knees and placed Jacob's arms over his chest, clenching his axe between them. "He will be safe here, for now. We must free the guards and soldiers, and prepare for the-"

A groan rose up behind her. Slow, deep, and dead. She stood and spun around, shaking from a mixture of grief, shock, and cold. The body of the beast was rising, slowly crawling to its feet, a continuous moan exhaling from its deformed mouth.

"His body couldn't fight it in death," Bayard whispered. "The plague got through, he is one of them now." Gendrina screamed and drew her bow, firing one of the siege arrows at its forehead. It pierced the skin, but would not penetrate the skull. She fired another at its eye, but its unsteady motions and her own dulled movement would not allow for it. Christopher started walking towards Helmet, the closest target. It moved faster than any other plaguewalker, but infinitely slower than it had prior to its death. "It is alright," Bayard called. "We can trap and burn it now, its mind is gone. We will lure it to the dungeons."

"No," Thomas said shakily. "The blasting powder, we cannot risk it."

"The kitchens then," Helmet said, jogging away from the seemingly immortal creature.

"That will not work either," Bayard said. "The door is solid, flames would be snuffed before they harmed it, and I'm sure the chimney is sealed."

"What are we to do then?" Uriel shouted. "The barracks are blocked off, there is nothing left-" His question was soon answered by the skies themselves. A blinding flash of light illuminated the city, and they were all knocked back by a massive pressure wave. The wall shook and stone crumbled, and Bayard felt like he had been struck in the chest by a charging bull. The madness ceased as suddenly as it had started, and Bayard forced himself to his feet, deafened and nearly blind. Blinking rapidly, he shook his head and gritted his teeth. His vision slowly faded back in, and he exhaled with exhaustion as he saw the charred husk that had been Christopher.

The sword still protruded from his chest, scorched from the heat of the lightning. Bayard grasped the tang and pulled it from what was left of the beast, holding it out in front of him as the others got to their feet. At the very base of the blade was a simple design, a curved line topped with a flattened circle that could have signified an anvil or a hammer. "This blade," Bayard said. "Bare steel, water, and lightning. Not a good combination for anyone who's holding the sword. Helmet, have you ever seen a forgemaster's mark like this?"

Helmet stepped up and took the steel from Bayard, blinking quickly. "This is not a forgemaster's mark. It means whoever forged this weapon is faithful to the Thunder God, Thor. There are very few of us left."

Bayard closed his eyes and shook his head in disbelief. "Now that is something else, isn't it?" he whispered. "I'll have to restore this weapon, and give it a proper place with us."

*****

"It won't budge," Sjarmir grunted, letting go of one of the large stones that blocked the exit. "We cannot get enough people in here to move them. We have no choice but to wait for rescue."

"There might be no rescue," one of the guards said worriedly. "Nearly all combatants are in here, that demon could have wiped out everyone else in the city by now."

"He is right," someone else whispered. "It has made no sound for a time, there may be nobody left."

"Silence," Sjarmir hissed. "There is enough food in here to last days, and we have air from the drainage tunnels where Jacob Carter escaped from. Hopefully he led the citizens through the dungeons to safety. We will find our way-" He was interrupted as the ground beneath them lurched, and more dirt fell from the ceiling of the underground tunnel. "We must wait out the storm further underground, the entrance may not be finished collapsing."

"Why do you get to give the orders?" a guard shouted at him. "Yer a bleedin' blacksmith!"

"Well nobody else seems to be doing it, and I was a guard once," Sjarmir asserted, holding his arms out challengingly. "King's missing, Barric is missing, even that kid Kerren is nowhere to be seen. So come with me, or stay here and get crushed like a bug." Sjarmir pushed through the group and retreated around a corner. He walked into the first armory and sat himself on a stool in the corner, inwardly grinning as soldiers and guards began to trickle into the room after him. They sat silently for nearly an hour, listening to the thunder booming above them. Just as he started to nod off, Sjarmir heard a crackle and a crash from the hallway.

He jogged from the armory, expecting a more grievous cave-in, but instead he saw three armored men standing shadowed in the moonlight, one of whom was big enough to lift a boulder. Soon, two more people stepped up behind them. The rest of the soldiers gathered in the hall, squinting at the group through the darkness.

"Good job, Helmet," the smallest of them said to the big one. He spotted Sjarmir and the rest, raising his hand in a wave. As the brightness eased off of Sjarmir's eyes, he could see that it was Bayard Travers and his own people from Valdus. "Good to see you are all alive," Bayard said. "You all likely know our names by now, so I will not bother with introductions. I regret to tell you that King Alvor has perished to the plague, as has Barric Eathellen. The city is safe, for now. We killed the monster, but an army of plaguewalkers approaches, numbering in the thousands. They will be at our gates by midday tomorrow, and if you wish to save yourselves and the people you love, you must do as I say. Bring every weapon there is in here to the gates, light armors too. Send five men to retrieve a new lock bar, and if there are any bolts for the ballistae in the siege garage, get them to the top of the wall with haste. There is a dead man there, he should be carried to the castle and left somewhere safe until we are able to bury him. Uriel, get to the castle and retrieve any and all combat-capable civilians, including women, then bring them to the gates. Leave the children and any mothers. When you get everyone together, lead a band of twenty outside the gate and dig a trench, at least five feet wide and deep, across the road about twenty meters away from the gate."

"Guess we know who's giving the orders now," someone whispered in Sjarmir's ear with a nudge.

*****

"Will you two be able to fight?" Bayard asked Thomas and Gendrina.

"Aye," Thomas said. "We've known this whole way that any of us could fall at any time, and he was ready to die in service to the living. We will mourn our brother after those who still live are made safe."

Bayard gave him a nod. "Then I am putting you in charge of training the people of Sinead. After the soldiers get everything in place and join the civilians at the gates, teach them all how the walkers must be killed. Do not coddle them, tell them the facts. For now though, locate Lilith and find out how Sefu is doing, then get to the gate." Thomas waved his hand in confirmation and climbed out over the rubble.

"What do you wish of me?" Gendrina asked.

"Accompany Uriel to the castle and watch as he informs the women there. If any of them seem particularly frail, tell them to stay put. Then find Pierre, and the both of you work on repairing the mead hall doors. That will be our last line of defense before we are forced to flee the city through the tunnel." Bayard turned to Helmet. "I know we always make you do the mule work, but you never seem to mind. Go to the top of the wall and position all the ballistae to face south, then get them pulled. Even if there is no stock of bolts, we can fire spears from them since they are useless against the dead while held in hand." Helmet saluted him and ran off. "That is all for now," Bayard rose his voice as he hollered over the soldiers. "Do your jobs, and do them quickly."

Chapter Twenty-Six
Autumn of 1513 A.D
City of Sinead
Morning

The sun showed ten hours past midnight when the sound of the dead could first be heard on the winds. Bayard stood up, stretching his legs after an hour on the grindstone. He held his new weapon out in front of him. Exactly his own height from tip to pommel, newly mirror-polished, and coated with the thinnest oil he could find, it was the most impressive weapon that he had ever seen. The lightning had traveled from the base of the tang to the tip of the blade, causing an incredible, almost frost-like design to be etched into the steel. The new handle was polished oak, held to the tang with thick iron pegs, wrapped in dark leather and studded to the wood.

Bayard heard the door of the smithy creak open behind him, and he placed the flat of the blade over his shoulder as he turned towards it. Sjarmir, Sinead's civilian smith, stepped through carrying a plate of beef and bread along with a large goblet of water. He set it all down on the anvil and sat on one of the small stools that were scattered around the room. "You did that blade an honor," Sjarmir said. "I would have thought it finished, seeing the state it was in when you showed it to me."

"Once I ground the rust off, the blade itself was flawless," Bayard said. "Admittedly, it is far better craftsmanship than I could have ever produced at my best. Am I to assume you are the one who forged this?"

Sjarmir shook his head with a grin. "There are people, even in this city, who would see one burned for worshiping a pagan god. Officially, I have never seen this weapon in my life. Under the table, I hope it serves you well. What will you name it?"

"I have never named a sword," Bayard said softly, looking to the symbol at the base of the blade. "Being a smith, I have crafted swords only to be named by others."

"It is yours now, give it a name worthy of your cause."

Bayard thought silently for a long moment. "Life," he finally said. "The strongest power there is. The limitless cycle that forces its way through every challenge that it is faced with, that will defeat even death itself. The sword shall be named Life."

"It is a good name," Sjarmir said. "A powerful name. Eat now, we need our strength."

Bayard set Life in a rack and pulled a stool near the anvil, across from Sjarmir. He picked up the largest cut of beef and bit into it, feeling the juices soak into his mouth. "I wonder if they feel *anything,*" Bayard said suddenly. "Do they enjoy the taste of us, do they think they must feed to survive? What logic could there possibly be in a plague that can only be spread through such contact? There are so many questions that I feel compelled to find answers to, and yet the only thing that can be done is to slay each and every one of them. As a man of science, this plague is my bane, far more than any religion or false wise man."

"What the fuck are you prattling on about?" Sjarmir groaned.

Bayard looked down and shook his head. "I apologize for that. I just needed to let that out. Nothing matters but defeating the plague." They finished eating in silence, and they soon made their way outside and into the cold morning air. The storm had faded three hours past, and while there was no more thunder and rain, the ground was still thick mud that grasped at Bayard's boots as he walked towards the gates. The further south he got, the more the moans of the dead were drowned out by the sounds of soldiers and the shouts of Thomas. Bayard smiled when he saw citizens of Valdus and Peydenal scattered in the crowd. He had barely seen any of them since their arrival, as they had been lodged in taverns and brothels throughout the city since there was no room in the castle for all of them. Soon Thomas's voice became fully audible.

"-And remember what I said about watching your legs. The infected are clumsy, always falling all over the place. It is not uncommon for them to decide to crawl at you rather than bothering to stand back up. Also, ballista fire will likely take a lot of their legs off, so keep an eye on the ground. You might see some that still carry the helmets they wore when they died. If you must attack a plaguewalker as such, strike at the upper center of its back. This will not *kill* it, so to speak, but it will completely disable them. If it wears armor on its torso as well, retreat and allow someone with a war hammer or mace to handle it. Breaking the neck is the only way to bring one of these sorts down. If you carry a bow, be sure to use arrows with heavy broadheads, or it may not pierce the skull when fired from-"

Bayard sneaked around the crowd as they took in Thomas's surprisingly well-constructed speech. He looked over his shoulder and saw Sjarmir joining the crowd, and Bayard began his climb to the top of the wall. Ten meters may not seem too far when you look up at it, but looking down was another story. Bayard had never been particularly afraid of heights, but it was an unsettling climb. The rickety wooden steps creaked under his feet with nothing below to save him.

Soon enough he stepped onto the stone wall, and was glad to see Helmet fast asleep, using a stone brick as a pillow. Bayard walked the southern wall, examining the ballistae and the contents of the five crates that had been lined up behind them. Each of the ballistae had been pulled and loaded with a proper bolt, and one of the crates contained dozens of spares. The other crates carried siege arrows, torches, small barrels of oil, and a number of folded, loose-knit fishing nets. Bayard turned away from the crates and strode over to Helmet.

Bayard gently nudged Helmet with his boot, and the large man shifted with a grunt. "Sorry friend," Bayard said loudly, over the din from below. "Time to wake up, we need to set defenses outside the gates before the dead arrive. Have you any idea if the soldiers finished with the trench?"

"Yeh," Helmet grunted sleepily. "Trench got done...eh, what time is it?"

"Ten hours past."

"Aye, it got done about three hours ago then, that's when I came up 'ere and passed out. Pierre and Gen were rollin' the barrels of oil, and Uriel and those three young squires were draggin' the trunk of ruined swords and spears."

"That is good," Bayard said with a nod. "Have you heard any news of Sefu?"

"Mm-hmm," Helmet confirmed. "The young Princess came with a message for you, but nobody knew where you were. She said 'Lilith says that Sefu will be fine after a long recovery. He is already awake and men...menal...'"

"Mentally stable," Bayard finished for him with a wide grin.

"Tha's the one," Helmet mumbled. "And that he has been taken into the dungeons next to the escape tunnel, along with Jacob's body."

Bayard's smile faded quickly. "It was me, you know," Bayard whispered. "I'm the one that got him involved in all of this. Jacob was the first person I saw when I arrived at Valdus. He wanted to get his siblings and escape the city. The first thing I did to him was tie him up and keep him hostage in a barn. But somehow, he ended up following me to the very end, as a warrior and as one of the best friends I've ever had. When I first met Christopher, he immediately tried to kill me. Only three months after that, he sacrificed himself so we could escape. In turn, he lost his mind and became the biggest enemy of everything we tried to accomplish. Not five minutes after I met Gendrina, she put an arrow in the shoulder of a knight, and now she is a knight. She went from a rash and violent child, to the best warrior that I know. And you, Helmet. You had everything torn away from you by this city, but you forgave them and now you fight for them."

"It was not Sinead, it was the Drydens," Helmet growled. "I will not blame an entire city for the actions of five people. Besides, if I wanted to choose a city to hate, it would be Valdus. It means nothing now, though. Valdus is gone, Sinead is pretty much under your control, and you are the one I am loyal to."

"That means much to me," Bayard said, holding out his hand to Helmet. The giant man took it but got to his feet on his own, knowing that he was likely to haul Bayard off the wall if he applied any actual pull. "However, I have no control over the city. Queen Gillian still holds reign over Sinead, though I hope she will allow me to lead them through this battle."

"Erm," Helmet said worriedly, shifting his eyes to his right.

Bayard sighed. "What's all that about? Out with it."

"At about two past midnight," Helmet started, "we assembled the citizens of the castle, includin' the Queen, and Uriel informed 'em of Alvor and Barric's death."

"And?"

"And the Queen retreated to 'er chambers and jumped from the balcony."

Bayard sat down on one of the ballista platforms, his mouth hanging slightly open. "Well, that isn't good."

"Yuh-huh," Helmet agreed.

"We needed a figurehead," Bayard said softly. "Someone to hold stability while we give the true orders before and during combat.

With nobody official to keep the peace, the soldiers may break into anarchy, and we absolutely cannot have that."

Surprisingly, Helmet stifled a chuckle and his face broke into a grin. "You've been gone for a long while, Bayard. Decisions were made, votes were had. Where were you, anyway?"

Bayard stood straight, reaching over his shoulder and pulling the greatsword from his back and holding it out to Helmet. "I was doing this. Many Kings and other leaders believe that they must always be active, controlling every move their men make. However, I believe that if a leader makes his choices in fear, anger, or grief, all he will lead his companions to is an early grave. I had to isolate myself, center my thoughts, let go of my fear. I had to accept Jacob's death, and forgive myself for all the mistakes that I have made. I will lead as who I truly am, unimpaired by negativity and regret."

Helmet stepped forward and embraced Bayard with a painful bear hug. "Tha's exactly why the choice was made," he grunted as he set Bayard back on the wall. "Come with me, there's somethin' you need to see." Helmet turned and started down the wooden steps; how they managed to support him, Bayard would never know. He followed carefully as Helmet reached the bottom and began clearing a path through the crowd.

There were hushed whispers as people began to notice Bayard, and Helmet soon stood aside and motioned him onto the wooden stage where Thomas still stood. *"And here he is now!"* Thomas was shouting at the top of his lungs. Bayard stepped up onto the platform, dirty, tired, and battered. Thomas had his arm raised in a salute, and he lowered it towards Bayard as he fell to one knee. *"The man who has come from nothing and now works to protect everything, the man who will save this city, and who will save all of England! Behold, Lord Bayard Travers, the King of the Living!"*

As one, all the soldiers and citizens of Sinead and Valdus combined got on their knees. The guards and soldiers held their swords along the ground in front of them, bowing their heads in fealty. Bayard looked over them, stunned. He knew he had to do *something,* but no words of glory came to him. Instead, he raised his sword in front of him and knelt down, placing it along the floor of the platform.

"An army should not exist to serve one King," Bayard said, trying to make his voice solid yet loud enough to reach the entire crowd.

"A King should exist to serve one army. As long as you place your trust in me, I will put everything I am into protecting the lives of you and your families. You will learn how to survive this plague, and we will take back England from its grasp. There is no time for any sort of a speech from me, so just heed these words: This city is the bastion of life, and I will *never* let it fall. Do not applaud me, do not bow to me. Rise up and steel your hearts and souls for battle against death itself. Anyone who still holds no weapon, find one, quickly. I am sure that Thomas already told you what to look for. Everyone else, get outside the gates. You will find a trunk full of ruined swords, stripped of their hilts, and spears that have been cut in two. Climb into the trench and insert the weapons into the mud, pointy ends up. Then pour the barrels of oil evenly along the bottom of the trench. The first wave of infected will fall into this trap, and be set alight. Soon they will fill the trench, and the others will walk over them to our gates. That is when we fight."

Two hours later, the first of the plaguewalkers stepped out of the trees in the distance. Bayard and all his companions stood atop the wall, staring at the encroaching plague through ornate brass spyglasses. "Damn rain," Gendrina spat from her place next to Bayard as they looked over the edge of the wall. "That's an isolated patch of trees, had it stayed dry we could have burned the whole thing down with flaming ballista fire."

"I had that exact same thought last night," Bayard said. "It is alright though, it would have only stopped a few hundred of them, and the smoke cloud might have attracted unwanted attention. We do not need another city attempting to come to our aid, uninformed of what they face."

"Do you really think that we can defeat thousands of them?" Uriel asked. "Of course, I will fight to my own death, but it would be regrettable to send untrained civilians to theirs."

Bayard clapped Uriel on his armored shoulder. "I told the civilians to arm themselves to raise their morale. Everyone feels better with a weapon in their hand. In truth, not one of them will have to lift a finger against the dead."

"What are you getting at?" Thomas asked, looking to Bayard and tilting his head.

"The infected will come to the city," Bayard started. "Many of them will fall to the razor wire, trench, and ballista and archer fire. When the main mass of their army reaches Sinead, our gates will fall within minutes. There is nothing we can do to stop that after the damage Christopher dealt to the hinges before the lock bar gave out. They cannot be repaired or replaced without days of work. I will sound the retreat, and everyone in here will run through the escape tunnel and out to safety. But I will not seal the door, I will let the infected follow us in, I will let them fill the tunnels until there is not one bit of room left in there. And then I will bring the mountain down on top of them."

"Bloody hell, Bayard," Thomas whispered. "You will never cease to amaze me."

"I have a feeling it would not amaze Sinead's people," Bayard said. "They would fear the destruction of their city from such a tactic, that is why it must appear as though there is no choice. However, we need someone who can stay behind and ignite the blasting powder when the time comes. I will not send anyone to their deaths, so it must be someone who can hold their own and make a fast escape."

"I'll do it," Pierre said quickly. "I have the most experience surviving the dead by myself, and I am a skilled climber. I'll be able to get over any part of the wall with ease."

"Very well, the task will be yours," Bayard agreed. "Uriel, head down and find the best archers, either military or hunters. Bring them up here and help them fill quivers with the siege arrows. Thomas, find guards who are familiar with the ballistae. We'd be better off with nobody firing them than someone who's never handled one before. As soon as they're up here, have them start firing into the horde. Target large groups rather than the ones in front." The two men saluted and retreated down the steps. "Everyone else, wait by the gates, and be ready for battle when they are breached. We must hold the line while the civilians escape, before we retreat for ourselves."

It was eleven hours past midnight when the first of the plaguewalkers toppled into the trench. It was pierced by numerous blades and it squirmed pathetically at the bottom as more soon began to fall in. Ballistae thundered in Bayard's ear as he pulled his longbow for what felt like the hundredth time. His fingers were raw and it felt like the entirety of his right shoulder had stopped existing long ago, but still he fired into the horde. He had found his aim and was easily landing more than half his shots in their heads, dropping them instantly. He had never used archery in combat, however he had trained with every weapon imaginable throughout his life, and it came to him quickly.

Gendrina and Uriel stood at his sides, firing their own bows. On either side of them stood twenty more Sinead men, and a few civilians from Valdus who had once made their living on the hunt. The line of archers had done an incredible job holding back the army of walkers, but now the center of the horde had reached them and the crate of arrows was on its last layer. Lines of infected were mowed down by ballista fire, splattering across the mud and knocking over any that walked nearby.

The trench was quickly filled with the writhing bodies, and the rest of the horde was able to walk over them on the final stretch to the gates of Sinead. "Gendrina, ignite it, now!" Bayard hollered over the ballistae. She nodded and spun, running to a small barrel which contained the special arrows, their tips wrapped in cotton cloth and soaked in oil. She nocked it and held the tip in the flame of a torch that hung from the wall of the guard tower. It blazed up instantly, and she pulled the bow and took aim. She had to wait a few moments for a clear shot, but soon she released the flaming arrow.

It landed perfectly, sticking into the oil-filled barrel on the left side of the trench. It took nearly half a minute for the flame to take hold, burning the outside of the barrel before the oil inside caught with spectacular effect. A plume of flame flew twenty meters into the sky, and the trench went up in an absolute inferno. More and more infected passed through the flames, igniting themselves in the process. The tactic cleared out a massive chunk of the horde, but in time the fires died, and the dead began to pile up against the gates of Sinead.

"They are at the gates!" Bayard roared to the people below. "Archers, keep firing! Skirmishers, prepare for close combat!" Bayard turned and stepped close to Uriel. "You are in charge up here until they breach the gates. When they do, get off the wall quickly and start cutting them down. Send the civilians who are up here to the mead hall as soon as the dead get through."

Uriel nodded, and Bayard ran off and made his way down the

steps. He pushed his way to the front of the crowd and turned to face his subjects. "There are too many at the gates," Bayard called over them. "We are low on arrows, and we cannot set them aflame when they are right outside like this. They will break through soon, but do not be afraid. All civilians, make your way to the mead hall with haste, and wait outside the dungeons. I am not sure if it is common knowledge among the citizens here, but there is an escape tunnel that leads out of the city, to the other side of the mountain. It is lined with blasting powder, we will use it to wipe out the army of plaguewalkers."

"Are you mad?" someone shouted. "You'll destroy the whole city!"

"I do not believe so," Bayard said. "The dungeons and mead hall will likely not survive the blast, but the castle proper and the rest of the city should be unaffected. Either way, there will soon be no other choice. That is my order, retreat to the mead hall. All combatants, form a line and prepare to hold them back while the civilians escape." Thankfully, the citizens accepted his order. The civilians turned and trudged through the mud back towards the castle, as the soldiers stepped back and got into formation.

Bayard took his place in front of them, and the gates began to buckle as he was joined by Thomas, Pierre, and Helmet. The gate began to groan, and Bayard could see the hinges shuddering. A motion of red caught Bayard's eye, and he saw Gendrina, Uriel, and the rest of the archers descend the steps. "Arrows are gone," Gendrina yelled. The ballistae still sounded from above; they took so long to reload that the crate of bolts was lasting a long time. "The guards on the ballistae will follow the wall around the city and rope down when they are out of bolts."

"Helmet, you are in charge of the civilians," Bayard said, pointing towards the retreating crowd. "Get them through the tunnel, and help them pile every large stone they can find near the exit. We need to be able to block off the infected from escaping." Helmet nodded and took off after them. There was another strained groan from the lock bar. "Pierre, find a place to hide near the mead hall. Do not draw any attention until you hear their moans fade, and you know they are in the escape tunnel. There is an oil barrel near the dungeon entrance, ignite it and roll it in there after them, then shut the door and *get out*. There may be stragglers in the city, so be cautious."

"Always am," Pierre said seriously, and he strode away after Helmet. It was three minutes later that the hinges gave out, and the deathly army began to crawl over the fallen gates and into the city.

"Prepare yourselves!" Bayard roared, holding his new weapon out in front of him. "Fight smart, and you will live to see a new dawn! Remember Thomas's words, and do not fear them! FOR THE LIVING!" Bayard grasped the long hilt of his blade and brought it thundering down into the skull of the first plaguewalker, splitting it through to its stomach. He slid the sword free from its corpse and spun, beheading two more with a single sweeping slash. A collective cry of battle sounded from behind him, and Bayard stepped back as his army engaged the enemy.

Bayard was surprised at the skill with which Sinead's soldiers fought the dead. They stayed at arm's length, hacking into their skulls with the pikes of axes and hammers. They were forced to break the line soon after the walkers entered the city. They backed away slowly, always making sure to not get cornered, and danced around groups of the infected as they methodically cut them down. A few had fallen, overwhelmed by the sheer number of enemies, but the horde was being effectively held back.

Bayard was keeping away from the main congregation of soldiers, running between groups of the plaguewalkers and slaying them in droves with Life. The length of the weapon would not allow for combat in close proximity with his men, so he supported those in need of aid and finished off any infected that were still in motion but too damaged to be a threat. It had been twenty minutes of battle, and Bayard knew they would have to retreat soon or else the casualties would grow too high. "Ten more minutes, men!" Bayard yelled. "Start making your way further towards the mead hall, but do not stop attacking!"

Slowly, carefully, they made their way up the hill. Bayard glanced behind him, seeing the mead hall rising up into the castle. The doors were shut, and Bayard ran to the back of his soldiers and pushed. They were locked.

"WHAT THE FUCK IS THIS?" Bayard roared, pounding on the thick doors with the hilt of his blade. A second later, he heard a lock unlatch, and the door creaked inwards. Lilith stood there, and behind her was Jenara, Helmet, and Pierre. All the citizens of Sinead and Valdus stood within the mead hall, huddled together with their families. Lilith was shaking head to toe, and tears streamed down her smooth face.

"Bayard," she cried. "The wall to the dungeons is closed. That *bastard* squire, Kerren...he ran into the dungeons with a crossbow, forced me and Jenara to drag Sefu out, and he shut the wall. Jacob's body is still in there. Pierre climbed in through the window when he saw the mead hall doors close, but it was too late."

Bayard screamed his absolute fury to the uncaring dead, slamming his boot into the stone wall. "Get inside," he hissed. "Everyone in the mead hall. Brace the doors with one of the tables in here." Two Sinead men started pushing shut the heavy doors. Bayard turned towards Lilith, but got knocked aside by a large force. He spun to see Helmet's back charging out the doors just as they clicked shut.

*****

Helmet heard Bayard yell after him as the doors closed behind him, but there was no going back. Sinead was his city at birth, and it was his city now, and he would not let its people fall. He barreled through the plaguewalkers like a horse through tall grass, spiking one every second that passed. He physically *threw* smaller ones into groups, sending them sprawling out of his way. The biggest concentration of them was still focused on the mead hall, but many had broken off to give chase. As he jumped onto the fallen gate, he stopped and turned. *I can't let them follow me out of the city. Have to make sure that they are either dead or focused on the mead hall.*

He dropped off of the gate and walked back into Sinead, splitting the skull of his nearest follower with the axe head. He landed a side kick on one that approached his left, spiked another, and turned to slam his boot through the skull of the fallen first. Forty of them fell to his power before no more came for him, and he ran out of the city. Disabled, crawling infected nearly carpeted the mud outside of the gates, unable to get over the thick wood into the city.

Helmet kicked and stomped his way through them until he reached the edge of the forest that lead around Sinead's mountain. There were many walkers here as well, that apparently couldn't manage to find their way to the gates and instead decided to dig their way into the city through the foundation of the mountain. Their hands were bloody from pounding against the stone, and Helmet executed each of them before he began the open run towards the escape tunnel.

It took nearly an hour to make his way there, switching between jogging and sprinting. The stone slab rested against the tunnel, and Helmet grasped it around middle and hauled it off to the side. Helmet had no torch, and the darkness of the tunnel loomed in front of him. *I just have to hold to the wall, it's pretty much a straight line.* He pressed his left elbow against the wall and started walking as quickly as he could in the darkness. He tripped and stumbled over fallen stones and changes in the ground, and he fell over twice, scraping his hands and forehead before he finally felt the ground angle upwards into the final ascent to the dungeons.

I have to be in time, the doors will hold, Bayard will protect them. His thoughts distracted him, and he barely heard the *click* and *twang* of the crossbow before the bolt slammed dead-center in his chest. Helmet stumbled backwards with a gasp, sure that he was going to die. He felt a piercing pain, and he was certain that ribs had broken. He grasped at the shaft and slid his hand down, and to his immense relief, he felt the end of the steel tip sticking from his armor.

"Nice try, yeh traitorous animal!" Helmet roared down the stone hall. "Never fire razor-heads into armor, the weight is too spread out!" Helmet ran forwards, crouching down and opening his arms to prevent the squire from sneaking past him. Sure enough, he felt something brush his left arm, and he reached down and caught the small man by his hair.

"Release me, filth!" Kerren hissed, uselessly slamming the butt of his crossbow into Helmet's side. "I should have been King, not some Valdus *pig*! I served King Alvor the Wolf for twenty years!"

"Both Alvors would 'ave given you the Blood Eagle had they seen you like this," Helmet growled. "Sadly, there's no time for that now." He pressed Kerren against the stone wall and ran his hands up until they wrapped around his little throat. With one powerful twist, Kerren collapsed dead at Helmet's feet. Helmet snapped the shaft of the bolt with his axe and started moving again, up the slanting hall.

*****

"It's not going to hold, the lock is going to give out!" Ringlef shouted. Bayard leaned all his weight against the wooden table, feeling it shake as the countless plaguewalkers pressed against the mead hall doors. It creaked and groaned, and Bayard heard the crack as the lock splintered free of the wood. Uriel and Thomas joined Bayard, pushing back against the dead through the table. Bayard felt the ground shake beneath him, but he could not let his mind wander from the task at hand. More soldiers joined the three, holding the thin wood that was the only thing between them and thousands of ravenous monsters.

Seconds later, a loud voice boomed out from behind the crowd. "If yeh're all done hugging that table, it might be a good idea to get out of 'ere."

Helmet. Bayard motioned at a Valdus soldier to take his place against the barrier, and he pushed through the civilians to see the giant of a blacksmith leaning against the frame of the dungeon hall. "Helmet, there are no words," Bayard whispered.

"Just teach me how to make tha' spiral thing you do on yer pommels, and we'll call it even," Helmet said with a grin.

"Deal," Bayard agreed. "Pierre, get into the kitchens and make no sound. Our first plan still stands, with a few changes. Once all the walkers get into the tunnel, bolt the door and get outside. When you hear three blows of the war horn, it means we are clear of the tunnel. That is when you will ignite the powder. Ringlef, have you any idea how long the fuse is?"

"'Bout thirty seconds, last I knew," the old man said. "Should be enough time to get clear of the mead hall. I should warn you all that nobody is *quite* sure how big the blast will be, so I would not stop running until it goes off."

"Obviously," Pierre mumbled. "I'm not sure if I'm going to live or die here, so I'll just say 'See you on the other side', it seems to work both ways." Bayard gave him a nod of respect as he retreated into the kitchens.

"Anyone who is not holding the table, make your way to the dungeons. Ringlef will lead you through, nobody else should handle a torch in there. Lilith will lead the transport of Sefu and Jacob, so do what she says. We'll handle the barricade for as long as we can, and join you then."

Many of the soldiers saluted Bayard, and started shepherding the civilians towards the dungeons. They disappeared down the steep stairs, and Bayard took his place against the table again.

"This gives a new meaning to 'Late to the dinner table', doesn't it?" Gendrina said softly.

"What are you on about?" Uriel grunted.

"Get it? Late, because they're dead. And it's a table...and we would be their dinner."

"Oh shut it, Gen," Thomas groaned, obviously struggling not to laugh in light of their current situation.

"Oh shit," Sjarmir whispered. "The window!"

Bayard looked to his left, and saw the arms and head of a plaguewalker writhing within the shattered window of the mead hall. "They've piled high enough where they can just climb right over each other," Bayard whispered. "The hall is lost, we must retreat right now. Release the table and run for it on my command." Bayard waited until the first of the infected toppled through the window, and then he shouted: "NOW!" The ten warriors who held the barricade released the wood and sprinted for the dungeons as the table toppled behind them, and the moans of the dead doubled in volume as they flowed into the mead hall.

The group made their way down the stairs, through the halls and dungeons, and finally into the escape tunnel. They moved as quickly as they could in the dark, and soon the sounds of speech could be heard echoing ahead of them, growing louder by the second. Eventually, Bayard blindly crashed into a woman's back to the response of a loud shriek, but for the first time in more than four months, he smiled in true triumph. The groans and howls of the plaguewalkers followed after them, and Bayard knew that they were pouring into the tunnel behind them. He had done it, he had saved Sinead.

Soon after his arrival was made known, a light started moving towards him and Jenara nudged her way out of the crowd, handing him a torch. "Christopher would be so proud of what you've done," she whispered to Bayard.

"I know he would," Bayard lied. Jenara still had no idea as to the identity of the abomination that had nearly destroyed Sinead the night before. Exclamations of disgust started spreading among the crowd, and Bayard soon realized why as his torchlight spread over the body of Kerren, slumped against the wall with his head twisted grossly to the side. Bayard bent over and took his crossbow, handing it to Gendrina. "No need to abandon a good weapon," he said.

It was an hour later that the rectangle of sunlight could be seen ahead of them, and Bayard breathed in deeply as they stepped out into the clean air, untainted by the scent of the dead. The guards who had been firing the ballistae were leaning against the mountain base, and they jumped to their feet at Bayard's appearance. Uriel and Gendrina shoved the stone slab back into place in light of Helmet's injuries, then began piling even more heavy stones in front of the slab. After they finished, Bayard led his people nearly a mile away from the tunnel before he reached into his rucksack, pulling out the war horn that had once belonged to King Alvor. He inhaled deeply and bellowed thrice into it towards Sinead, then looked to the mountain.

The single minute that passed felt like it could have been a year, and Bayard was starting to feel worried just before he was knocked off his feet by the force of the explosion. Everyone in the crowd collapsed over each other, and Bayard watched the stone slab launch hundreds of meters across the open field, followed by the bodies of hundreds of infected. Many were on fire, and very few were in one piece. The whole mountain rumbled, and massive boulders shook free from it as the tunnel completely collapsed, sending dust and gravel flying in every direction.

"It is done," Bayard said just loudly enough for everyone to hear. There were a few seconds of silence as the people of Sinead and Valdus got to their feet and began to comprehend what had happened. Laughter and shouts started lightly at first, but it was soon a full-fledged riot of celebration. The warriors of Sinead tore off their cuirasses and pounded on their chests in victory, and civilians and soldiers of Valdus and Sinead alike embraced as brothers and sisters, their past uneasiness knocked from their minds in this one glorious moment.

Bayard let them have this, but he himself stayed still. He knew the day was not over, and there was still darkness to come.

Nearly two hours passed before a Valdus woman called out, pointing into the woods nearby. A blackened shape shambled from the trees, stumbling over a root. Bayard stood, grasping his sword, before the figure raised his hand in a wave. "Hello!" Pierre called. "Don't bother returning the greeting, I would not hear it anyway."

Bayard leaned back while the battered man made his way to them and fell to the ground next to him. Thomas, Gendrina, Lilith, Uriel, Helmet, and Jenara all joined them while the people of the two cities celebrated behind them. "Are you alright, Pierre?" Bayard asked, looking over him.

"Aye, I think," Pierre moaned. "I really can hardly hear, but that will fix itself soon enough. And my arse is badly burned, but I think

I'll live."

"You are missing an eyebrow," Jenara whispered, rubbing her thumb along Pierre's forehead.

Pierre batted her hand away. "Never liked em anyway," he mumbled. He leaned back in the grass and stared up into the sky. "So, Bayard...have you handled the bitten yet?"

"No," Bayard said softly. "It will need to be soon though, before they start showing their sickness."

"I will do it, if you wish it," Uriel offered.

"It has to be me," Bayard asserted. "Their King should be the one to perform such a task. They were told it would be done, and I believe they are prepared for it." Bayard got to his feet and walked towards the still-cheering crowd. "People of Valdus and Sinead," Bayard shouted over them. Their noise died down slowly as they turned their attention to him. "I understand that this should be a time for celebration, but there is something that still must be done. If you were bitten, you know what has to happen. You are all great and honorable warriors, and I know that you can all be trusted to accept what needs to be done. Please step forward."

There was a murmur through the crowd, but soon six men stepped out towards Bayard. Four soldiers of Sinead who Bayard did not know by name, a castle guard from Valdus who was of the name Conner Mellway, and to Bayard's immense sadness, Sjarmir. "We accept our fate," Sjarmir said for the rest. "Do what you must."

"I give you a choice," Bayard said to them. "Die by my sword, here and now, or be restrained until the plague takes you to a natural death. What is your say?"

Sjarmir stood straight, looking into Bayard's eyes. "We are men of Sinead. It would be shameful for us to die anywhere but at the end of a blade."

"Aye," Conner Mellway agreed.

"Very well," Bayard whispered. "Please get to your knees." As one, the six men knelt down and leaned forwards, holding their necks out and their hands by their sides. Bayard pulled Life from his back, and one by one he gave the six warriors their mercy. None of them flinched as their time came, and they, along with Jacob, were buried under the city that they died to protect.

Epilogue
Winter of 1513 A.D
The City of Sinead
A New Day

Bayard sat in his chambers, the same room that had once belonged to King Alvor. The morning sun streamed through his window, the cold air refreshing him after a nearly restless night. Lilith still slept, wrapped under the thick red blankets of the King's bed. A sheet of parchment lay in front of him, held open by small stones as he stared at the blank letter, quill in hand. Bayard took a deep breath, and began to write.

To the Kings and Lords of England-
A plague is coming. I am sure that you are aware of it by now. They have attacked your towns, some may already be at your gates. The dead walk among us, and they will not stop. Many of you are at war with other Kingdoms, and all of you wish to protect your homes and your people. However, the dead care nothing for that. They will spread out, increasing in number as they feed on everyone in their path. You know that both Valdus and Haarn have fallen to them, and they will arrive at each of your cities in time. My name is Bayard Travers, and I am offering you a chance against this plague. The cities of Valdus and Sinead have merged, and we have formed an alliance. Our loyalty is with the living. Our faith is in ourselves. If you are besieged, send your messenger to the city of Sinead. We will come to your aid, and we will slay all the dead that surround you. In return, we ask that you pledge your allegiance to our cause and join our crusade against the plague. We hold no prejudices, no hate, no fear. We are the living, and with our combined strength, we will wipe the plague off the face of our Earth.
-Bayard Travers, King of the Living

Bayard stood and rolled the parchment, sliding it into a small scrollbox and placing it on his side of the bed, next to seventeen more of the same. He walked quietly across the bedchamber and took his large rucksack, stuffing the scrollboxes into it. He brushed Lilith's hair aside, smiling as she shifted in her sleep. He sneaked from the chamber and down the long staircase until he reached the ground, and he started making his way towards the gates. He looked over at the ruins of the mead hall, shattered stone and wood still scattered around the building.

The streets were empty aside from a few guards, and it was a quiet, peaceful walk. He heard the whinnies of horses before he saw them, and soon enough he found the eighteen messengers, all riding large and healthy beasts. He passed a scrollbox to each of them, instructing them of their tasks. Two scrolls to each city, should one of the messengers lose their way or otherwise fail to reach his destination. Bayard thanked them for their service, handing each of them five gold coins, and he watched as they rode off into the morning fog.

Made in the USA
San Bernardino, CA
13 September 2019